A Women Like That is Constance Bartel's first novel. She lives in Phillipsburg, New Jersey.

CONSTANCE BARTEL

A Woman Like That

GRAFTON BOOKS

A Division of the Collins Publishing Group

LONDON GLASGOW
TORONTO SYDNEY AUCKLAND

Grafton Books
A Division of the Collins Publishing Group
8 Grafton Street, London W1X 3LA

Published by Grafton Books 1987
Reprinted 1987, 1988

First published in Great Britain by
Judy Piatkus Ltd 1986

Copyright © Constance Bartel 1985

ISBN 0-586-06974-7

Printed and bound in Great Britain by
Collins, Glasgow

Set in Times

For Bonnie and Jimmy

Part I

1

Roberta must have missed his call by seconds. Mattie met her at the door.

'Mr Marston just called, Mrs Marston. He said something has come up; he can't get away. He said for you to go on to the country yourself.'

'He *did*!' That had never happened before. 'Did he say how late he'll be?' Roberta was already reaching for the hall phone.

'He said he was out of the office – that he might be tied up quite late. He said would you please give the Bruces his apologies.'

Damn. For a moment she had forgotten the Bruces. She would prefer to wait for Brad, no matter how late, but the Bruces were coming to dinner.

'Oh, Mattie . . . isn't that rotten luck! Stuck working on a Friday in summer!'

'It's a shame, 'specially with you and the mister so crazy about that farm.'

'Didn't he have *any* idea when he can get away?'

'He said he'd try for the last bus, but if he wasn't there by midnight, not to worry, he'll come early tomorrow.'

'Oh, dear. Well, thanks, Mattie.' Roberta picked up the insulated hamper of food Mattie had prepared for that night.

'Oh, and one more thing, Mrs Marston . . . Mr Marston said seeing you don't have to pick him up midtown, like usual, that you should cut across the park and take the West Side, to beat the traffic.'

Roberta nodded. 'See you Monday, Mattie.'

It seemed perfectly fitting that Brad should leave driving instructions for her.

She had always been the sort of woman who finds it natural to say 'I'll ask my husband.'

She did make good time from East Seventy-ninth Street to the Lincoln Tunnel, but she ran into traffic at the entrance. Stuck through two green lights, she happened to catch the eye of a truck driver. He grinned, made a gesture, mouthed some words. Confused, Roberta looked up at him. Was he warning her that she was in the wrong lane, or that her brake lights weren't working?

She leaned over to roll down the window just in time to hear 'Hey, baby!' as the light changed and the truck moved forward. Roberta was amused. Nothing wrong with the car, thank heaven. Just the simple sexual tribute of the road. She could almost hear her daughter Susan claiming she was 'weird' for not recognizing that in the first place. Well, it was true, Roberta supposed. She did tend to be oblivious of men, males. Males in relation to herself, anyway. But why not, when she had Brad?

By the time she reached Route 78, where she no longer had to concentrate on traffic, she was missing him acutely. Heading for the farm alone was not at all the same, and it was not just that Brad usually did the driving. The trip itself was a ritual part of their weekends. Despite the many times they had taken this familiar route, they still marveled at the transition from city canyon to open farmland in a mere ninety minutes. Who on the upper East Side, they asked each other, would believe red barns, grazing cows, and rustling cornfields? So close? And they admitted to a preemptive sense of proprietorship: this surprisingly rural part of New Jersey was *their* private discovery. Their township was actually called Greenwillow.

Laughing at herself, Roberta tapped the horn in salute to a certain silvery silo. Brad always did that. He said it marked the spot where the good life began.

It was not yet five-thirty when Roberta swung onto the creek road. As she caught the first glint of the stream, she remembered how they had stumbled, accidentally, onto this road seven years before, how they had instantly agreed: 'This is it. This is where to buy a country place – if there's one available.'

There had been one available. An 1800 stone house in a state of near ruin, approached by a little bridge, surrounded by one hundred overgrown acres sloping to the creek, and rimmed at the horizon by gentle hills. It had been a dairy farm. Naturally they called it the Farm.

Roberta crossed the bridge, pulled into the curving driveway, and parked next to the stone wall. Housekey in hand, she ran up the front steps. She could bring in the food hamper later. Right now she could not wait to greet the beloved house and to feel the warm sense of homecoming she always experienced.

She turned the key in the handsome brass lock she and Brad had agreed was extravagant, but worth it, and stepped into the wide hall which ran the depth of the house. As always, the mellowed, random pine floors, the deep window embrasures, the beamed ceilings, and the rosy brick of the fireplaces gave joy to her eye, but something deeper to her heart.

She and Brad had often speculated on why they, New Yorkers to the bone, had responded so strongly to this quiet, isolated place. 'Don't you think it has something to do with continuity?' she had asked him. 'Roots into the past, even if not literally our roots? A sense of enduringness? After all, these walls have been standing a century and a half.'

'I agree,' Brad had said. 'It's unchanging – in a changing

11

world. But I think there's something else,' he'd added musingly. 'Don't you think we tend to love what we have rescued? This house was at peril when we found it. Another year or two of standing empty, and it would have begun to topple. Remember what a disaster it was.'

Roberta, indeed, remembered. As she climbed the broad stairway, she saw again the ragged wallpaper, the scarred floors, the missing windows, the primitive plumbing they had originally found.

She remembered, too, their first day of ownership. After they had concluded the 'closing' in the lawyer's office and had been handed the key, they had driven back to the house and Brad had, absurdly, carried her over the threshold. Then they had found themselves speaking in whispers and tiptoeing around the empty, echoing rooms like intruders, as though they'd expected their right to be there to be challenged. They'd gotten lost in the house too, having been unsure of where each of the three stairways led, or which doors opened onto what. As the full impact of the terrible state of the house had hit them, they'd looked at each other aghast.

'My God, are we *mad*?'

'Marston's Folly!' But soon their initial sense of the worth of the place had reasserted itself. The foundation and thick stone walls were sound. The roof was slate. The proportions were good. There was dignity and beauty beneath the surface neglect. All they had to do was reveal it.

Later that first day – Roberta smiled as she remembered – they had climbed the hill to the barn. Gingerly, they'd pushed open the little side door next to the massive sliding doors, tentatively stepping inside. The rafters had soared high above them, the interior space had seemed limitless, and from somewhere a shaft of sunlight had slanted over them.

'Know what it reminds me of?' Roberta had whispered. 'Something crazy.'

'Yes,' Brad had replied. 'Grand Central. The height . . . and that beam of light. But not the silence. You can *hear* it.'

Later Brad had tested, rung by rung, the tall ladder to the hayloft. Roberta had followed. Arm in arm they'd stood in silent awe, gazing at the panoramic view from the high dusty window: green valley, winding stream, distant blue hills. Then Brad had taken off his jacket, spread it over the pile of fragrant hay, and grinned. 'It *was* called "a roll in the hay" wasn't it? Lie down!' And there, as the motes danced in the sunlight, they had made love. It had been Roberta's fortieth birthday.

Now, in the large square bedroom with the spool bed and the patchwork quilt. Roberta thought how sound their instincts had been. It's not just a house. It's stability. It is *abiding*. And when Brad retires, it is where we will abide. It will be here, for the kids. Wistfully, she hoped that their grandchildren would want to live in it; then she sternly reminded herself that one generation cannot choose for another.

She changed from city clothes to jeans and shirt, and then lingered a moment at the window. I'm so privileged, she thought. A happy marriage in *this* day and age . . . a daughter . . . a son . . . and all this beauty. She closed her eyes and felt deep gratitude.

The chime of the clock on the landing reminded her that the Bruces were coming. She flew downstairs to retrieve Mattie's salmon mousse and the wine from the ice chest in the car, then headed out to the garden for lettuce.

She was putting the candles on the table when Peg Bruce called. 'Roberta, I'm so sorry to cancel at the last minute, but Ed has one of his migraines. It just hit him

13

out of nowhere. We had to pull off the road. Forgive us, but I really think I should get him straight to Doylestown and into bed.'

Roberta hung up, ashamed of feeling slightly relieved. Still, there *was* a difference between having your husband mix the drinks, hold the fort while you slipped out to the kitchen, and keeping things going on your own. But what would Women's Lib think of that attitude?

By twelve, Brad had not arrived. Obviously he had not made the last bus. As she switched off the lights before going upstairs, Roberta suddenly realized that she had never spent a night alone in this house, not once since they'd bought the place. Brad had occasionally been on business trips that had kept him away over the weekend, but she had always had houseguests, or the kids, or the kids' guests. She felt a moment of uneasiness. It was a big house, and now it seemed very silent.

'Nonsense!' she told herself. 'How can anyone who walks the streets of Manhattan feel nervous here?' But she did decide to leave some lamps burning.

The big bed seemed empty. Suddenly she felt too small for it. And she had trouble falling asleep; she missed Brad's shoulder.

She opened her eyes to the early morning sun blazing through the windows. The birds were making a racket in the hemlock. A heavenly day. She was glad they would be alone this weekend. Brad could work on his precious stone wall to his heart's content.

The clock said six. She thought briefly of going back to sleep, then rejected the idea. The day was too good to waste. Before the sun was much higher in the sky, she was sitting in the garden savoring her first cup of coffee, again amazed that this green peace could exist seventy-five miles from Manhattan.

As she poured more coffee, Roberta reminded herself

to take the eggs out of the refrigerator so they would be at room temperature for Brad's breakfast. She would offer him a choice of herbed omelet or French pancakes. Having decided that, her eye was caught by a strange car on the far side of the creek. Early for a passenger car, she thought idly. There were so few people using 'their' road that she and Brad were familiar with every car and farm truck which 'belonged' on it. The strange car crossed the bridge and turned into the driveway. Someone lost, no doubt. No wonder, on these backroads.

She crossed the terrace, hoping she would know the place the stranger was seeking. The countryside was peppered with tiny crossroad hamlets, each with a name nobody except its immediate inhabitants ever recognized.

Before she got to the steps, the driver turned off his ignition and got out of the car.

It was Brad.

Her expectation of a stranger was so total that for a split second she assumed this was a man who looked like Brad, that double everyone is supposed to have.

But it was Brad. He raised his hand in a funny little salute, then dropped it again.

What's *wrong*? she wondered, in a panic.

She flew down the steps and into his arms. His arms encircled her without embracing her, as though he were trying not to touch her. He was stiff, wooden. He *was* a stranger.

She stepped back and looked at him. 'Brad. What's wrong? Is it Jim? Susan?' Her heart seemed to stop beating while she waited for his answer.

'Susan? Jim?' he repeated. 'No, no. No, of course not. Don't be silly. No.'

Her heart flooded with relief, only to be wrung with a new fear.

'Then it's *you*. What is it? Are you ill?' Dear God, her

15

mind raced, he's been to a doctor. He's keeping it from me. He's had terrible news. Some awful, awful prognosis – I'm going to lose him. Dear God, please . . .'

'Me?' If only he would stop repeating what she said.

'Yes. *You*. Are you ill?'

'No. I'm all right.'

Thank God, thank God, she thought. Then what is it? Something wrong at the office? One of the plants in trouble? But Brad wouldn't look so haunted about business. He's too strong. Too confident.

Confusion swept over her, then anger. 'For God's sake, Brad, what *is* this? Why are you here at this hour? Why do you look so strange? And what's this car? Whose is it and where did you get it?'

For the first time he really looked at her. 'The car? It's a Hertz. I rented it.'

'But why?'

'Oh, because I have to get right back to the city.'

In a minute I'll scream, she thought. No. It's a nightmare. It's the scream you scream just as you wake from a nightmare. At any second, I'll wake up . . .

But the next thing he said sounded real enough. 'Have you any coffee?'

'In the garden.'

She poured. He drank. Brad looked at the house lovingly, sadly. He looked at the glittering creek. He looked at the pile of stones with which he'd been making his wall. Finally he looked at her.

'Robbie.'

She met his eyes silently.

'There's to way – *no way* not to be cruel. I suppose the best way is the quickest way.'

Now Roberta could not have spoken had she tried.

'Roberta. I must leave you.'

16

The words had no meaning. It was as though he were speaking a strange language.

'What did you say?'

'Roberta . . . Oh, Robbie, I'm in hell. Jesus, please try to understand.' He put his head in his hands.

Roberta stared at him. She felt nothing. She was anesthetized, numb, but at the center of the numbness was a sense of craziness, of unreality. The world had spun off its axis. Either she had gone mad, or he had.

'Brad.'

He looked up.

'Are you on drugs?'

He stared at her. 'Roberta! For God's *sake* – '

'No, of course that's ridiculous,' she agreed, speaking in a conversational tone. 'Absurd. Are you sure you're not ill then? Something frightening – a brain tumor? Brad, darling, you know we can face anything . . .'

Brad rose and walked to the wall he had been building. He stared at the pile of stones, picked one up, hefted it, stared at it thoughtfully, discarded it. He picked up another. It was as though we were making a careful choice. He picked up a third stone and placed it precisely on the wall. Then he came back, put his hands on her shoulders, then stiffly removed them.

'Roberta. I'm involved with another woman.'

'Oh,' said Roberta.

'Yes.' He said it as though reporting a surprising fact they must both look at, objectively.

'You're kidding,' said Roberta, insanely.

Then it came – a torrent of agonized words from Brad: explaining, self-accusing, self-excusing, pleading for understanding.

'Robbie! You must believe me – I didn't mean it to happen – no man does. It started so innocently – please believe me. Nothing was further from my mind. As a

17

'matter of fact, I rather disliked her, can you believe it?' For a moment Brad seemed to forget he was speaking to her, his wife. He had the wondering air of a man recounting something surprising to an uninvolved acquaintance. 'Amazing, isn't it. As a matter of fact, she *irritated* me, but then – I don't know how it happened . . . So you see, Roberta, I have no choice.'

Now the numbness was gone. She took the full impact. First the blow. Then the waves of pain.

'Roberta! Don't look like that. Are you all right? Sit down, darling.' Tenderly he put his arm around her, guided her to a chair. 'We both need a drink. Don't move – I'll be right back.'

Roberta sat. Brad came back with brandy. He poured. She did not take the glass he offered. He held it to her lips. 'Drink, darling.' She sipped, pushed the glass away. I'm dying, she thought. I'm being killed . . . Please. Why can't I die faster?'

He frowned at his snifter, cradling to in his hands. 'I was up all last night, Roberta. Trying to break it off. I had decided. I knew what I would be losing . . . you . . . the kids . . . our life. It *has* been a good life, Robbie, hasn't it?' He seemed to plead for her agreement. She said nothing.

'But, Robbie, I couldn't – couldn't end it. It's as though something outside me has taken over, as though I'm powerless.'

Roberta was staring unseeingly at the willow tree.

'You know, Roberta,' he said quietly. 'I will always love you. I know you won't believe it – how could you? – but it's true. You are everything I ever wanted in a wife. You understand me.'

He rose and tipped her face toward his. 'And that's why I know you'll understand now – after the shock wears off. But you see, she . . . she needs me.'

'Look,' said Roberta. 'The oriole!'

'You're in shock, darling. Why wouldn't you be? If only there were a way to make a situation like this less brutal. You shouldn't be alone. Shall I call Mingo? Ask her to come?'

'What for?'

'To stand *by*, darling. Moral support.'

'Oh . . . I see. No. No, thank you.'

'Are you sure?'

She did not answer.

'I must go, Roberta.'

'Go? Go where?'

'Back to the city.'

'Why?'

'You see, Roberta, she's expecting me.'

'Expecting you,' said Roberta.

Brad put his arm around her, kissed her on the cheek. 'Roberta, I'd give a great deal to spare you this, but I can't help myself.'

He waited. She did not answer.

'I'll be in touch,' he said.

Then he left. He went down the stone steps, got into the Hertz car, crossed the bridge, turned onto the Creek Road.

Roberta watched him disappear around the curve.

2

Later, Roberta could never remember the rest of that day. It was as though a button had been pushed, switching her to Automatic. She neither saw nor heard. Her mind was blank. But from somewhere in the core of her being pain radiated in slow, relentless waves.

As strong as the pain was the sense of disorientation. She felt as though the very building blocks of her life, the fundamental 'Givens,' had proved illusory. Given: the sun rises in the east. Given: Roberta loves Brad, Brad loves Roberta. Given: their closeness, their knitted-together experience, their shared lives. Given: their marriage was forever.

'None of that is true?' screamed a voice inside Roberta. 'The truth is not true? Everything I have always believed, have always *known*, I didn't *really* know? Because it doesn't exist?' It was as though something uncompromisingly solid – Brad's stones, perhaps – had turned hideously weightless in her hand.

Sometime during the day the farmer who sold eggs delivered their order. Roberta could not remember paying him, but she must have. The eggs and some change were on the hall table. Sometime during the day Peg Bruce must have called from Doylestown. There was a notation in Roberta's handwriting: 'Call Bruces re 9th.' Roberta had apparently sounded all right, because no one had said '*Are you all right*?'

Mechanically she moved from room to room in the silent house. She plumped a pillow, lifted a pewter pitcher and carefully replaced it, pushed the antique doorstop an inch to the left, then back again.

'Why?' she said aloud. 'Why?'

Oddly, she did not once wonder who the other woman was. The shock of learning that she, Roberta, was not to Brad what Brad was to her – the other half of self – obliterated the existence of another woman. Nor did she think of divorce, settlements, money. She did not even think of her children.

She did not think at all. She simply suffered the rending of a closeness she had believed indestructible. And in the destruction of it, she felt she could not survive.

At some point, exhausted, she fell asleep. Or perhaps, unable to bear more, she escaped into unconsciousness.

When she awoke, she reached, as always, for Brad. She enjoyed only a few seconds of forgetfulness before the untouched pillow brought back yesterday. But now the searing pain was gone. It was as though her unconscious had fought for survival in her sleep. The first shock was over.

It is ten o'clock, she noted. What day? Of course, Sunday. Right. I'll put everything on Hold, she thought. I won't feel; I'll just move. First, change my clothes. (She had apparently fallen asleep fully dressed.) Then, coffee. Then . . . eat something, I suppose. She was not hungry. But she had not eaten for twenty-four hours, so she supposed she should. Right. One foot before the other. First things first. Go through the motions.

In the kitchen she found the coffee cups and brandy glasses from yesterday morning. Was it only yesterday? It seemed aeons since the world had changed. And Brad's cup, Brad's glass – which his lips had touched, and his hand had held – seemed remote, from another time, unconnected with the present. She pushed the tray aside almost absent-mindedly.

21

She carried her coffee and toast, from habit, toward the garden and then stopped short. No. Of course not. Not the place to sit. Now where *yesterday* had taken place. She headed, instead, for the little table under the big sycamore behind the house.

She sipped her coffee in a state of suspension, her eyes traveling idly up the field to the barn. Was that a slate missing from the roof? There in the corner? Must tell Brad about that.

That woke her up. Reality returned to her slowly awakening mind, but this time her mind promptly declared it to be *un*reality. It simply could not be.

Brad and I break up? Preposterous. After twenty-five years? Impossible. Whatever this situation is, it can't be serious. A fling on his part? Well, there's a lot of that going on. Midlife crisis. Could he really be going through that state we hear so much about, when he feels he's getting older and wonders if he's still attractive? *Brad*? But he's so strong. So take-charge. Could he really have a secret little area of insecurity I never knew about? Should I have realized?

At this point Roberta was quite ready to blame herself. She must have failed Brad somehow, been insensitive to his needs. She did not know where or how, nevertheless, she must have been lacking in something. Well, she had only to ask him. Then, of course, she would try to fill the bill, whatever it was. The great thing was that she and Brad could – wasn't there a better word than *communicate*? – *commune*, maybe. They had always been able to share their innermost feelings. And wasn't that rather rare? Of course it is, thought Roberta. Brad knows that. Oh, this is just a crazy incident. We'll laugh about it . . . a month from now.

As for *you*, Roberta, she addressed herself sternly, what happened to *you* yesterday? Falling apart. Going out of your mind. Climbing the walls. Where's your perspective? Collapsing over what many a woman goes through – some more than once. Like Judith Bevan and that philanderer husband of hers. Look how strong she is.

Roberta felt something like shame. Can it be, she thought that I'm weak? Or worse, childish? That I'm so spoiled by a good marriage, I go to pieces at the first cloud in a blue sky? For shame, Roberta. Let's see you show some courage. Let's see you rise to the occasion.

A half-hour later she was on her way back to New York. The thing to do, obviously, was to get to Brad. She would act perfectly normal. She wouldn't say a word. Then, when he brought up the Subject, she would simply ask him to tell her, his nearest and dearest confidante, what it was he hungered for. And if it should be just male ego, Roberta thought, the need for confirmation of his male magnetism – well, *I'll* show him what a wonderful lover he is. Because he *is*.

Roberta had always felt that she and Brad had an unusually satisfying sex life. From what other women said, she knew this was by no means true in many marriages. She and Brad no longer felt the compelling urgencies of their twenties and thirties, but they had active, healthy passions and they fulfilled each other completely – or so she had always believed.

For a moment she felt a doubt. Could she be mistaken? No, I'm not, she told herself. I'm sure. A wife can tell . . . unless . . . maybe today's rampant sexuality has gotten to Brad? Even to *Brad*? Can it be that the prevailing emphasis on sex as the be-all and end-all of experience has sold Brad a bill of goods? Just as it brainwashes the hapless young, forcing them to be sexy whether they want to or not?

Why should Brad be immune? Maybe he's stuck with

the worst idea of all: that he's *missing* something. Variety? Varieties of sexual experience? She felt herself flush. One hundred and one positions?

Okay, Brad, I'm game! Try me. She thought of her new nightgown, as yet unworn. Black, slit, see-through bodice. A gift from Brad. Had that been a message? Teach me, Brad.

She was approaching the city before she realized, belatedly, that of course Brad might not be in the apartment when she got there. The dashboard clock said twelve-twenty. He might at that moment be dressing to go out to lunch. With her. I'll just miss him. But what am I thinking of? Of course he probably did not go home at all. He's at her place. The apartment will be empty. I won't be able to find him. *Find* him. My *husband*.

It was at that point, more than twenty-four hours after Brad had dropped his bombshell, that Roberta finally felt rage. When she realized that just moments before she had been planning to ask Brad where she had failed – to make amends – outrage finally detonated in Roberta. She literally saw red.

Whereas a moment ago she had been fantasizing a transcendent sexual coupling with Brad, now her inner image was of attacking Brad. Physically. She saw herself pummeling him with fists, raking his cheek with her nails, drawing blood. She heard herself screaming: I hate you. I'll always hate you. And I'll fight you. How dare you think you can simply end our marriage overnight? What do you take me for? Do you think you can discard me? Throw me aside like yesterday's paper? Traitor! Deceiver! Cheat! *Bastard*!

There was no hurt left. Just a blazing determination to show Bradford Marston that he could not summarily reject her and expect her to accept it – because she had 'always understood' him – while at the same time he

expected her to believe that he 'would always love' her
. . . in a way. Bullshit. She said aloud, for the first time
in her life. She would hurt him, as much as he had hurt
her. She would fight divorce with every means at her
command. But she would not live with him – ever again.

At the entrance to the East Seventy-ninth Street apartment building, George, the doorman, was whistling down
a cab for a couple waiting at the curb. When he saw
Roberta, he abruptly left the couple, came toward her,
and removed his gold-braided cap.

'Oh, Mrs Marston,' he said. Looking almost as though
he were about to offer his arm to support her, he
solicitously held the door and then followed her into the
lobby. 'Oh, Mrs Marston,' he said. 'I'm so sorry, Mrs
Marston.'

Roberta stared at him. Did he *know*? How *could* he
know? Did she *look* like a woman whose husband wanted
to leave her for another woman?

She felt hot humiliation. 'Thank you, George,' she
said.

'Shall I take you up, Mrs Marston?'

'That won't be necessary, thank you George.' She
stepped into the elevator, pressed twenty-four, and leaned
against the wall. She felt as though she had been publicly
pilloried.

Her hand was shaking so violently that she had difficulty
taking her keyring from her handbag. But before she
could get her key in the lock, the door opened.

It was not Brad. It was Paul Reston, Brad's oldest
friend and a close family friend of the Marstons.

Before Roberta could utter a sound, Paul embraced
her. 'Oh, Roberta, I am so desperately sorry.' Gripping
her firmly by the shoulder, he propelled her through the
foyer into the living room. 'But Roberta, you're not
alone? Didn't the Bruces come with you? Are they

parking the car?' He was guiding her to the sofa. 'Sit down, dear . . .'

Roberta felt she was going mad.

'What are you talking about? The Bruces? Why should they? . . .'

'But we called them in Doylestown. They said they'd leave for your place immediately . . .'

'Immediately?' repeated Roberta. 'The Bruces? But what *for*? And why are *you* here, Paul? What? . . .'

A look of pure horror passed over Paul Reston's face.

'Oh, my God. Roberta . . . Roberta, then you don't – You haven't heard? . . .'

Dear God, thought Roberta. My daughter. Or my son. Dear God, no, no, no . . .

'Is it Susie?' she whispered. 'Jimmy?'

Paul Reston shook his head. 'No, Roberta.' He sat down beside her and gripped her hand hard.

She stared at him.

'Roberta. It's Brad. An accident . . . two hours ago . . .'

She tried to speak. She could not.

The silence seemed fixed in eternity. Then Roberta heard an unearthly scream which spiraled higher and higher until it reached an unbearable peak and descended, in diminishing echoes, to nothingness.

When she opened her eyes, her son Jimmy was sitting beside her.

'I'm right here, Mom,' he said. He smiled at her. She saw the tears tangled in his lashes. 'Mom, you've got me . . . and Susie.'

She tried to smile back, but failed. He was barely twenty-one. There were signs of emerging manhood on his face. But right now, poignantly visible, there were still traces of the young boy he had so recently been. He looked so vulnerable – and so heartbreakingly brave. She

26

wept for her son's loss of the father he loved. And for her daughter's. She and Susan were close, but there was no question that for Susan, the sun had risen and set in Brad.

'Is Susan here?'

'She's on her way, Mother' – Jim put his arm around her – 'please. It'll be okay.'

Yes. She must be strong. For him. For Susie. She mopped her eyes with the handkerchief he offered. She managed a shaky smile.

And then a new fear struck her. The name Nelson Rockefeller suddenly floated across her mind, as though printed in a headline. A wave of nausea swept over her. How had Brad? . . . Where had Brad? . . . God, please spare the children *that* . . .

'Jim.' She could hardly speak. 'Jim . . . how did Daddy . . . die?'

He had to fight for control. She waited.

'Car,' he said. 'Out of control. Daddy was on the curb, waiting for the light to change. The car jumped the curb. They think the driver had a heart attack.'

'Oh . . .' She closed her eyes. Relief flooded through her.

'Lenox Hill said it was instantaneous.' He was trying to comfort her. 'The doctor said Dad didn't suffer.'

'Was he . . . alone? When it happened?'

'Alone?' He looked puzzled. 'Yes. He must have been. It was the police who notified the Restons. When they didn't get an answer here, they tried Paul Reston. His name was in Dad's address book, under In Case of Emergency.'

She nodded mutely. The details didn't matter. What mattered was that the children need never know their father had wanted to leave their mother. That he loved someone else . . . or thought he did.

* * *

27

Bradshaw Marston, fifty, was buried on a beautiful summer day in a small Connecticut cemetery where his grandparents were buried. 'Unless you prefer otherwise, my dear?' Brad's mother had asked, meticulously honoring Roberta's right to choose.

Roberta had looked at the frail, aristocratic face and had seen the anxiety in the faded blue eyes. Having Brad in the family plot meant so much to his mother. The elder Mrs Marston had behaved bravely, as befitted her staunch Yankee code, but Roberta knew she had suffered a mortal blow at the loss of her only son.

'Of course, Mother Marston,' Roberta had agreed. 'I'm sure Brad would have wanted it that way.'

The children wanted it that way, too. They were fond of their paternal grandparents. They had spent many happy childhood vacations in the dignified old house Brad had grown up in. They knew and liked the quiet New England town. 'Daddy will be home,' Susie had said.

For herself, Roberta found that, except for the children's wishes, she was quite indifferent. She had no emotional reaction to the matter. She simply let herself to swept along on the tide of arrangements made on her behalf by others. Her widowed father, who had flown up from Florida, and Paul Reston, who had also been Brad's lawyer, took quiet, efficient charge. They spared her details, but gently consulted her for her approval. She said yes to everything.

Others, stunned by the suddenness of Brad's death, and deeply concerned for her, formed a protective cordon around her. Mingo Darcy, her close friend from childhood; Brad's sister Ann and her husband, who rushed home from a European vacation; Brad's senior business associate, whose job as head of a chemical firm Brad had been expected to inherit – all had been solicitous, eager

28

to do whatever was in their power to ease Roberta's suffering.

Roberta had expressed her gratitude. But underneath, in her wounded heart, she was bitter. All these kind, caring people naturally thought she was a stricken widow. But she was a widow denied a widow's grief. She could not feel the healing balm of true mourning. She was not a woman who had lost her husband to death. She was a woman who had lost her husband to another woman. But she must play the role of bereavement. She must 'walk through the part' for the children's sake. For everyone's sake.

The little church was crowded, with friends and neighbors of the elder Marstons; many of whom had known Brad as a boy. There was Brad's parents' house-keeper, red-eyed from weeping, as well as Roberta's own Mattie. There were friends from New York, some of them from Susan's and Jimmy's circles, touchingly, awkwardly solemn. There was a large contingent from Brad's com-pany, including those who had flown in from out-of-town branches to pay their respects. Roberta was glad for the children's sake. It was good that they should know how well liked their father had been. People were still arriving as the minister began the service. Many had to stand quietly against the back wall.

Roberta sat through the service numbly. She seemed to see it and hear it from a remote distance, but her mind noted irrelevancies. She saw the sunshine lighting Dr Holcombe's white hair as he said, 'We do not know why Brad has been taken from us, but we did know Brad, the man, and we are richer for it . . .'

Dr Holcombe had confirmed Brad and had co-officiated at their wedding, although not in this same church. She saw again her wedding day, remembered the total joy she had felt as she walked down the aisle – ''till death do us part . . .' But this was not death that had parted them.

No! Don't think, she told herself. Don't *think*. 'Wipe your mind!' Her grandmother had said that to her as a child when she had been upset over a disappointment. 'Wipe your mind, child.' Roberta tried. She took a deep breath. Then an unbidden thought struck her forcibly. Is *she* here? In this church? Someone I've met? From Brad's office? Or someone I know well? 'A *friend* of mine? Somebody's wife?

She felt her control slipping. She wanted to get up, push down the pew, run up the aisle – flee. For a split second she considered it.

There was a small stifled sob to her right. Susie. Susie was breaking down. Roberta put her arm around her weeping daughter and held her close. Susie needed her, and so did Jim. Thank God for that.

That night she lay alone in a small guest room in Brad's parents' house. The elder Marstons had begged Roberta to stay, with Susan and Jim, for a few days. 'It would mean so much to us,' Brad's mother had said. 'And you should not be alone,' Brad's father had added. 'You need someone to stand by' – his voice had threatened to break, and he'd fought to control it – 'and so do we. We must sustain each other.' Roberta had looked at her father-in-law, suddenly so much older looking. Poor man. He was indeed stricken. She'd kissed him lightly on the cheek. 'We'd like to stay, Father Marston,' she had replied.

But when Mrs Marston, as a matter of course, had shown Roberta to the room she and Brad had always shared, Roberta had been unable to cross the threshold. 'Please, Mother Marston,' she'd said, 'may I sleep in the little back room? . . . I can't – '

'Of course.' Hastily, as if she had been guilty of

insensitivity, Mrs Marston had added, 'I quite understand . . . yes, yes, I know how you feel – oh, my dear . . .'

'Besides' – even to her own ears Roberta's voice had sounded hard, brittle, 'I must get used to being on my own. Mustn't I?'

She lay staring at the moving shadow of a pine bough on the window blind. But what she saw were images of Brad, a succession of them, like home photos on a projection screen. Click. Brad opening a bottle of champagne with a flourish. The occasion, the six months' anniversary of their marriage. Click. Brad on a ladder, building kitchen shelves for her, in their first tiny apartment in a Murray Hill brownstone. Click. Brad, over a lazy Sunday morning breakfast, outlining his plans for their future: they'd wait awhile for children. No child of his would come into the world until he was making X amount of dollars. When he'd had at least two promotions, then, darling, they would begin a family. Later, Brad in Central Park, pulling Susie on a sled. When Jimmy came along, Brad deciding they must move again, to a larger apartment. Brad the decision maker. Roberta trusting always in his decisions, happy to lean against his broad chest. The safest place to be, she had always thought.

At last, and for the first time, Roberta wept. She wept for the lost past, lost love, lost life. As the first light paled the window, she slept.

She awakened with a lucid thought: 'I must leave New York.'

3

Roberta took a last look around the apartment. Stripped of all personal possessions, it looked as sterile as a hotel suite. She was leaving it forever, leaving it like an empty shell which had once contained life but was now hollow. And, like a shell, it contained within its empty heart echoes of the past. If you held it to your ear, you could hear the murmur of what had been. She was fleeing from that murmur.

Paul Reston, who was executor of Brad's estate, was convinced she would be back. Roberta had wanted to sell the apartment at once, to have done with it. He had persuaded her to hang on to it for at least a year. 'Roberta,' he'd said gently, a look of deep concern in his eyes, 'I simply can't let you make a rash decision. It's never wise to make drastic changes at a time like this. Your judgement, naturally, is not at its best.'

Her father had agreed. 'Roberta, child,' he'd said. 'You have had a terrible loss. You must not also lose everything that's familiar to you. This is your home, your accustomed place. Perhaps later, when things have healed a bit . . .' He'd sighed. 'Later, perhaps, you may want a smaller place. But for now, the more things stay the same, surely the easier it will be for you?'

'Poor Daddy,' she'd said, patting his cheek. 'I know you're thinking of when Mother died. I know how much comfort you got from staying on where you had been together so long. But for me, I feel I must get away, at least for a while.'

Impossible to explain. Impossible to say: But you don't

understand. I am not the usual widow you think I am.' She could not make it clear that she never intended to live in New York again. Too many memories . . . reminders on every street corner . . . and the agonizing, nonstop thought that, unknown to her, she might meet the woman Brad had loved. Everywhere she went she would look for her. Any woman she encountered would provoke that question: Is this the one?

So, in the end, she had gone along with Paul Reston's advice. The Erskines, who were eager to leave their apartment hotel, would be delighted to take over Roberta's cooperative apartment, furnished, for a year. Technically, they would be Roberta's guests, because subletting was not permitted. But since the Erskines were already on a waiting list for Roberta's building, Paul was sure he could square it with the board. He would take care of everything.

Both Paul and her father had seemed relieved that she was willing to keep her options open, as Paul put it. But then Paul raised another issue.

'But, Roberta, even if you feel you must get away, why the farm? *Living* in the country isn't like weekending in the country, you know. Two different things. You're a New Yorker, Roberta – a native New Yorker, at that. Don't you think the contrast is going to be rather staggering? Why choose a remote place like the farm?'

Roberta responded with a weak joke. 'Because it's there.'

'But you'll be so damned isolated! Exactly what do you visualize? What will you do with yourself?'

'I don't know exactly. I haven't . . . I'll need some time . . . to find my way.' She felt a small sense of panic. Paul was right. She was rushing away from something. But what was she rushing *toward*?

'Anyway, Paul,' she said, 'it won't be *that* isolated.

Don't forget that Jim will be only a half-hour away. Lafayette is very close to the farm, you know. He'll be very busy in his senior year, it's true, but he'll be within shouting distance.'

Yes, thought Paul. Thank God Roberta's son is at Easton, instead of New Haven or Cambridge. But Jim was only a twenty-one-year-old kid, and next year he'd be going off to law school. Well, by that time, Roberta would be back in the city, if Paul had anything to do with it. And in time, of course, she would remarry.

Paul hoped his face did not betray his feeling for Roberta. Three years ago Paul had had the shocking realization that he'd fallen in love with his best friend's wife. He had been appalled. It was unthinkable, of course. A man in command of himself, Paul had succeeded in repressing his feelings, living with them. Not out of loyalty to his wife, who had a lover. Out of loyalty to Brad. And then, not long before Brad died, he'd had shock number two. He'd discovered that Brad had another woman.

Now Brad was gone, and Roberta was free. But there was Alicia . . . Well, there has to be a way, he thought grimly.

Fortunately, he would be seeing a lot of Roberta in connection with Brad's estate. That was another source of concern. Paul was not at all sure of Roberta's financial security. Bradford Marston had been a corporate executive with high earning power, but he had long enjoyed the affluent life of the upper East Side. He'd had every reason to be confident his income would rise when he stepped into the presidency of his company, as he'd been clearly slated to do.

But Brad had not been a rich man, and knowing Brad's easy optimism – 'there's always more where that came from' – Paul suspected that Brad had lived pretty much to the hilt. He doubted Marston had accumulated much in the way of capital. Roberta's exact financial position would not be known until the will was probated and the taxes were paid. That would take a little time. Brad's life insurance was immediately available. And that, although it would have been substantial only five years ago, was now diminished by inflation. As a matter of fact, Paul recalled, he had only last year mentioned to Brad that it would be a good idea to increase his insurance. Brad had agreed, but apparently he had not gotten around to it.

For the immediate future, at least, the insurance would provide sufficient funds for Roberta to live as comfortably as she always had. Paul had already told her this, to reassure her.

Roberta only half listened. 'Then it's all right, about money?'

'Roberta,' said Paul gently. 'You are in a good position, for now. But later, you will want to make some . . . adjustments.'

'Yes, I see. Of course, Paul.'

Money was the last thing on Roberta's mind. In the three weeks since Brad's funeral, she had been intent only on closing this chapter of her life and turning to the next page, blank though it was.

She was glad the job of dismantling the apartment had kept her too busy to think, and grateful for the supportive presence of her father, Jim, and, whenever she could steal time from her busy life as editor of *Cachet*, her dear friend Mingo. Her father had insisted on standing by until she was settled at the farm. Jim pitched in and did everything he could to help. Mingo lent a brisk, competent hand, but most of all she offered the balm of her sympathetic presence.

It had all gone smoothly enough, considering, except for Susan. Susan had been stunned by the shock of her father's death. She had wept until it seemed she could weep no more. And then she'd wept again. She'd sat huddled in a chair, refusing to eat, her lovely young face tragic. Obviously she was in no shape to return to her job, her first job after college, a very junior one at NBC.

Roberta had been alarmed, and so had her father and Jim. They had all tried to console Susan, to help her accept the reality of Brad's death, to convince her that life went on. But only Jim could reach her. He spent hours in her room. 'Just rapping,' he told Roberta. 'She'll be all right. But she does feel the world has ended right now.' Although Susan was two years older than Jim, Jim seemed by far the more mature.

At the end of a week, at Jim's urging, a wan Susan had gone back to work. At the end of the second week, she had gone back to the apartment she'd been sharing for just six months with two other girls.

'But Susie, dear,' Roberta had said, 'why go now? Why not stay home with us for these last few days?'

'Home?' said Susan. 'I'm going to have to get used to not having this home sooner or later. I might as well start now, right?'

Roberta was shocked by her tone. Susan sounded . . . accusing. 'But Susan' – Roberta faltered – 'of course you have a home. It is just a change of home, isn't it? The farm is home, too. It's always there for you. Right now, if you like. You know I'd love to have you there with me . . . but I thought your job – '

'Mother,' said Susan, 'I don't think you understand.' And she left.

Now, making a final tour of the apartment, Roberta lingered at the door of Susan's room. It was so bare, without Susan's things. Without Susan. She felt a deeply troubling doubt. Had she been too precipitous in this headlong flight from the city? Had she pulled the rug out from under Susan? Was it too much for Susan, the loss of her father plus the abrupt loss of the home which had always been there?

It was true that Susan had already technically 'left home.' But that was only a gesture really. She had moved into the apartment because her friends had invited her, and because it was the thing to do. You got your first job and then, as soon as possible, you got your own pad. That was standard procedure with Susan's peer group.

But, Roberta now realized, Susan had not really left home. Not emotionally. She had obviously considered East Seventy-ninth her true home, a safe place in the family circle. She had thought nothing of arriving, unannounced, for dinner, laughingly saying that Mattie's cooking beat Hamburger Heaven any day, or of bringing her laundry for Mattie to do.

She must be feeling lost, thought Roberta, betrayed. Have I been selfish, thinking only of my own pain? Have I hurt my daughter? Oh, Susan, I didn't realize. Perhaps I should have made this change more gradually . . .

But it was too late now. Within minutes Roberta's father would be returning from last-minute errands, waiting for her in the lobby, and Jim would be bringing the car around for the trip to the farm. She could only hope and pray that her daughter would find her way back to her usual lighthearted self.

The buzzer sounded. It was the doorman, announcing that her father and Jim were downstairs.

Roberta picked up her bag, and stepped out into the hall. For a few seconds she kept her hand on the knob, holding the door open, reluctant to let go of her last link with the life she had lived there. Then she closed the door and the lock snapped with a click of finality.

* * *

On the thirtieth floor of a Wall Street skyscraper, Paul Reston checked the figures again; then he snapped shut the file labeled Marston, Bradford. It looked serious. There was definitely not going to be enough money for Roberta to live as she was accustomed to living. It would take a hell of a lot of capital to generate enough income to equal the one Brad had enjoyed annually. That capital simply wasn't there. As Paul had suspected, the country property, the house set on a hundred acres, was the estate's chief asset. He knew Brad had poured enormous amounts of money into its renovation and maintenance. Still, unless it were turned back into cash, it was a liability.

He noted that the real-estate tax had jumped another forty percent last year. He shuddered to think what it cost to heat that place, and to guess what heat would cost next year. No. His duty was clear. He must find a way to persuade Roberta to sell the place.

In the meantime, how long would the available cash last, given Roberta's standard of living? Two years? No, with inflation, probably less. After that, she would be in 'reduced circumstances,' and that was unthinkable, for a woman like Roberta. Not that she was mercenary, God knew. Not like money-loving Alicia. It was just that Roberta didn't know a goddam think about money, because she'd never had to. She was not the kind of woman who should suddenly be faced with having to cut corners and pinch pennies.

Paul was determined to prevent that. But give her a little time, he thought. She's still in shock. And he was glad, for her sake, that she'd never known about Brad's affair.

Paul had found Brad's infidelity incomprehensible. His feeling for Brad had been brotherly. They'd been college roommates, best man at each other's wedding. And Paul

38

had envied Brad for being one of the few happily married men he knew. That morning when Paul had stepped out of a Chicago hotel room just as Brad and a strange woman had emerged from the room next door had been one of the shocks of his life. His eyes had met Brad's for a split second. Neither had spoken.

Two days later Brad had called. 'When are you free for lunch?'

'You don't have to explain,' Paul had said.

'I know I don't have to explain,' Brad had snapped, 'but I'm in trouble. For Christ's sake, you're my big buddy, aren't you? I've got to talk to someone.'

At lunch, Brad had said that he loved Roberta. *Knew* he did. Always would. How could he not? Roberta had made him happy dammit. But this was different. He didn't know what the hell it was. He'd had no intention – it had been entirely accidental – it had started absolutely innocently – Paul must believe him. But now he found himself trapped in a feeling he couldn't understand – and couldn't conquer.

'Bigger than both of you?' said Paul.

'Don't be sarcastic,' said Brad. 'You gotta *be* there to know what it's like.'

He looked so miserable that Paul had to feel sorry for the poor son of a bitch. He was in hell; that was clear.

'It's not just a run-of-the-mill affair,' Brad went on.

'Better if it were.'

'Thanks for the obvious.'

'Then what *is* it, Brad?' Paul said, compassionate in spite of himself.

'I don't *know* That's the hell of it. It's . . . it's like a compulsion. I don't seem to have any will . . . I'm driven . . .'

'Then let it run its course. If you can't fight, float. Easy does it . . .'

'That's what I thought, at first. But it's gone deeper than that. You see, I feel so goddamned *responsible*. In the beginning I thought she was just someone given a raw deal by life. I was just trying to be decent, but I was misinterpreted. She thought I meant far more than I did mean. And then, God help me, I did mean it, in a way. Because there's something else . . . something . . .' He trailed off.

'Are you talking about sex?'

Brad put down his fork and looked straight at Paul. 'Jesus, Paul . . . I never experienced . . . I didn't know . . . I wasn't looking for it . . . but it happened . . .'

'I see,' said Paul. Bradford Marston was too much of a gentleman to go into detail, but he had obviously been hard hit by a new dimension of sexual experience. Harder hit, in his early fifties, than would have been true earlier.

'Now she says it's all – or nothing,' said Brad. 'I'm afraid she might harm herself.'

'Who is she, by the way?'

'Just a woman in the office.'

That conversation had occurred a month before Brad's death. In spite of everything, Paul missed Brad and mourned his loss. But he couldn't help feeling that if Brad had had to die, it was fortunate it happened before he'd done anything rash, anything that would have been devastating to Roberta.

Paul's thoughts turned to his wife Alicia. There was always Alicia, Alicia and her great, good friend Rena. Alicia who had told him bluntly that she would no longer share his bed . . . or any man's. Who'd said that she had reached a higher plane of human relationship. At first he had tried not to know what she meant, but of course the realization was inescapable. Alicia, fluffy, fragile little Alicia, had turned lesbian.

'But then. Alicia, why not end our marriage? There's

40

nothing in it for you apparently, and certainly not for me. Why not a divorce?'

'Because I need a cover, old boy. It's that simple.' She had smiled her childlike, big-eyed innocent smile – the one he had fallen in love with. 'No, I like things just as they are. Respectability, stuffy as it is. Social position. Financial security. And Grandmother's money later. You know very well, Paul darling, how Grand'mère would react to a divorce. A Catholic Boston dowager who has a private audience with the pope?' She shrugged. 'So you *see* my position, surely? For now I'll live happily on your money. Rena doesn't make much, you know,' she added conversationally. 'Sculptors don't, especially women sculptors, not in this man's world. So I can't afford a divorce. Maybe later.'

Paul rose to leave the room without replying.

'Oh, and Paul,' she added, as he reached the door, 'I'll do whatever's necessary, keep up appearances, and all that. Don't worry; I'll be discreet. And of *course*' – she smiled maliciously – 'you're free to hop into as many beds as you like. Fair's fair.'

She hates me, he realized. Pure unadulterated hostility – to me and the entire male sex. Eventually, he did hop into a bed or two, for closeness, for human contact, and to quiet his healthy male hungers. Nothing serious. No real emotional involvement.

Of course, Paul Reston could have secured a divorce, but not without scandal. He was a Wall Street lawyer with a respected reputation. And even had he been John Doe, he had an inbred distaste for the unsavory. Alicia knew this, and was quite willing to exploit it.

Paul weighed the pros and cons and decided to let things ride. At the time, he had no urgent motivation to free himself. When Alicia had first revealed her hostility, Paul had had no interest in any particular woman. Later, when he fell in love with Roberta, his freedom would have been equally meaningless. Indeed, he found being married an additional defense against his desire for another man's wife.

So his legal tie to Alicia didn't much matter. And Alicia had kept her end of her self-dictated 'bargain.' Paul had to admit she was a consummate actress. When he needed a wife and hostess, Alicia played the part beautifully. She was ever the feminine, the charming, the gracious Mrs Paul Reston. Meantime, her real life was lived in Rena LaSala's SoHo studio, in the more experimental art galleries, and in the coffee houses of SoHo and the Village. Paul and Alicia had been separated, although they lived under the same roof, for more than five years.

Now Paul turned back to the Marston folder on his desk. He thought of Roberta alone, in need of a man's protection. Involuntarily his hand went to the telephone. He had a strong impulse to call her, to hear her voice. But no. It was too soon. He did not have anything to offer her, not yet, anyway. And it was too soon for her too. After all, she was a newly grieving widow.

4

During that first week at the farm, Roberta felt that she was living between two worlds. On the one hand, with both Jim and her father in the familiar house, the days seemed curiously normal, almost like any quiet vacation week in late summer. On the other hand, they would be leaving – and she would be staying. To her surprise, both men made a last-ditch effort to change her mind.

'Spend the winter with me in Florida,' her father urged. 'Close the place. It will be waiting for you in the spring, if you still want it by then. But don't try to face all this alone.'

'Mother, winter can be *rugged*,' said Jimmy.

'Roberta dear,' said her father, 'I'm afraid you don't realize what is involved in a large place like this.'

'You two!' said Roberta. 'I thought everything had been decided. I can always change my mind later. But for now, really, I want to stay.'

'Then I'll stay with you,' said her father decisively.

'No, Granddad. I will' said Jim.

Roberta was touched. She looked at the two men she loved. Both were offering to make a considerable sacrifice for her. Her father, bless him, at seventy-four, was really comfortable only in Florida. He had found kindred spirits there, he still enjoyed golf, he would miss it terribly. And Jim. Manfully offering to live off campus in his important senior year.

'Thank you, darling.' She patted her son's hand. 'But I won't *hear* of your giving up your last year of campus

43

life. Off you go to College Hill next Tuesday. I promise you if I need help I'll holler.'

When it was quite clear that Roberta could not be dissuaded, Jim and her father made a great to-do about checking the oil burner, the storm windows, the pump in the vast cellar.

'Who is your fuel-oil supplier?' asked her father.

Roberta did not know. For the first time it sank in that she had no idea of the practical working of the place. Brad, of course, had taken care of everything. 'Maybe they're right?' she thought. 'Maybe I am being fool-hardy?' Then she recovered. 'Surely it's ridiculous to worry about not knowing the name of an oil company? I'll find out, or I'll get a new one.'

Jim remembered that his father had kept farm records in the desk in the hall. Yes, there it was, a fat folder of utility bills and records of the plumbers, electricians, and masons who had worked on the restoration of the house. In the end, Jimmy made her a neat telephone pad with bold headings: Electric Company, Electrician, Carpenter, Oil, Plumber, Water Softener, Fire Department, Police.

And unknown to Roberta, her father made a call to the tiny township police department. He wanted them to know that his daughter, recently widowed, would be living alone in the old Van Kirk place on Creek Road. He would so much appreciate it if they would cast an eye in that direction on their rounds. And did the police have an annual fund raiser for a local charity? He would like to contribute . . .

On a lovely day in early September Roberta drove her father to Newark Airport to catch his plane to Florida. As they waited for his flight to be announced, Thomas Barclay said, 'You know, perhaps you're right, Roberta . . . about staying on alone at the farm. It *is* a private matter, adjusting to life's great changes. But it's possible, you know. You learn to . . . adapt.'

'I know.'

The loudspeaker announced his flight. At the boarding gate, he kissed her. 'I'll see you at Christmas,' she said. She watched him walk up the ramp until he was out of sight. Then she was alone.

She drove back to the farm slowly. For the first time, no one was waiting for her. No one expected her. The fall term at Lafayette had begun three days ago so Jim had already left. The house was empty.

She thought of her son's and her father's concern for her. It was love, of course, love that sustained and warmed her. But there was a troubling aspect to it. Did she really appear so totally helpless? She thought briefly of Paul Reston. He, too, had advised strongly against her living alone. Did she impress them all as a woman who could not be expected to fend for herself? A woman unable to cope, even with something so elementary as having fuel oil delivered? That was an image she didn't much care for.

But I suppose it's a reasonable assumption, she admitted to herself. I never have fended for myself. I've never had to.

She pulled into the driveway, turned off the ignition, and sat, musing. It struck her forcibly how totally she was, as the Internal Revenue put it, a dependent. She had always had someone to lean on: first as the only child of her devoted parents, and then as Brad's wife. She had married a year out of college. Then Brad had provided for her, materially and in every other way.

Strong, take-charge Brad had simply taken over. He had set the emotional basis of their marriage: he, the protector; she, the protected. He had established their style of living, their social orbit, even their political views.

It was he who'd decided which obstetrician she should consult, and in which hospital she'd give birth. She had always worn her hair the way he liked it, even when she'd felt the urge to switch.

It was not that he dominated for domination's sake. It was rather that he considered himself qualified to act in her best interest . . . and she had agreed. What Brad thought best must *be* best. She had consulted him in all things, big and little.

Now she had no one to consult but herself.

Aware that she was forcing herself to do so, Roberta entered the empty house. The silence was deafening. The slow, inexorable ticktock of the clock on the landing emphasized the quiet. She went into the living room. The sofas, the pictures, the treasured bibelots, the fireplace – all seemed to stare at her mutely, indifferently. They were things – dead, inanimate things.

This house had always seemed so warm and welcoming. Now it was . . . noncommittal. In a flash of painful insight, she saw that the house's warmth had sprung from the spirit animating it, the spirit of involved people. Without that spirit, it was just a house.

At that moment, Roberta panicked. I can't do it; what made me think I could? They were right – all of them – Father – and Jim – and Paul. What was I thinking of? Of course I can't stay here alone – not for a minute – I'd die. I must have been mad.

She rushed to the phone, driven by an urgent need to hear a human voice – any voice. But whose? She couldn't call her father, to tell him perhaps she would go to Florida after all. At the moment, he was en route. She'd call Susan. Just to hear her voice. Maybe Susan could be persuaded to join her in the country? No. Susan was in no condition to be pressured. Mingo, then. No. Mingo was out of town. Paul. She'd call Paul Reston.

46

She dialed, waited, and was put through to Paul's secretary. 'Mr Reston will not be back until Friday.' Roberta said she'd call again, but she didn't leave her name. What would she have said to Paul? she wondered. 'Help! SOS! Rescue me!' She sat staring at the phone. The physical act of making the call had taken the blind edge off her panic. Now she felt embarrassed. Thank heaven, she had not reached Paul. How humiliating it would be to admit defeat on the very first day she was on her own, especially when he had warned her so strongly against it.

Looking up, Roberta saw herself reflected in the Hepplewhite mirror above the desk. Have you no courage at all? she silently asked her image. The question shamed her.

She stood up. Keep moving. Do something practical. Practical? Let's see . . . The silence. Of course, turn on the radio.

She tuned in to an interview. Voices. That took care of the silence. Next? The house was too large, certainly, for one person. Very well. Close all the doors on one side of the center hall. Live on just one side. That's more fitting for a single woman. A single woman? The phrase struck her as exotic when applied to her. She had never been 'a single woman.' But I am *now*, she reflected. A single woman, living appropriately in smaller quarters.

What next? Quick, think of something. Oh, yes, the phone book Jim had prepared for her – plumbers and such, things she should know. There was no one else to know them for her. She dug out the book and studied it. The oil people were in Thomasville, the well people in Flemington, and the utility company was called Jersey Central, as opposed to Con Ed.

She closed the book as the clock chimed six. Time to make dinner. Dinner? For one? Did anyone really make

47

dinner for one? She would fix a sandwich and let it go at that. But no, she shouldn't. She thought of the Englishman dressing for dinner in the jungle, keeping up morale and not letting standards slip. She must set the table as she always did, even light the candles, meaningless as it seemed. Deliberately she selected from the refrigerator – Jim and her father had stocked it to the hilt – a small steak, asparagus, and peaches.

But she barely touched the food, and she stared unseeingly at the book propped in front of her. When she had cleared the few dishes, it was still only eight o'clock in the evening.

At eight-thirty Jim called, at nine her father called, at ten-thirty Mingo called from San Francisco. She heard herself assure them all that everything was fine.

But, at eleven, desolation set in again. Feeling her aloneness as acutely as if it were an actual presence, she went slowly upstairs to the back guest room. She had not yet been able to use the room she and Brad had shared.

She lay awake, the bedside radio nattering softly beside her, wondering how to fill a blank future.

5

Over the telephone, Paul Reston's voice sounded disappointed. 'Of course, Roberta, whatever suits you. But I looked forward to seeing you, over and above business, I mean.'

'Oh, Paul, what a good friend you are.' Roberta hesitated. Paul had proposed that he drive to the farm. He wanted her approval for investing half of Brad's insurance on a short-term basis. 'But Paul, driving here would be such a waste of your time. Couldn't you just go ahead and arrange it, whatever it is, on my behalf? Whatever you think best?'

She doesn't want to see me, thought Paul. Well, naturally. Too vivid a reminder . . . of everything. Of Brad.

'Yes, of course. I can handle it that way,' he said. 'I'll go ahead then, Roberta.'

Roberta was contrite. She wasn't being very cooperative. 'You see, Paul, I'm just sort of digging in here, just getting used to it . . .'

'And you don't want to lose your momentum. I understand.'

'You *do* understand,' she said gratefully. 'Anyway, we'll be meeting soon, won't we? When everything is finally settled, I mean. Six weeks or so?'

'It might take a little longer. I'll call you. Meantime, if you have any problems . . .'

'I'll call *you*. Thanks for being so patient, Paul. Best to Alicia.'

Momentum, he had said. That was the right word. She

was trying to set her life in motion. And the effort was so uncertain, so *shaky*, that any interruption, no matter how valid, could throw her off course.

I certainly wasn't going to tell him I've decided to look for a job, she thought. Not that he'd laugh, he's much too chivalrous. But he would certainly wonder what I thought I could *do*, as I wonder myself, she thought ruefully.

Roberta had been alone one full week . . . and had survived. She'd learned that eating alone, sleeping alone, and getting up alone does not kill you – even when you do it all over again the next day. The experience was bittersweet. Bitter, because it had been thrust upon her. Sweet, because she'd lived through it.

Moving through the unnaturally orderly, eerily quiet rooms – no footsteps but her own, no jacket flung on a chair – she struggled to find herself. Her self. She tried to face solitude not only in the sense of being unmarried – incredible enough – but in the deeper sense of being a one. An only. Not twinned to another. Separate. For the first time in her life, she glimpsed herself as a someone. It was almost like meeting a stranger.

Of course, there were moments when all the violent emotions of the past two months hit her without warning. Then, helpless to control them, she relived them. The aching longing for the past. The stab-wound hurt of Brad's betrayal. The hot fury at him for *dying* and thus *cheating* her, forever, of knowing why he had left her. And for whom.

In one of these moments of anger, she rushed through the house, collecting photos of Brad, and marched them into the attic, where she shoved them into the darkest corner.

Then she flew downstairs and flung open the door of

the room she and Brad had shared. She had not slept there since . . . before.

It was *her* room now, and she could move back into it. She would not give up the corner fireplace and the beautiful view. Why should she? She would rearrange everything, make it a woman's room, and she would sure as hell get rid of the double bed and substitute a single one.

Roberta emerged from her seven days in solitary with a nascent sense of strength. Very small, very new, but alive and kicking. It was strange to perceive herself as a . . . person. Roberta Marston, person. Other than daughter, wife, mother. Funny feeling.

Trying to summon courage, she told herself she would not settle for an empty life. Although she was alone, she would not be 'lone.' First she would join, somehow, that vast majority of the human race who work, stand on their own two feet. As for those who worried about her well-being, well, she'd show them. Here Roberta's sense of humor stirred, and she had to laugh at herself. 'I'll show them.' Like a kid, fist clenched. But maybe not a bad slogan, at that. No, she thought more soberly. No, it should be I'll Show Me. That is the essence of it.

Roberta had never worked, unless you counted that one brief year between college and marriage when she had worked at Lord & Taylor, an offshoot of being on *Mademoiselle*'s College Board in her senior year. No, that couldn't possible count. Not twenty-five years later. Face it, she said to herself. You are without training and experience, and you are forty-seven.

But there must be *something* an adult woman, not exactly decrepit, with a B.A. in English Lit and an Art minor, could do for a living? Here in the country? she thought doubtfully. Among these farms and woodlands and meadows? Of course, there were nearby towns.

Clinton, Fleminton. A little farther away, Lambertville and New Hope.

The trouble was that she knew nothing about them. She had never set foot in Flemington, for example, even though it was only twenty miles away. Surprising, considering how long they had owned the farm. But she and Brad, like most people in love with country property, had begrudged every moment away from their own acres. Other than country auctions and flea markets, she had never even shopped locally, except for food. So for all practical purposes, Roberta was a stranger to the area, as if she had just arrived.

She bought the local weekly papers, the *Hunterdon Democrat* and the *Delaware Valley News*, and scanned the short help-wanted columns. Wanted: riding instructor, fast food cook, experienced bookkeeper, dairy hand, tractor salesman. Nothing.

The best bet for someone totally inexperienced must surely be some sort of selling job, she reasoned. Her obvious first step was to explore the area to see what sort of shops existed. It would be logical to start with Clinton, because it was closest.

On Saturday morning she methodically browsed from one end of Clinton's charming Main Street to the other. Lots of arts and crafts, dress shops, a gift shop, a book store. Most were small, and appeared to be owner operated. Appealing, but not very promising.

In Flemington, however, Roberta was amazed at the size of the glass and china place, the fur shop, and the vast pottery store that was housed on the site of a towering old brick kiln. She was unprepared for bustling Turntable Junction, an enclave of artfully restored old buildings that housed shops selling all kinds of merchandise: antiques, reproductions, linens, specialized foods, plants, leathers, fashions, party accessories. To heighten the effect of Americana, an old steam engine train huffed to and fro at regular intervals.

Why, the place is teeming, thought Roberta. The parking lot was crowded and lots of people were shopping. When a special excursion bus pulled up, Roberta realized the place was something of a tourist attraction. With that much active business, there probably was also an active turnover in help.

Encouraged, she entered one of the restaurants in the complex for lunch. She had picked up a 'Guide to Flemington,' and she studied it as she waited for her order. All the shops were listed, complete with phone numbers. On Monday she would call each one on the list and ask for the name of the owner. Then she would send letters of application. Her first job applications, at this late date.

She spent the rest of the afternoon exploring the shops and noting which ones had the larger sales staff. She wound up buying some hand-dipped candles and six wineglasses. It was hard to resist Flemington's wares, and she noticed that almost nobody was empty-handed. All these people trooping from shop to shop were actively buying. She made her way back to the car exhilarated and optimistic.

In the interest of familiarizing herself with the area, Roberta decided to take a different route home. Her map showed that she could take Route 12 west, then follow the Delaware River north.

A half-hour later as she drove slowly down the main street of a tiny town, looking for the turnoff, her eye was caught by a discreetly lighted gold-lettered sign saying only Cheese. Interesting, she thought. Not Fine Cheese, or Choice Cheese, or even Good Cheese. Whoever ordered that sign obviously thinks less is more. I agree. On impulse, she pulled up and parked. Might as well check out this place to round off the day, she thought. Leave no stone unturned. Besides, the sign had done its work. She had a sudden hankering for cheese.

Inside, the shop was handsome and sophisticated, and the wares were more extensive than she'd expected. Good-looking kitchen utensils of gleaming copper and steel, many imported from the look of them, were on display.

'You look so surprised.' A small chic woman with a crop of crisp gray curls was looking at Roberta with amusement.

'Forgive me,' laughed Roberta. 'But I am. Such an impressive shop. I didn't expect to find it in . . . what *is* the name of this town?'

'Smith's Mill. Population fifteen hundred. People are always surprised.'

'Well, it has been an afternoon of surprises. I've just been in Flemington, for the first time. I didn't expect to find all that, either.'

'Yes, isn't Flemington something?' The woman moved toward the door to lock it.

'Oh, you were about to close,' Roberta said apologetically.

'Yes, but do browse, if you like. I'll be with you in three minutes.' She sank into a little chintz chair, took off her high-heeled pumps, put her feet up, and lit a cigarette. 'Forgive the informality, but I *must* have a breather. What a day!'

'That busy?' asked Roberta.

'That busy. Thank heaven, of course. But I am *beat*.'

'I can imagine. But tell me, where does your clientele come from?' Roberta was wandering among the Robot-Coupes and espresso makers. 'I had no idea that this area could support such a shop.'

'People find you. Somehow they find you. They come

54

from across the river in Bucks County, and there are a lot of city people hidden in the back roads and up the lanes in Hunterdon County and Warren County. Even some of the farmers come in – those with a taste for cheese, that is. By the way, I'm Jane Whitford.'

'I'm Roberta Marston. And I do congratulate you, Mrs Whitford. Your shop is fantastic. Did you start it yourself?'

'In a little hole-in-the-wall in the next town. Just cheese at first, and a small selection of good biscuits and bread to go with it. It was very hard going in the beginning. Not a soul showed up the entire first week.'

'And you didn't lose your nerve?'

'We came close. By the end of that first week, my partner and I thought we were facing ruin. And then, on Saturday morning, in came our first customer, God bless her. And she bought like there was no tomorrow. She walked out with sixty dollars worth of cheese, ten boxes of Carr's Water Biscuits, and a lot of our special bread. She was giving a huge party. Maggie and I thought we were dreaming.'

'I'll bet you were pinching yourselves, but you must have felt it was a good omen.'

'We made ourselves think it was. We figured if there was one party giver, there might be another. We especially hoped to attract city people like Margaret Rumford – she was our historic first – who entertain in their country places but don't like to lug everything from town. But it took a whole year for us to break even. Neither one of us made a cent during that first year.'

'How triumphant you must feel now.' Roberta had tremendous respect for this small hard-working woman, tinged with something akin to envy.

'Well, yes. But now there's another huge problem. My partner's husband has been transferred to Atlanta. I'm prepared to buy her out – thank heaven, I can swing it – but I can't manage alone. I need help, and not just anybody. I need someone at home with expensive stuff like this; the locals just won't do. You don't know anyone, do you?' She seemed to ask the question routinely, not really expecting an answer.

'I'm looking for work,' said Roberta.

'You?' Jane Whitford looked incredulous. She eyed Roberta's clothes. 'But surely you're a weekender?'

'I was, but now I'm here to stay. I was recently widowed, and I've decided to leave the city and stay on in the house my husband and I bought in Greenwillow Township.'

'Really? Alone?' Roberta could see Mrs Whtiford was curious. 'This can be a terribly isolated place as *I* can tell you, especially for someone used to Manhattan. You *are* from Manhattan, of course?'

Roberta nodded. 'I realize it can take a lot of adjustment, but I have made up my mind. And I'm not totally alone. My son is at Lafayette.'

'Do you really want a job?'

'That is why I was in Flemington today. I wanted to look at the shops there. I planned to make some initial contacts on Monday.'

Mrs Whitford looked at Roberta appraisingly. She hesitated; then she said abruptly, 'Look, Mrs Marston. You are obviously the type I'm looking for, but frankly, it's very hard work and pays very little, at least to start. You see, when I buy out my partner, I'll be reinvesting the profits to pay for her equity. Naturally an assistant will be in a different position from a partner who made an investment and knocked herself out to get the thing started.'

'Of *course*,' said Roberta.

'And I need someone I can count on.' Mrs Whitford

56

was all business now, very much the prospective employer. That's why she's made it, Roberta thought admiringly. 'I don't want to put time into training someone who'll get bored and quit just when I need her most, or someone who'll decide to spend the winter in Jamaica.'

'That would never occur to me.'

Somewhere in the shop a clock chimed seven.

'My God, is that seven?' cried Mrs Whitford. 'My daughter will be getting anxious. Excuse me.' She got up, rushed to the phone, and dialed. 'Patty? I'm leaving now. Be home in fifteen minutes.'

She turned back to Roberta. 'Mrs Marston, you'd be an absolute godsend – if you're serious. But before we decide anything, I should really give you a clear picture of what's involved. What about coming to my place for breakfast tomorrow? Sunday's my only day off, and I try to stay at home with my daughter. Okay? Third house on Chimney Stone Road.' She gave instructions. 'Eleven o'clock?'

'I'd love to. I'll be there, Mrs Whitford.'

'Good.' Mrs Whitford was briskly turning out lights. 'See you tomorrow.'

She didn't mention a husband, thought Roberta on the way home, and from the way she spoke of her child, it sounds as though she's a woman on her own, too.

6

Jane Whitford's house was a small saltbox with an eagle over the door and blue shutters. She greeted Roberta in jeans and a T-shirt. 'My chore clothes,' she said. 'My day for the damned housework. Come on in.'

Roberta followed her down a braid-rugged hall into a sunny kitchen, where a table was laid for two.

'You'd be surprised how quickly you settle for eating in the kitchen when you're busy,' said Mrs Whitford. 'Anything to save time.'

'But who wouldn't, with a view like that?'

'It is nice, isn't it? One of the reasons I bought this house after my divorce. As different from New York as possible.'

Another fugitive from the city, thought Roberta.

'Here, let me pour you a cup of coffee while I whip up some eggs.' She waved Roberta to a chair. 'Patty is at a neighbor's. So we can talk in peace.'

Over a puffy omelet and flaky biscuits, they chatted about the city, discovering they had lived two blocks from each other, and compared notes on how they had stumbled on this unheard-of part of New Jersey. Then they traded information on their children.

Pouring a final cup of coffee, Mrs Whitford said, 'And now to brass tacks.'

For the next hour, she laid out for Roberta a detailed picture of what running a retail food shop involves. Sanitary codes, for starters. You had to have a permit, be inspected by the Board of Health, and meet prescribed standards in your refrigeration, behind-the-scenes sink, and restroom. Commercial refrigeration was one of the biggest single investments, and if the electricity was cut off during a storm – you could lose your entire stock to spoilage.

As for the cheese, that was a study in itself: country of origin, correct storing temperature, correct serving temperature, lasting properties . . . Cheese was as tricky as wine, and people were as self-conscious about cheese as they were about wine. They wanted to know what cheese went with what, but were shy about asking. And afraid of mispronouncing the names. Was *that* an art, said Jane Whitford – telling the customer what he wanted to know, without making him feel ignorant.

Then there were the suppliers. Finding the right ones in the first place. Establishing credit. Then hounding them, sometimes for promised deliveries. More than once Jane or her partner had to spend half a day picking up an order when they were running short and facing a big weekend.

The paperwork never stopped, either, Jane Whitford went on. Checking the invoices, to be sure orders were complete. Paying the wholesalers. Balancing the receipts. Taking inventory. Billing charge customers.

And all that applied to the kitchenware too, except for perishability. On the other hand, the kitchen stuff came from entirely different markets, so that meant buying trips, wholesale catalogues, and a different pricing structure – to say nothing of the damned retail sales-tax forms.

'My God!' said Roberta, awed.

'Complicated, right? You do have to keep a lot of balls in the air, but of course, you catch on. It gets easier with time. After all, every little Mom and Pop store does basically the same thing. Still, it isn't as simple as it looks to the customer, not by half.'

'I'll *never* go into a store with the same feeling again,' said Roberta fervently.

Mrs Whitford laughed. 'And I haven't even mentioned the blasted menial work. Opening cartons, unpacking them, sticking on price labels. That's really tiring – and *very* boring. I have a boy for that, but he doesn't always show up. When he doesn't, Martha or I have to pry up all those staples, and get rid of the excelsior. Even the cleaning is a problem. Sometimes we just grab a broom and dustcloth, and go at it.' She smiled. 'I wouldn't ask anybody to do what I wouldn't do myself, but neither would I let anybody in for that sort of thing without due warning.'

'*Got it*,' said Roberta.

'Are you game?'

'I'm game.'

'Would you accept two hundred dollars a week?'

'I certainly would, Mrs Whitford.'

'Oh, Roberta!' Mrs Whitford jumped up impulsively and hugged Roberta. '*May* I call you Roberta? I'm Jane. Listen, I'm so pleased. You're exactly the sort of dame I wanted, but didn't dare hope for. I had to give you that long song and dance so you'd know what to expect, but it's not all struggle, you know. It's a lot of fun too, a lot of laughs sometimes. You and I are going to get along beautifully . . . I feel it.'

'I'm thrilled,' said Roberta. Should she say she had never worked before? Why not? 'It's practically my first job.'

'I figured! When can you start?'

'Tomorrow?'

'Tomorrow it is. Nine o'clock.'

As Roberta was going down the front path, Jane called from the doorway. 'You don't happen to type, do you?'

'I do. I took a course. I typed all through college.'

Jane made a circle with her thumb and first finger, signifying *terrific*! 'I knew it was my lucky day! See you tomorrow.'

Roberta flew home on a high of stimulation. I have a job! I'm a working woman – and I only started to look yesterday. It was luck of course. If she hadn't happened to notice that Cheese sign, if she hadn't tried a new way home . . . How many of life's major turns are decided by chance? she wondered. On the other hand, if she hadn't been *looking* for work, she'd never have *taken* that back road.

Still, it was definitely luck to meet a dynamo like Jane Whitford. What an inspiration she was to a woman facing life alone for the first time.

Wait until I tell the kids, she thought. She called Jim that night.

'A job? In a cheese shop? Doing what?'

'Just learning, at first,' Roberta replied humbly, 'then selling cheese, of course . . . and kitchen stuff . . . and making out bills – everything.'

There was a pause while Jim let it sink in. Then he said, 'Wow! Right on, Mother!'

But when she called Susan, her daughter said: 'A *what*? A *cheese* shop? Father would have had a *fit*!'

On Monday morning Roberta found both Jane Whitford and her departing partner at the shop. Molly Fields greeted Roberta warmly. 'Am I glad you're here, Mrs Marston. I was worried sick about leaving Jane without help. But you know what husband's transfers are. When the corporation calls, you *go*.'

'This poor woman has a huge house to pack and move,' Jane explained to Roberta. 'By rights, she should be gone by now. But trouper that she is, she insisted on standing by this week.'

'Least I could do.' Molly smiled. 'But let's get going. What's first for Mrs Marston, Jane? Cheese?'

'Right! Come on, Roberta. You're about to get your feet wet.'

Molly disappeared into the little office in back. And for the next couple of hours, Jane gave Roberta an education in cheese. Soft, semisoft, hard, runny on the inside. Cheeses with herbs, nuts, seeds, or wine. How different things looked from the other side of the counter, Roberta thought. During that time there were no customers; Jane said Monday mornings were always slow. The first customer was just entering, a young man in jeans.

'The lunch trade,' Jane whispered to Roberta.

'Hi,' said the young man. 'Can I have a pound of feta and a loaf of . . . What's the name of that bread I always buy?'

'Kommisbrot. Here you are.' Roberta watched as Jane took a cardboard carton, lined it with wax paper, then lifted a chunk of feta from its brine, and placed it on the scale. 'One pound and one ounce. Close enough?'

'Close enough,' said the young man.

'He's a clerk at the post office,' said Jane, after the customer left. 'Funny, Martha and I never thought of this as a lunch stop. But people who work in the area have caught on to cheese as a switch from hamburgers and potato chips. We get quite a few from the paper mill, too. In fact, here come a couple of them now.'

Roberta noted that Jane greeted the two girls by name. Rather nice, she thought, the neighborliness. While Jane was busy, a burly man in heavy workclothes, obviously a farmer, came in. Instantly, Molly appeared smoothly from the back room. 'May I help you, sir?' She must have ears in the back of her head, thought Roberta.

'I want to get my missus one of them machines,' said the farmer.

'Machine?' Roberta could see Molly trying to guess: salad spinner, coffee maker, cheese grater?

'I don't know what you call it. But she's dead set on it for our anniversary. Supposed to do everything. What does she call it? Sounds like Robert Coop.'

'Certainly, sir. Right over here.' Roberta remembered what Jane had said about people being embarrassed at using unfamiliar names. Molly did not say, 'Oh, you mean *Robot Coupe*.' Instead, she said, 'Yes, the food-processing machine. It does chop and blend and mix dough.'

'That it?' said the farmer. 'How much?'

He's going to fall over when he hears the price, thought Roberta.

Molly turned the box over to get the exact price with tax. She named it.

'Okay,' said the farmer, pulling a roll of bills from his pocket.

'Would you like me to gift-wrap it?'

'Sure.'

'How *about* that!' said Molly, after the man had left. 'Now who would guess that he would buy our most expensive item without blinking an eye? One thing you learn in retailing, Roberta, is that you really can't judge who'll buy what. You think you can. Somebody well dressed and well spoken looks like a better bet than someone who is not, but it doesn't always work that way. Some of the best-heeled are positively chintzy, and vice versa.'

'Lord, its one-thirty,' said Jane. 'I forgot to tell you what we do about lunch. The truth is, Molly and I just grab a bite in the back room when we have a chance. Then, if either of us has a personal errand we want to do,

63

we take turns dashing out before noon or after two. We both try to be here in the middle of the day. That's hardly your conventional lunch hour. But is it all right with you?'

'Of course.' Roberta hadn't given a thought to lunch.

Molly made coffee on the hot plate in the back room, while Jane served chicken salad on paper plates. Between bites, Jane and Molly took turns in the complicated business of training a new assistant.

'I'm going to have to be in New York Wednesday and Thursday for buying,' said Jane worriedly. 'Actually, I should have been in the market last week. While I'm gone, Molly can break you in on the kitchen stuff. Then Friday, when I'm back, Molly can give you a preliminary idea of the paperwork. Don't you think that's best, Molly?'

'Look,' said Roberta. 'What about my staying awhile at night, after we're closed . . . if you have time?'

'*Would* you?' said Jane. 'I didn't want to suggest it, but it really is the only way to cover a lot of ground without interruption.'

'I'd be happy to.'

'Jane,' said Molly, 'you're in luck. And did you notice the way Roberta said "when *we're* closed"? She's got the old team spirit already!'

On Saturday night Roberta drove home from the shop dead tired. Molly had finished up on Friday, and she and Jane had been alone. There had been a rush of customers so the day had flown. She had enjoyed it immensely, and she was intensely conscious of the paycheck in her handbag. Funny, she thought, I've never been especially money conscious. But I love that check, I'll hate to cash it. Ridiculous, I suppose. But it is the first money I've ever earned entirely on my own. Simultaneously very tired and very stimulated, she wished she weren't going home to an empty house. She wanted to share her success with someone, to tell someone about her new experience. Suddenly she had a flash of understanding about the contribution she'd made to Brad's career. Of course! She had always been there to *listen*, to act as a sounding board. From the very beginning of his climb up the corporate ladder, she had cheered him every rung of the way, had cheered him even during setbacks. How nice it would be to have someone waiting for *her* now.

There *was* someone at home. As her house came into view, she saw warm, welcoming lights. Her heart lifted. It could only be Jim. Bless him.

He was standing, grinning, in the doorway, two cocktails on a tray in his hand. 'Welcome home, working lady!'

'Jim!' She flew at him, and flung her arms around his neck. 'I've never been so glad to see anyone!'

'Careful. You'll spill the drinks.' He set down the tray and gave her a bear hug. 'I figured you'd want to report on your career – and I've got some grub ready.' She could see candles flickering in the dining room. 'Only TV dinners, I'm afraid. But edible, I hope.'

'Sounds delicious. I'm famished. But, Jim, I thought we made a deal. You're not to pass up your weekends.'

'Don't worry. They'll keep. I *do* have a date tomorrow, if that makes you feel any better.'

'Oh, good. It does.'

Over their TV dinners, which Jim had removed from their foil trays and served ceremoniously on dinner plates, Roberta poured out all her impressions of her first week on the job.

'Have you ever been in Smith's Mill? You can go down the entire main street in five minutes. Doesn't it strike you as amazing that a really rather sophisticated shop could exist there?'

'I guess wine and cheese parties have come to the hinterland.'

'That's *right*! We had a customer today, about your age, who mentioned he was giving a party. He bought about eight different kinds of cheese. And there's a fairly good wine shop not too far away.'

'I'll pass the word around the campus.' Jim smiled. 'Tell everybody to pick up party stuff at my ma's place of business.'

'Oh, do! I understand that's called a "following," when an employee brings in customers who are friends of hers. I'd love to bring Jane Whitford a following. She works so *hard*.'

'I'll do my best to drum up some trade.'

'You know, Jim, I don't feel I've been much real help yet. You have no idea how complicated it is – the buying and pricing, shipments and deliveries, all the paperwork.' She looked at him wide-eyed. 'You have no *idea* . . .'

Why, she's as enthusiastic as a kid, thought Jim. She's sparkling, and she looks so young. Almost young enough to be taken for his older sister. Well, not quite. But an incongruously young aunt, at the very least.

Jim rose to change the plates. 'Dessert and coffee in the living room, madam. Go in and put your feet up.'

Jim could not really see his mother cutting pieces of cheese and making change, or even selling quite expensive kitchen stuff and gifts. Not for long. It was too radically different from the life she was used to, but for now, she seemed to be thriving on it. Jim was too loyal to the memory of his father to easily imagine his mother close to another man. Still, looking at her as he brought in the coffee, so slim and pretty in that big chair, he did allow himself to think that she'd probably remarry, someday. It was hard to picture a woman like his mother living alone for very long.

'And another thing, Jim' – Roberta was happily chattering on – 'just this one tiny week in a shop has opened my eyes so. You remember our Gristede's, around the corner from Seventy-ninth Street on York Avenue?' Jim nodded. 'Well, I must have been in there hundreds of times. And I never gave a thought to how all those cans and packages got onto the shelves. I passed people unpacking big cartons and stamping prices on things, without ever even *seeing* them. *Oblivious*. And now! Why, I can't tell you what respect I have for the manager of a supermarket. He has to know and do so many different kinds of things. Really, I'm awed.'

'Learning how the other ninety-five percent lives, right?'

'You're teasing. I *have* been on a soapbox, haven't I? And I know I sound naive, babbling on about a job as though it's a new invention. But it is new to *me*.'

Roberta was seized by a tremendous yawn. 'Forgive me! I haven't even mentioned college. How is it going, Jim?'

'Fine, mother. Everything's under control. But I can see you're falling asleep. To bed with you.'

'I *am* beat,' confessed Roberta. 'Dead tired. You don't mind?'

'Of course not. As a matter of fact, there's a party on College Hill that's probably just getting into high gear.'

'Good.' She kissed him good night. 'It was dear of you to surprise me, Jim. I loved dinner.'

She waved him off at the door, and in ten minutes was sleeping like someone who had put in an honest day's work.

* * *

Six weeks later Roberta was astonished to catch herself in a moment of – could it be? – *happiness*? At least, a sense of well-being, contentment of a kind. It was Saturday. She and Jane had just closed the shop. She was rushing home because Mingo was coming to spend the night and all day Sunday. We'll probably sit up half the night talking, she thought happily, and we can sleep tomorrow, which will be heavenly.

You can't know what a day off *means* until you work, she thought, to say nothing of appreciating the simple act of sitting *down*. Now she knew what it was to stand up most of the day. It had been excruciating in the beginning; she had now known that fatigue could make the body ache so. But now that she'd found her working legs, she was feeling the need of something to do to fill her evenings.

For the past few weeks Roberta had done nothing but work, eat a scrappy dinner, and sleep. She was beginning to feel at home in the shop, and it was already clear that she and Jane complemented each other well. Jane's great strength was her business acumen, her steady eye on the profit margin. But Roberta was developing a latent gift for display, for the presentation of the 'merch,' as Jane called it.

Jane had struggled all one morning with a window display of dark blue enamel cookware which had just arrived. 'Damn it!' she said when she finished. 'It looks terrible. Roberta, can you see what's wrong with this window?'

Roberta studied it. 'Perhaps it's a matter of scale? That huge basket in the corner dwarfs the stockpot. And maybe the color values are wrong? Perhaps a gray blue cloth, if we have one, would show up the dark blue better?'

'Try it, will you, Roberta?'

Roberta had redone the window, and had been absurdly gratified to have a passing car slow, stop, and look. A woman had come in to inquire about prices. She had bought a saucepan, but had said she'd be back for a larger piece when she could afford it.

'Terrific!' said Jane, when the customer left. 'That's called "pulling power." Listen, Roberta, if you have any ideas about display, or anything else, speak up, will you? I need all the talent I can get.'

Roberta smiled to herself. Jane was so infectiously ambitious. More than once she'd seen a visionary gleam in Jane's eye. 'Why not a branch shop?' she'd asked. 'When this one gets to the saturation point for its location, why not another one?'

What a break to have a boss as stimulating as Jane. And how good it was to be rushing home to meet another special woman, her dearest friend Mingo.

7

Her best friends invariably described Mingo Darcy's face as 'interesting.' Those who envied her said maliciously, 'Such *unfortunate* features.' But her body was something else again. She had the long attenuated lines of a fashion sketch – a few bold strokes in black and white – understated, elegant. 'Best bones in the business,' said the fashion designers who adored her.

Roberta looked at her affectionately. Although it was October and there had already been a frost, the temperature on this Indian summer day was an incredible eighty degrees. Mingo was stretched out on the garden chaise in a tiny black bikini, every inch of long length gleaming with suntan lotion, her hair yanked back in the severe chignon she always wore, tiny white herbal eye pads on her eyelids.

Underneath that facade, Roberta knew, beat the heart of a hausfrau. There was no one like Mingo to fuss over you when you were sick, to roll up her sleeves and plunge in when there was a disaster in your kitchen, or to cheer you when you felt low.

But today Mingo seemed a little low herself. She was not at all her usual wisecracking, irreverent self. Does her glamorous, globe-trotting life pall sometimes? Roberta wondered. As fashion editor of *Cachet*, Mingo knew everyone who was anyone on both sides of the Atlantic. She was at home in Paris, Florence, Rome, and New York. She had been the first of the fashion press to get to China, she had been in Russia and Japan, she had photographed furs in Mongolia and bathing suits by the

Red Sea. If anyone had a pressed-down and overflowing life, it was Mingo.

Last night, as Roberta had expected, they had talked half the night. Roberta had told Mingo all about her new job and her new life. Mingo had reported the latest from the jet set, and had brought Roberta up-to-date on their mutual friends in town. Even after they had reluctantly gone upstairs to bed, Mingo had wandered into Roberta's room, and they had talked still more, like girls in a dormitory.

Mingo had been very much her customary amusing self. But now, as they lapsed into a momentary, companionable silence, Roberta saw a hint of sadness on Mingo's expertly made-up mouth.

'Ming?'

'Um?'

'Penny.'

'Not worth it.'

'Something worrying you?'

'Nothing more than your basic everyday *Angst* – the secret hang-up with your very own name on it.'

'Oh, Mingo, don't I *know*.'

'It's partly *Weltschmerz*, I suppose. Wondering what it's all about, what it's all for.'

'Everyone feels that at times. Even teenage kids, from what I hear.'

'Well, I'm no teenage kid. I'm Madame Chic, of a certain age, known in every overpriced restaurant, bistro, beauty spa, and watering spot from here to Taormina. To say nothing of the Avenue Matignon *and* Seventh Avenue. And I know everyone with a name that's a *Name*. But where am I going? What's the last act of this scenario?'

'You mean you're worrying about getting older?'

'Not older. Not even *old*. With a face like this, what

have I got to lose?' Her lips twisted in a travesty of a smile. 'No, I'm not afraid of being old. I'm afraid of being old *alone*.'

Mingo sat up and whipped off the eye pads. Roberta was dismayed to see unshed tears.

'Mingo, *darling*, surely that doesn't have to be. You've bowled over at least three nice men that I know. *Real men*, I mean,' she added hastily. Mingo often chose her escorts from among the more distinguished gays. 'And I'm sure there must have been others. Like that diplomat your letters were so full of a couple of years ago, the one you met in London.'

'Right. I've had my chances.' Mingo lapsed into silence, her eyes fixed on the curve of the creek in the distance.

Roberta had always wondered what went wrong with Mingo's men. A certain kind of man, usually an urbane, older man, could fall hard for Mingo. These men preferred her worldly elegance to mere young prettiness, and they were turned on by her low, beautiful contralto voice, her other great natural asset. Doubtless, they also thought she would make a superb hostess for their impressive establishments.

Roberta remembered the well-known architect who had pursued Mingo when she was just beginning her career. 'She's as elegant as a blueprint,' he had confided to Roberta. Then there was that industrialist, the king of a conglomerate with a logo familiar around the world. But Mingo's relationships with men always followed the same course. She would be seen everywhere with the same man for months at a time. The fashion world would consider a wedding invitation so inevitable that people would begin to plan what to wear. *Women's Wear* would speculate on who would design Miss Darcy's gown, and secretaries at *Cachet* would wonder wistfully where in the world Miss Darcy could possibly go for a honeymoon that she had not already been. Then, abruptly, the man would disappear, and Mingo would again be seen with a different escort every night – a friend or associate, obviously not a lover. When people were bold enough to ask her what happened, Mingo would laugh and say, 'It wasn't made in heaven, darling' or 'Oh, did you think that was *serious*?'

Roberta looked at her friend with concern. They had been close since childhood. They had gone to Brearley together, had spent the night at each other's homes, had vacationed at their families' respective summer places. They had progressed from kids' lunches at the Central Park Zoo, under supervision of a parent or a maid, to lunching alone at Schrafft's in their teens and then catching an exciting Broadway matinee or going on a shopping spree at Lord & Taylor.

But close as they had been, they weren't close enough for Roberta to undertand what had happened between Mingo and the men who had seemed to love her. Somehow Mingo conveyed, without every saying it in so many words, that the part of her life which concerned love and sex had a large No Trespassing sign on it.

Roberta would not have dreamed of probing, but during her years with Brad, she had often wished that her dear friend could experience the same happiness she had. The situation was all the more puzzling because Mingo had such a pronounced leaning toward domesticity, incongruous as that seemed. Even after Roberta and Mingo were well established on their respective paths – Roberta, a traditional wife and mother; Mingo, a spectacular career success – Mingo spent a great deal of time with the Marstons. Christmas, always. Sunday mornings, often. She seemed to prefer sitting around with the *Times* crosswork puzzle at Roberta's to the endless fashionable brunches to which she was invited. And she doted on the

73

children hung over their bassinets, plied them with gifts, even pushed the pram in the park. Once when Roberta asked her how she could possibly choose to do what the most loving mothers considered a chore and a bore, Mingo answered flippantly, 'Real life, darling. A change from make-believe.'

'Roberta.'

She turned. Mingo's long fingers were tensely gripping the arms of the chaise.

'Roberta, you must have wondered why I never married when more than one gentleman asked me.'

Roberta started to speak, but Mingo stopped her with a gesture.

'Roberta, I'm frigid – frozen . . . ice . . . can't feel.'

'Oh, my *dear*. But, Mingo, there is help, there are ways . . .'

Mingo shook her head. 'Not for my kind of frigidity.'

This time Roberta did not attempt to speak. She sat silent, her eyes on Mingo's, trying to convey support, affection.

'Because do you know what kind of frigidity I've got, Roberta?'

Roberta waited.'

'*Incest*-induced frigidity, Roberta. Frigidity induced by incest.'

Roberta heard her own sharp intake of breath.

Mingo looked at her with pained eyes. For a moment, Roberta saw again the homely, ungainly child Mingo had been at twelve, the suffering child who knew she would never be pretty.

'Mingo . . . surely not,' Roberta heard herself stutter.

'Yes, Roberta. Surely . . . Yes. It happened.'

'Tom?' whispered Roberta. 'Your . . .' she could not say 'your brother.'

'My . . . father.'

Roberta closed her eyes in shock. Mr Darcy. That tall, stiff, stern, formal, correct man who had always seemed so ill at ease when Roberta had visited the Darcys. That man who had always attempted to make small talk with Roberta and Mingo, as if he were trying to do what a father is supposed to do but found it painfully difficult. After a few stilted remarks, he would pull out his billfold, give them each five dollars, and ask Roberta 'Do you like ice cream?' Then he would disappear down the hall to his library. Mr Darcy.

'Do you remember when my mother went to Europe for a whole year and I stayed at home with just Daddy and the housekeeper? When you and I were about fourteen?'

Roberta nodded mutely.

'That was supposed to be so that Tom could study in England. But it was really because Mother was considering a divorce. They didn't get along at all, you know. They always had separate bedrooms. They put up a good front, publicly, but I always thought Mother hated him.'

Roberta remembered Mingo's mother, a dazzlingly beautiful woman.

'Mother never cared much about me either. How could she? She was so lovely. I used to catch her looking at me, wondering where *I* came from.'

Yes, the classic case of the swan giving birth to the ugly duckling, thought Roberta. Mrs Darcy had done all the correct parental things for Mingo: the clothes, the dentists, the summer camps, the parties, the museum trips. But she had never been *motherly*. And, it was true, she had often looked at Mingo's lanky body and homely face with an I-can't-believe-this expression.

'Mother was always crazy about Tom. Of course, he was a lot older than I was. And when he got old enough to be a sort of companion, it was as though Mother felt,

Thank God, there is at least one person who speaks my language! So that sort of left Father and me on the other side of the fence. A house divided.'

Poor kid, thought Roberta. Poor, poor little rich girl.

'So that's how it was. After Mother and Tom left, Father tried to make a companion of me, but he seemed to be so miserable. And he had such a hard time talking to me. When we sat at the dinner table, he'd try to make conversation. He'd ask about school, and I'd answer. Then he couldn't think of a thing to say, so we'd lapse into these awful silences. Finally he'd just give up and say "If you'll excuse me, my dear."'

Roberta sensed that Mingo was no longer aware of her presence. She was lost in an internal scene, reliving it moment by moment.

'It was a Sunday. A rainy Sunday. You know what a rainy Sunday in New York can be for a kid, or for a parent with a kid. Father had planned to take me for a ride in one of the carriages at the Plaza, but it was pouring. He read the papers, and I fooled around in my room. Mrs Robertson had the afternoon off. She'd left things for lunch. Cold veal. I've never eaten it since. I put the food on a tray and set the table. I guess I felt important, taking my beautiful mother's place.'

Roberta felt she couldn't bear what she knew was coming.

'We sat there alone, Father and I, in that big dining room. He had a brandy with his coffee, but even then lunch didn't last long enough. There was that endless afternoon ahead. When Father had finished his coffee and brandy he said, 'What do you say to a game of chess?' We went into the library. He brought the brandy decanter with him. He set up the board and we began to play. Suddenly, without warning, he swept all the pieces off the board and onto the floor. He put his head in his hands and began to cry. I felt so sorry for him, yet I was terrified. He was all I had to hang on to – and he was falling apart. I sat beside him on the sofa and patted his back. All I could say was "Father don't. Father, please don't." He put his arm around my shoulder and pulled me close to him . . .'

Mingo's face revealed her naked anguish.

'Then . . . it happened,' she whispered.

Roberta felt she could hardly bear this.

'It . . . happened,' repeated Mingo. 'And I responded. Responded. *Responded*!'

Tragedy, thought Roberta. What unspeakable tragedy. Two lonely people, grasping in the dark for warmth. Elektra. Poor, poor Mingo.

'The next day Father acted as usual. So did I, But, of course, I was in torment. Hell. Finally, I convinced myself that I had dreamed it. I really convinced myself that it had not happened; then I felt guilty for even dreaming such a thing. Finally, I buried it, simply wiped it out of my consciousness. But of course it just sank into my unconscious – and stayed there, festering. God, the guilt. And you know what happened to Father.'

Roberta did know. Mr Darcy – she remembered hearing her parents talk about it – had had 'a nervous breakdown.' He had gone away for a 'rest,' but he had never come back. Something had snapped in Mr Darcy's brain. For years he had been living in an extremely expensive, extremely discreet private hospital for the mentally ill – an insane asylum. At the time, Mingo's mother had flown back from Europe and then had returned to Paris. An aunt and uncle had stepped into the breach until Mingo went to college.

How can I help? thought Roberta. What can I *do*? She was powerless in the face of Mingo's suffering. Anything she could say would be a cliché – useless – but she did say the obvious things.

'Mingo, Mingo . . . you must not blame yourself. You were a child, a lonely child. Don't punish yourself so . . .'

'Oh, I know, I know. That's what Dr Baird said, over and over . . .'

Roberta knew that Mingo had had a prolonged analysis. 'And it didn't help?'

'It helped, if you can call it that, by getting me to face the fact that it really did happen, that it wasn't a sick fantasy but a sick *fact*. But it took ten years to uncover it, can you believe that? Ten years on a shrink's couch five days a week. It was like giving birth to jagged glass . . .'

'But getting it out in the open – '

'That's as far as we got. Getting it out in the open. It's not true,' said Mingo passionately, 'that finding out what warped you gets rid of the warp. It only lets you know *why* you are warped. That's where I am, warped and knowing why. Dr Baird tried so hard to get me past that point, to help me to feel acceptable as a woman – or even just as a . . . humanoid. He even told me that . . .' – Mingo struggled with the word – 'incest is not the rare, terrible, unspeakable aberration we think it is. It happens more often than most people know, and in' – she tried to smile – 'some of our very "best families." "Look at royalty," he kept saying.'

I suppose that's true, thought Roberta.

'In the end, the good doctor and I settled for sublimation, for the fine art of compensating. Therefore, me and my famous lifestyle.'

'But doesn't that – '

'Make up for a lot? Dashing around the world, seeing my name in print, nonstop fun and games? Plus, I must admit, really hard work. That's the best part. I do get a kick out of keeping *Cachet* the most authoritative magazine going. And I do get my jollies out of spotting talent, finding an obscure designer or artist or photographer and giving him the recognition he deserves. That's a kick. But you know, Roberta . . .' – she hesitated – 'I'd toss the whole thing in tomorrow for closeness . . . for love.'

In her long recital Mingo had regun to recover from the strong emotion which had wracked her earlier. Now she wavered again.

She looked at Roberta starkly, her heart in her eyes. 'In spite of how I look and how I live, I've always wanted the man, the home, the kids – even grandchildren. Like you and Brad, and Jim and Susie. But it's too late for all that, of course. Even if it weren't, I can't *feel*, not in that way. It wouldn't be fair to a man.'

For a second she looked as though she were threatened with tears again. Then, making a visible effort, she forced a smile. 'And that's where you came in!'

'Mingo, I want you to know – '

'I'm going to hate myself in the morning,' said Mingo lightly, ending the conversation. Her familiar amused expression, her protective mask, Roberta realized, slid smoothly over her face. She was Mingo again.

Roberta was sure she would never mention the subject again.

Lying in bed that night after Mingo had left for the city, Roberta thought sadly about her friend's unhappiness. How terrible to hunger for human warmth, and be too frozen to accept it. Did everyone hide a secret pain that the world never guessed? she wondered. Like her own secret pain over Brad?

Even so, Roberta had had twenty-five years of the happiness Mingo had never experienced. Maybe it was true, what they said. If you had to choose your troubles, in the end you'd choose your own. Because other people's were so much worse, once you learned what they were.

8

The young woman on the doorstep was very pretty. What unusual coloring, thought Roberta, such dark eyes with that pale wheat hair.

'Mrs Marston? I'm Terry Fenton. I live on River Road. I hope I'm not disturbing you? I meant to phone first, but then I saw your lights . . .'

'Not at all. Won't you come in?'

'Thank you. Oh, how beautiful you've made this house!' Terry looked around with open admiration as Roberta led her into the living room. 'It's lovely. I used to visit here when I was a kid. I always hoped someone would really restore it.'

'Then you've always lived here . . . is it Mrs Fenton?'

'Mrs, yes. I lived in Thomasville, worse luck. But now we're in Greenwillow, and that's really why I'm here. It's about the proposed development on the hill. Have you heard about it?'

'I'm afraid I haven't. Which hill is it?'

'That one.' Terry Fenton gestured toward the front windows. 'The one across the creek, facing your house.'

'That one? A development?'

'Five houses to an acre, Mrs Marston. Twenty-five houses to start with and more to come.'

Roberta was aghast. Twenty-five houses directly opposite? Why, that would destroy this peaceful country road completely.

'But can they do that? I thought this land was considered agricultural?'

'It is, but our Town Council wants to change it. They've already given it first approval.'

'But that's awful!'

'Disastrous.' Terry Fenton had seemed quite shy at first, but now she was the picture of indignation. 'You see, Mrs Marston, it isn't just a question of ruining a beautiful view. I've done some homework. I checked it out with the environmental protection people. They say the whole *hill* could be undermined. It couldn't stand that much bulldozing. We'd wind up with erosion and mud slides and probably pollution. Forget mere beauty.'

'But I don't understand. How could that be allowed?'

'Lots of things are allowed that shouldn't be,' said Mrs Fenton darkly. 'You wouldn't *believe* how carelessly these things are decided around here.'

Quickly she sketched the facts. The township was run by three men, part-time. They were hardly knowledgeable about this sort of thing – how could they be expected to be – and the public did not get involved. Almost nobody ever showed up at town meetings, so a mere three men could easily make a terrible blunder affecting the whole area.

'. . . And that's why I'm out ringing doorbells,' she concluded. 'To try to get people to turn out and speak up. Could you possibly come, Mrs Marston?'

'Yes, of course I'll come. When is it?'

'Next Tuesday, seven o'clock, at Township Hall.'

'But what can I actually do to help?'

'Just voice your objections, as a taxpayer. After all, your property would be directly affected. So would the Harcourts'. Have you met them?'

'No. I haven't.'

'They're new. They're going to be neighbors of yours. They just bought the house up the road from you, just after you turn into Rimble's Lane. The big Victorian with all the porches.'

'Oh, yes, I've admired it.'

'The Harcourts are going to use it for a weekend place. I was lucky enough to catch Mr Harcourt just as he was pulling in last week. He was very upset when I told him about the development. So they'll be at the meeting too. They're coming all the way from New York just to attend.' She rose. 'I should be getting on. I have three more stops to make.'

Roberta saw her to the door. 'You must be putting in a lot of hard work on this cause, Mrs Fenton.'

'Please call me Terry, Mrs Marston. I *am* spending a lot of time on it. But someone has to do it. You certainly can't trust the countryside to the *locals*.'

'I'm very grateful that you alerted me. And I'll be there, for what it's worth.'

'It's worth plenty. I'll look for you at the meeting, Mrs Marston.'

Roberta closed the door thinking that Terry Fenton was the first Greenwillowite she had ever met, even semisocially. Although she and Brad had strongly identified with their farm, they had been more or less oblivious of the township. It had never occurred to them to seek out their 'neighbors.' Probably that was due to their ingrained New Yorkishness. Everybody knew you could live in a Manhattan apartment building for decades and never speak to the people next door except to say good morning in the elevator.

But now Terry Fenton's visit had jolted her into realizing that she, Roberta, was now also a local – a Greenwillow resident – even though she had no feeling of belonging.

Nonetheless, she would certainly go to the town meeting, not only because the hill opposite, with its beautiful, evergreens, was what she opened her eyes to every morning, but because she owed it to Terry Fenton. It wasn't fair to let someone like Mrs Fenton work so hard on a common cause without lending a hand.

She wondered what Terry Fenton was like, aside from her civic-mindedness. Maybe she would get to know her. Now that I'm used to working, thought Roberta, I could use a few new acquaintances. I need something to do *after* work. I wonder what those new people up the road are like . . . Harcourt, didn't she say?

The little township hall was crowded. People stood against walls as two boys set up extra folding chairs. Terry Fenton hurried over as Roberta entered.

'I've saved a seat for you.'

Roberta looked around curiously. Motley. The local people were by no means all of a piece. Some were obviously farmers. Red-necked and blue-shirted, they sat stolidly, their faces impassive under their duckbill caps. Others were workers at the paper mill. They sported rather loud jackets and their haircuts aimed at the latest fashion but missed. The women were surprising. Lots of overtinted, overpermanented hair. Lots of pastel polyester, worn with 'gold-tone' jewelry. Hardly Grant Wood, thought Roberta.

In strong contrast, a number of people stood out. The small redhead with the Vuitton bag was accompanied by a good-looking man wearing the kind of country clothes that can only be bought in the city. That thoughtful-looking man in elbow-patched tweed was frowning over a document he was reading. An older man had a decidedly aristocratic look. A graceful young man wearing a dangling scarf caught Roberta's eye. As he raised his arm to greet someone across the room, Roberta's mind automatically registered *gay*.

The three men on the platform, the Township Council, looked uneasy, as though they were not used to confronting so many people, yet self-important.

The mayor, a bantam cock of a man, yanked at his purple turtleneck, banged his gavel, and opened the meeting.

The issue was quickly drawn. One by one, those who opposed the rezoning voiced their objections. Roberta rose to say the development could pose a threat to her property through potential flooding, an argument supplied by Terry Fenton. The factory workers and the shopowners supported the proposal. Anything that brought more ratables to the township was good. Anything that brought business was good. You can't stop progress, they said. The argument became heated. Then the man in tweeds stood up.

'I'm John Blair. I live on Creeley's Mountain. I'm here neither to oppose nor support. But I feel the available information is inadequate for a sound judgment.' His voice was calm, objective, authoritative. He had everyone's full attention. 'There are some questions perhaps the council can answer.'

The mayor nodded.

Could the council show the public an accurate map, precisely drawn and surveyed, of the proposed subdivision? Had the first reading, at which the proposal was originally offered, been properly advertised, according to law? Had a geological survey been made? Had the relevant aquifer been located, and was it adequate?

With a few dispassionate questions, John Blair threw the project into doubt. The council members looked at each other, and one literally scratched his head. Then the mayor said that they did not have the documentation, but it was in the works.

'May I suggest, then,' said John Blair, 'that this matter

84

be indefinitely tabled until the additional data is available?'

His tone made it quite clear that unless this were done, John Blair was prepared to throw up legal roadblocks.

'Oh, good, *good*!' whispered Terry Fenton to Roberta. 'Isn't he terrific?'

'Masterly. A lawyer, of course?'

'No, a doctor. An internist. Supposed to be a diagnostic genius.'

John Blair had stopped the rezoning process cold, at least for the time being. The meeting was adjourned. People were milling around, greeting each other, gathering in clumps. Roberta began to slip on her coat.

'Oh, Mrs Marston,' said Terry. 'Don't go! Stick around for the postmortem. Come meet your neighbors.'

Terry headed straight for the redhead Roberta had noticed. 'Mrs Marston, Mrs Harcourt.' – Mid-forties? Roberta guessed. Anyway, a contemporary. And very attractive – 'and Mr Harcourt.'

'Welcome to the Outsiders' Club,' said Carole Harcourt. 'I can tell at a glance *you're* a city mouse.'

'One of *us*, thank God.' Greg Harcourt had a charmer's smile and the looks to match.

'Hello. It's so good to meet you.' What an outgoing couple! 'But I'm afraid all this is over my head. I don't know Thing One about land use or zoning – '

'You'll learn,' said Greg Harcourt easily, 'especially with land as beautiful as yours.'

Roberta was surprised. How did he know where her land was?

Mrs Harcourt guessed her thought. 'There's no anonymity in the country, Mrs Marston. We've learned that already. Even though we're such newcomers, we know your smashing house. In fact, it was one of the things that attracted us to the area. We positively *lusted* after one just like it.'

'And I've always admired yours,' Roberta laughed. 'All those wonderful porches. And that marvelous gingerbread.'

'Try having it painted!' joked Greg Harcourt. 'But seriously, now that we've landed in this neck of the woods, we have to keep after the town fathers. They strike us as clowns, but with a stroke of the pen, they're in a position to alter the whole future of this area.'

'For the worse!' said a newcomer at their elbow. 'We need an entirely new form of government in this township.'

'Oh, Sarah!' said Terry. 'Meet Mrs Marston, and . . .'

Sarah Smith was white-haired, blue-eyed, about seventy, and feisty. Roberta liked her at once.

'Forgive my barging in,' said Sarah. 'But we must get some competence at the helm, otherwise – '

'Sarah is a fighter,' said Terry.

'Great,' said Greg Harcourt. 'Why don't you form a committee, Mrs Smith, and – '

'*Ms* Smith, as it happens, and I might just do that. If you're serious, why not come to my house right now, all of you, to discuss it? It's only nine-thirty.'

'Ms Smith, I'm with you. I'll join any group you set up, but unfortunately, we have to head back to New York,' Greg replied.

'I have a shoot early tomorrow morning,' explained Carole Harcourt. Seeing Terry's puzzled look, she added, 'A TV commercial. That's my job, heaven help me.'

'You mean you came all the way from the city just for this meeting?' asked Carole Smith. 'Does great credit to your sense of commitment, I must say. Okay. I'll hold you to it. I'll count on your support.'

'Listen,' Carole Harcourt said impulsively. 'Why don't

you all come to our place Sunday for brunch? You can let us know what you've decided and tell us what we can do to help. Besides, Greg and I don't know a soul here. We'd love to get acquainted. You'd be doing us a favor.' Her impish smile was irresistible.

'That's a handsome offer,' said Sarah Smith. 'Love to.'

'And bring everybody else you round up for your watchdog committee – *our* watchdog committee.'

Terry Fenton and Roberta accepted gladly.

'Terrific! See you Sunday,' Greg said. The Harcourts left.

'Well, should we go on over to my house?' asked Sarah Smith. 'Terry? Mrs Marston? I'll round up John Blair and Luther Hodges; will you come?'

She hurried off without waiting for an answer. But who can resist such energy? thought Roberta.

As she and Terry waited for Sarah to come back, they were joined by the young man Roberta had automatically labeled gay.

'This is my husband Tim,' said Terry.

Roberta hoped she concealed her astonishment.

'Oh, Mrs Marston,' said Tim warmly, 'we've been *hoping* to meet you. But we natives don't get much chance to mingle with you *city* people. We'd love to, you know – '

'Now, come on, Timothy!' Sarah Smith was back. 'Cut out that "native" stuff. If there were more natives like you, we'd have no problem. Well, John Blair has flown the coop. That man is like quicksilver. But here's Luther, he's got a head on his shoulders. Mrs Marston, Luther Hodges. Shall we go?'

'Sarah,' said Terry, 'do you mind if we switch to our house, instead? We have a baby-sitter and we promised to be back by ten.'

'Anywhere,' said Sarah. 'As long as we get going.'

In the parking lot, Tim gave Roberta directions. 'It's about four miles. Down your road, and then left along the river. Just follow us.'

As they were about to pull out, a distracted-looking young woman rushed up to the Fentons' car.

'Terry, have you seen John?'

'Why, Mary, I didn't know *you* were here.'

'I was in the back, but I can't find John . . .'

'I was looking for him myself,' called Sarah from her car, 'but apparently he left immediately. Did he know you were here?'

'I *thought* he did,' replied the young woman, 'since he brought me.'

'Well, no problem,' said Tim. 'Hop in. We'll take you home.'

Idly, Roberta wondered what that was all about.

The Fentons lived in an old clapboard house backed up against a cliff and facing Pennsylvania across the Delaware.

Terry settled her guests around a long trestle table in the kitchen. As she set out coffee and cake, Tim lighted a fire. How pleasant this is, thought Roberta. And how different these people are from anyone I've known before.

The Fentons did seem rather ingenuously eager. During the social chitchat before they got down to business, Terry mentioned a current piece in *New York Magazine*, and Tim referred to a recent Broadway play, adding 'We try to keep up, even if we do live in the sticks.' But the most striking thing about the Fentons was the obvious harmony between them. Their mutual devotion was obvious.

'What a beautiful fireplace,' Roberta remarked to Terry.

'It is, isn't it? Luther built it.'

'Really?' Roberta turned to Luther Hodges. A stone-mason? His strong and rather work-worn hands did suggest manual work, but his noble head and cultivated speech belied it. You could have taken him for a scholar, or a scientist.

Seeing her look of surprise, Luther Hodges laughed. 'An avocation, Mrs Marston.'

'Luther sets stones the way Winston Churchill laid bricks,' said Sarah. 'For the joy of it. In real life, Luther is a banker.'

'Now, Sarah, you and I have often argued the point. Which *is* real life? Lasting stuff like stone or illusory stuff like money?'

What a fascinating viewpoint for a banker to have, thought Roberta.

Finally, in response to Sarah's goading, they stopped socializing and got down to forming an activist group. Luther Hodges proved to be as amusing as he was articulate. The Fentons were impassioned, and Sarah was tough and practical. The last member of the group, the young woman who had needed a ride home and whom the Fentons had persuaded to join them, said almost nothing. She sat quietly listening, and merely responded, 'Really, I know so little about it,' when the others tried to include her in the discussion.

She seems shy and terribly ill at ease, thought Roberta. But when they'd unanimously decided that the one man to head the group was Dr John Blair, and Sarah asked, 'Do you think he would, Mary?' the shy young woman showed signs of spirit. 'I'm afraid you'll have to ask *him*,' she said.

Why, this must be John Blair's *wife*, Roberta realized. That impressive man. This mousy girl. How strange.

* * *

89

After her guests had left, Terry Fenton lay in bed waiting for Tim to return from driving Mary Blair home. Arms cradled under her head, she looked with satisfaction around their bedroom. She and Tim had hung every inch of the Williamsburg wallpaper – Williamsburg *type*, they couldn't afford the real thing. They had scraped the floors, 'taken down' the fourposter bed, refinished the washstand. And Terry had painstakingly mended the wedding-ring quilt. It could be in *House Beautiful*, thought Terry. I know it could. But of course the people who live around here think it's *weird*. They'd rather have an iridescent taffeta bedspread and a Mediterranean *suite*.

It was an old, bitter theme of hers. Terry had always felt like a fish out of water. She had hated blue-collar, working-class Thomasville, where she was born, since she'd been old enough to be conscious of it. And she had hated what she perceived to be the narrowness and prejudice of its crimp-haired, print-dressed women and its burly macho men. Of course, nobody used the word *macho* then. They were called red-blooded he-men. *He-man*! What a hideous, primitive, chauvinist expression.

Her father had been the biggest he-man of all. Driving a big brute of a truck, drinking beer, yelling his head off at football games – '*Kill 'em!*' – and hunting. Sending cruel razor-edged arrows into the helpless flesh of beautiful, quivering deer and then bragging about the antlers. 'How many points to your buck, Buck?' Of course his name was Buck.

And of course the other kids thought she was 'funny.' She didn't fit in, didn't like what they liked, didn't laugh at what they thought was hilarious. Eventually, they excluded her. Finally, they made fun of her.

She had tried to escape. She had managed to put herself through a community college, and had earned a degree in home economics. Then she had headed for

New York. She thought she might get a job on one of the women's magazines: *McCalls, Good Housekeeping*. But the best she could manage was a receptionist's job. New York had been a terrible blow to her pride. It was so cold, so fast, and so indifferent. After a year, she had fled home in humiliation.

It was a miracle that she had found Tim. He, too, had grown up in Thomasville. He, too, felt alien, different. She had not known him in school, because he'd been a senior when she was a freshman. They met when Tim was twenty-nine and she was twenty-seven, at a church fair. Afterward, he asked her out for a drink. Tentatively, they sounded each other out.

'You don't seem at all as though you come from Thomasville,' she said.

'Neither do you.'

'You seem much too . . . sensitive.'

'The word they use here is "sissy".'

'They would!'

A year later, they were married. Now, seven years and two daughters later, they had escaped to rural Greenwillow. But they were still close enough to Thomasville's factory-town radius to run into people who had scorned them when they were kids – and still did. We have no status, thought Terry resentfully. And the damnable thing is that those clods don't know what status *is*.

She heard the bedroom door open quietly, and Tim tiptoed in. 'I'm awake,' she said.

'It turned out to be a nice evening, didn't it?'

'I thought so. What did you think of Mrs Marston?'

'Super.'

'Yes. Class. Those clothes.'

'It was a sweater dress, wasn't it?' Tim was very fashion conscious. They both were.

'Cashmere. And the way her scarf was knotted, the

91

way she *carried* it.' Terry made all of her own clothes, from *Vogue* patterns. 'Tim?'

He was getting into bed. 'Yes?'

'Do you think we'll get to know Roberta Marston? And the Harcourts?'

'Maybe. But don't get carried away.' Tim was basically cautious. He had learned not to expect too much. 'We don't really know them yet. They're from another world, remember. And, let's face it, I'm really just a kind of clerk – not in their league.'

'You're talented and amusing, when you let yourself be. And you're *nice*. If they don't appreciate that, to hell with them.'

She fell asleep with her head on his shoulder. They were very good friends.

When Tim Fenton drove Mary Blair home, she asked him to drop her at the top of the Blair's lane. 'Of course not. It's too dark,' Tim protested. 'I'll take you to your door.'

'No. Really, Tim. Thanks anyway, but I feel like walking.'

Tim drove off wondering if Mary Blair was really stuck up, as some people said. Somehow, he sensed that she was not. But it was strange that she never invited anyone to visit. He and Terry had stopped making friendly overtures because Mary always politely turned them down. She invariably said she couldn't get away because of the children. But why doesn't she get a sitter, the way we do? Tim thought. She can certainly afford it – better than we can, God knows.

The Blair's place lay at the bottom of a deep valley. Trudging down the lane, Mary reflected that Tim would never guess she'd rather walk a black half-mile than have

92

anyone see her awful house – even anyone as friendly as the Fentons.

Beat-up and shabby hardly described it. It was positively *substandard*, in screaming need of repair and modernization. Nobody would buy it without major restoration in mind, which was the reason Mary thought her husband *had* bought it. But the restoration had never taken place, and they had been there twelve years. Mary Blair was almost used to it by now. But occasionally, like tonight, when she was in someone else's house, the awful condition of her own struck her with fresh force.

And doctors' wives are supposed to live in the lap of luxury! she thought bitterly.

She had tried. She'd called in a kitchen contractor on her own. John had barely glanced at the plan for a beautiful new kitchen. He'd looked at the estimate and said he couldn't afford it.

Mary was bewildered. 'But I don't understand. Your practice is so busy. And you're doing so well.'

Then he told her what he hadn't bothered to tell her before, that he had bought another fifty acres adjacent to the land they already owned and that he was angling for another parcel on the opposite side. He was short of cash because he was investing in property.

Mary was even more bewildered. 'More *land*? But why? Why do we need more land when we already have seventy-five acres?'

'Because owning land is the only way to keep it from being developed. And because someday I'd like to build a small private medical center.' He had never mentioned that either.

Mary climbed the front steps, avoiding, from long habit, the shaky third step where the wood was rotting. As usual, it was a struggle to open the front door. It had been out of kilter when they'd moved in.

But John never seemed to *notice*. As he never seemed to notice her. Again she felt the hot embarrassment that had overwhelmed her at the meeting. To have her husband simply drive off and leave her! She knew he had not done it deliberately. No. They went out so rarely as a couple, and he was so engrossed in the zoning, he had simply *forgotten* her.

A couple. Did John know the meaning of that word? Had he ever? Looking back, she tried to remember if John had ever shown real awareness of her, let alone love? Had she merely assumed that he had, believing what she wanted to believe? She, a Bryn Mawr junior from Maryland's Eastern Shore, had instantly fallen in love with the Johns Hopkins medical student from the midwest. His brilliance had dazzled her, his fervor about medicine and the exalted light in his eye when he told her his dreams of serving suffering humanity. What a romantic she had been. To her, John had been the knight in shining armor, carrying not a lance but a lancet.

He had asked her to marry him without ever once saying he loved her. 'Oh, John. I love you so much,' she'd said and then she had waited. He had merely tightened his arm around her shoulder. Finally she'd dared. 'Do you love me, John?' 'Naturally,' he'd said. She had asked a dumb question. With a man like John, you didn't press him to state what he considered self-evident. She felt she had failed him, not met his standards. Oh, John, I'll try to be worthy of you.

Midge was born a year after their marriage. John was interning at New York Hospital, working long hours, making little money. Mary was struggling with a baby in a fourth-floor walk-up when she found herself pregnant again. By the time she was twenty-six, Mary Blair had four children and John had decided they should leave the city. He had finished his residency, and was on fire to establish a private practice in an area where better medical service was needed. He had picked this area, this house. Mary still had faith. She thought that, with John better able to control his time, they would begin to *live*. Together.

But it had never happened. John never got around to the house, or to her. In a suburb, of course, John would have been forced to provide a better home for his family. Status would have demanded it. But here in the country, where properties were so scattered and hidden from view, no one saw Dr John Blair's home . . . or his wife.

Her hope and her faith had died slowly. And her love? She no longer knew. But she did know that John's true love – his only love – was medicine. It would always come first.

Creeping miserably into bed next to her oblivious husband, Mary Blair wondered how long she could stand nonstop unhappiness.

On the way back to New York, Carole Harcourt turned to her husband. 'What did you think of Roberta Marston?'

Greg took his hands off the wheel, palms up, and shrugged. 'Ech. What can I tell you? Just your run-of-the-mill Upper East Side Wasp matron. A dime a dozen.'

Carole's fingers tightened on her handbag. Mr Putdown. When would she learn? She looked at her husband's handsome face, the careless, negligent way he sat at the wheel. Every line of his body bespoke male superiority. But how did he get that way? What did he have to be superior *about*? Considering.

At the Lincoln Tunnel toll booth Greg extended his hand. 'Have you got change? And by the way, I need money.'

What happened to the check I gave you four days ago? Carole thought. But she didn't say it. She knew better.

No, she'd stick to the policy she had learned was best for getting along with Greg.

'Yes, dear. Right,' she said.

But tell me, she asked herself, why do I need this man? Why? But she did, and she knew it. Carole Harcourt, dynamo career woman, able to support herself luxuriously, could not face life without a man. And Greg was *there*. It was that simple.

A determined and disciplined positive thinker, Carole forced her mind to the people she had met at the Greenwillow town hall. What a mixed bag! But an interesting change from the high-pressure barracudas she knew in the ad business. The country would be a whole new scene. She'd have fun, stir up some excitement. She'd see to it. And if Greg put on his lord-of-the-manor act, and the local yokels all assumed that the house, the horse, and the pool were all *his* doing – with Greg, of course, doing nothing to dispel that impression – well, let them. Let him. What was the difference? The important thing was to get a few laughs out of life.

Roberta got home from the Fentons at one in the morning. As she got into bed she thought how varied these people were. Tim, for example. So very likable, but so clearly not masculine. Bisexual? Latent? Did he even *know*? And what of Terry? Did she know? Apparently, they were very devoted. And that mystifying incident with Mary Blair. Dr Blair was obviously a brilliant man, but how could he possibly accompany his wife somewhere and then simply *leave* her there? Extraordinary. How nice it was that the Harcourts were just up the road. As she drifted off she thought it was no longer true that she didn't 'know a soul' in Greenwillow. She now knew several. She'd see them again Sunday, at the Harcourts.

For the first time since she had been at the farm, Roberta fell asleep without thinking of Brad.

9

Paul Reston realized he was being compulsive. It was capricious, to say the least, to abruptly cancel his last two afternoon apointments and tell his secretary he did not know when he would be back tomorrow. Well, compulsive or not, he thought grimly, he was going to make certain that Roberta was all right. Anxiety rose in him as he maneuvered through the traffic into the tunnel. His secretary had tried to reach Roberta for two solid days. Then he had dialed her at regular intervals last night. His last attempt had been made after midnight. As he'd listened, long past any reasonable hope of an answer, to the indifferent mechanical ringing sound, he had imagined all sorts of mishaps – or worse. Could she have been in the barn for some crazy reason, and fallen from a height? Could she have been in a car accident, be lying unconscious in a hospital? Was there crime in the country? A shady character or a downright crazy might spot Roberta as a woman alone on a remote property, and be intent on robbery or rape.

His hands clenched the wheel. Goddammit! It is insane for a woman like her to be alone in a place like that, he thought savagely. Well, now he had solid arguments for her to sell the place – in black and white. The bottom line was that there was not enough money for Roberta to go on living as she had been living. It was just as he'd feared. But was *feared* the right word? Not exactly, he admitted to himself. He had hoped Roberta would come back to New York, so that he would have a fighting chance to prove his love. But knowing Roberta, he would have to be free first. Well, he was going to set that in motion next week. He already had an appointment with Sam Strauss who specialized in sticky divorces. Of course, Alicia would contest. Even so, he was going to file. He could no longer endure wanting one woman and being tied to another.

But first things first, he told himself. Right now he felt an urgent need to see Roberta, to be sure she was safe. As he turned onto Route 78, his foot pressed the accelerator to the floor.

After work, Roberta picked up a bottle of wine to take to the Fentons. She was due there at seven-thirty for dinner. She would have to hurry to shower and change. But how nice to have something to change *for*, she thought. And how amazing that she now found herself in a kind of modest social whirl. Instant friends-and-neighbors, she thought happily. All due to that one Greenwillow meeting.

There was a strange car in her driveway, with a New York license, she noted as she pulled in. At that same moment, a tall figure came forward from the terrace. Who in the world? Paul Reston. She stood stock-still. Immediately, the sight of Paul Reston evoked Brad, New York, East Seventy-ninth Street, her whole past life – everything she was trying to forget. She had been succeeding too, if not in forgetting, at least in diminishing the memories, the hurt. But now, because Paul was such a vivid symbol of the past, the old pain swept over her, as sharp as ever.

'Roberta!' He gripped both her hands. 'I'm so relieved to see you. Thank God you're all right!'

'All right? What do you mean? . . .'

'I've been trying to get you on the phone. And when there was no answer, I thought . . .'

'Paul. I'm so sorry . . .' She saw the concern in his eyes. He was such a loyal friend that it was unfair to look on him as merely a reminder of the past. Obviously he was just trying to be protective. 'Paul, I'm so surprised to see you that I haven't said I'm *delighted*. And I'm sorry you were worried . . . how thoughtless of me. I should have let you know. I'm out all day because I work – '

'You have a job?'

She laughed. 'You look so astonished. But why are we standing out here? Come in, Paul, and I'll tell you all about it.'

Inside she snapped on lights and settled Paul in the living room. 'Excuse me just a minute, will you, Paul? I have to make a quick phone call, and then I'll make you a martini.'

'Let me make it.'

'Will you? You remember where the liquor cabinet is? The jam cupboard in the dining room. Ice in the usual place. I'll be right back.'

She called the Fentons on her bedroom telephone and quickly explained. Tim sounded disappointed, but understanding. Besides, Roberta knew they were expecting another couple, so she wasn't leaving them completely high and dry. She freshened her face, and then went down to join Paul.

'I'm afraid I have interfered with your plans for the evening,' he said as he rose when she entered. While she'd been phoning, he had wondered if she was breaking a date. Could she possible have met another man already? Would it be too late, when he was finally free? He tensed at the thought.

'Just a little get-together with some neighbors,' said Roberta easily, accepting the martini he offered her. 'No problem at all. But tell me, how are *you*, Paul.'

'I'd much rather you told me about your job.'

She told him. His reaction was predictable.

'A *cheese* shop? You?'

Looking at Paul now, with the urbanity of Manhattan clinging almost palpably to him, she realized how strange it must sound. And looking at herself, through her own ex-Manhattanite's eyes, what she was doing seemed distinctly offbeat even to her. But from her new Greenwillow point of view, it seemed quite natural, even desirable.

'I know it sounds wild, Paul, but you'd be surprised how used to it I am already. It happens to be a rather elegant shop. And so is the owner. Another Ex-New Yorker, by the way.'

'I'm sure it's extremely smart, if you say so. But standing behind a counter?'

'I don't just stand behind a counter,' she said rather defensively. 'There's a lot to learn. And I *love* it!'

Mixed as his own feelings were, Paul sensed that, for Roberta, getting a job was, indeed, breaking new ground. For a woman who had very recently lost her husband with brutal suddenness, a husband with whom she had been totally happy, as Paul had every reason to believe, Roberta was showing remarkable courage. He lifted his glass to her. 'I salute you, Roberta. Here's to true grit, to going job hunting from a standing start.'

'Oh, I sort of lucked into it,' she said modestly.

'But what about evenings, Roberta? Don't you get lonely? Bored? You're far from everything you're used to.'

'Well, I did, Paul. I was beginning to feel a little marooned in the middle of nowhere in the evenings. Then – you'll never believe this – I got involved in a local zoning battle. I joined a citizens' group and helped frame bylaws, got petitions signed, and such. And through that, I've met the most interesting collection of people, people I normally would not have met in a million years. Really a wild mix of backgrounds and ages, come to think of it. I must say, I didn't realize how *insular* we were in New York. You know, corporate types hobnobbing with other corporate types, show-biz people sticking together.'

'Yes, melting pot or not, New York *is* stratified,' agreed Paul. 'So you're not feeling too isolated?'

'Not at all. And you know, Paul, the countryside itself is growing on me. The birds and bees etcetera. Waking up very early and seeing the creek sparkle. Falling asleep listening to it. I used to love all that, on weekends, of course. But I never thought I'd get *addicted* to it. Now I'd miss it terribly if I were deprived of it.'

This is going to make it even harder to tell her about the money situation, Paul thought. She's not just enduring it here, she's enjoying it. He glanced at his watch. 'Roberta, let me take you to dinner. Is there a place nearby?'

'Paul, I ought to be giving *you* dinner. I'll rustle something up.'

'Of course not,' he said. 'I looked forward to taking you to dinner. But you'll have to tell me where . . .'

'All right. I'd love it. There's a place on the other side of the river, quite pleasant. About a half-hour away.'

'Should I call? See if they have a table?'

'Perhaps you'd better.' She gave him the phone book and the name. 'I'll just rush up and put on a dress. Back in three minutes.'

Over dinner, Roberta said apologetically, 'Paul, I've been chattering on and on about *me*. I haven't asked about you. And Alicia.'

He hesitated. Should he tell her about Alicia and himself now? No. Better wait until it was a *fait accompli*.

'Alicia's been out a lot lately.' He would go that far.

'She's very . . . busy. She's bought a small art gallery, you know.'

'*Has* she!' Roberta knew of Alicia's interest in modern art, but it was hard to think of her actually working at it. But then, she thought, I've never felt I really knew Alicia. I don't think she's ever once let her hair down with me. Funny, considering the years we've known each other and the time we've spent together. But it had always been Brad and Paul who were great friends, and we wives just completed the foursome. Not that Alicia and I didn't put in our fair share of girl talk. But we were never what you'd call close.

'An art gallery of her own?' Roberta repeated to Paul. 'How exciting for her.'

'Yes, it is. Exciting.' He didn't want to think about Alicia. And he must get to the matter at hand. There was no really good time to break the news to Roberta that she was financially hard up. So it might as well be now.

'Roberta, my dear. Brad's estate has now been settled. And I'd give a great deal if I didn't have to tell you that there is very little capital. There is not enough income for you to live as you have always lived.'

She stared at him. 'But that's hard to believe. I always thought – '

'I know, I know. Brad's earnings were in the upper brackets. But you see, Roberta. Brad spent to the limit of his income. You and Brad lived very well, Roberta.'

'I suppose that's true.'

'As a matter of fact, Brad's only major investment was your farm.'

'But I never thought of the farm as an *investment*. It was just a place to go in the country.'

Paul smiled. 'I know. But it has proved to be an investment, all the same. A very sound one. You see, Brad poured enormous amounts of money into restoring the house and maintaining the property instead of build-ing a portfolio of other investments. And the money he put in was well invested, because the farm has appreciated in value. It is now worth a great deal of money.'

'Well, that's good at least, isn't it?'

'Yes and no. You see, the farm represents capital that isn't producing income. And income is what you need. Right now, the farm is *costing* money instead of yielding money. In fact, it's costing more money than you have.'

'But how can that be, when I already own it?'

Paul was finding this more painful by the moment. With each cold fact he presented, he felt that he was assaulting a helpless woman, and he felt a hot resentment against Brad, for making all this necessary.

'Roberta, he said very gently, 'have you any idea what it costs to heat your house?'

'I'm very ashamed to say that I haven't.'

He told her. 'That's several times as much as when you bought the place, and fuel prices will rise.'

Of course Roberta knew about the astronomical cost of fuel, but she had never felt the direct impact in cold figures. She had never written a check for an oil bill. In New York, Brad had made regular deposits into her checking account. They had been for food, the maid's salary, and her personal 'walking around money.' All other bills, even her beauty-salon account, had gone to Brad's office. When Brad had died, Paul had offered to have all bills switched to his office, and Roberta had gratefully accepted. Now she realized, belatedly, how much time and effort this man was spending on her behalf.

'Paul,' she said, 'I hadn't realized what a *burden* all this is. To you.'

'No burden at all. I just wish I didn't have to put you through this, Roberta, but there's no cause to be frightened. You do have considerable assets if you turn them into income. But as things are now . . .' He sighed. 'I suppose I really should show you the figures.' He took a paper from his inside pocket and handed it to Roberta.

She studied it. Real-estate taxes, fire insurance, homeowners insurance, water conditioner service, snow removal . . .

Roberta handed the paper back. 'I feel like a financial moron. I had no idea – '

He patted her hand. 'How could you? Why should you? But the point is, Roberta, that these are only this year's figures. High as they are, next year they'll be higher.'

'Yes. I do see. What are you recommendations, Paul?'

Lawyerlike, he ticked them off. 'First, sell the co-op in New York to the Erskines. They're eager to buy. That will give you some capital. Two, sell the farm. Then invest both those amounts as conservatively as possible. That should give you enough income to keep you comfortably secure in a suitable place without all the burdens you have here. Perhaps a small co-op.' Paul did not add until *I* can take care of you, but that was what he meant.

Roberta looked thoughtful. 'But suppose I just sold the apartment and not the farm? How far would that carry me?'

'Not far at all. Not if you spent the proceeds. You must *invest* them.'

'Yes, of course you're right.' She sat turning her wineglass, thinking hard.

'Paul, how long could I last with whatever cash is available right now?'

'Barely a year, Roberta. Based on current expenses and allowing for inflation.'

'A year. A lot could happen in a year. And if I cut expenses, I could last longer?'

'Somewhat longer. But I don't see how you could cut your expenses.'

'I could try.' She stopped playing with her glass and looked at him. 'Paul, I don't want to give up the farm. I've just begun to put down roots. I've made friends. I'm beginning to feel as though I belong in Greenwillow. I couldn't face being uprooted again. Besides, I always wanted the kids to have the place. No. I want to hang on, make a fight for it. I don't know how, but there must be a way.'

Paul had been afraid she would feel that way, but at least he had planted a seed in her mind. The idea of selling her beloved farm had at least been broached. He picked his words carefully. 'Nothing has to be done tomorrow, Roberta. We do have a little leeway. As a matter of fact, it wouldn't be easy to sell the farm overnight, anyway. Valuable as it is, not many people can afford it today. We might have to wait a year or more for the right buyer – a retiring doctor of someone looking for a tax shelter. It would take some time.'

Roberta looked as though she had been given a reprieve.

'Well, it's certainly a challenge, isn't it? One year to save the old homestead! Just like an old movie.'

Paul looked at her. He had just spent two hours telling her she had serious money problems, that she must reduce her standard of living. Her response was to call it a 'challenge.'

'Roberta,' he said, his heart in his eyes, 'may I tell you you're wonderful?'

On the way home, Roberta said little. Paul knew she was thinking hard about a problem she had never faced before, and he was lost in his own thoughts. Suddenly Roberta clutched Paul's arm, exhibiting more alarm than she'd shown all evening. 'Paul! There's one item we didn't discuss. Jimmy. Jimmy's college expenses. What about them?'

'They're taken care of, Roberta. Brad had a separate fund for that. I'm sorry, I thought you knew that.'

'Thank God. No, I didn't know that. I've been an absolute *illiterate* about money. Really, Paul, I'm so ashamed. How could I be so oblivious?'

'Don't feel like that. People only learn about money when they have to.'

'Well, they *should*!' she said severely. '*I* should have. There's no excuse to be so ignorant.'

She was silent again, thinking. Then she said, 'For example, Paul. I do earn some money now. In my job. And do you know, I never once thought of that money in connection with bills? Isn't that incredible? I just thought of it as a sort of . . . prize, I suppose. A nice little extra. But of course, it should at least help to pay the taxes, shouldn't it?'

'Absolutely.'

'So you see, I've already bridged some of the gap between Out and In. Now, I've got to work on some additional approaches.'

'Such as?'

'Oh, I don't know. Maybe take in roomers? Make the place yield a return, as you said?'

'Roberta, that's ridiculous. What an unthinkable idea.' He couldn't help imagining how Alicia would have reacted in a similar situation.

'Maybe. But it's a thought.'

When they got back to the farm, Paul accompanied Roberta to the door and began to say good night.

'Paul, it's late. Why don't the spend the night and get an early start in the morning?'

Paul felt a pang at the casualness of her invitation. It

was all too clear that to Roberta he was simply an old family friend she was sparing a late drive back to the city. Had she felt slightly differently, he knew she would not issue the invitation. As for him, he could not bear to spend a night alone in a house with Roberta. It would be too painful. He didn't need that.

'Thanks, Roberta, but I really must get back . . .'

She laughed. She thought he was concerned with old-fashioned propriety. 'Paul! Don't be silly. Look, there's the carriage house, private as you please. If you leave at seven, you'll be in the city at eight-thirty. And it's really lovely driving along these roads as the sun comes up.'

He hesitated.

'Oh, come on, Paul! Surely you'll let me show you a little hospitality. Have you got an overnight bag in the car?'

He nodded. 'Well, go and get it, while I get the key to the carriage house. Find out what it's like to wake up to the farmer's rooster!'

He decided to stay. 'Thanks. I'd like to.' At least he'd see her in the morning.

Roberta came back with the key. 'There are you. Drive up the lane and park next to that big tree. I'm afraid it will be a little chilly at first, but the thermostat is just inside the door. There's a phone downstairs and one in the bedroom, so you can call Alicia. I'll be up at six. If you're not down by six-thirty. I'll throw pebbles at your window.'

Paul appeared next morning just as Roberta was carrying the coffee into the dining room. 'Good morning,' she said. 'Sleep well?'

'Like a top.' He smiled. Actually, he had spent the night in sleepless thoughts of Roberta, and he had not turned on the heat, to spare Roberta's oil bill.

'You know,' she said, pouring his coffee, 'I had an idea last night. About income.'

'So did I. I want to suggest it to you.'

'Something tells me it's the same idea. You tell first.'

'No, you.'

'Okay. It's renting the carriage house.'

'Exactly! It's very attractive. And it's completely self-contained. It should bring a decent rent.'

'That's just what I thought.'

'If' – he frowned – 'if you got the right sort of person.' He didn't want to think of Roberta being exposed to anyone irresponsible or crude. It had better be a woman, he thought. On the other hand, a man would be a kind of protection for her. She really needed a man around the place in case of snowstorms, or power blackouts and such. But might not a man? . . . He suddenly realized that he had assumed Roberta was as irresistibly appealing to other men as she was to him. But how could she not be?

'Oh, the right sort of person, of course,' said Roberta blithely. 'I'll put an ad in the paper right away.'

'Better let me check the references.'

As she walked him to his car, he hated to leave.

'Paul, I don't know how to thank you for all your help. You have spent so much time on my problems, but I can't let you go on doing that. Look, could you send me a monthly budget figure, the amount I should live within? And won't you please have all my bills forwarded to me? It's time I faced them myself.'

But how will I see you then, Roberta? he thought.

'Certainly, Roberta. Eventually. There are still a few loose ends. I'll be calling you often.'

'Thank you, Paul.' She kissed him on the cheek.

'Can't lure you into the city for lunch?'

'Not anytime soon, I'm afraid. I don't feel I could face New York. Right now, anyway.'

Of course not, thought Paul, as he pulled out. He had been clumsy. Brad had been dead only three months. New York would be painful for Roberta.

He looked back from the road to wave. But she had already disappeared into the house. Of course, he thought, she has to get to work. But he was disappointed.

As for a monthly income for Roberta to live on, that figure, he knew, would be barely more than *half* of the amount currently going into her account. How could she possibly cut expenses by fifty percent? Still, he thought, if she got some additional income from the carriage house, she just might manage. Temporarily. Perhaps it would be just as well for her to stay at the farm for a while, after all. She had made it clear it would be an emotional wrench to leave it. That would give him a little time to – to gain the freedom to tell her he loved her.

The following Wednesday, at ten in the evening, the lights in Roberta's kitchen and dining room suddenly went out, and the refrigerator went dead. So did the dishwasher, which she had been running. Roberta groped her way into the hall and living room, where the lights were on.

In New York, you simply called the super. But here? Well, of course, she had to get an electrician. She blessed Jim for having foreseen such a situation when he'd listed vital services in her telephone book. She found the electrician's number, then wondered if it was too late to call. She had better call first thing in the morning.

She called at seven the next day. The electrician's wife said he had already left, but she took the message. In the end, the man did not show up until Friday, the same day

Roberta was paid. The bill amounted to three-quarters of her weekly pay check.

She was shocked to her roots. 'My God, *now* I know what Paul was talking about.' For the first time, the problem of money really hit home. Shaken, she thought, Maybe this is crazy? Maybe it's impossible for me to try to survive here, just as everyone warned me? She had a moment of terrible self-doubt. But where would I go? What would I do instead? Where else could I live?

Then she made a conscious effort to steady herself. Wait a minute. I haven't really come to grips with this yet. I can't give up until I give it a try. I've got to find out about costs, put figures on paper, find out where I really stand. And I've got to advertise the carriage house – immediately.

10

Jane Whitford looked worried when Roberta told her about Paul's advice that she sell the farm. 'My God, Roberta you're not going to leave just when I've found you?'

'Of course not, not if I can help it. But Paul says I can't afford to keep it. There isn't enough cash. It seems that I've got to get what Paul calls a return on my investment.' Briefly she summed up the situation.

'Oh, Roberta. I am sorry. You see, I just took it for granted that money was no problem for you.'

'So did I. But Paul broke it to me that I'm really rather hard-up.'

'Well, I know all about that,' said Jane grimly. 'But there are ways to wiggle through, if you try. Did he have any suggestions?'

'Yes. Funny, we both thought of the same thing – to rent my carriage house. I've already put an ad in the paper.'

'That is a good idea. That should help pay the taxes, at least.'

'That's what Paul said.'

'But be careful, Roberta. Be sure to get security and references. And have the tenant sign a year's lease.'

'That's also what Paul said.'

'Tell you what,' said Jane, throwing herself into Roberta's problem. 'Your ad won't be out until next week, right? So let's put up a little notice in the shop, right now. You never know who might see it. That will

111

give you a head start. Go on; type it up. We'll put it where it can't be missed, right near the cash register.'

On Thursday evening the phone was ringing just as Roberta returned from work. It was Jane, very excited. 'Roberta, I think I've got a live one for you, a tenant for the carriage house. He walked in right after you left. He saw the notice and asked me if I could tell him anything about it. He was *very* interested, said it sounded like what he was looking for. He's just been transferred here to that big new PetroFax thing in Clinton. He needs a place for a year.'

'Good! Is he going to call me?'

'Better than that. He's on his way to see the place right now. He just left. His name is Owen. I didn't want him to get away, so I took the liberty of sending him. I hope you don't mind?'

'Mind! I'm grateful.'

'But listen, Roberta. Don't commit yourself until you check his references. He seems to be a very decent guy, obviously educated and well spoken. But a lone lady can't take chances. Remember.'

'I'll remember. Thanks, Jane.'

'Call me back and tell me what happened?'

'Right.'

She liked him the minute she saw him. A humorous face, she noted. Sandy hair, quirky eyebrows. Not good-looking, but somehow appealing. Not especially tall either, but muscular and very masculine.

'Mrs Marston?' Nice smile, too. 'I'm Zachary Owen.'

'Hello, Mr Owen.'

'Mrs Whitford was kind enough to tell me about your carriage house.'

'Yes, she telephoned. Mr Owen, the carriage house is up the lane a bit. You can drive up, or perhaps you'd like to walk?'

'Oh, let's walk, if it's all right with you, Mrs Marston?'

As they turned from the lane and the carriage house came into view, Zachary Owen said, 'Very nice. A later period than your own house, isn't it?'

'Yes, about 1890. We were told the original burned down. That's why this one is late Victorian. It's this door on the side.' She unlocked the door and switched on the lights.

Zachary Owen took in the spacious inviting room at a glance: the large windows which had been installed at each end, the bookshelves, the fireplace, the stairway against one wall.

'And here, you see, is a small kitchen.' Roberta led him to a kitchen area, open to the room but separated from it by a large wood work counter.

He said, 'You must have had a very good cabinetmaker. It's a handsome job.'

'I suppose he was good. An oldtimer. You see, we intended the carriage house to be a guesthouse, but my children gradually took it over. We put in the kitchen for their parties, at their urgent suggestion, of course.'

'I can imagine. Mountains of pizza and rivers of Coke.'

Roberta laughed. 'Exactly! Now, upstairs . . .'

She showed him the big bedroom with one slanted wall forming a separate alcove, two smaller rooms and the large bathroom.

'Where did you ever find that old pedestal sink?' he asked admiringly. 'And the old porcelain wall fixtures?'

Roberta was pleased that he had noticed the lights. It had taken her a year to find them. 'In New York, on Third Avenue. And my son lugged the sink home in the trunk of his car. He rescued it just as it was being carried out of a house they were demolishing in Easton.'

'Where it would certainly have been crushed and thrown on a heap of rubble.' He shook his head.

He seems to have an eye for old things, she thought. That would make it much nicer. Jane had warned her about tenants who think nothing of taking down your prize oldies and substituting chrome. 'And they think they're doing you a favor,' she had added.

Back downstairs, Zachary Owen said, 'Mrs Marston, this is the sort of place I'd been hoping for, but didn't expect to find. I'd like very much to rent it.'

This is where I must be careful, Roberta remembered. 'There are some details to be discussed, Mr Owen, but won't you sit down?'

She said the place was available on a yearly basis, with a lease; then she named the rent. And the amount of the security deposit. 'And of course I'll require references.'

'Of course, Mrs Marston. I'm an engineer with Petro-Fax. I'm based mostly in Dallas, and I'm subject to a lot of travel, often on short notice. But I'll be spending a great deal of this coming year working on the research and development plant we're putting up in Clinton.'

'I've passed it. It looks gigantic.'

'It's quite a project.' He took out a business card, and scribbled on the back. 'Here you are, Mrs Marston. Employer, bank, personal references.' He handed her the card. 'And oh yes, I'd be occupying the place alone. I'm staying with friends in Bedminster now, so I could move in at any time.'

He stood up. 'Thank you for showing me through, Mrs Marston. I'll be hoping to hear from you.'

Zachary Owen moved into the carriage house ten days later. It seemed strange to see lights on the hill through the trees, and it was strange to hear another car going up and down the lane. Strangest of all was the notion of being a landlady. Roberta thought ruefully of the familiar image of a landlady in fiction, a forbidding harridan. She shuddered. But when she held the first crisp rent check in her hand, it seemed like found money. Money in the bank! and in the bank was where she put it. In a special account earmarked for the quarterly real estate taxes.

Paul Reston was painfully aware of his raw desire to put his hands around his wife's creamy throat and strangle her. She looked so fragile, so ethereal, and so small, curled like a kitten on her mile-long pale sofa. But inside she was . . . what? Stone? Ice? No, she was more like a deadly serpent. That was it – venom. She was venomous.

She had just responded to his renewed request for a divorce with a quietly, deadly *no*. The word hung in the silence. Paul looked around the vast open apartment high in United Nations Plaza. Open space flowed from one free-standing curved wall to another. Alicia and her architect had created a sense of infinite emptiness, infinitely repeated by mirrors reflecting muted non-colors, Alicia's art and sculpture collections, and the East River. It's like living in limbo, Paul thought, as I am in fact living.

Alicia was watching him quizzically. She took a cigarette from the stark glass box on the stark glass table, inserted it in a slender vermeil holder which was itself a work of art, and snapped the crystal lighter.

'You're such a fool, darling,' she said. 'Why don't you simply have an affair with her?'

He looked at her.

'With Roberta. Did you think I didn't guess?'

Paul kept his face impassive. How *did* she know? Intuitive witch-bitch! But it hardly mattered.

'I don't want to have an affair with Roberta.'

'You mean you want to marry her.'

'Yes.'

'Hm. You have a point. Roberta *is* the marrying kind. The perfect type for all those filthy little male-female

115

games. Dominant male. Passive female.' Her lips curled with scorn.

'You wouldn't understand that, Alicia.'

'Perhaps I do, only too well. It's what the male brute lusts for – bondage of the female. At any rate, I'm afraid you'll have to make do with an affair . . . or nothing.'

Before he knew it, Paul was across the room. He pulled Alicia roughly from her chair. His fingers dug into her shoulders.

'Alicia. God damn it. Listen to me. I am going to divorce you. We can have a civilized divorce, or a dirty, slanderous one. Which do you prefer?'

Alicia stood perfectly still, a triumphant gleam in her eye. 'You have proved my point perfectly. About brutal man. Aren't you going to hit me?'

Paul loosened his grip. Controlling his frustration and fury, he said, 'Alicia, for Christ's sake, you have nothing to gain by this. You have more than enough money for anything you want to do. You can travel, entertain, collect art. What is your motive for hanging onto a marriage that means nothing to you?'

'Paul, darling, sit down like a good boy. And I'll tell you.'

Paul moved away a little but remained standing. Alicia looked at him, shrugged, and sat down on the sofa. She kept him waiting while she lighted another cigarette, inhaled, and blew a contemptuous little smoke ring.

Then she turned to Paul and looked at him seriously.

'You ask why I won't agree to a divorce. I have already told you one reason. But there are two. One' – she ticked it off on her slender finger – 'I want a great deal more money than I already have. I want my grandmother's millions. And you know, Paul, how she feels about divorce. Let alone one based on my . . . my private choices.'

116

Paul thought of that devout old lady. Alicia was right about that. She would cut off her only grandchild without a qualm. Nevertheless, he would not let Alicia's lust for money stand in his way.

'And reason two?'

'To punish you. For being a man.' For a second Alicia's mask slipped. Her eyes blazed, her mouth twisted, her voice was distilled poison. 'For all you men, with your brutal pricks!'

She's mad, thought Paul, shocked. Unbalanced. Incisively intelligent as she is, in the area of her red rage against men, she's off the wall. His own anger drained away. She was almost pitiable.

'I see,' he said. 'Even so, I'm going to file for divorce. And about your grandmother's will, you can always contest it. In any case I'm leaving. Now.'

'I don't think so, Paul.' Alicia was her cool, exquisite self again. 'Not when you hear what else I have to say.'

'And that is?'

'I'm sure you would not want Roberta hurt, would you, Paul? That poor, defenseless woman, so in need of a man's protection?'

Paul sensed danger. The very thought of a threat to Roberta made his heart pound. But it made no sense. How could Alicia hurt Roberta?

'Alicia,' he said roughly, 'no games. What are you talking about?'

'Would you say, Paul, that Roberta and Brad Marston were happily married?'

Paul thought of Brad's affair, but he knew that for years, before that incident, the Marstons had been manifestly devoted to each other. Thank God Roberta had never learned of Brad's deception.

'They certainly seemed happily married.'

'They did, didn't they? The only couple in our set still

117

married to original spouses and not keeping marriages of convenience, like us.' She smiled maliciously. 'But *you* knew, didn't you, Paul, that Brad was having an affair with another woman?'

He was too surprised to conceal it. He knew his face gave him away. How did she know? He had revealed it to no one.

'I see you did know. And I did, too.'

Paul said nothing.

'Do you remember that ghastly business trip you dragged me on – to Chicago? You had gone up to our room for something and I waited for you in the lobby. I saw Brad and a woman. And when you came downstairs, I knew you had seen them, too. You looked as though you were in shock.'

'Strange you didn't mention it.'

'Not strange *you* didn't. The conspiracy of men. As for me, I tend to keep little nuggets of information to myself. For times when they might be useful. Like now.'

'Go on,' he said.

'Why, it's so simple. I propose to pass this little nugget on to Roberta. Don't you think it would be devastating?'

'Roberta would not believe you.'

'Oh, I don't know. If I proved it? I did a little sleuthing. You'd be surprised how easy that is, in the small world we live in. Found out the woman's name, and so forth. Yes, I could present Roberta with some certifiable facts.'

'You're despicable,' he said.

'No, just fighting for what I want. Using any weapon handy, as men do. Well, think about it, Paul. Here is Roberta, mourning the loss of her beloved husband, but sustained by the memory of a perfect marriage. What would it do to her to find out that her husband had been spending his time in someone else's bed? What would all that good, clean, healthy grief turn to? . . . Well, who knows what it would do to her, maybe rock her reason. And wouldn't she lose all faith in men? Be afraid ever to trust again? Be afraid to trust *you*, Paul?'

'Even you wouldn't do anything so gratuitously cruel.'

'Wouldn't I? Shall I show you?' She reached for her little leather phone book, flipped through. 'Let's see . . . her number is 201 . . .' She picked up the phone.

'Don't' said Paul.

Alicia replaced the receiver. She smiled.

On Sunday morning Roberta opened her eyes to snow fluffed high on the hemlock outside her window. The first snow of the season. There was a streak of red, and a cardinal alighted three feet away. She could see his crest, his bright eye. Then he was off, vivid against the white dazzle. Roberta giggled. Too much! Nature showing off. But how beautiful.

She stretched contendedly, thinking of last night at the Harcourts. It had been fun. Everyone had stayed late: the Fentons, Luther Hodges, Sarah Smith. There had also been a couple from New York, houseguests.

It was amazing how all these people established such an easy, familiar footing in so short a time. Carole Harcourt was the catalyst, of course. Gregarious to her fingertips, she had created instant camaraderie. Ever since that first brunch at the Harcourts, Carole had projected an open-door, come-anytime policy. More than that, she had gotten across the idea that her country weekends wouldn't *be* country weekends without seeing her newfound friends. The Greenwillow Gang she called it.

The feeling had spilled over to the full-time residents. Probably, without Carole's contagious example, they would all have remained mere fellow committee members. But now, with the exception of Dr John Blair, who ran the committee but didn't socialize, and Mary Blair, who'd never attended another meeting, they were inviting each other to impromptu meals, dropping in on each other, calling to say there was a good movie in Easton and asking her to go. Roberta felt that she need never face another empty evening; she had only to pick up the phone.

Eleven o'clock. This was a fringe benefit of working, the deliciousness of lying in bed on Sunday. But the day was too beautiful to waste; she had an urge to go outdoors. First, however, like any working woman, she had weekend chores. And Jim was bringing a college friend to dinner. Perhaps if she got dinner well underway in advance, there would be time for a long walk.

In the late afternoon she pulled on boots, parka, and a fur cap. She climbed the lane and then struck off on the rough path which ran the length of the property. If you walked to the far boundary, you walked a mile. With each few feet she ascended, the view widened and changed. From here, you could just see the dome of the silo. From there, the creek below, now black against the snow. It was hushed and untouched. She felt a quiet joy which surprised her.

Funny, she had never been an outdoor type, certainly not a nature-lover. But now, more and more, the land was tugging at her. She was noticing more, *seeing* more. That lovely dried weed, whatever it was, with dangling pale papery pods. And those bright red berries, or were they seeds? Could they be rose hips? If she had something to clip them with, she'd gather an armful for the house.

She walked on past the grove of pines, toward the cornfield with the big lone tree in its center. She turned a curve in the path, and there was her new tenant, sitting on a rock, looking at the view. He seemed delighted to see her. 'Mrs Marston! Hello! I can't believe this countryside!'

He jumped up, brushed snow off the rock, and gestured for her to sit down. 'There's going to be a sunset. Look.'

'Thank you.' Roberta sat down. 'It is rather spectacular, isn't it? All that untouched snow. But you must have come the other way round, Mr Owen. I didn't see footprints.'

'I followed the creek . . . and wished I had snowshoes.'

Roberta laughed. He was fun.

Together they watched the sky fill with shifting color, mutate from gold to green to pink, reach a dazzling crescendo, then begin to fade.

'Awesome,' he said. 'For once the word applied, don't you think?'

'Yes. That was glorious.'

It was pleasant to walk back through the quiet fields. Zack Owen seemed to have no need to make small talk, he was quite at ease. Roberta considered his companionable silence a sign of inner assurance.

He did not turn in at the carriage house, but walked her politely to her door.

It would have been nice to invite him in for a drink, Roberta thought. But I suppose it's not done, under the circumstances.

I wish I had asked her to join me, Zack Owen said to himself later as he splashed water onto his Scotch, but it would have been exploiting a circumstance. I mustn't intrude on the lady, attractive as she is.

Three days later, when Roberta was ready to leave for work, she put her coffee cup under the faucet to rinse it. When she had done so the water refused to turn off. It was flowing full force in the off position. She tried to

121

tighten the faucet, jiggled it, banged on it. The water kept pouring.

She rushed to the phone and called the plumber. While she was praying she could reach him, she heard the pump go on in the basement. Jim had told her that prolonged demand on the pump would burn it out. She *had* to get the water turned off before she went to work, and she had to get to work. The plumber's number finally answered. 'This is a recorded message. If you will leave your – ' She hung up, frantic. It seemed an absurdly small thing, yet it wasn't. God only knew what it would cost to replace the pump. On top of that, there was a drought. Wells were low, and she had heard that a dry well was catastrophic.

Another plumber? She grabbed the phone book, turned to the yellow pages. There was a knock on the door. It was Zachary Owen. 'Pump doesn't sound right,' he said. 'I heard it driving past. Shall I have a look?'

'*Would* you?' She told him about the un-turn-offable water.

'Are there tools somewhere?'

'Right hand side of the cellar door.'

'Right.' He disappeared toward the outside cellar door, then returned within minutes. 'Now let's see that faucet.'

Within fifteen minutes he had removed the faucet, replaced it, and turned the main line back on again. It was fixed.

'Oh, Mr Owen, I can't tell you how grateful I am. The plumber had already left. I don't know what I would have done. What caused it? Why should water suddenly not turn off?'

He showed her a grain of sand.

'That?'

'That. It was just enough to keep the valve from seating

securely. It happens with wells, especially when they're low.'

'But you did it so deftly, so quickly. How in the world did you know?'

'I grew up in an old house' – he smiled – 'with a well.'

Of course, idiot, Roberta thought on the way to work, he's an engineer. But how kind of him to volunteer. A tenant is a tenant. The owner's problems have nothing to do with him. But the incident did make Roberta aware again of the perils of a large old house. Apparently anything could go wrong without warning. She had been lucky so far, except for that staggering electrician's bill. But it was reassuring to have a Zachary Owen nearby. Not that she would impose upon him. Still when there was an emergency like this morning's . . . She felt warmly grateful. She hoped she hadn't made him too late at his office.

Strange for her to be living alone in that big place, thought Zachary Owen. The well could have gone dry. He decided to keep an eye out for anything amiss. Even find some tenant's pretext to telephone, to make sure she was all right. A woman like that.

'How goes it with your tenant?' Jane Whitford asked Roberta.

Roberta told her about the water.

'Lucky you,' said Jane. 'A good man is hard to find.'

123

11

Roberta could feel herself growing tense as Christmas approached. It was three weeks away and expectation was in the air. She was determined to have the traditional Christmas the Marstons had always had. Jim would be home for ten days, Susan for a long weekend, and her father was coming from Florida. Mingo would join them, as always.

Roberta looked forward eagerly to the holiday. But she also felt nervous flutters. It would be her first Christmas without Brad, and she was afraid that the impact of the season would rekindle more memories than she could bear. She was also worried about Susan. Her daughter's behavior hurt her, baffled her. Susan had not snapped out of her extreme reaction of her father's death. She had not once visited Roberta at the farm, and she was uncommunicative on the telephone. When the Harcourts had invited Roberta, Jim and Susan for Thanksgiving dinner, Susan had coldly declined.

And when, on the phone, Roberta had said, 'And of course, Susie, bring Gil for Christmas, too,' Susan had replied 'Gil who?'

Gil who! Gil Rutherford, the young man Roberta and Brad had hoped Susan would marry. Susan had always been attractive to boys, but during the year that preceded Brad's death, she had been seeing Gil Rutherford steadily and exclusively. Last summer Gil had been at the farm nearly every weekend.

'You are not seeing Gil anymore, Susan?'

'You got it, Mother.'

'But why, Susan. I thought . . .'

'Does there have to be a why? But since you ask, he's such a kid.'

'I see,' said Roberta faintly. Susan's slangy delivery and let-me-alone tone certainly precluded further discussion. At the moment, anyway. She fervently hoped that during the holidays she could get closer to her daughter. But she was apprehensive. She was afraid that the poignancy of Christmas, with her father gone, would be rough on Susan.

Jim was thinking along the same lines. 'Since this is our first Christmas without' – he paused, swallowed – 'without Dad, what would you think of making it the same as usual, but a little different. To take the edge off it?'

'How do you mean, Jim?'

'I thought we might go to the candle-light service in Bethlehem. Bethlehem, Pennsylvania. It's quite well known. People come long distances to see it, but it's a fairly short ride from here.'

'That's a wonderful idea. I'm sure your grandfather and Mingo would like that very much, but I don't know about Susan.'

'I'll talk Susan into it.'

Roberta was glad they were very busy at the shop. It was easier to keep your problems at bay when you were too rushed to think about them. Jane had taken on two part-timers, and the shop was open evenings. They frequently had a line at the cheese counter, and there were always customers for the kitchenware and the gifts and handsome wrappings Jane had added.

'But I'm drawing the line at Christmas Eve,' Jane told Roberta. 'We're closing at four sharp on the twenty-fourth – and staying closed until the twenty-seventh. That will give us both a chance to recover.'

Working in the shop was **fun** as the holiday buying accelerated. Christmas presents are, after all, happy things to sell. A few customers were demanding or curt, but most were aglow with the festive spirit. Still, the pace was exhausting. Each night Roberta sank like a stone into deep sleep as soon as she got home at ten, and on Sundays she tidied the house and went shopping.

At four on the twenty-fourth, Roberta and Jane toasted each other with a quick drink in the back room, exchanged small gifts, and then Jane handed Roberta an envelope. 'A little bonus, Robbie,' said Jane. Then she laughed at the expression on Roberta's face. 'It's customary, silly, and you earned it. We did fifteen percent better than last year. Hosannas for *that*!'

Roberta raced home, full of Christmas cheer and positively merry. The drink? The unexpected bonus? Maybe. Or partly. But most of all she couldn't wait to see her family.

Jim had arrived yesterday and had promptly headed for the back field to chop down a Christmas tree and cut greens for garlands. Then, bless him, he had set up the tree and had asked his mother to put him to work at whatever needed doing. That afternoon he had picked up his grandfather at the airport. They were both waiting for her now. And Mingo had offered Susan a ride from the city. It's going to be all right, thought Roberta.

And it was . . . until noon on Christmas Day. They had all enjoyed the candlelight service in Bethlehem, and the late supper at home in front of the fire. Christmas morning had been as always – the gifts, the tangle of paper and ribbons, and the chorus of thank-yous. Roberta had been tremendously relieved to find Susan subdued, but not as withdrawn as she had been. However, just as Roberta was basting the turkey, flushed and happy that things were going so well, Susan stormed into the kitchen.

'Where are the pictures?' she demanded.

Startled, Roberta said, 'Pictures? What pictures?'

'Pictures of Daddy! The photos. The one of him on the horse. And the one when he was in college, and the one that was in the *Times* when he was made vice-president – all of them. I thought there was something different about this house, and that's it! They're gone! Where are they?'

Roberta had forgotten the day when, in a rush of acute anger at Brad, she had furiously dumped the pictures in a corner of the attic. Now, looking at her daughter's accusing eyes, she felt her heart thumping. How could she explain?

'Susan,' she said slowly, groping for the right words, 'we don't all . . . react to loss in the same way. For me, it was easier not to have so many reminders. Your father's pictures are safely stored upstairs.'

'Stored,' said Susan. 'I see. Well, then, Mother' – she was elaborately polite – 'you wouldn't mind very much, would you, if *I* took them?'

'Of course not.'

'And may I say something, Mother?'

'Yes, Susan?'

'You're a funny kind of widow, Mother!'

She turned and left the kitchen, her very back radiating hostility. Roberta leaned against the table, shaken. A funny kind of widow! It was clear that Susan, hurt as she was, was seeking someone to blame. She had settled on her mother. Roberta was not grieving for Susan's father as Susan was: Does she *resent* my making a new life for myself? Roberta wondered. Apparently she does. It's her way of defending herself against pain. It's easier to lash out than to accept. Oh, Susan, Susan, she thought. If only you understood.

The next day friends of Susan's stopped at the farm en route to skiing in the Poconos. Susan decided to join them. Roberta was bitterly disappointed. She had hoped to spend some time alone with Susan, and she had looked forward to introducing her daughter to her Greenwillow friends. But Susan was over twenty-one, free to do as she chose. If only she weren't so unhappy, thought her mother miserably, but that is beyond my power. I can't 'kiss it and make it well' as I did when she was a little girl.

The thought of Susan as a small child brought back the past. Roberta felt tears rising and fought them off. No. Think of the present. Right now, I have my son, my father and my best friend. That's something to be grateful for. And my daughter will be my daughter again – eventually. I must believe that.

The rest of the holiday week was warm and loving.

January was a letdown. The house was especially quiet and empty after a week filled with voices and footsteps, and temporarily, company was hard to come by. The Harcourts, who had entertained exuberantly during the holidays would not be coming to the country for a month. The Fentons were laid low with flu, and Sarah Smith was off visiting. Roberta was glad that she and Jane were working nights, taking inventory.

But what was she going to do with this long empty Sunday? Restless and feeling more lonely than she had in months, Roberta wandered through the big house thinking that maybe living alone was impossible after all.

She was ridiculously glad when the telephone rang.

It was Zachary Owen.

'I hope you had a nice Christmas, Mrs Marston?'

'Very nice, thank you. And yours?' He had thoughtfully let her know beforehand that he would be away, so that she wouldn't wonder at his dark windows.

'Very pleasant, thank you. Mrs Marston, there are a

couple of dead trees on the hill. They should really be taken down, and they'd make good firewood. Would you care to have me cut them?'

'Dead trees? Why, of course, if you like, Mr Owen.' He certainly knew more about trees than she did. 'But isn't that a great deal of work?'

He laughed. 'Only if you *have* to do it. I'd *like* to do it. Thanks, Mrs Marston.'

Three hours later Zachary Owen arrived at the front door with a huge basket of logs, and Roberta could see more wood in the open trunk of his car.

'Your firewood, Mrs Marston.'

'Mine? But of course I thought it was for your fireplace, Mr Owen?'

'That's not done. It's an unwritten law: you cut a lady's wood, you deliver it to the lady.'

'Why, thank you. I *was* running rather low.'

'May I stack it for you?'

He filled the wood baskets in the two downstairs fireplaces, and piled the rest neatly behind the back door.

The wood was heavy, so the chore took a little time. When he had finished, Roberta thought she should show some appreciation. This was the second kindness Zachary Owen had done her. Should she offer him a drink? Some lunch? Well, why not? He was an extremely pleasant young man.

'I was about to have lunch,' she said. 'May I offer you some? The remains of the holiday ham.'

'I'd like that very much.'

'Good. Please excuse me a few minutes. Make yourself comfortable, Mr Owen.'

As she left the room to go to the kitchen. Roberta switched up the thermostat. She had been training herself to keep the heat low to save on oil bills. But the room was chilly for a guest.

'Oh, don't do that!' Zachary Owen protested. 'Perhaps you'd like me to build a fire?'

'That *would* be nice on a day like this.'

By the time she came back, with the food and drink, the bright fire made the room a warm refuge against the gray bleakness outside the windows. He sprang up, took the tray from her and placed it on the coffee table. When she reached for the bottle opener, he said, 'Let me,' and quickly drew the cork from the wine bottle. How easily and naturally he does things, Roberta thought. So effortlessly.

They talked about the things people who don't know each other do talk about: books, travel and music.

'I see you have a lot of Vivaldi,' he said, indicating the shelves of tapes near the built-in stereo. 'You like Baroque, then?'

'Very much.'

'Really?' His eyes lighted up. 'I do, too.'

'Oh, then you must try WFLN radio – out of Philadelhia. Do you know that station? Classical music around the clock – and the Met on Saturdays.'

In New York, Roberta had regularly held subscriptions to Carnegie Hall and the Met. Brad had cheerfully confessed to a tin ear, but Susan shared her mother's love of music. Now it was oddly pleasing to learn that Zach Owen was a fellow classics buff.

'WFLN. Good. Another attraction to this surprising part of New Jersey.'

'How are you finding it here, Mr Owen? You're comfortable in the carriage house?'

'Oh, I like it here, Mrs Marston. It's a great place to live, especially after Texas. I missed the seasons.'

'I feel the same way. The winter is so beautiful, deep freeze or not. It's worth it, to look forward to spring, the green on the willows, the first robin.' She broke off laughing. 'Etcetera. Did you ever hear such clichés? Still, I'd hate to think I'd never see another robin.'

'Me, too. Unthinkable.' He glanced at his watch and stood up. 'It can't be quarter to four? And I'm due in the city at five. I've enjoyed this so much, Mrs Marston. Thank you.'

Seeing him off at the door, Roberta thanked him for the firewood. It had been kind of him.

'Mr Owen, I hope if there is any favor I can do for you . . .' She hesitated. What favor could she do for him? 'I don't know exactly what, perhaps sign for a package for you? Pick up something in Flemington? Please don't hesitate . . .'

He smiled down at her from the doorway. 'There *is* a favor you could do for me, Mrs Marston.'

'Oh, good. And that is? . . .

'Won't you please call me Zack?'

'Oh! Why, of course.' She looked uncertain. Was it her turn to say and please call me Roberta? She had never really liked everybody first-naming everybody else immediately after introductions. Besides, he must be ten years younger . . .

He seemed to guess what she was thinking.

'And may I call you Mrs M? That's the way I think of you. Mrs M. Friendly, but not impertinent.'

She couldn't help laughing. 'Okay . . . Zack.'

He grinned. 'Thank you, Mrs M.'

The rest of the day did not seem nearly as empty as its beginning. Roberta hummed as she cleared the coffee table. She would do one chore, maybe pack away the extra silver and china from the holidays. Then she'd wash her hair and get into a housecoat. Then she'd turn on some music – Vivaldi, why not? – and if she was hungry by that time, she'd eat something virtuously light – soup, fruit, tea – over her still unopened Sunday *Times*. First, the *Book Review*, then *The Week in Review*, then *Arts and Leisure, Travel,* the display ads, and the front page. And she'd go to bed nice and early.

She went to bed at nine-thirty. Not a bad day at all. On balance, as they said. Drowsily she wondered what Zachary Owen was doing in New York.

12

'More coffee?' asked Roberta.

'Let me get it.' Terry Fenton jumped up and went into Roberta's kitchen.

'You can't say we don't make ourselves at home,' said Tim Fenton.

'But I love it,' said Roberta. 'I never had neighbors before. Neighbors who are good friends – and bring goodies.' The Fentons and Sarah Smith had dropped in, bearing armfuls of budded forsythia to blossom indoors. 'I didn't know what I was missing in the city. Nobody ever drops in on you there.'

'But it goes two ways, Roberta,' said Tim. 'It's a kick for Terry and me to know you and the Harcourts. You bring a breath of fresh air to the country.'

Everybody laughed. Tim was so ingenuously sincere. Indeed, both Fentons were guileless in their open admiration of what they perceived as city glamour, and so modest about themselves. They seemed to have no idea of how attractive *they* were.

'Listen, Tim,' said Roberta. 'It would be impossible for a newcomer to be happy here without the friendliness of people like you. You make me feel *connected*. And that makes all the difference.'

They do make a difference, she thought later, after they left. Especially their easy, comfortable informality. When people feel free to walk into your kitchen for more coffee, you feel free to walk into theirs. And when people are relaxed enough to call at the last moment and say. 'We've got more leftover roast that we can eat, will you join us?' that allows you to offer them potluck on a night when you don't want to eat alone. It certainly relieved the pressure of 'having people in.' An asset for a working woman. It's not like New York, where the standard response to an invitation is 'Let me look at my book.'

Besides, the Fentons and the others had introduced her to new pleasures, simple, almost naïve ones but definitely pleasures. The apple fritter place, for example. She could hear a New Yorker saying 'Apple *fritters*? You're kidding!' But there was a place, on the opposite side of the river, near a covered bridge, where they made hot, fresh sugar-dusted fritters. She had gone there with the Fentons after a long walk on the towpath beside the canal, and it was delightful. The country mice had also initiated the city mice into that rural institution, the Sunday morning firehouse breakfast. You sat at long tables laden with homecooked food, and hobnobbed with the farmers. 'I love it!' said Carole Harcourt. 'When's the next one?' And Sarah had introduced Roberta to Reading, Pennsylvania, a mecca for discount shopping.

Not that all their get-togethers were so casual. Luther Hodges gave the group a superb dinner, complete with vintage wines, and served by the couple who looked after him. He lived in a formal brick Federal house, a town house really, set incongruously in the country and hidden by tall hedges.

Roberta had wondered if there was a Mrs Hodges until Sarah had told her that Luther's wife was a victim of Alzheimer's disease. 'It hit her when she was only forty-two,' said Sarah. 'Unusually young. She was a beautiful woman. She's been institutionalized for nearly ten years. Luther has to live with that, and he does heroically, I think.' Roberta agreed. The more she learned about these new friends, the more she respected and liked them.

134

In a way, she thought, as she slipped into the tub in preparation for a leisurely manicure and pedicure, I feel as though I've been here forever. I feel at *home*. Secure. And that's incredible. It has only been six months, after all.

Besides, she mused, I'm not really secure at all. I still have money worries, and inflation's getting worse. God knows, in a big place like this it's crazy to live without a man to help me cope, as everyone certainly warned me. So how come I feel so . . . so safe?

As she toweled herself dry and rubbed fragrant body oil onto her warm skin, she tried to analyze her feelings and she slowly realized that her sense of safety was based on the advent of Zachary Owen. His mere presence in the carriage house made her feel protected. That made no sense, of course, because Zack had no responsibility for her in any way.

Yet she felt she could count on him. Funny. Was it because their relationship had progressed beyond that of tenant and landlady, even beyond that of neighbors? No matter how she looked at it, Roberta would now have to describe Zack Owen as a friend.

And that, too, had happened so quickly, without Roberta's knowing quite how it had come about. Ever since the lunch they had shared in front of the fire, Zack had become a presence in her life. A week later he'd called to say he had a new recording, would she care to come up and hear it? She hesitated, then told herself that was silly. He liked music, she liked music. She went, and the time passed very agreeably. He was pleasant company, a man – she had sensed it that day they had walked through the snow – at ease with himself. He called again. Would she consider sharing a crust with a lonely bachelor? As an act of kindness? She laughed at the 'crust.' Veal birds. He liked to cook.

Occasionally, he simply turned up on her doorstep, but never intrusively, always ready to vanish if she was busy. Usually he offered some service. Did she need anything from the city, should he spread some rock salt on the icy front steps?

But neither Zack's amusing company, nor his generosity in rescuing her from home-owner dilemmas entirely explained her sense of security when she saw his lights from her window. Nor did they explain why, when he was out, she felt relieved when she heard his car drive up the lane.

Slipping into bed and turning out the light, Roberta pulled up the quilt, feeling grateful that Zack had turned out to be Zack. How different it would be if her tenant were merely a tenant. She would miss him when he left at the end of the year, and not just because of the invaluable services he performed for her. No. She found the time she spent with him stimulating, but so easy and natural. Probably because it's without sexual overtones, she thought. After all, he's much younger.

One week later, Roberta spent the night in Zachary Owen's arms. Much later, she tried to understand how it had happened. Certainly, she had had no such instincts toward Zack. Well, she amended honestly, no *conscious* instincts. Who knew what went on in her unconscious?

He had asked her if she could pick up a Melita coffee pot for him at the shop. Glad to be able to do him a favor, for a change, she walked up to the carriage house to deliver it. He took it for granted she'd stay awhile. He offered her a drink, showed her his plan for a garden, asked what she thought of a recent piece in *The New Yorker*. They always seemed to have a lot to talk about.

They were both surprised at the hour when Roberta looked at the clock. 'Midnight! Have I been here *four hours*! I must go.' She stood up.

'Roberta.'

She turned, startled at the change in his voice.

'Roberta. Don't go. Stay. Stay with me.'

She looked at him. He did not touch her. His eyes questioned hers. Her heart pounded. She could not look away.

'Zack . . .'

'Roberta?' He moved toward her, took her in his arms, held her close. She could feel his heart. 'Will you stay? Do you want to?'

Yes, I want to, I want to, I want to, sang Roberta's blood.

'Yes, I do Zack. Yes.'

Only then did he kiss her. Then he led her upstairs.

'Cathedral under the Sea.' The image drifted across her consciousness. Like the booming of a great bell in the deep. Resonances, repeated until she herself was the resonance, the bell.

When she opened her eyes, for a moment she did not know where she was. She had traveled a vast distance to an unknown place, and now had to find her way back. And she felt a fulfillment she had never experienced before. But she also felt astonishment. How could this be?

Zack's arm was tightly around her shoulder. He was wide awake, staring at the ceiling. When he felt her stir, he lifted his head and smiled at her.

'Hello,' he said.

'Hello,' she said weakly.

He dropped his head back on the pillow.

'Zack . . .'

He tightened his grip on her shoulder. 'Let it be . . .'

'Yes,' she thought drowsily. 'Let it be . . . for now . . .'

* * *

137

The next morning the sun had barely risen when Roberta let herself silently out of the carriage house, leaving a sleeping man upstairs. She felt an urgent need to move. Her body tingled with life, its every sense awakened. It was a glorious morning. The sight of a spider web, every spoke perfect, strung with dew, struck her as unbearably beautiful. At the same time, her emotions were a whirlpool of confusion. She must get away alone to think. She went into the back door of her house and straight out the front, snatching up her car keys in passing. Thank goodness it was Sunday.

She pulled the car out onto the road, no destination in mind. But the sun was so bright as she faced into it, that she was blinded. She thought of a fanciful analogy. It was like last night, so blindingly brilliant that she couldn't see. Yet she *must* see.

She made an abrupt U-turn and headed west, so that the light would illuminate rather than dazzle. She needed illumination. What had happened to her? She had spent the night in a man's arms. And she had never experienced such joy. It was a revelation. While her body still echoed with the physical pleasure of the night, it was Brad who was most vivid in her mind. Brad's arms, Brad's kisses, the close warm intimacy of Brad. In Roberta's psyche, sex was Brad and only Brad. No wonder last night had brought him back to life despite all her struggles to banish him from her memory.

She hardly saw the Pennsylvania countryside she was now speeding past. Her mind was turned on an inner, confusing landscape. She and Brad had had a good sex life, she'd always thought. They had always 'wanted' each other. Sometimes they had even rather smugly congratulated each other on their compatibility. When they'd witnessed the breakup of other marriages and seen evidence of infidelities in both wives and husbands, Brad had often said ribaldly, 'They don't know that the family that lays together stays together, do they baby?'

But in the end, Brad had rejected her for sex with someone else, or presumably for sex. Now she, too, had experienced someone else, and her pleasure had been greater than she had known before. Is it possible that I have lived most of my life without knowing what passion really is? she wondered.

Of course, she acknowledged, I'm not what you'd call experienced, even after twenty-five years of marriage. Not by today's standards. I reached my twenties before the sexual revolution, and I behaved accordingly.

Roberta had not known any man other than her husband. But when Roberta and Brad were in their twenties many, many girls still 'waited.' Some did not, of course, but their sex lives had to be clandestine and were accordingly attended by guilt. The prevailing mores were still very much that 'nice girls didn't.'

Roberta had necked with boys she'd dated before Brad. But she had never 'petted,' which was considered several degrees 'worse' than necking. And she had certainly never 'gone all the way' the euphemism used then for 'having sex.'

And when Brad had come along, from a background as conservative as her own, he had taken it for granted that they would wait for marriage. They had.

Consequently Roberta had had no basis for comparison. Some of her New York women friends had discussed sex openly, often in disconcertingly explicit terms. But Roberta, with what she considered simple fastidiousness, had never traded confidence for confidence. Indeed she had none to trade.

Until *now*. She felt her body grow warm, she caught her breath. For a split second she closed her eyes, then forced them open.

You're *driving*. Have you taken leave of your senses? . . .

Perhaps I've found them, she thought.

Is last night the way it is for most women . . . most of the time? But no. Such peaks couldn't be usual, could they? If so, why all the sex manuals? No. Last night must have been rare, like a shooting star.

But what now? She had been so shaken, so intent on the experience itself, that she had not yet thought of the consequences. Now she did. But what consequences? Was it the beginning of an affair, or just a spontaneous encounter, perfect but complete in itself? If it was more than an encounter, did she want to have an affair?

Zack was younger than she, perhaps by ten years. And that bothered her. And, absurdly, their landlady-tenant relationship bothered her. 'The accommodating landlady.' She felt herself flush. No, that's nonsense. But she also thought, against all logic and her own intelligence – *what will he think of me*? Given her background and the standards which had molded her, it was impossible for her *not* to think that. A reflex from her conditioning. But her good sense reasserted itself. That's absurd. Old-think. *Archaic*. I'm free and over twenty-one. So is he.

But that didn't answer the question of what now. Where *am* I? Roberta wondered figuratively. As if giving her a literal answer, a sign read Shartlesville. She had driven all the way to the Pennsylvania Dutch country. She should turn back. She stopped for coffee. A man in the restaurant looked at her with an openly inviting eye. Does it really show? she wondered. The way they say it does?

As she crossed back over the Delaware and neared the farm, she found herself driving more and more slowly. She realized she was postponing meeting Zack. In a fit of . . . what? A crazy kind of shyness. That's what it felt like, childish as it was. But she didn't know what to expect. How would Zack behave? Would he take her in his arms or would he be as before, friendly but impersonal? What tone would he set?

What tone would you like him to set? she asked herself. Facing the question head-on, as honestly as she could, Roberta thought, I'd like to get right back into bed with him.

But Zack was not there. Looking toward the carriage house, she could see that his car was gone. Still more confused, she noted that it was only eleven in the morning. She had traveled so many light years in her thoughts; it felt much later. Perhaps he had gone to pick up the Sunday papers. He'll be right back, surely? He'll knock on the door? He'll call, won't he?

Zack did not show up. At five o'clock, Roberta drove to Sarah Smith's. Better to be out of the house, and not know if the phone had rung, than to be in it and know it hadn't.

When she returned at eleven, the carriage house was dark. Lying sleepless, Roberta went into a tailspin. She even wondered whether Zack had moved out. The fantasy was so vivid, she could see him packing his tapes, his books – decamping. She fought against her fear. It was irrational, absurd. He could be anywhere for any reason. It was none of her business where he was. Where was it written that a man had to be waiting at your door just because you had spent the night with him? Nevertheless, she was haunted by the phrase 'one-night stand' and was half-convinced she would never see him again.

In the morning, in the space between the storm door and the front door, she found the note he had left the day before. Apparently, she had stepped unseeingly right over it, stunned as she had been to find him gone.

'Dear Mrs M, my very dear . . .

Roberta, where are you? I reached for you – you were gone. Oh, Roberta, what hellish timing this is. Dallas called an 8 A.M. rush meeting early tomorrow. I'm on my way to the airport. *Not* what I had in mind for today, Roberta. I'll call you Monday night.

Zack

She leaned against the doorway in relief. She had been foolish to let her imagination play such tricks on her. But her anxieties had clearly shown how vulnerable she was. Having been rejected by her husband, she was hardly secure enough to be confident with another man. No matter what her relationship with Zack Owen turned out to be – if anything – she would avoid making assumptions. She would have to, for self-protection. Closeness was not a sure thing, as she had learned.

Zack came back at the end of the week and immediately took her into his arms. It seemed the most natural thing in the world.

If you're going to be in love, Roberta exulted, spring is the time. She couldn't remember a more beautiful April and she felt that she herself was in blossom, in harmony with the bursting-with-life world. I'm happy, she thought – happy!

She no longer doubted what her relationship with Zack was. She was having a full-fledged affair. And she marveled at how easy, how right, and how good it was. That was due to Zack, she thought. No games, no tricks, no maneuvering for the upper hand. When Zack expressed his feelings, you knew they were truly his feelings, and when he asked you about yours, he took it for granted that you meant what you said. The word which came to Roberta most often when she thought about Zack was *natural*. She also thought him witty and sweet and strong.

He said he was in love, and she said the same. But neither said 'I love you' except *in extremis*, in bed. Funny distinction. But a real one. 'I love you,' she supposed, implied a commitment – lasting commitment – and there was no such commitment between her and Zack. The age difference precluded it. Eventually, Zack would choose a woman his own age. That was inevitable, and right. He would want to have children.

'Zack,' she had asked him curiously, when they were lying idly in bed after making love, 'have you ever been married?' He had described himself as 'single,' when she'd first met him, but he had never mentioned whether he'd been divorced.

'Yes, I was married, Roberta,' he answered. 'I'm a widower.'

'A widower!' Her eyes opened wide in surprise. 'So young? Oh, Zack! I'm so sorry . . .'

'Plane crash,' he said. 'Small private plane. My brother-in-law's. They were going to see my wife's parents. My little girl was aboard. She was six.'

'Oh, *Zack*!' Pity made her throat tight. 'My dear . . .' She kissed him on the cheek, tightened her arm around his neck.

'There's nothing to be said, Roberta. Idiot chance, Idiot, idiot chance. We're all subject to it, at any minute. At every minute. The present is all we have. That's why it's so foolish to waste it.'

Yes. Idiot chance. Like the snapping off of Brad's life before Roberta had a chance to . . . No. That was past. And Zack, too, had had a terrible loss.

Did you love her very much? Roberta wanted to ask. It was a question one always wanted to ask a lover about a previous love, but Roberta resisted. She knew the

143

answer. Of course Zack had loved his wife. He was a man capable of love. In a way it was a celebration of past happiness, a tribute to it, that he could make Roberta so happy.

So she was living in the present – the only way to go, as Zack had said – and she was loving it. There was such a powerful animal magnetism between them, and that alone was worth the price of admission, she conceded, feeling sensuous at the mere thought; but they were also good companions.

Like today, she giggled to herself. Whoever heard of conducting a – well, it wasn't a courtship, but an *affaire de coeur* – on your knees in the garden, transplanting day lilies? But that was what they had done, starting early, working late, and both enjoying it.

And when she had pulled a weed and remarked 'Wouldn't you hate to be a weed? After all, they were here first,' Zack had snatched up her hand and kissed it, grubby with garden dirt and all.

He's so spontaneous, so life-loving, Roberta thought, touching her wrists and earlobes with perfume. She was dressing to go to dinner – he was taking her to a new place in Bucks county – and she liked the way she looked, because she knew Zack would.

They had a standing, taken-for-granted date every Saturday night, and sometimes, like today, they spent Sunday together. But not always, and not every weekday evening either. Roberta was disciplining herself on that score. It was hard to do. Zack wanted to spend every free moment he had with her, and she urgently wanted to be with him. But she would not permit herself to forget that perfect as their love was, it was temporary. She had to remember that. She had to reserve part of herself against the time when, inevitably, he would be gone. And she couldn't jeopardize her friendship with the

Harcourts and her Greenwillow friends, either. They were too important to her. So she made a point of keeping her end up socially, even though Zack was always in her thoughts, no matter where she was.

Of course she could have introduced Zack to her friends, she had even thought it would be natural to do so. But she shied away from doing it. She was not ready to declare herself publicly as half of a couple. She was too new to dating, too out of practice. Most of all, she felt that what she and Zack had was intensely private. She wanted to keep it that way.

She heard Zack's car in the driveway. Nothing could make me admit it, she thought, but I feel about eighteen. She ran downstairs to greet him.

13

Jim graduated from Lafayette in May. The family turned out in force to attend the ceremony: Brad's parents, Roberta's father, Susan, and, of course, Mingo.

As they watched Jim receive his diploma, all of them, in varying ways, were wishing his father were alive to witness it. Roberta's feelings, however, were mixed. She, too, as she looked at Jim's serious young face, regretted that her son could not share this moment with his father, but thinking of Brad rekindled her own pain. At the same time she was experiencing another conflict. Jim would be spending the summer with her at the farm, and that gave her joy. But what of Zack? Jim's presence would make it difficult, if not impossible, for her to continue their affair. Every fiber of her being protested against giving him up. As long as their affair lasted, she wanted him, but she would not resort to subterfuge. Her relationship with Zack was based on mutual respect and honesty. The need to arrange secret meetings and practice deception, particularly in regard to her own son, would cheapen it, would even introduce an element of guiltiness, where guilt should not exist.

How am I going to handle this? she thought. Then she regretted that her mind had wandered to her own concerns while she was witnessing a milestone event in her son's life. He was being graduated *magna cum laude*, and she was so proud of him. She would put off deciding her own personal course until later. Today was Jim's day. Later, God willing, perhaps she could get closer to her daughter. As she had so dismally failed to do at Christmas.

After the ceremony they all gathered festively at home, and corks popped as they toasted Jim. Both the elder Mr Marston and Roberta's father had come bearing champagne. The gala dinner Roberta had planned was a warm, merry occasion. Mingo beamed every bit as proudly at her godson as did Jim's mother and grandparents. Only Susie, Roberta noted, was not relaxed. Although she, too, paid affectionate tribute to her brother, it was obvious that she was feeling no happier.

The next morning, Susan did not come down for breakfast. As the others lingered over their coffee, Roberta excused herself and went to her daughter's room. She found her staring at the ceiling.

'Don't you feel well, dear?'

'I'm okay, Mother.'

'They why? . . . Don't you want breakfast? Everyone is still at the table.'

'I didn't feel I'd fit into the prevailing atmosphere of good cheer.' Susan tried to bring her answer off flippantly, but in spite of herself, her mouth trembled.

'Susan, I know you are unhappy. Can't I help?'

'What did you have in mind?'

Roberta hid her hurt. She looked at her young daughter, a delicate, feminine version of Brad. She lay in the long T-shirt she wore as a nightie. It was bunched up around her slender body, and her shining hair tousled the pillow. Across her small firm breasts the T-shirt read, 'But what is the question?'

Roberta pulled a chair close to the bed and sat down. 'Maybe you're right, Susie. Maybe I can't help. But I'd like to, if you'll let me.'

Silence.

147

Dared she mention Susan's breakup with her boy-friend? Roberta wondered uneasily. 'Is it Gil, Susan?'

Susan looked at the ceiling. 'Naturally you'd think that. No. It's not Gil. You can relax about that. Gil didn't brush me off. *I* broke up with *him*.'

'I see.'

Now Susan sat up. 'No, you don't, Mother. You don't see at all. Gil is neither here nor there. A nice boy, but a boy. I already *told* you that. Don't you remember? Who wants a boy? I want a man. A grownup. Some-body strong, somebody sure of who he is, someone like Daddy . . .'

She broke off and flushed. She hadn't meant to put it like that.

'Oh, I know what you're thinking! Father complex, right?'

That wasn't what Roberta had been thinking. 'Wrong, Susan. It struck me as a tribute to your father.'

'Yeah. Right. You could say that.'

She dropped her head back onto the pillow. She was silent. Then she said, 'Do you want to know what's really bugging me?'

'If you'll tell me.'

'All that fun and games downstairs. Is nobody *mourning* Daddy? How can everyone laugh and joke so, when Daddy has been gone less than a year?'

Fun and games? 'Susie, it's your brother's graduation. Surely – '

'I know, I know. Life goes on, so they say. But it's not the same. Everything is changed. I *miss* Daddy.'

And you *don't*, her tone said.

Roberta's heart sank. Her instinct had been right at Christmas. Resentment of her mother was tying Susan up in knots. Unmistakably, she was grieving for her father. But in true grief, you turn to those closest, for comfort.

Somehow this had been short-circuited in Susan. She had changed the hurt to hate. Of her mother. And wasn't it a truism of psychology that depression, like Susan's, is always based on suppressed hostility?

Perhaps confronting her anger head-on would be best. 'Susan, I know you are very, very grieved at your father's death. I also know you are hostile to me. Can we have this out? Can you tell me what is at the bottom of this?'

Susan sat bolt upright. 'All right, Mother. I will, since you ask for it. I can't understand your . . . your gung ho attitude, your everything-is-rosy bit. All that happy chatter last night – about your *job* and your new *friends*. The Mentons, or Fentons, or whatever their name is. And the committee to save the township, whatever that is. You don't even mention Dad's name. And you look so happy! How *can* you?'Now her hostility was blazing from her eyes. She might have been pointing a finger and saying *J'accuse*! 'Didn't you *love* Dad?'

Roberta felt sick. 'Yes,' she said slowly. 'I did love your father . . . very much. As I love you very much. But your father is gone. Forever,' she added deliberately.

'But do you have to be so . . . so blithe about it? So *up*?'

Up! Now Roberta sensed another element in her daughter's hot challenge. Envy. Roberta, in Susie's parlance, was 'doing okay for herself.' Susan was falling apart. Susan's real question was: Where do *you* get off, Mother, to be making it, when I'm not?

'Would it serve any purpose, Susan, if I pulled down the blinds and wept behind them? Would it do you any good? Or me? As for my job, I need the money. I'm trying to hang on to this place, for you and Jim. Paul Reston says I can't afford it. He says I should sell it. Your father left very little, you know.'

149

Susan looked shocked. 'Very little? How could that be? I thought . . .'

'So did I. But I have very little money.'

'Sorry about that,' Susan muttered. 'I didn't know.'

'Perhaps because you never asked? Perhaps because you were so absorbed in your own feelings, you gave no thought to anyone else? Your grandparents, for instance. Can you imagine how hard it is for them to accept the loss of their son? As for me, has it occurred to you that I, too, have had to make some very tough adjustments?'

'Sorry.'

'Susan. You are a bright, beautiful young woman. Your life is before you. I would do anything to ensure that that life will be happy and fulfilling, but of course I can't. Only you can. Think about it.'

Roberta rose and quietly left the room.

As soon as Susan heard her mother's footsteps safely recede down the front stairway, she flung herself from the bed, yanked on jeans and shirt, sneaked down the backstairs, and left the house. Her chaotic feelings drove her to action, but *what* action? She struck off blindly along the creek. Then she stopped to pick up a fallen willow wand, unconsciously whacking away at the wild grass as she strode through it. Her intelligence told her she was being unreasonable, but her intelligence was no match for her feelings. Her feelings! They were more like torments. She felt lost, alone, with nothing solid to hang on to. She didn't even know what it was she wanted. Yes, she did. Life as it used to be. But that was impossible. And her mother! Lecturing her . . . and being so *with* it. While she, Susan, was so miserably out of it.

Where the creek met the far hedgerow, Susan turned to climb the slope to the back acres. She walked unseeingly through the fields to the property line, then reluctantly turned into the path which led back to the house. She was sure of one thing. She couldn't stand much more of this country scene. Could she leave for the city right now? No. Not with the family here. Not when it was Jim's graduation. But she wouldn't be back in a hurry. In fact, who knew where she would be.

The barn door was open as she passed. Someone inside was whistling. It took a second for it to register. Then, in a double take, Susan stopped. *Don Giovanni*. In the barn? She went inside. 'Hello?' she called. 'Hello!'

'Hello yourself!' What a great voice. A man came from behind a tractor, a tool in his hand. 'I don't think we've met,' he said. 'I'm Zack Owen.'

'Hi. I'm Susan Marston.'

Roberta's daughter. Instantly, Zack felt a warm almost proprietary interest in this pretty kid. She she must look like her father. She certainly did not resemble Roberta.

He reminds me of someone, thought Susan. Someone terrific. Spencer Tracy. Susan went for the men in the late, late movies. The grownup men, not the guys in jeans commercials. Yes, Spencer Tracy in his younger days. Not handsome – who wants a narcissist? – but powerful. You could feel it a mile away. She realized she was staring.

'I couldn't believe what I was hearing,' she said.

'Hearing? Sorry, I – '

'*Don Giovanni*. You were whistling.'

'Was I? My mind must have been somewhere else. Do you like Mozart?'

'Crazy about it.'

'That makes two of us.'

Two of us. How nice that sounded. But she couldn't just stand there like an idiot.

'Do you live around here, uh, Zack?'

'Why, yes – I live in the carriage house.'

151

'Oh! You're the *tenant*.'

'You look so surprised.'

Susan felt like a fool. Roberta had told her, of course, that she had rented the carriage house – when was it? – months ago. But it had barely registered. Susan had not even known whether the tenant was a man or woman, and she hadn't really cared. She had been too involved with her own problems. Bumping into Zack in the barn, she had vaguely assumed that he had something or other to do with the tractor, that he was a hired hand or repairman, although he certainly didn't look or sound like one.

'How dumb of me,' she said. 'It was because you were working. I didn't think tenants – '

'Fiddled with tractors? It's the lure of machinery. Some men just can't resist.'

'Then I guess I'm keeping you from fiddling.'

'No, I had just finished.' He stowed away the tools, and then waited for her to precede him out of the barn. She watched while he slid the huge door along its track and secured it with a metal pin. Quick. Graceful. God, those *shoulders*.

'Wonderful old barn,' he said, as they started down the lane together. 'And what a view, isn't it?'

'Yes. Great view. But doesn't it get . . . boring?'

'Not to me.' They had come to the little box-edged path which led to the carriage house. Zack stopped. '*Very* nice to meet you, Susan.'

Could she say 'I'd love to see what you've done to the place' or 'May I look at your garden?' No. She supposed not.

She said, 'Me, too. Nice to meet *you*, Zack.' Then she headed on down the lane.

Nice girl, thought Zack. Roberta had mentioned, in passing, that her daughter had been hard hit by the loss

152

of her father. He wondered if there was anything he could do to help Roberta cheer up her child.

'What's up with Susan?' Mingo asked Roberta when they had a few moments alone. 'Boy trouble?'

'More like mother trouble,' Roberta replied. 'At least, that's what it looks like. And I don't know what to do about it.'

'But that's terrible.' Mingo's face showed quick concern. 'Oh, Robbie. After the tough time *you've* just been through.'

'She doesn't see it that way. At the moment, she's blind to everything but herself, and she's still in pieces over her father.'

'Yes. But still . . .' Mingo frowned. 'Do you think a change of job might help, Robbie? Jolt her out of it? There's an assistant's job open in our Features department. I can pull a little rank, you know. And it would even be kosher, considering that Susan's degree is in journalism. What do you think?'

How like Mingo. 'It's sweet of you to suggest it, Mingo, but I don't think Susie's mood has anything to do with her job. She seems to like NBC – at least she did. Apparently the big dream of girls nowadays is to be an anchorwoman, the way we wanted to be movie stars. But come to think of it, she hasn't even mentioned her job lately. No, I think Susan's problem is with Susan. She needs to grow up.'

'Well, you'll let me know if I can do anything? Take her to lunch, spank her – anything?'

'Of course, Mingo. Bless you.'

Thank God for a good woman friend, thought Roberta, a woman who cares as much about my troubles as I do. Ever since Mingo poured out her own torment, Roberta

153

had ached to do something for *her*. What Susie has to learn, she thought, is that *everyone* has to bear *something*.

But when Susan came in from outside an hour later – Roberta had imagined her still huddled in bed – she greeted everyone cheerily, was charming to her grandparents, and challenged her brother to a game of Scrabble. Roberta and Mingo exchanged glances. Could that little talking-to have worked already? No, that would be a miracle. But, be grateful for small favors.

Jim Marston lay face down in bed, his stomach in a knot and his fists unconsciously clenched. Shit, was he *uptight*!

How come he hadn't realized *before*, the huge difference the loss of his father was going to make in his life? It had gone right over his head because, at first, there hadn't been that much change in his personal life. The shock had been a bitch, naturally, and the grief. He'd loved his father, respected him, even though he was probably closer to his mother. Susan was the one who had the big thing with Dad.

But his actual day-to-day routine had not been affected. He'd gone back to college, as he would have anyway. He'd spent Christmas at the farm, as he would have anyway. And he'd just graduated – everything according to original plan. But what was he supposed to do next?

He was *supposed* to spend the next six weeks sailing on Long Island Sound with Chuck Smith and Ben Cooper. That had been planned nearly a year ago, with all their parents in on it, as a kind of reward for graduating, a breather before the grind of law school.

But his mother had apparently forgotten all about it. She seemed to assume he'd be staying with her, seemed to be *counting* on it. How could he tell her he was taking off next Friday? Especially after what she'd told him last night about money? Without making a big deal of it, she'd let him know there wasn't much ready cash. He was furious at his father. How could you let that *happen*, Dad? That's a hell of a way to take care of Mother! Hold it, he thought. Dad hardly knew he was going to die young. Still, his mother was working because she had to, not just to keep busy as he'd supposed.

Where did that leave him?

In his twenty-two years, Jim Marston had never been faced with a hard choice. One had simply never come up. Everything had been cool without his having to think about it. His parents were firmly behind him, they lived a rather nice life, his path lay straight ahead. Grow up, get an education, become a lawyer, strike out on your own. In due time. Meanwhile, no sweat.

He sweated a little now as he realized how much he'd taken for granted. And that a lot of things he'd taken for granted were gone. He buried his head in the pillow and thought about them. The apartment in New York, for one. The great room he'd had, and Mattie serving dinner, and, way back, the parties his mother gave for him and Susan, with a clown or a ventriloquist and favors from Dennison's. And the city itself – skating at Rockefeller Center and the *Nutcracker* and a million movies and the Planetarium. Hopping a bus to spend the afternoon at a friend's apartment, and being sent home in a taxi. Ducking into Bloomingdale's to charge a sweater or something to his mother's charge account. And later, when he was old enough to drink beer, the Second Avenue hangouts where he met his pals – and tried pot in the john. And the vacations, not just having his friends here at the farm, but the special ones – the Easter vacation in Bermuda, the wild one at Fort Lauderdale.

He'd never thought about any of it. It was just *there*. Not that he was dumb enough to think *doesn't everyone*? But that was the way everyone *he* knew lived. Now it was all . . . wiped out. Jim Marston – nice kid, untried kid – felt the way he had when his bike was stolen. It hurt. He could have cried, if you must know . . . if he'd let himself.

Fuck it! He flung his man's body out of bed, yanked on his jeans, and stood staring out the window. He realized he had just made a decision. Of *course* he couldn't go sailing. Was he out of his mind? He had to stick around this summer, whether he wanted to or not. He *didn't* want to – the Smiths' boat was a beauty, and so was Chuck's sister – but he *had* to. Otherwise he'd be a jerk.

Scowling at the meadow, Jim forgot himself for a moment and thought about his mother. Not as *his mother*, for once, but as *her* – herself. It hit him how heavy all this must be for her. Worrying about bills. Lonely, too, probably. He remembered the night he'd surprised her with the TV dinners. She'd flipped so. The truth was, he'd really only come home to pick up his basketball shoes. The idea of their eating together had just been an afterthought, because it was nearly six. But his mother had assumed he'd shown up to hear about her new job. Well, maybe he *would* have, if he'd known she needed his company.

Needed. Kids need parents. But a parent needing *him*? He wasn't ready for it. Yes, he was. No choice.

So what are you going to do? Cancel the sailing. Look for a summer job. Earn spending money, at least. Maybe I should pay board? How weird that sounds – pay board in your own home. But my mother's buying and I'm eating. Yeah. Contribute something.

One good thing, Jim thought, cheering up slightly. I really dig the farm. The outdoors turned him on. And another good thing: it was just as well that he and Barbara had finally split. He had other stuff on his mind.

He called Chuck to cancel the sailing. Chuck was pissed, even though Jim explained. 'Can't you talk her into it?' Chuck persisted. 'Know what, Chuck?' Jim said. 'You talk like a fucking kid. Grow up, huh?'

It was wonderful to have Jim at home, to have breakfast with him, to have him greet her when she came home from work, and to hear the sounds she had missed: Jim taking the stairs two at a time. Jim running a shower. It made the house a home again, in spite of the awkward position with Zack.

She was touched when Jim announced he'd landed a summer job with the local Road Department, more touched when he handed her fifty dollars 'toward my weekly keep, Mom.' Roberta's first impulse was to refuse it. She'd never intended her kids to pay their own way, not until they were launched on real careers. But Jim seemed so serious. In fact, looking at him more closely, she was shocked to realize she was glimpsing the man Jim would soon become, not the boy she knew so well. There was something about his jaw, the set of his face. My God, he looks so much older all of a sudden. Have I just not noticed? she thought.

'Thank you, Jim,' she said. 'That will help.'

And realistically, it would.

She worried about him a little bit, though. He didn't seem down, exactly, but he was so quiet, not his usual high-spirited self. Of course, with his father gone, he was trying to adjust, too. So much had changed, for all of them.

But Jim's basically happy nature could not be quenched for long. Roberta was glad to see his old grin back when he showed off the hedge he had clipped.

'Jim, it looks terrific – so *even* – but it goes on forever. That must be a big job.'

'You said it, lady. My arms are killing me. But when

it's for the family place, that kind of eases the pain. This is quite a spread, when you think about it.'

'You like it, then, being at the farm?'

'Well, living here and just goofing off here are pretty different. But you know what?' Jim waved an encompassing arm toward the far field, the distant tree line. 'I think I'm getting as hooked as you are, Mom.'

That made her happy.

Roberta still hadn't figured out what to do about Zack. She missed him terribly, and sometimes, seeing his lights on the hill, her desire for him was so acute it almost frightened her. But with Jim recently arrived, she didn't see how she could avoid having dinner with him, nor could she say, after dinner, 'I'm going out for a while, dear.' It would be so highly unnatural not to say where she was going. And she could not bring herself to lie to her son. Practical as that might be, the words would stick in her throat.

She had seen Zack only twice since Jim had arrived: once for a quick drink after work and again, when at Zack's insistence, she'd called Jim and simply said that a friend had invited her to dinner. 'Have fun,' Jim had replied. She had not gone to the carriage house, and that was where she wanted to be.

Some women, she supposed, could simply say to their sons, 'I've met a nice man. I won't be back tonight.' Maybe at some point she could manage to do that, if she developed enough courage, and if she did a little consciousness-raising first. After all, she told herself, you're not committing adultery. You're free. She might be able to do it, she thought, if her son and the man were not on the same property. However, as it stood, disappearing into the carriage house seemed . . . indelicate. Silly, maybe. But she was stuck with it.

It wasn't fair to Zack either. He's not going to put up with my qualms forever, she thought.

In the end, it was Jim himself who provided a solution. 'Look, Mother,' he said one night. 'I hope you're not sticking around the house for me. Didn't you say you've met some people here? I'll bet you've been turning down invitations.'

'Well, I thought since you were settling in, Jim – '

'Sure. But the honeymoon's over. And I certainly don't want to cramp your style. Anyway, Mom, *I* have a date tomorrow night. I've met a girl, and I have a feeling I'll be seeing her often. I wanted to give you advance notice. Okay?'

'Okay!'

Within five minutes she was calling Zack from the phone in her bedroom. 'I'll be up tomorrow night. If you like, that is.'

'That's the dumbest "if" I ever heard,' Zack said.

Zack brought up the subject at dinner. They were on the porch of a country restaurant overlooking Spruce Run.

'Roberta, I know you feel having Jim home changes things.'

She looked at him gratefully. His fine-tuned sensitivity to her feelings astonished her. She and Zack seemed to communicate without words. Even Brad had not known her so intuitively.

'Yes, I do feel that.'

'I thought so.' Zack frowned thoughtfully toward the reservoir shining in the distance. 'I understand your feeling, Roberta. But it doesn't make sense, darling.'

'Meaning? . .'

'Do you feel there's something shameful . . . about us, Roberta?'

She was indignant. 'Of *course* not.'

159

'But you're uneasy about what we share, in regard to Jim.'

Yes, she was. Now it was Roberta who frowned. It *didn't* make sense. How could she feel 'funny,' maybe even guilty, about something to which she had every right? She and Zack had found unexpected happiness together. At least temporarily, she reminded herself. Perhaps the fact that it was temporary made it all the more precious. So why should she feel to uptight?

Zack was smiling at her, half-amused, but dead serious.

'Hang-ups, die hard, don't they, darling? All those old "thou shalt nots" we grew up with, all of us over thirty-five.'

Thirty-five. Was he being tactful?

'Zack, I'm over *forty*-five. Almost forty-eight, in fact.'

There! It was out.

'Right. You must tell me when your birthday is.' Zack's face did not change by a flicker. 'But let's not dodge the issue. Back to Jim. To you and me – and Jim. We must get this straight, Robbie. I won't have you feeling guilty . . .'

Roberta wasn't listening. She had just fallen several more notches in love. Zack Owen had behaved as though he'd never seen the *young-is-better* commericals, or simply didn't buy them. She wanted to jump up and kiss him. But he was waiting for her answer.

'Yes, it's true. I agree it's silly. But I hate being secretive. It seems so sneaky.'

'Sneaky! Us? But that's a false equation, darling. Isn't this a case where secrecy really means privacy? You think your private life is not appropriate to share with your son. I agree. But just because circumstances dictate *discretion*, that doesn't make us thieves in the night.'

He was right. He had sorted out her conflicting feelings. She did believe that emotional love and sexual love were intensely private matters. But they were only furtive, as he'd pointed out, if you *felt* they were furtive.

'It's just that life is so damned tenuous, Roberta.' She knew he was thinking of the wife and child he had lost. 'The only moment we have is this one. It's stupid to waste happiness when life offers it.'

'Yes, Zack. Yes. I agree.'

'Then, my darling, let me put it in plain English.' He reached over and took her hand. 'I want you in my arms, Robbie. I think you want me too. But I sure as hell can't come to your house, so you must come to mine. Because discretion demands that, for now, you must wake up in your own bed, we can't escape a certain amount of . . . covert activity.'

'Covert activity.' She laughed.

'Right.' He grinned. 'Like the CIA. We've got to get you back down the lane at a decent hour. A deprivation, but in a good cause. The question is: how will you feel? Merely realistic? Or tacky? If tacky, it's no go. I won't permit it.'

'I'll feel happy.'

He tightened his grip on her hand, and the flame between them leaped high.

'Shall we go?' said Zack, a roughness in his voice.

Later, in the carriage house, Roberta stirred reluctantly. 'Tell me one thing,' she murmured into Zack's ear. 'Did you ever take acting lessons?'

'What?' Zack opened his eyes.

'Or do you *really* not care that I'm older than you?'

'What?' he said again. 'Oh, that. Well, I never saw the allure of the child-girl. Give me a woman. You, in fact.' He buried his face in her hair.

'How old are you, Zack?'

'Thirty-seven.'

'That's ten years.'

'Correct.' He pulled her toward him. 'But you're so silly. And so lovely.' He kissed her. 'And so young.'

Roberta stroked his chest. 'I must go, Zack.'

'Yes.'

'Time for covert activity.' She found herself giggling at the phrase. At that moment, it didn't seem to matter who was what age. And it didn't seem tacky at all, walking down the lane with Zack before Jim returned. It merely seemed sensible.

When he left her at the door, Zack said, 'But I reserve the right to take you out to dinner, in full view of your son. I'll do that next Tuesday, darling.'

'Please *do*,' said Roberta.

After that, it was all right. When she mentioned to Jim, for the first time, that Zack Owen had invited her out to dinner, he replied 'Good, Mom. *Time* you got out. I hope he takes you someplace classy. My guess is he will. He seems like that kind of guy.'

14

Roberta leaned her head against the seat of Zack's car. What a perfect birthday, she thought dreamily. And what luck it had fallen on her day off. Zack had had business in New York, or had he maneuvered that? She suspected so, which made it that much nicer. If you have to be forty-eight, she thought, this is the way.

The day had begun with Jim absurdly ringing the old cowbell outside her bedroom door, to celebrate her being born, he'd said. He'd had a festive breakfast ready for her, complete with flowers and best china. Propped at her plate she'd found a gift certificate from the White Flower Farm for a dozen Bright Eyes phlox. The thoughtfulness of the gift had moved her to tears. Weeks had passed since she'd admired the flower in the catalog and remarked that she would love to add it to her collection. But Jim had made a point of remembering.

Then Jim had driven her to the bus for New York, where she was to meet Mingo for lunch. She'd spent the morning happily puttering through Bendel's and Bergdorf's. Not that she could afford to buy anything, but just for the hell of it. Had she ever actually shopped there, not only for her clothes but for all those little luxuries like wickedly expensive bath soaps and little gold pencils and extravagant notepapers and frivolous mules? As the pampered, protected Mrs Bradford Marston, in another life, on another planet.

The woman behind the counter in The Gilded Cage greeted her. 'Why, Mrs Marston, we haven't seen you in some time. Have you been away?' 'Yes, away.' Roberta smiled. It suddenly struck her as hilarious that she, too, was now a saleslady. What would this nice woman think if she knew I belong on her side of the counter? Roberta wondered. Probably that I now know what real life is about. And she'd be right. But it's not so bad, real life, not on a day like this.

At one, she met Mingo at Le Cirque. As she followed the captain to the table where Mingo was waiting, there was Susie as a birthday surprise. Even though Mingo had undoubtedly twisted Susie's arm, Roberta's heart lifted at the sight of her daughter. And from the way Susan greeted her, it was evident she was on her best behavior at least for today.

It was a long, gay lunch. Mingo and Susie toasted Roberta, and Mingo kept them laughing with her sardonic commentary on the beautiful, posturing people. Several stopped to speak to Mingo: the king of a retail empire, a famous designer, *the* fashion photographer, a Seventh Avenue Name. 'Do you know *everybody*?' Susan asked. 'Everybody,' said Mingo. 'But to know them is not to love them. Listen, we're in a sea of sharks. The trouble is, they're such talented sharks. You don't trust them, but you have to respect them.'

Roberta found it great fun to be in the Manhattan whirl again. It was nearly three when Mingo looked at her watch and said to her, 'You have exactly twenty-five minutes to get to Arden's.'

'Arden's? I'm not going to Arden's.

'Yes, you are. You're booked for three-fifteen. Massage, facial, hair, the works. Birthday present.'

'Mingo! That's too much. You're too much! You've already given me that smashing negligee . . .' United Parcel had delivered the negligee to the farm yesterday, with a note from Mingo: 'So you shouldn't schlepp it around town tomorrow. See you at lunch.'

'Come on, Roberta,' Mingo said. 'You *know* I get everything, but everything, at a monster discount. And you know Arden's, and every other shop in town, is dying to do me favors. So get along with you . . . Not that you need Arden all that much, with your assets. Still, a little cossetting can't hurt, can it? Come on, I've got a limo waiting. I'll drop you.'

As the car pulled up to the familiar red door, Roberta said, 'Oh, Mingo. If I could only do something for *you*.'

'You do, kid, you do. Have fun.'

Lying in quiet, fragrant privacy in the world-famous temple of beauty, feeling deft, skillful fingers knead and pat her body, enjoying the pull of a facial masque, Roberta let her thoughts wander in blissful mindlessness. Zack. Zack would be waiting for her at five-thirty. She was a woman being made beautiful for her lover. She would meet him, and then . . . Totally relaxed, she slid into a delicious dream.

She knew she looked her best as she stepped into Barbetta's, and the glances of strangers confirmed it. But she wasn't prepared for the fervor of Zack's greeting. 'Roberta! My God, you're incandescent.'

'Well, I've had a lovely day,' she said lightly, to counter the impact of the look in his eye. She hoped she wasn't blushing.

Over drinks, he took a small wallet-size package from his pocket. 'Happy birthday, darling Mrs M. For you. Open it.'

Inside was a photograph of what appeared to be a primitive painting. He said the original was uptown being framed.

'Why, it's the farm,' she said delightedly. 'My house. From the east, so you see the creek and the barn and the top of the silo. Zack, it's enchanting. I *love* it. But where on earth did you get it?'

'You know that little gallery in Clinton? I happened to see something in the window – a snow scene. It reminded me of that first Sunday when we met in the snow, remember? I went in and found out the artist is local, quite an old man. People are beginning to collect him.'

'A kind of Grandpa Moses. And you saw this and recognized the farm?'

'Not exactly. I tracked down the artist, and asked if he'd consider . . .'

Roberta sat back in her chair. 'You mean you *commissioned* it? Oh, Zack! But how? When did he paint it?'

'I sneaked him in on Saturdays while you were at work.'

'How – how unbelievable of you.' The time and thought he had put into the gift moved her. But it was his perceptiveness which touched her heart, as Jim's garden gift had. 'Zack, I'm touched.'

'That was the general idea, Mrs M dear, to touch you.' He reached across the table and took her hand. *Besides, I knew damned well you wouldn't accept the bracelet I wanted to give you. You're such a lady, Roberta, as well as such a woman.*

'Have I said thank you? Thank you, Zack. No gift has ever pleased me more.' That was true. 'I'll . . . I'll treasure it.'

For the rest of the evening, Roberta walked on air. The possessive way Zack gripped her elbow as they went down the aisle of the theater, the attentive way he lighted her cigarette at intermission, made her feel cherished. Like a pearl nestled in velvet.

Afterward, Zack said. 'What's your pleasure, darling? Shall we do the traditional, Sardi's?'

She hesitated. The last time she'd been in Sardi's she had been with Brad. Could she take the memories? Yes, she could. She wouldn't let herself have memories. This

166

was her night. Hers and Zack's. Why should she let the past spoil the present, especially when the present was so temporary?

'Yes, let's. Sardi's.

Their reactions were almost identical as they hashed over the play they had just seen.

'That second act curtain rang a little false, didn't you think?'

'Absolutely. Too contrived.'

'But that bit of business with the luggage, did you notice?'

'Wasn't he marvelous with that?'

Now, at two in the morning, they were driving home along a deserted route 78, the darkness broken only by their headlights. Zack had been silent for the last ten minutes, his face thoughtful in the dim glow of the dashboard. Roberta watched the trees fly past, lulled by their rhythm. Life can be good, she thought. You somehow survive the blows and hurts, and then a perfect day like this drops into your lap. So what if it didn't guarantee one against future blows and hurts? It was heaven while it lasted. While it . . . lasted. But suppose it could last? No, don't dream, she warned herself. Still, contained in this quiet closeness, her shoulder touching his, she could not resist dreaming. *Could* it last? Or put another way, how could it *end*? They *fitted* so well. Not only the chemistry, the companionship. The harmony . . .

The car turned onto the Creek Road, and she came to. And a good thing, she told herself reluctantly. The perfect day was over. She had been foolishly woolgathering. This was a wonderful interlude, but only an interlude. Her path and Zack's had happily intersected, and she should be grateful for that. But they could never run on parallel lines, reality was against it. She must remember that.

Still, what a shame that they couldn't end this evening

properly – in bed. Impossible, though. Jim was home, perhaps awake. That would be blatantly indiscreet.

Zack saw her to the door. Roberta turned on the top step to kiss him good night. 'May I come in, Roberta?'

She hated to part with him. But wouldn't it be harder to be so close, and not be in each other's arms? 'Zack, it's so late . . .'

'Never mind.' He took the key from her hand, unlocked the door, and stood aside for her. 'Come, Roberta.'

Jim had left a lamp burning in the living room. Roberta led the way to the far end, where they would be least likely to disturb Jim, and sat down on a loveseat. Zack walked past her and sat on a chair opposite.

He saw her look of surprise. 'I'm deliberately putting a distance between us,' he said, in a low voice, 'because I can't trust myself to be close to you. And because I want to reach you, not with my body, but with my heart and mind.'

'Zack?' Her own voice was tremulous. 'Zack, I . . .' Had she known it was coming, really, in the depths of her being? Or had she been afraid it would never come? She was uncertain. But she knew that this man was now going to make demands on her.

Much as she wanted him, she had a blind instinct to fend off whatever he was going to say.

'Zack,' she said again. 'My dear, can't we . . . couldn't we – '

'Stay as we are: Lovers? Uncommitted lovers? No.'

She looked at him. No words came.

'Roberta. I love you. Will you marry me?'

She could feel joy coursing through her veins in a sweet, sweet flood of exultation. He wanted her. He wanted her seriously, permanently. And only a half-hour before she had been warning herself that all things begin and end, especially affairs. But now, with the joy, she felt icy fear. *Marriages also begin and end*. Even Rock-of-Gibraltar marriages. Even twenty-five-year marriages. How could she make herself vulnerable again, risk disillusion a second time – especially with a man she had known only a few months? Yet she felt she'd known him forever. No, it was crazy. It was foolish. It was *perilous*.

But I want him.

Zack broke the silence. 'Well, Roberta?'

'Oh, Zack . . . Zack, forgive me. I didn't answer because I couldn't. I was thinking of you, and me, and life and what happens to people. Zack, I think I love you. No, I *know* I love you. And I'm happy that you want to marry me. But I'm afraid. Afraid of the risk, afraid it's not wise for *you*, darling, for *you* as well as for me. It's so dangerous to assume that something wonderful . . . can stay wonderful.'

'Roberta, goddammit.' Zack's voice was intense, impatient. Roberta, you fool. You and I are passionately attracted to each other. I cannot be near you without desiring you.'

Me, too, thought Roberta.

'And when I'm away from you, the mere thought of you makes me desire you. That doesn't happen with every man and woman, you know. It's rare enough. But that's only a fraction of what we have, Roberta. We have the same values, react in the same way. Surely you see that? Compatibility is too pale a word. We *rhyme*, dammit! You and I respond in unison. I want to make that unity complete. I want to share life with you in every way. Marry me, Roberta.'

If you knew how much I want to believe that's possible, she thought. But what about our ages? You can't laugh that off. Bravely she forced herself to say it aloud.

'Zack, I'm ten years older than you,'

'Balls!' he said crudely, to shock her. 'Irrelevant.'

169

'But how can you say that? Today I'm forty-eight. And you're not quite thirty-eight. Ten years from now – '

'Arithmetic. Numbers. Nonsense.'

Roberta felt now, as she often had before, that Zack was more life-wise than she was. Life-smarts? Was he right? Were age hang-ups only for those insecure enough to buy what the culture sold? Was the youth cult a bill of goods, like the emperor's clothes?

'Roberta, listen to me. This isn't young love. I've had that. So have you. I was totally in love with my young wife, as I'm sure you were with your husband. But what I feel for you is quite different. We're not a boy and girl, starting out in life. You're a grown woman. I'm a grown man. We've both survived life's low blows. And because we've survived them, we should have the good sense to grab happiness when it's grabable. The moment is now. I won't let us waste it.'

Roberta moved to Zack's side and took his hand. 'Zack, Zack. I love you . . . I treasure you. But I must think. There are so many angles . . . so many questions . . .'

He looked contrite. 'Robbie, dearest, I didn't mean to pressure you. Of course, you need time to think. You're not the kind of woman who would ever say "This is so sudden," but I realize it *is* sudden in a sense. I know that it's less then a year since you lost your husband, and that leaving the city was another major upheaval for you.'

He stood up, gently drew her to her feet, and put his hands on her shoulders. 'Look, Roberta, I've got to go to Japan in about three weeks. I'll be gone six weeks or so. That should give you plenty of time. But I'll expect an answer when I come back, darling. I'm unwilling to go on like this. I want you for my *wife*. I love you. Happy birthday, my darling.' Tenderly he kissed her forehead, and was gone.

She stood motionless a long time, her hand pressed to the spot Zack had kissed.

15

In the days that followed Zack's proposal, Roberta swung helplessly between joy and fear. While she went through the motions of daily life with one part of her mind, the deeper part carried on a ceaseless dialogue: Do I dare? Or is this crazy?

She had thought that she'd recovered from the wound Brad had inflicted, that her busy new life in Greenwillow had healed that hurt. Not entirely, of course. That was impossible. But enough to find some gratification in living.

Now, paradoxically, Zack's declaration had reawakened the old pain. The happiness she felt was counteracted by a strong, once-burned fear of trusting love a second time. Twice shy indeed.

Zack said, 'Let's not discuss it, darling. Let's not over-analyze. You know what I want. Now you must decide what you want.'

He made it sound so simple. And seeing the steady flame of love in his eyes, everything in her cried out Yes! Yes, I want it too, Zack.

Then, in the middle of the night, she awoke from a dream clearly hearing Brad's voice saying 'Roberta, I must leave you.' But the face in the dream was Zack's.

Ice-cold, heart thumping, she felt she had just escaped a terrible danger. How could she even think of marrying again? Hadn't she learned from experience? 'Those who don't learn from history are doomed to repeat it.'

Staring into the darkness, she was still in the dark about the failure of her marriage. The hideous blankness

171

of it. The namelessness and facelessness of the other woman. It was fatal enough to be abandoned. But to be denied the solace, if solace it was, of knowing why? Or for whom? Where she had failed? Of one thing she was convinced: it had been a younger woman. Wasn't that what all the bitter jokes were about?' 'He turned me in for a newer model.'

That brought her back to the ten years between Zack and herself. When I was married at twenty-two, he was a kid of twelve. It's preposterous. What would people think? The kids, my father, people like Paula and Alicia Reston? Do I care what people think? Yes, I do. I'm a conventional woman.

Nevertheless, the very next morning she swung in the opposite direction. In clear daylight, anything seemed possible. And instead of fearing to take a second chance, she saw that chance not as a *risk*, but as an *opportunity*. Age difference? They were both adults.

Thus Roberta, seesawed between yes and no, pro and con; a woman who couldn't make up her mind. No sooner did she think she saw clearly, than doubt confronted her, and she was again undecided.

On that Sunday morning in June, she was on the up side of the seesaw. She felt a rush of euphoria as she pulled out of the driveway. She was only on her way to the shopping center for detergents and scouring pads, but the world looked glorious. Remembering last night with Zack, the future looked glorious too. She loved and was loved.

And things might even be better with Susie, she now thought hopefully. After Susie's surliness last month at Jim's graduation, she had turned up unannounced at the farm two weeks in a row. Strangely, she had only stayed for Saturday, while her mother was at work. But it was nice to have her at home on any terms. And she had been sweet at Roberta's birthday lunch. Good signs, surely?

Roberta decided it was just as well, probably, that Zack was going to be away for a while. It would give her a chance to sober up. How can I think straight when I'm on such a high? she asked herself.

On her way back, she passed the Harcourts' house just as they were pulling in. Greg honked and Roberta stopped. 'What luck!' Carole said. 'We've got people coming for lunch; come and join us.'

'I'd love to, Carole, but I shouldn't. I've got to tackle the cleaning today, or else pay for my sins all next week.'

'Cleaning!' Carole didn't know one end of a broom from the other. 'Come *on*! It will keep.'

'That's what I said last week, but it lies in wait for you. Or so I'm learning.'

Carole's perky face, complete with false eyelashes even at this hour of the morning, looked disappointed. 'Well, come in for a cup of coffee, at *least*. We haven't seen you for a week.'

'Might as well give in, Roberta,' said Greg. 'You can't turn down Miss Conviviality. She won't take no for an answer.'

'Okay,' said Roberta. 'But please throw me out in an hour, will you?'

She had grown immensely fond of Carole. Apart from the cordiality the Harcourts offered as a couple, the two women had developed a chummy, just-us-girls rapport. 'Come on over and dish,' she would urge Roberta on the phone. 'Greg's out doing his thing on the tractor, and I need company.' That's Carole for you, Roberta thought affectionately. Roberta had the impression that Carole could not stand being alone, not even for an hour. And Roberta wondered about Carole's hunger for people. Did she and Greg ever have a chance to be alone together?

Now Roberta sipped coffee on the Harcourts' ferny, wickery porch, trading local news for Carole's chitchat about the Big Apple. Greg had excused himself and headed for the stable. 'My husband, John Wayne,' Carole said. Both women watched Greg's tall, faintly swaggering figure cross the field. 'I'm scared to death of that big beast of a horse, but Greg dotes on him.'

She turned back to Roberta. 'Roberta, you look lit from within today. And about thirty-five, tops! What's your secret? Blow some my way.'

Roberta laughed, pleased. 'Thanks, Carole. What an ego-booster you are.' She glanced at her watch and stood up. 'I must get going. It's almost noon; your guests will be arriving.'

'Not to worry. The food's all ready; I bought out Zabar's. Anyway, they're all old friends. Except for a cousin or something the Johnsons asked to bring along. Some kind of hard-luck story, I gathered. They wanted to give her a day in the country.'

Just as Carole was walking Roberta to the door, two cars pulled in under the porte-cochère.

'And here they are,' said Carole. 'Sure you won't stay, Roberta?' Roberta shook her head. 'Well, now you've got to meet them, at least.'

Two couples got out of one car, and a man and two women got out of the other. Greg joined them at the door, and there was the usual babble of greetings and introductions. One of the women introduced the extra woman to the Harcourts as 'my cousin, Jean Culver,' and then Carole introduced Roberta. 'Our great friend and neighbor, Roberta Marston, who lives just down the road.'

As Carole said 'Roberta Marston,' Jean Culver's eyes widened and she looked full into Roberta's. Roberta distinctly saw her face pale. In the chatter of small talk, everyone speaking at once, no one else seemed to notice. But Roberta had recognized shock and fright. Startled, she wondered whether the woman was ill.

And then she knew.

This was the woman Brad had left her for.

Five minutes later, Roberta struggled to control the trembling of her hand as she tried to insert her car key. Blindly, she drove the short distance home, entered her house, ran upstairs, and flung herself on the bed.

That woman? That ordinary woman with the plain face and not-very-good figure and no style at all? That woman of forty or so – a woman you wouldn't look at once, let alone twice?

The shock was almost as great as the initial shock when Brad had left – and almost as impossible to believe. This couldn't be. It made no sense. She must be wrong about the woman's identity. But no. The reaction to Roberta's name had been unmistakable. She was sure.

And when the knocker sounded on the front door, Roberta was just as sure who it would be.

Jean Culver stood there, looking frightened. 'Mrs Marston, may I speak to you?'

Roberta's mouth was so dry she could hardly speak. 'Yes?' she finally managed.

The woman dropped her eyes, then raised them again. 'I want to speak to you about your husband.' There was a long pause. 'I told the others I was going to take a walk. I looked for your name on the mailbox on the road.'

The jealous female in Roberta wanted to close the door in the woman's face. But the questions which had endlessly haunted her – who? why? where did *I* fail? – made that impossible. It would be unbearable to be so close to the truth without learning it.

'Come in,' she said stiffly.

She led the way to the living room and gestured toward

a chair. Jean Culver sat rigidly on the edge of the seat. Roberta sat opposite her.

'Mrs Marston. How can I begin?'

Roberta said nothing.

'I had an affair with your husband.'

'I know.'

'You knew?'

'The minute I met you. Yes, I knew.'

Now Jean Culver was silent. She looked at her lap. She flexed and unflexed her ringless left hand. Then she looked up and faced Roberta.

'I came to tell you that Brad – Mr Marston – loved you.'

Roberta simply stared.

'You never lost your husband's love.'

'And why should *you* tell me *that*?'

Jean Culver's eyes flashed. 'You are not making it any easier, Mrs Marston. This is as painful for me as it is for you. I wanted to reach you, woman to woman. If you don't want to hear what I have to say, I'll go.'

'Go on,' Roberta said.

'Brad never meant it to happen – what did happen. I am certain of that. I worked for him for five years. In all that time there was never the slightest hint of anything personal, but I was in love with him from almost the beginning. He had no idea. I was just another member of his staff, and not a very important one at that.

'Then the acquisition of The Taylor Company came up. Perhaps you remember it. Brad – Mr Marston – believed in it. But some of the board members were against it. Mr Marston had to put together a lot of marketing data and a lot of financial figures to prove his point. It had to be done in a hurry. We all put in a great deal of overtime.

'Then, one night, I was the only one who could work

really late, so Mr Marston and I were alone together. Oh, Mrs Marston' – Jean Culver made a hopeless gesture, as though she didn't expect to be believed – 'I know how hackneyed that sounds. "One night we were working late, and one thing led to another." But it wasn't like that at all. Mr Marston was so absorbed in the work, he didn't know I was there. I was just a machine organizing the data as he needed it.

'But when he finally finished, he insisted on taking me out for some food, out of pure courtesy. We had skipped dinner, except for a sandwich at the desk.

'We had one drink, and while we were waiting for our order, Brad – Mr Marston – asked me about myself. Just making polite small talk. Well, maybe it was the martini, or maybe it was that I knew so well that the man two feet away was really a million miles away – from me. Anyway, before I knew it – I'm very disciplined, usually – I lost control. I cried on your husband's shoulder. I told him I lived alone in a dreary little apartment on the West Side, that my husband had walked out on me, and that I have a Down's Syndrome child. What used to be called Mongoloid.'

Instantly, Roberta thought of Susan and Jim.

'She's twelve now. In an institution. I visit every Saturday.'

Roberta thought of the abnormally large head, the slanted eyes, the mental retardation . . .

'Mr Marston looked just as you did just now. Horrified. Sickened. And I suppose he felt the usual "There but for the grace of God . . ." Down's Syndrome can happen to anybody, you know. He was very kind. He tried to express sympathy. But as you know, what can you say? Well, that was that, except that the next day there were roses on my desk when I came back from lunch. The card

said "Thank you for your help. I wish *I* could help. Brad"
Just "Brad". He had always been Mr Marston.

'Mrs Marston, those red roses triggered something in me. I had done a lot of daydreaming about your husband, but I'd always known it was daydreaming. I was aware of the gap between dream and reality. The trouble was that the roses were real, and I deliberately let myself pretend they meant what roses usually mean. I escaped into fantasy. Deliberate self-delusion.

'Then the roses faded. I woke up to reality . . . and I couldn't *bear* it. I saw my life for what it was: work, movie with a girl friend, visit to my child. Around the clock, the month, the year, the *years*. Something snapped. I decided that I would *fight* for some happiness, the way other women do. They do, you know. They simply go after a man, with no encouragement at all from the man. Have you any idea how common affairs are in the corporate world? Half the men in those dark, rich, expense-account restaurants are lunching with girlfriends. I've always thought that's why they're so dark.

'As a loser, I had nothing to lose. So I psyched myself up with some of those get-yours books: *How to Get What You Want, You Come First*, that sort of thing. And I actually took a course in assertiveness training.

'Then I deliberately tried to get Brad – your husband – to realize I existed. I asked him to have lunch with me, to get advice on my ridiculously small savings. I asked if he had any medical contacts who might know of a better place for my child. I brought him trumped-up work problems.

'Mr Marston tried to help, tried to buck me up. He even tried to convince me a nice man was bound to come along. He was simply being a good Samaritan, a decent man trying to help a woman in distress.'

Yes, Roberta thought. That was entirely consistent

178

with Brad's character. He had a strong sense of *noblesse oblige*. He had believed it was the duty of the strong and fortunate to succor the weak and unfortunate, and he had clung stubbornly to the old sex roles. To him man was the protector of defenseless woman. Yes, that fit.

'But I could see Brad had no more personal interest in me than he had in his desk, and I guess I went a little insane, Mrs Marston. When he had to go to Chigaco, I followed him. I just showed up at his hotel-room door. I burst out that I was hopelessly in love with him. I threw myself at him. I begged him to go to bed with me. I told him it would be heaven for me . . . and would cost him very little.

'I could almost see the wheels go round in Brad's mind. How can you turn down a woman begging for crumbs? Brad was trapped in his own compassion. If he'd sent me packing, that would have been the ultimate rejection. Mrs Marston, it was an act of charity on your husband's part.'

Roberta caught her breath sharply. Ultimate rejection! This woman could talk of 'ultimate rejection'? What would she call the brutal, abrupt ending of a long marriage? She wanted to throw Jean Culver out of the house – and Brad with her, if that were possible. She hated them both. But she *had* to hear the rest.

'That is how it started, Mrs Marston. My doing, entirely.'

'I see,' said Roberta icily. 'You are saying you fell in love with my husband, deliberately set out to involve him, and then, by playing on his sympathies, you did. Is that it?'

Jean Culver flushed. 'Not pretty, from your point of view, Mrs Marston. Indefensible. But from mine, it was a desperate grab for happiness. I loved him.'

Roberta believed her. That part was convincing. She

could accept the fact that Jean Culver had loved her husband, but she did not want to believe that he had been putty in her hands.

'You're wondering how a man like Mr Marston could fall for anything so . . . so calculated. Maybe the strongest of us can be had, if someone pushes the right button. At first, Brad simply felt pity for me, but then there was something else . . .' She did not meet Roberta's eyes.

'And that was? . . .'

'Sex.' Jean Culver's voice was almost inaudible. 'I . . . I don't understand it. Something happened, between us.'

Roberta felt her heart pounding, her face growing hot. No! She did not want to listen to this. But at the very moment she was hearing Brad's other woman unthinkably telling Brad's wife about sex, Zack leaped into her mind. She remembered her own astonishment at the heights she and Zack had scaled. Had it been like that for Brad? Was it possible that she and Brad, smugly believing they 'had everything' had never known supreme pleasure with each other, and that he, too, had found it with someone else? But he could *not* have loved this woman. She had none of the qualities he had always valued most.

'He never loved me, Mrs Marston. He never said so, and he never did. To him, it was just an . . . affair. He wanted to end it, almost as soon as it started. He said it never should have happened, and it would be better if I worked somewhere else. He offered to get me another job, a better one. But I threw a scene and cried all over his office. I said in that case I wouldn't want to live. In the end, I did something even worse.'

'Worse? What could be worse than what you've already said?'

'I told him I was pregnant.'

This was unbearable. Roberta had to force out the words. '*Were you?*'

'No. And then . . . he died. That was two days before the accident.'

Two days before. Then it was the night before that terrible Saturday when Brad had turned into a stranger, when he'd said he was leaving . . . and left.

'I still have one of those red roses,' said Jean Culver. Without warning, she began to cry.

Roberta looked at this plain, mature woman shaking with sobs. I should want to punish her, call her names. Slut, schemer, liar, homewrecker . . . I should drive her away with sticks and stones.

But all the anger had drained away. Roberta watched the woman fumble blindly for a handkerchief. She thought of the abnormal child. She thought of the loneliness. She thought of Brad's magnetism, his warmth. No wonder, she thought sadly. Maybe if I were Jean Culver, I'd act like Jean Culver, too.

'I'll make some tea,' she said. She left the weeping woman alone to regain her composure.

When she returned with the tea, Jean Culver had mopped her face, but it looked streaked and puffy and miserable.

'Kind of you,' she muttered, as Roberta handed her a cup.

They sipped in silence. Then Roberta said, 'I wonder if you would tell me one thing?'

'If I can, Mrs Marston.'

'Were you at the services? Brad's services?'

Jean Culver looked shocked. 'Oh, *no*! Of course not! I hadn't the *right*.'

'Thank you.'

'As a matter of fact, I spent that morning at St Patrick's, praying.'

For the first time Roberta realized that for this woman, too, Brad's death had been a devastating loss. Like

181

Roberta, who felt she could not truly mourn as a widow because Brad had left her, this woman could not openly mourn, because she had no mourning status.

'Brad's death must have been very hard on you,' Roberta said quietly.

'Yes.'

There seemed no more to say. They sat silently, each with her own thoughts.

Then Roberta had a final question. 'But why did you come to see me? Why did you tell me all this?'

Jean Culver smiled shakily. 'Conscience. Old-fashioned word, isn't it? Nobody uses it anymore. Today we talk about guilt. But guilt is something we're urged to get rid of. Conscience was something we were taught to develop. I had you on my conscience, Mrs Marston. I've gone back to my church, and I couldn't rest, knowing that Brad had died while you thought he loved someone else. I wanted to tell you that was not true. So when I met you today, it was a clear sign that God was giving me the opportunity. You never really lost Brad, Mrs Marston. It was all just a temporary . . . something. He would have been back, and very soon.' She stood up. 'And you are exactly as I imagined you, Mrs Marston.'

At the door Roberta hesitated; then she said, 'I hope things will be better for you, Miss Culver.'

She watched the woman go down the path. She had imagined a thousand women, but never a Jean Culver.

Roberta sat motionless for a long time. So many conflicting emotions were fighting for dominance she could not sort them out. It was as though her perceptions of her marriage and its breakup had been violently shaken in a kaleidoscope and rearranged. It was hard to read the new pattern.

Slowly, she recognized that one feeling was dominant.

That feeling was relief – relief at being free at last of the torturing question: where did I fail? She had not failed. Rather, Brad had been weak, not the man she had thought him to be. Still, did that diminish him so very much? He had done what most married men do sooner or later; he'd become involved with another woman. Most men did it sooner. In this case, his first motivation had been a compulsion to play Sir Galahad. That was his real weakness, an inability to resist a hard-luck story. But that wasn't the most awful characteristic in the world. Some men, apparently civilized, were subtle sadists.

Then, of course, there was . . . the sex part. That was hard to take, and hard to believe, when the woman looked and acted like Jean Culver. But perhaps such naked desperation produced a kind of abandon. Well, no point in thinking about *that*. Maybe she and Brad had been born too soon, given their generation and upbringing, to be completely free of sexual inhibition? Wistfully she wished that she and Brad had reached the 'wilder shores' of sex – together.

You were supposed to want to scratch the other woman's eyes out, and I did, she thought. But Jean Culver? Most people would think Roberta the world's biggest fool to offer tea and sympathy, but the woman was pathetic. And somehow she believed her, believed that had Brad's life not been snipped short, it would have turned out to be just an incident as Jean Culver had insisted. Many marriages had survived such incidents.

It would take time, Roberta realized, to come to terms with all this, but already the pain she had kept hidden so long was beginning to ease. The marriage she had believed in *had* been happy, *had* been real. It had not been wiped out, as a sponge erases writing on a blackboard. She and Brad had been lucky to have had it so good for so long. And then? Well, fate had hit. Why should they have been immune?

In a way, Jean Culver had been an instrument of fate or of God, as she herself had said. She had restored to Roberta the faith she'd lost.

Now she could begin to feel like a loving widow, rather than a rejected woman. And she might, as a woman who had had a good marriage, eventually dare to risk another.

16

Roberta opened her front door after work to find a pile of luggage in the hall: two suitcases, a raffish duffle bag, and a huge tote bag. Susan's, she recognized at a glance.

Susan herself appeared at the top of the stairs. 'It's me, Mother.'

Roberta felt instant alarm. 'Susan! What has happened?'

Susan raced down the stairs and gave her mother a perfunctory peck on the cheek. 'Your chick has come home to roost. I'm here to stay. Okay with you?'

Roberta's maternal side gladdened. Perhaps her daughter was at last returning to her old lovable self. But Roberta's woman-in-love side rebelled. No! *Not* Okay! Ghastly timing. Zack would be leaving so soon. She needed all the free time she could get.

'Well, Mother? Aren't you glad to see me?'

Roberta gave her a hug. 'Darling, of *course* I am. You know I love to have you with me. But you must admit, it's rather unexpected.'

'Yeah. It is. Unexpected to me too. It's just that . . .'

Roberta could see Susan struggling to explain. It would be better to wait until later, when Susie got her bearings and when Roberta got hers, as well. What *had* happened? Roberta wondered uneasily.

'Susie dear, let me get into some other clothes. I'll be right down. Then we'll talk while I make dinner.'

'Okay,' said Susie. She picked up the suitcases and headed up the stairs with them. Roberta followed with the tote and the duffle.

'My word, these are heavy,' she said. 'How did you ever manage all this stuff on the bus?'

'I hired a couple of those scary urchins who hang around the Port Authority bus terminal. They carried it down the escalator.'

'But how did you manage at this end?'

'Oh, I called that guy in the carriage house . . . Mr Owen.'

Roberta stood stock-still on the stairs. 'You called Zack Owen?'

'Yes. Is that such a big deal?'

'But Susan, you don't even know him.'

'I've met him.'

Zack had told Roberta about meeting Susan in the barn. She had been glad. She knew that Zack and Jim liked each other. She wanted Zack to know her daughter too. But still . . .

'Is that a federal offense, Mother?'

Don't make an issue of it, Roberta thought. She didn't want to create a conflict with Susan when the girl had barely arrived.

'Of course not. It's just that Mr Owen is a tenant. We're supposed to respect a tenant's privacy. We shouldn't impose on him.'

'Got it. But I don't think it killed him. He was awfully nice about it.'

Susan led the way to the big back corner bedroom with the red toile wallpaper. Without asking, Roberta noted. She saw that Susan had already scattered her toilet things on the mahogany lowboy.

'Okay with you?' Susan asked belatedly. 'This room, it's my favorite. I love the view.' The view took in the hill, the barn, and a corner of the carriage house.

'Of course, Susan. I'll help you with your things later. See you in the kitchen in a few minutes.'

There was a note from Jim on the kitchen table. 'Mom, went to Allentown. Won't be home for dinner.' Good. That would give Roberta and Susan a chance to talk privately.

But Susan seemed to have difficulty in getting to the point. She chattered inconsequently as she set the table and Roberta mixed a salad. Patience, thought Roberta.

It was only when they were sitting over coffee that Susan began, hesitantly, to talk about what was uppermost in Roberta's mind, why she was here.

'Mother, I know you're wondering – '

'Yes, I am, Susan. Naturally.'

'Naturally. Right. It's just that . . . Oh, Mother, it's so hard to explain . . .'

Roberta waited.

'Oh, Mother!' Susan's young face was a picture of confusion. 'Oh, Mother. I don't know who I am, or what I'm doing . . . or why. I just know one thing. I've *had* it with New York: the singles bars, the game playing, the one upping and the status seeking, and the so-called *men* who turn out to be little boys.'

Susan looked like a little girl as she said 'little boys.'

'I'm tired of waking up with a guy I met the night before.'

Roberta felt the generation gap yawn before her. She had uneasily assumed that Susan was sleeping with Gil Rutherford, but even though she and Brad had believed Susan would marry Gil, they had not permitted Gil to share Susan's room when he visited them. They knew many of their friends threw up their hands and said, 'We know they're doing it *anyway*, they might as well do it at home.' But Roberta and Brad had been more conservative. Even though they fully realized that Susan and Jim were children of the liberated age, they were not liberated parents.

187

What Roberta felt now was not so much shock as pity, and fear; pity at the joylessness of casual sex, fear of its potential to hurt a girl as vulnerable as Susan. But she could not express this to Susan right now. Susan would take it as preaching.

So she simply said, 'Yes. I understand. But what about your job?'

'I quit.'

'You *quit*? But I don't understand. You were so thrilled when you got it. I thought you loved working at NBC.'

'I do. I did. I'm really interested in news. It's what's happening. But even news has turned into show biz. At least on TV. Everything is *image*.'

'But didn't you always say you thought being a newscaster was the most exciting job a woman could have and that being an anchorwoman was the absolute top?'

'Yes, I did say that.' For a moment Susan looked doubtful. Had she made a hideous mistake in throwing up her job? Would she regret it? She was so mixed up! 'But that was before everything began to seem so . . . meaningless. Anyway, it was pretty stupid of me. How many anchorwomen are there? Crazy to think I could make it. There's a long way between working as assistant floor manager and being on camera. Anyway, I don't have the motivation. You have to be really single-minded. I'm not sure I *want* a career. I don't know what I want . . .'

'Susan . . . Susie, dear . . .'

'Oh, Mummy!' When she said 'Mummy' Roberta knew she was again a little girl wanting and needing her mother's comfort. 'Oh, Mummy. Maybe I've made a terrible mistake, quitting my job, because maybe I'll never find what I *really* want. But it's not true that I don't know what it is. I *do* know.'

'And that is?'

'Someone to love me, Mother,' Susan burst out. 'Really love me. Love *me*. The way Daddy loved you.'

'Susan, darling. You'll meet – '

'Mr Right? Not at the rate I'm going.'

'Give yourself time . . .'

'Isn't it funny? Here I am, born into the age of liberation, and what do I want? I want to get *married*. I want to have a *baby*. I even want a wedding, with a damned white veil.' Susan tried to laugh. 'Isn't that a switcheroo?' She was attempting to satirize the subject, to hide the depth of her feelings. 'What am I, a *throwback*?'

Roberta's heart melted. As mothers have always done, she wished she could absorb some of her daughter's pain.

'Susan,' she said hesitantly, 'what about Gil? I thought you and he – '

'I pretty much expected to marry Gil. He kept pressing me to announce our engagement last summer, and I was on the verge of telling you and Daddy . . . when everything fell apart. When Daddy died. After that I felt differently. Suddenly, Gil seemed such a kid. A nice kid, but I couldn't imagine him as my *husband*. I suppose I hurt him, a lot. I felt rotten about that, but he just didn't seem like a *man* to me.'

'I understand. And I think I understand what you want. I still believe it's what most women want, even successful career women. But, darling, why do you feel that living here will be better? Won't you feel isolated? In a way, this is the middle of nowhere.'

Susan looked away from her mother. She stared at her coffee cup, turned it slowly on its saucer. 'Oh, I don't know. I just thought it would be nice to be with you and Jim for a while. Peaceful.'

Roberta sensed instantly that her daughter had become evasive. She was no longer pouring out her naked feelings, spontaneously and without reservation. There was another factor in her abrupt decision to come to the farm. Uneasily, Roberta wondered what it could be. Could she be pregnant? Surely that would not devastate a girl nowadays. Roberta had an even wilder thought. Could Susan be working up to announcing that she intended to have her baby as so many girls did today? But that made no sense. She had just said, poignantly enough, that she wanted love and marriage. There's something she's holding back, Roberta thought. But I'd better not probe, or she'll simply go into her shell again.

Roberta took a deep breath. 'Susan. I love you. I'm here to help, if I can. I know you are *hurting*, and that hurts me. But I don't think you can plunge from one world to another without having some clear idea of where you're going. Darling, what do you visualize? What do you intend to *do* all day? I'm at work, as you know. And Jim is busy outside most of the time. Won't you be at loose ends?'

'I haven't quite thought it through yet. I'll find something to do. Scrub the floor, maybe' – she laughed shakily – 'keep house for you.'

'That's silly, Susie. That would hardly satisfy you. And there's another problem.'

'What's that?'

'Money.'

'Money?'

'Yes, darling, dollars and cents. Don't you remember? I did tell you.' Roberta experienced a moment of exasperation. She had told Susan that money was tight on the weekend of Jim's graduation. Apparently it had not sunk in.

'Gee, Mother, I'm sorry. You *did* mention it.' Susan looked genuinely contrite. 'I guess it just didn't penetrate. It's so hard to believe. I mean, we never gave money a thought before.'

'I know. But it's very different now. The cold fact is that I'm living on a fixed income, a very small one. It doesn't get any bigger, but the bills do – every single month. You know, this is a very expensive place. Taxes, heat, insurance – things you've never had to think about, nor had I until now. Inflation has made me . . . well, near-poor.'

'Mother, I didn't realize.'

'I know you didn't, Susan, you have no idea of the little economies I go in for nowadays. I *have* to. Don't be surprised if the peas left over from this meal turn up in soup next week. I try not to waste a *crumb*, and I turn out lights, don't use the dish dryer, think twice about driving – to save gas. God knows I don't buy any clothes. Remember this blouse? It's five years old.'

'That's terrible.'

'Not so terrible. It's a challenge. As I mentioned, Susie, Paul Reston had told me over and over that I should sell the farm. He says it's much too expensive for my income. But I want to hang on as long as possible, so I cut corners like mad.'

'Are you saying you can't afford to have me stay here?'

'Darling I'm saying you'll have to earn some money. Contribute to your own support.'

Now Susie's inherent sweetness showed itself. For a moment, she forgot her own needs and thought of her mother's.

'Oh, Mummy! Of *course*. I don't want to be a free-loader. I just never gave money a thought. But of course I'll pay my way. I'll get a job, maybe on a newspaper. There must be some sort of little rag around here, isn't there? Or maybe a local radio station?'

'That might be a possibility,' said Roberta

But as fast as Susan's momentary animation had appeared, it fled. A look of unhappy-self-absorption slid over her face again, and Roberta could see she was already thinking of something else.

Oh, Susan, she thought, you need more than a job. You need to grow up. And I need to break my date with Zack for tomorrow night.

She called him from the shop the next day. He came on the line saying, 'I know, darling. You can't make it tonight.'

'Zack, I'm sorry. And I'm sorry Susan imposed on you yesterday by asking you to pick her up.'

'Roberta, don't be absurd. But what now? When can we meet?'

'I don't know, Zack. Susan has come to stay, and she seems to be at such loose ends . . .'

You needn't tell me. Roberta. I could see it, thought Zack.

'She's chucked her job,' Roberta went on. 'Oh, Zack, it's so awkward. I can't just go off and leave her alone when she's just arrived.'

'Right. I understand. It's damnable timing. But listen, Roberta. Next Tuesday you're going to meet me at the Golden Pheasant. Six-thirty. Make any excuse you can think of. Your boss wants you for dinner, you'll be at a housewares show, whatever. And you'll be late getting back. Golden Pheasant. Six-thirty.'

'I'll be there, darling.'

On Tuesday night Roberta and Zack went to a motel. Roberta had to overcome an inborn distaste for the very word *motel*. 'Do you know,' she told Zack, 'I've never been in one in my life, not even in legitimate travel?'

'And you feel this is *illegitimate*? Have you forgotten I want you for my *wife*?'

Lying in his arms, she felt she *was* his wife.

192

On the way back to where she had parked her car, Zack said, 'Look, darling. Would it be easier for you if I kept a low profile the next couple of weeks? Would it be easier to deal with Susan? God knows, it's the last thing I want. But I can't have you pulled apart like this.'

'Oh, Zack, how I love you for that.' His concern for her and his intuitive understanding of her feelings made her feel so cherished, to say nothing of the wonderful two hours they'd spent. 'I had the same idea. But I didn't know how to say it.'

'Right. Let's consider it settled. I'll make myself scarce until I leave for Japan. But there's a catch, darling.'

'What's the catch?'

'I want us to have a weekend together. Forty-eight whole hours with you, darling, not just these little scraps of time. I have a friend with a place in Vermont, a mountain hideaway. I have the key. Plan for it, darling. If you can't manage a Saturday off, we could make it Sunday and Monday. Will you?'

'You know I will, Zack.'

'I'll call you at the shop. Good night, Mrs M, dearest.'

Driving the rest of the way home, Roberta felt absolutely sure that she loved this man – she knew he loved her – and yes, she wanted to marry him. Since her new insights into Brad's defection and since her slow understanding and acceptance of it, she had regained her faith in commitment. She no longer felt that every bond had a built-in betrayal. She knew she had had a good marriage, and she felt she could have a good second marriage. But then the age difference raised its mocking head again. Did that make the whole affair pure folly? Or could it be ignored, as Zack claimed? She'd have to face that, really face it, while Zack was in Japan. Meantime, she had the weekend in Vermont to look forward to.

* * *

It was discouraging that Susan, after pouring her heart out, slipped so quickly back into her withdrawn, moody self. She did make a cursory effort to do some of the housework, and she did have dinner ready when Roberta came home from work. But she was polite, remote. She seemed to be somewhere else.

Well, give her a little time, Roberta thought. She remembered her own first week at the farm, when she had wandered around in limbo. It *was* rather disorienting to switch from Manhattan to Greenwillow. I'll wait until next week, she decided, before I approach her.

But by the end of the week Susan had shown no signs of moving in any direction. Roberta could not imagine what she did all day. Since she had no car, she was tied to the place, except when Jim gave her a ride.

Worried, Roberta consulted Jim at breakfast. Susan was still in bed. 'Jim, has Susan confided in you? Have you any idea what she plans to do?'

'All I know is that she's miserable, Mom.' Jim looked miserable himself as he said it. 'I don't understand it, but I think she's still suffering from Dad's death. And – it's only a guess – I think she can't handle Women's Lib. You know how big she was on independent women and lady corporation presidents and all that. But I think she was strong for freedom when she had you and Dad and Seventy-ninth Street to back her up. Now I think she's scared to be on her own. I think she wants some strong guy to take over and solve all her problems for her.'

'But what does she do all day, Jim? Surely she must be bored.'

'She mopes. That's my guess. And she takes long walks into the back fields late in the afternoon. I ran into her up near the barn the other day. I thought maybe she was getting into nature, you know, back-to-the-land stuff; but when I asked her if she wanted to learn to drive the tractor, she turned off.' He shrugged.

'Has she mentioned looking for a job?'

'She made vague noises about looking for work on the *Hunterdon Democrat*, but she hasn't taken step one, as far as I can see. And when I brought it up the other day – she's so *touchy* – she said she wasn't in shape to look for work yet. She said she had to get her head together first. But she shouldn't be sponging on you like this, Mom. Doesn't she realize, about cold cash, I mean?'

'Yes. I made it very clear.' Roberta sighed. 'But I don't want to *push* her. After all, she grew up with the idea that the family home was always there. And I suppose my giving up the New York apartment so abruptly did rather pull the rug out from under her. Anyway, money is the least of it, although heaven knows it counts. The important thing is for Susie to find herself, to stop being so miserable.'

'To stop being so selfish, you mean. I could kick her, Mom. She's *wasted*. She's got everything: looks and brains, a degree from Smith, dean's list. And she's really a great girl, Mom, when you can *reach* her. But right now she's so wrapped up in herself she's sort of sleepwalking. Something's got to jolt her out of it, wake her up.'

'Yes. But *what*?' Roberta rose and rinsed the coffee cups. 'I've got to get to work. But not before I tell you you're a huge comfort, Jim.' She kissed him on the cheek. 'As for Susie . . . well, we'll have to play it by ear, I suppose.'

As she crossed the bridge, Roberta caught a glimpse of Zack's car backing out from the carriage house. Strange how her preoccupation with her daughter could have made her forget Zack for a whole hour. Now she forget Susan and thought only of Zack, of last night in his arms, and of the coming weekend in Vermont. Forty-eight nonstop, unhurried hours with Zack. Her heart beat faster at the thought.

Two nights later when she arrived home, Roberta was greeted by a transformed Susan. Instead of her usual T-shirt and shorts, Susie was wearing a skirt, delicate sandals, and a clinging crepe blouse which made no secret of her upthrust young breasts. Her hair was freshly washed and shining, and she was wearing a teasing, insistent fragrance.

'Susan! How pretty you look! But what's this? A party?' From the hall Roberta could see the dining-room table, unmistakably festive and formal looking. Silver candelabra, the silver epergne bright with flowers. It was set for four. And there were good smells coming from the kitchen.

'Susan, you're having a guest from the city. How nice! Who is it?'

'Oh, just what's-his-name. Your tenant.'

'*Zack Owen*?'

Susan stared at her. 'Why do you look so shocked? He's our neighbor, isn't he? And didn't you tell me he and Jim are on very friendly terms?'

'Yes, I did,' said Roberta lamely. 'But you might have told me . . .' So I could have prevented it, she thought.

'*Sorry*,' said Susan tartly. 'I just felt in the mood for cooking up a storm. But what fun is cooking if you don't have an audience? I thought it would vary the monotony a little. I don't understand you, Mother.' She looked at Roberta with some of the old hostility. 'Aren't you and Jim always hinting I should get out and meet people and circulate?'

'Yes, of course,' said Roberta hastily. 'It was a nice idea, and something smells delicious. It's just that you

196

took me by surprise. When did you invite . . . our guest? Was it spur of the moment?'

'Oh, I just waited until I saw his car go up the lane. Then I called and invited him, that's all. And he accepted, for seven-thirty.'

And did he sound surprised? Roberta wanted to ask.

'Oh, don't worry, Mother. Of course I did it *properly* I asked him in your name, of course.'

'In my *name?*' You had no right! she wanted to add.

'Yes. You are the lady of the house, aren't you? Doesn't a daughter usually issue an invitation in her mother's name?'

'I must change my clothes,' said Roberta. She mounted the stairs trying to control her embarrassment and alarm. But under the shower, she struggled to be reasonable. Susan had no inkling of her relationship with Zack, of course. Inviting their nearest neighbor to dinner would seem only natural to her.

The thing now was to get through the evening, some-how. But what would Zack think? After they had agreed not to see each other? She could hardly get him in a corner and explain in a whisper. He's going to be thoroughly confused, she thought anxiously. As she dressed, she wished the evening were already over.

Zack arrived at seven-thirty. Roberta opened the door for him.

'Roberta!' Zack's eyebrow had that quizzical lift, and his eyes questioned hers.

'Zack.' She offered her hand, feeling ridiculous. 'How good to see you.'

Before she had a chance to say more Susie appeared in the hall. 'Oh, hi!' she said.

'Susan. How pretty you look,' Zack responded.

'Oh, thanks.' She tried to hide her pleasure. 'Listen,

it's Mom's party, but I'm cook and bartender. Want to get out the ice cubes?'

'At your service,' said Zack.

Roberta waited in the living room, like a guest. She could hear Susan's laughter from the kitchen. Jim arrived. He saw the gala dining table. 'Mom?' he called.

'In here,' said Roberta.

He poked his head into the living room. 'What's going on?'

'We have a dinner guest.'

'Oh? Who? Who's in the kitchen?'

'Susan. And Zack Owen.'

She couldn't read Jim's expression. 'Oh,' he said. 'Well, back in ten minutes. Have to wash up.'

Dinner was as painful as Roberta feared it would be. Zack's manner was perfect. As a punctilious guest he divided his attention between all three Marstons. He chatted with Jim about farm matters, asked Roberta about the shop, and made small talk with Susan about her work at NBC. But Roberta vividly sensed the unspoken question Zack was beaming at her – *Roberta. What the hell is this all about*? – and she was not able to beam back. *It's all right, darling, it's not what you think*. Instead, she was forced to mask her turbulent feelings and play the gracious, uninvolved hostess.

Only Susan, oblivious, was in top form. She sparkled. She was heartbreakingly beautiful. How proud she would be, thought Roberta miserably, to show off her lovely daughter to Zack, under other circumstances.

Now Susan was giving Zack the flattery of her undivided attention. She kept her huge eyes focused on him, said she was fascinated by big engineering projects like the one Zack was involved in, tried to draw him out about his past, present, and future. It was clear that she considered Zack her date. Roberta lent the occasion formality, in Susan's view, as mother, hostess, and chaperon.

Charmingly and gracefully, Susan served coffee and brandy in the living room. In spite of her bright chatter, conversation began to lag. Zack valiantly introduced the subject of politics, bringing up a current hotly debated issue, but before either Jim or Roberta could make a response, Susan turned to Zack.

'There's a terrific flick in Easton,' she said. 'Care to go?'

When Zack hesitated a moment, Jim attempted to intervene. 'Susie, you're putting Zack on the spot. Maybe he isn't in the mood for a movie.'

Susan smiled beguilingly at Zack. 'Is there anything bossier than a kid brother?'

Zack turned to Roberta. 'Roberta, would you care to take in a movie?' *Please come!* his eyes urged.

But Susie's eyes were also on Roberta. *Say no!* her look implored. Instead, Roberta forced herself to say lightly, 'Thank you, but I think I'll make it an early evening. Tomorrow is going to be busy at the shop.'

Roberta saw the flicker of anger on Zack's face. But he quickly controlled it and turned to Jim. 'Jim? Movie?'

'Sure,' said Jim deliberately. 'Don't mind if I do.'

Roberta saw the look of acute disappointment on Susan's face. This was one more painful thrust to her bitterly conflicted emotions.

Tired as she was, Roberta lay awake for hours until she heard Zack's car drop off Jim and Susan. Jim went straight to his room, but Susan stayed up playing rock at a low volume in the living room. All Roberta could hear was the muffled insistent beat. Like the heartbeat of the troubled, demanding young.

The next day Zack called her at Jane Whitford's, as she knew he would. His voice was chilly. 'Roberta? Zack. Can you meet me tonight after work? The little place in Kintersville?'

'Yes, of course.' She wanted to say more, but Jane was nearby, and there were customers. 'What time?'

'Can you make it at six-thirty?'

'Yes.'

'Right.' He hung up.

He was waiting at 'their' table when she entered the inn. He couldn't conceal the love in his eyes as he rose to greet her. But he also looked angry.

'What will you drink?' he inquired formally when the waiter appeared, and when the man left he said, 'I must thank you for a delightful dinner party.'

She stared at him. 'Don't be silly.'

'Silly?' Then his anger took over. 'What in hell are you trying to do, Roberta? Dramatize the difference in our ages, prove to me that's the big barrier you claim it is? Was that your way of putting it over?'

'What are you *talking* about, Zack?'

'Goddam it, Roberta! I love you. I want to marry you. This last couple of weeks has been hell, having you so near, but not seeing you. I thought we had a gentleman's agreement. You were going to search your soul and decide whether a *lady of a certain age*' – he emphasized the words, the better to make them absurd – 'could risk marriage with a *kid* like me.' But he looked anything but a kid. He looked like a madder-than-hell man. It was Roberta who felt like a kid, a kid being bawled out.

'So you staged that *charade*,' Zack went on furiously. 'to remind me of the attractions of youth, to send me a message. What are you trying to tell me, Roberta? That I'm nearer your daughter's age than yours? Untrue, of course. Damn it, Roberta.'

When the full meaning of Zack's words sank in, Roberta began to laugh. She could not help herself. Almost hysterically, she thought, that possibility never occurred to me, that Zack should imagine . . . He was glowering at her.

'Forgive me,' she gasped, wiping the tears from her eyes. She reached across the table the took his hand. 'Oh, Zack, forgive me for laughing. But what you said was so bizarre . . . it struck me as so ludicrous . . .' Laughter threatened to overcome her again.

Zack gripped her hand hard. 'Steady.'

'Yes, steady,' she said gratefully. 'Sorry to be so giddy. But I've been under a bit of strain, too.' She took a sip of her drink. 'Zack. I had nothing to do with that dinner. It was as much a surprise to me as to you. Susan . . . Susan is bored and at loose ends. She wanted to stir up a little excitement, so she staged a company dinner – as a surprise to all of us.' She wanted to add: *And I'm sorry you were stuck taking my kids to the movies*. But she couldn't be that disloyal to her daughter, even with Zack.

'Roberta.' Zack's voice was contrition itself. 'Oh, darling, can you forgive me for being such an ass? I guess a man in love is so damned sensitive he's irrational.' He smiled that homely-attractive grin she could never resist. 'Look, Roberta. How's the decision-making coming? Don't I deserve a progress report?'

'Oh, Zack.' She frowned a little, at the seriousness of what she wanted to say. 'Zack, I feel . . . almost embarrassed. If you knew how much I hate *coyness* and game playing . . . I love you, I know that. And I want to marry you. I know *that*. But I'm still not sure it would be right, for you or for me. And the truth is that Susan, showing up so unexpectedly, has rather thrown me. I can't think about *us* for worrying about *her*. She's very unhappy, and I don't know what to do about it.'

Zack looked grim. 'Roberta, let me get this straight. Are you saying you'd sacrifice your happiness to your daughter's? Make a maternal martyr of yourself? You surprise me. I thought you were stronger than that.'

His words stung. 'No, I *don't* mean that,' said Roberta hotly. 'I have as much contempt for self-made martyrs as you apparently have. And I don't believe in "sacrifice" for sacrifice's sake. But it's a fact that Susan's life changed very drastically when Brad died.' She didn't notice that this was the first time she'd been able to say Brad's name naturally, a sign of the inner healing which had begun, so oddly, with Jean Culver's visit. 'Susan seems so . . . so lost. And naturally it hurts me to see it. Wouldn't it hurt you, with *your* daughter?'

She saw him flinch. She was aghast. How could she have forgotten that he had lost his daughter? 'Oh, Zack, Zack – I'm so sorry . . .'

He gripped her hand hard. 'It's okay, Roberta.' He was silent a moment, then he said quietly. 'Do you realize we're quarreling?'

'I suppose we are,' she said miserably. 'I didn't mean to burden you with my problems, Zack. I was only trying to explain why – '

'You can't give your undivided attention to *me*. I understand, Roberta. Susan's state of mind *is* a problem. Hard on you. And hard to know how to handle.' She loved him for not saying the easy, obvious things: *She'll grow out* or *It's just a phase*. Instead he said, 'Kids seem to be caught in an emotional wringer today, don't they? They've been sold such a bill of goods by the culture. Instant gratification . . . and other fairy tales.'

She smiled faintly. 'Yes. And "Stamp out Reality."'

He laughed. 'Exactly. Ah, Roberta, nothing's easy, is it? But anything that troubles you, troubles me. Maybe together, we can think of a way to make Susie happier. At least, I'm here for moral support.'

She felt her eyes grow misty. 'Zack . . . Oh, Zack, you are so *dear* . . . so very dear.'

'Ditto, Dear Mrs M. Meantime, keep your mind on Vermont.'

They said goodbye in the restaurant's parking lot. He watched her pull out; then he got into his own car and headed farther down the river. He did not want to arrive at the farm at the same moment she did. Besides, he was restless. He would have dinner alone in New Hope.

When he got back to the carriage house at nearly eleven, he was puzzled to hear music through the front door although the house was dark. He turned the knob and found the door unlocked. 'Hi,' said a voice from the corner. He snapped on the light. Susan was curled up in a chair, a Tab can beside her.

'I had an *uncontrollable* craving to hear your Mahler recording,' she said. 'I didn't think you would mind.'

'Susan, your mother would mind.'

'But who would tell her?' said Susan.

17

'Shit!' Susan muttered the word aloud and aimed a savage toe at a stone in the lane, Why does he treat me like a child? she thought. *Zack, what in hell is the matter with you?*

As baffled as she was frustrated, Susan tramped the back fields, hardly aware of the hot July sun. Can't you see I'm a woman? A woman who fell in love with you at first sight, up there in the barn when I heard you whistling? What would you think, Zack, if you knew that I'd chucked my job because of you? That you're the reason I'm *here*? And that I've spent every minute since, trying to get you to *see* me?

But nothing had worked. She had slaved over that damned dinner and she'd wound up with her kid brother and Zack, who'd treated them *both* as a couple of neighbor kids. And last week, when she had waited for him at his place, using his record collection as an excuse – well, I really *do* go for Mahler, she thought defensively – he had said she was welcome to stay, but if she would excuse him . . . big day tomorrow, etcetera. Naturally, she had split immediately. She was hardly about to sit downstairs, knowing he was in bed – alone – upstairs. No way.

Not that it was sex she wanted. Sex was easy – available, whenever. It was love she wanted. The whole bit, white veil and all. May all your troubles be little ones. She wanted a wedding photograph like the one of her mother and father. And the man in the picture had to be Zack, looking at her as her father had looked at her mother. As though he were handing her his heart on a silver salver. Oh, Daddy, she thought, if you were here, you'd make things right for me.

She paused a moment at the far fence, looking across the valley to the opposite hills, thinking of her father. She had not realized, until this moment, how fully her security had rested on her image of her father as all-powerful. He had been such a take-charge man. His existence had been her terra firma. And since she had lost him – the suddenness of it was brutal – she'd been falling through space.

And now she had met another take-charge man. Zack. You could feel his strength. If you were caught with him in a hurricane or a fire or a holdup, he'd know what to do. He'd do it. He'd save you. And I love his funny face, she thought, irrelevantly . . . and that he's not tall. The opposite of those New York jocks with their gorgeous faces and their narcissism. Zack is gorgeous inside. He has gorgeous guts. Masculine, my God. She caught her breath, feeling the power of Zack's animal magnetism.

She would like love to come first, *then* sex, she thought wistfully. But in this case, maybe it would have to be the other way around. She would use *her* animal magnetism, and afterward, she would convince him of her love. The real thing. She would tell him she would wash his socks – no, his *feet*. She would labor in the fields for him, bringing in the sheaves. She would care for him in sickness and in health. She would bear his children. Surely, pray God, he would recognize the real thing when he saw it?

Turning back, she passed the carriage house, and realized she even liked his trash can, because it was his.

But oh, Zack, why do you have to be away this weekend of all weekends, when you're leaving for Japan next Friday? There is so little time, for us, Zack, for me to let you know . . . everything.

And her mother was away this weekend, too. New England or somewhere . . . with a friend or something. That's why it was so frustrating. With nobody around, this would have been her opportunity to get through to Zack. Now there would be only four weekdays left. That wasn't much. Somehow, she'd have to catch Zack alone and make her move. Make her declaration. She had no doubt at all that he would let her make love to him, that he would make love to her. She thought no man could resist a direct invitation. But would he believe she was serious, and not just sensuous? He'd *have* to – because it was true. At least, his curiosity would be aroused, wouldn't it? And wouldn't he think about her while he was in Tokyo? Want to get back, to find out more about a woman who would offer herself so honestly, no games?

Back in the house, Susan dutifully got out the vacuum cleaner and carried it to the living room. Halfway through the job, she abandoned the vacuum, flung herself on the sofa, and slid from daydream to sleep. She dreamed she and Zack were living in a house he had built for her. It was mostly open decks with a panoramic view, sturdy and strong, but at the same time like a space ship, soaring. They made love every morning and every night. Between times she scrubbed, and tended Zack's son. But then Zack became a little jealous – of the baby. Possessive. He demanded they get away for a weekend. 'You're my woman,' he said. 'I want you all to myself.' Her mother was coming to baby-sit.

In the small white house hidden in a grove of maples in Vermont, Roberta Marston and Zackary Owen lost themselves in their swimming senses.

'You're my woman,' murmured Zack. 'Mine.'

Roberta, drifting on tides of happiness, whispered, 'Yes. Yes, I am.'

It was heaven not to have to separate, to fall asleep in each other's arms again.

'It can always be like this, Roberta. It must be. It's destined.'

Roberta's last delicious, drowsy thought was: It is.

Susan's heart was thumping. She didn't really want to do this, but she had to. It was her last chance. He was leaving early tomorrow. A drizzling rain fell as she climbed the lane to the carriage house. She hugged her raincoat around her. Shivering. It wasn't really cold. How could it be? It was summer. She was shivering inwardly. Timidly, she knocked on the door. No response. Zack must be upstairs. She knocked more loudly. She was scared to death. In a moment, Zack opened the door.

'I just came to say goodbye . . . before you leave.'

'How nice of you, Susan. Come in.' He stood aside to let her enter. She stopped just inside the door.

'And to see if I could help you pack or something, or take care of anything here in the house, while you're gone. Water your plants, maybe? Or . . .'

You sound like an idiot, she said to herself fiercely. How many excuses do you need?

'That's sweet of you, Susan. But everything's all set. Sit down. Take off your raincoat.'

Susan sat on the edge of a chair, still clutching her coat. 'Oh, thanks, but I won't stay long.' Now why did you say that, idiot? 'Are you . . . are you looking forward to Japan?'

Zack strugged. 'Tokyo is an interesting city, and the project is interesting, too – I'll be meeting with some Japanese engineers. But would you believe, I'm already looking forward to getting *back*.'

'You are?' How great – if he meant because of *her*. But of course he didn't, couldn't . . . yet.

Heavy going, this conversation, thought Zack. Still, he was relieved that this moody kid wasn't aiming her provocative sexiness at him, as she'd done previously. Of course he had picked up on it, as he was sure Jim had. He fervently hoped Roberta had not.

'So!' he said brightly, struggling for small talk. 'And what will you be doing, Susan? Job hunting?' Maybe he could give her a hint on *that* subject, for Roberta's sake.

'Do you like career women?'

'What?' Zack was thrown off balance. 'What a non sequitur! But to answer your question – it depends on the individual. I do admire achievement.'

'You do?' Okay. If that's what it takes, I'll be an achiever.

'But we were talking about you. Didn't you mention something about trying for a job on one of the papers here, or one of the local radio stations? Easy for a bright kid with New York experience, don't you think?'

'I'm not a kid.'

Said the wrong thing. 'Beg your pardon, Susan. Of course I meant bright newsperson.'

'And I'm not a Women's Libber, either.'

'My foot in my mouth again? Sorry again. Is it all right if I say I think you'd be terrific in any local spot lucky enough to get you?'

'Thank you.'

To break the tension he could feel rising almost palpably, Zack said: 'Like a cup of coffee? Or a drink?'

'Coffee, please.'

But when he came back, she wasn't there.

'Susan?' he called.

'I'm up here.' Her voice came from upstairs.

'Coffee's ready.'

She must be in the bathroom, he thought. When she didn't come down after five minutes, Zack sensed trouble.

Alarmed, he roared '*Susan*!' like a father putting his foot down. No answer. Jesus, he thought, how am I going to handle this? Complications with Roberta's daughter were unthinkable. The weekend they had spent in Vermont had confirmed his belief that Roberta would marry him, as soon as possible after his return. He did not intend to let anything stand in the way. Certainly not a grotesque situation with this mixed-up kid. His stepdaughter-to-be, in fact. But anything that hurt Susan would hurt Roberta. Catch 22, and then some

'Susan?' he called again, more gently this time. Should he simply outwait her? No, better get it over with. He would have to go upstairs and somehow, without hurting her pride too much, get her out of the house. He started up the stairs, deliberately making his tread slow and heavy. He hoped the sound would convey a no-nonsense implacability to the poor kid acting out whatever she was acting out.

Susan was sitting on the edge of his bed, still clutching her raincoat. He stood in the doorway. The imploring look on her face made him feel like a brute. But he knew he had to be tough, for her sake, for all their sakes.

'What the hell is this?'

She stood up slowly. 'I'm here to tell you I love you.' Then, with a visible effort at courage, she let the coat fall open and shrugged it into a heap on the floor. Stark and beautiful, she stood before him. 'Please. Won't you take me? Then you'll know how much I love you.'

For perhaps ten seconds the impact of the naked, taut young body by-passed Zack's mind and hit his instincts. Desire surged through him and he caught his breath. Then reason and his more profound desire reasserted themselves, and his mind raced, seeking the right approach.

'Susan, you are lovely. Very.' Seeing the look in her

eye, he added, 'And very, very tempting.' He had to salve her pride as best he could. 'But there's something you don't know about me. Come downstairs, and let me tell you. Right away.' Thank God, he hadn't said '. . . like a good girl.' Above all, he wanted to avoid treating her like a child. She was suffering enough. He turned and went downstairs.

Five endless minutes passed. She's fighting off her humiliation, he thought miserably. It's like a kick in the midriff, being rejected after such a blunt offering.

Eventually she came downstairs, coat now buttoned to the chin, collar turned up, hands in pockets. She tried valiantly to smile, but the look in her eyes was that of a child bewildered because nobody wants her.

'Sit down, Susan.' She remained standing, saying nothing. 'Susan, you're a damnably attractive woman . . . and an exciting one. You have your life – '

'Ahead of me? Please don't insult me with platitudes.'

Okay, thought Zack desperately. He'd have to be direct.

'Susan, I'm in love with another woman.'

She flinched as visibly as if she'd been slapped. She stared at him a second, lips trembling, face crumpling, eyes stricken. Then she ran past him, flung open the door and dashed out, leaving the door wide open to the rain.

Zack was sweating, Jesus. That wounded-doe look, as though he'd just killed something helpless. He felt like a brute, but he also felt rage. That willful, self-involved kid, indulging in childish fantasies, at other people's expense. He'd like to beat some sense into her.

But most of all, with cold, sick certainty, he felt that kooky Susan was destroying his future with Roberta. He couldn't deceive himself into thinking this fear was

210

unreasonable. It was eminently reasonable, and that was what was so hellish.

Knowing Roberta, he knew she would not sacrific her – their – happiness to her daughter's unhappiness. She was too rational for that. If Susan were falling apart about any *other* man, that would not stop Roberta from marrying *her* man . . . but when they were one and the same man?

That *would* make a difference to Roberta. Wouldn't it rip her apart to let her daughter know that *she* was the woman he loved? Wouldn't she feel that was the cruelest blow she could deal Susan? And might she not fear that this would push Susan's shaky emotional state over the edge into God knows what? At the very least, permanent estrangement from her mother. Roberta would *have* to feel that way. Reluctantly pushing his honesty to its limits, he had to admit she would be right. Especially thinking of his own lost daughter, he admitted she would be right.

And as of now Roberta doesn't even know, he thought. The shock, when she finds out. Perhaps Susan will blurt it out to her. If not, I will have to tell her. I owe it to her. He knew Roberta would never forgive him if he did not tell her the truth. But no matter how she learned it, the truth could mean nothing but pain for Roberta.

Zack Owen had begun the day believing happiness was within his grasp. Now he feared it had eluded him. He paced the floor until dawn, telling himself there had to be a way that two intelligent grownups who loved each other could overcome the offbeat fantasy of one mixed-up kid, without hurting the kid. He knew that his most cherished plans would have to be put on Hold – for who knew how long.

* * *

211

It was two in the morning when Roberta was awakened by a sound. She turned on the bedside lamp. Alarmed, she listened. What was it? Sobs . . . racking, heartbroken sobs. Susie! Frightened, she jumped out of bed and rushed to Susan's room, without stopping for a robe. The faint night light revealed Susan, knees drawn up, arms gripping her shoulders, body heaving. Roberta sat on the bed, pulled Susan toward her, and held her closely. Instinctively, she did not attempt to talk. She simply murmured, 'Susie, it's all right . . . whatever it is. It's all right. It will be all right, darling.'

Gradually, the girl's sobs diminished to explosive little gasps. Eventually she lay still in Roberta's arms. Roberta could see nothing but shining, tousled hair. Then Susan abruptly pulled away and flung herself back onto the pillow. Her eyes were swollen, her lashes spiked with tears, her face streaked. 'Mother, I'm so miserable. I want to die.'

'Stop that, Susan.'

'I'm such a loser. Born to lose, I guess. I thought . . . I was so sure . . .'

Roberta reached for her hand and held it firmly. 'Do you want to tell me about it?'

'Mother, I found the man for me . . . the only man. I love him. I'll always love him. He doesn't want me.'

'But how do you know? Perhaps – '

'He turned me down. After I offered myself to him . . . on a platter.'

'After you? . . .'

'Asked him to sleep with me, Mother, to go to bed with me. I was trying to be honest. No games. I thought if he saw that I'd go that far – not for sex, for *love* – if I'd risk my pride that much, he'd know I was truly in love with him. A man would *have* to get that message, wouldn't you think? He would have to respond.'

'Susan. Dearest. These things are . . .' – she picked her way – 'so . . . delicate, so complex . . .'

Susan suddenly sat up and looked at her mother. 'But it wasn't complex at all. It was *simple*. He said he was in love with another woman.'

'Oh, my dear. That hurt, I know. You think you won't survive, but you will, Susan. I know you will.'

'How do you know?' Susan flared. The old hostile note was back. 'How could *you* know? You've never been rejected in your life.'

Oh, but I have, Susan, Roberta thought, by your father. For a second she was back on the patio, hearing Brad say he was leaving her. Remembering the pain of that moment, she felt Susan's pain as her own.

'Susan.' She stroked her daughter's brow. 'I do know what you are feeling, truly, but Susie, believe me, it will heal.'

'Heal!' Susan burst into tears again. 'I'll never get over it,' she sobbed. 'Never. What will I do with my life? Without Zack.'

Without Zack. Zack? Roberta's heart seemed to stop beating; then it began to pound so violently she was sure Susan could hear it.

'Susan,' she was barely able to speak, 'I'm going to get you a cool drink.' Susan flung herself back on the pillow.

In the kitchen, Roberta stood stock-still. She felt a wave of nausea. Her daughter loved the man she loved. For the second time in her life, she thought, *This must be what hell is like*. Then she took a deep breath and forced herself to get out ice cubes.

But was it really a total surprise? Consciously, yes . . . but unconsciously? Not entirely, she forced herself to admit. She *had* uneasily noticed Susan's interest in Zack – it was too obvious not to notice – but she had simply diminished its importance. In her joy over Zack's love,

213

she had rationalized that Susan was simply testing her powers, flirting.

Numbly, Roberta carried the drink upstairs. She found Susan asleep, exhausted by the violence of her feelings. There was a puzzled frown on her face and her hands were clenched. Looking at her defenseless daughter, Roberta experienced an ambivalence so searing she felt cleft down the middle. One side of her found it unbearable to see her daughter so wounded. In every fiber of her maternal being she wanted to protect Susan from hurt, slay dragons for her. But the other side, the self side, raged. Damn you, Susan. You are ruining my life. You are an obstacle between me and what I want. *Get out of my way, Susan! Grow up, and live your own life.* Then, realizing that Susan had no inkling of her own involvement with Zack, Roberta was horrified at the unfairness of the thought.

As Zack paced the floor of the carriage house, Roberta restlessly prowled her bedroom. There was another thought she was struggling to suppress, but it rose torturingly in her mind. She could not escape it. Susan had said she had asked Zack to sleep with her. Roberta tried not to imagine the scene, but she failed. Pictures arose in her mind. She thought of Susan's lovely body. Had she actually?. . . And Zack . . . Had he responded? Could he have helped himself? Hotly, Roberta thought of her own body. She was slender and firm, but she was forty-eight. She did not have the sculptured gleam of youth. She was convinced that Zack would not have made any overt move toward her daughter, but had he *wanted* to? . . . That was the question.

She threw herself on the bed, her every muscle tensed in protest. It was unbearable – the thought of sexual competition with her daughter. By seven A.M., she had not slept at all. But her mind was made up. She had come to the decision Zack had foreseen. She could not marry Zack – she could not even see Zack – until Susan's life was on solid ground . . . whenever that might be.

No, she told herself bitterly, she was not playing the self-sacrificing, self-aggrandizing martyr. She had no taste for that at all. But in her best judgment, Susan might not withstand the blow of learning that it was her mother Zack loved. Besides, Roberta had a nagging guilt about the abrupt way she had broken up the family home base. She had been so intent on fleeing her own pain that she hadn't given enough consideration to Susan's loss and grief. She wouldn't make that mistake twice. Of course, she thought, plenty of people would think me a fool. They'd say Susan is twenty-three, for God's sake, old enough to stand on her own feet. But chronological age is no guarantee of maturity, heaven knows. I suppose you can be childish at any age. And the fact is, Susan *isn't* grown-up, emotionally, bright as she is. That is humiliating for a parent to admit.

Wearily, Roberta got up. She felt a hundred and one, but she had to get to work.

The phone was ringing as she unlocked the door of the shop. Zack, of course. She crossed slowly to the little office, dreading what she had to say.

'Roberta?' His voice was strained.

'I know about Susan, Zack.'

'You know?'

'She told me.'

'Darling, listen to me. We'll weather it. It must *not* make a difference – I won't let it!'

'Zack. Of course it makes a difference. Surely you see that?'

'No! I do *not* see that!' Zack was furious. 'I do not

see letting one flaky kid destroy what's between us, Gaddammit!'

Flaky kid. Another twist of the knife. Roberta's throat tightened. She couldn't speak for a moment.

'Roberta?'

'Oh, Zack . . . that hurts.'

'You see, Roberta? See what happens? Here I am, hurting *you*, damn it!' Zack struggled with his anger. 'I'm sorry, darling. Forgive me. This is hellish for you, but, Robbie, nothing's written in concrete. These things do pass, you know.'

'Yes . . . but when? Zack, this is such a *mess*, how can we take anything for granted? Oh, Zack, what I'm trying to say is . . .'

'All bets are off? No, Roberta. I won't accept that.'

'Susan's been upset since her father died, and that was only a year ago. I'm all she has to hang on to right now. She needs me, Zack.'

'And we need each other.'

Yes. If only she could put her head on his shoulder, if only . . .

'Zack, this conversation is too painful for both of us. We can't solve anything right now, anyway. Don't you think – '

'We should hang up? Not until I hear it from you again, Roberta. Do you love me?'

'You know the answer. I love you, Zack.'

'Then we'll make it.'

She wanted so to believe him.

'Darling, have a good trip. I'll write you.'

'I'll call you from Tokyo.'

'No, Zack.'

'Why the hell not?'

'Because . . .' It was too hard to explain, the torn-in-two feeling she'd have. 'Because it would be easier for me, Zack.'

He hesitated. Then he reluctantly agreed. 'Whatever's best for you, Robbie, if you really mean that. No calls, then . . . until I hear from you. And Mrs M, sweet?. . .'

'Yes, Zack?'

'Promise me you won't let anybody – not anybody – call you "Mrs M"?'

She managed a tremulous little laugh. Mrs M. It had become their code word for love and lovemaking, for closeness and everything important between them.

'Promise,' she whispered. 'Goodbye, Zack.'

18

Roberta was so apprehensive over Susan the first week after Zack's departure that she felt his absence was almost a bittersweet relief. She didn't know what to expect from Susan. Would she fall apart, take to her bed, do something rash? But to Roberta's surprise, Susan seemed to pull herself together almost overnight. She looked pale and somewhat chastened, but calm.

'Susan, would you like to meet me for lunch?'

'No, that's okay, Mother. I think I'd really better get going and look for a job.'

'Well, why don't you and I plan something for the evening? There's a concert at Waterloo village, would you like? . . .'

'Relax, Mother. I'm okay. Sorry I spilled my guts.' Her tone said: *Please forget it, will you? And please don't mention it, ever*.

Roberta was amazed. Was this the resilience of youth? Could Susan really recover from a blow so quickly? Or had her feeling for Zack just been a moment of self-drama. Thinking it over, remembering Susan's broken sobs, Roberta decided not. She did not doubt that Susan believed she had met the one and only for her, and had lost him. Was Susan being brave, accepting the hurt, growing up at last?

Somewhat relieved, Roberta still felt uneasy. It seemed too good to be true. Too quick, too easy. But when, ten days later, Susan announced that she had landed a job on the weekly *Clarion* – 'just local social stuff, taking down wedding and engagements on the phone' – Roberta allowed herself to hope that maybe, mercifully, things would work out for Susan, and for her.

. . . Until she happened on Susan's calender. She'd gone into Susan's room to close the windows against a pelting summer shower. The calendar was on the table in front of the window. There was no escaping it nor the red Xs crossing off the past twelve days. September first, a date engraved on Roberta's heart, was marked with a Z.

Susan was counting the days until Zack's return. Looking toward the empty carriage house, Roberta felt sick. Susan was still hoping. She had refused to accept Zack's statement that he was involved elsewhere, or she had accepted it, but believed she could change his feelings. Far from recovering from her infatuation, Susan was locked into it.

Roberta went slowly downstairs, thinking Susan's apparent about-face had indeed been too good to be true. It was clear now that Susan's new job, and her new, serious demeanor were preparations for Zack's return. She probably had some notion of becoming a mature young woman he'd have to take seriously. She probably felt that as long as Zack was single there were no holds barred.

Now what do I do, thought Roberta. What do I *do*?

Picking up his mail in the Miyako Hotel in Tokyo, Zack knew what Roberta's letter said before he opened it. Something about her writing – something forced and reluctant, as though she had had to push the pen against her will – was as clear as the letter within:

Zack, Zack – oh, Zack!
 I have been writing this letter for hours. I have torn up pages and pages even though I know so many words are not necessary between you and me. One of the many reasons I love you is that you understand without words.

219

Therefore, before I lose my courage, I must end what is between us. What I'm trying to say is that you must not feel in any way committed or involved or bound by the hopes we shared. Because I see no hope of fulfilling them.

Zack, Susan is counting the days until your return. She has either blotted out what you told her, does not believe it, or thinks it need not matter. She's a different girl, Zack – serious, quiet. She has a job; and it's all for *you*, Zack. I'm absolutely sure of this. You can imagine how this tears me apart, how I weep for her – and for us.

And you'll understand how miserably *deceitful* I feel to be lending Susie moral support while at the same time I'm dreaming about you. So I must give up dreaming.

I know you'll say Susan will get over this. Of course she will . . . sometime. But 'sometime' is too vague for either of us. Anyway, I can't bear the thought of keeping you – well, wouldn't it be *dangling*? – especially over a problem that's all mine and in no way yours.

I'm sure you'll consider this next bit absurd. I always did feel peculiar about being a landlady, especially yours. But I am one and you do have a lease.

But, Zack, could you 'forgive' it – cancel the rest of it? Wouldn't it be wise? Could you write me a sort of official 'tenant' letter – your plans have changed, you'll be away longer than you thought, whatever? . . . Something that would make sense to Susan and Jim?

Silver lining, darling. No more worry about the younger-man–older-woman questions. I was never sure about that, although you almost convinced me.

Zack, what happiness you gave me.

Roberta

Zack's reply came within ten days, in two separate envelopes. The first said:

My Roberta:

No, we don't need a lot of words.

And no, I have no intention of giving you up.

Darling, you feel trapped by a terrible conflict of interest. And you're handing me my 'freedom' because you can't see a way out and feel it's not fair to keep me 'dangling.'

220

But you don't really believe you can keep a man from being involved just by saying he isn't, do you? Mrs M, you know better than that.

Look, Robbie, if it makes it easier with Susan for you to feel you've canceled *us*, okay. Noted. We're both free as birds, which leaves me free to go on planning and dreaming of the day I hold you in my arms again. Robbie, this is just a setback. Believe it.

I won't write again, Robbie, because I sense you'd prefer I didn't right now. I know you won't write me, either. But I'll be back, Roberta, after a decent interval, when my sixth sense tells me it's the right moment.

I'm sending a separate letter about the carriage house. I wish you knew what hell it is to give it up. What am I saying? Of course you know. But oh, Mrs M, what a *waste*!

You can always reach me through the New York office. I *trust* you, Roberta, to let me know if you need me – or want me – for anything.

> Abidingly yours,
> Zack

Abidingly. 'Abide with me.' How like Zack. The word blurred through her tears.

The second letter hit the perfect note. It said his plans had changed, he did not know how long he would be away, and therefore . . .

He wrote how much he had enjoyed the carriage house, thanked Mrs Marston for her kindness, and sent his regards to Susan and Jim. If Jim would be so kind as to pack his books and his other belongings, he would arrange to have his office pick them up.

Dreading what Susan would have to experience as another blow, Roberta tacked the letter on the kitchen bulletin board.

Two days after Zack's letter arrived, Susan left.

'Gone?' Roberta stared at Jim. 'Gone where?'

'She left a note.' He handed it to her.

Mother and Jim: I'm taking off. There's nothing for me here. I don't know where I'm going – but somewhere. I'll let you know where later. Don't worry about me. S.
P.S. I called the newspaper to quit my job.

Roberta sat down. She was aware that she should be feeling something, but she was numb. It was as though her power to absorb shock was used up. She was null and void.

'Mother, relax.'

'I am relaxed. Where do you think she went, Jim?'

'New York is my guess.'

'But she hates New York nowadays.'

'As a starting point, I mean. To take off for somewhere else. She probably called the Thomasville taxi to get to the bus station, or maybe she hitched a ride.'

'Did she take all her things?'

'No. I looked. She just took a few clothes. Most of her stuff is there.'

'But she has no money.'

'I thought of that. She *does* have some money, the money Grandpa Marston has been giving us every Christmas. We were supposed to keep it until "the need arises." It's in C/Ds, remember? I wouldn't put it past Susan to cash them in, even if she loses on the deal.'

'I'd forgotten that.'

'So she's not penniless.'

'But we've got to find her, Jim.' The reality of the situation was beginning to sink in. She could feel anxiety taking over. 'We can't *not* know where Susan *is*! It's unthinkable!'

Jim was fed up with Susie's selfishness. He was breaking his back as it was: working at his job, spending Saturdays mowing acres of lawn, doing his best to be 'the man of the family.' Did his sister *have* to throw them another curve? She needed a swat in the behind. Besides, even though Susan had been doing a number on them recently, he knew she had good sense. Jim wasn't really worried about her, but his mother was falling apart.

'Easy, Mother. It's going to be okay. Listen. You must know that Susan had a big thing for Zack. It was obvious. That's what all that early-to-bed and early-to-rise stuff was about. My guess is that Susan was trying to make herself over so she could knock Zack dead when he came back.'

Yes, thought Roberta. Just what I thought.

'And when Zack wrote that he wouldn't *be* back, that clobbered Susan.'

'But that's just it! In that state of mind, don't you think she might do something – '

'Rash? No. I honestly don't. You know what happens when you're hurt. You want to run away from it. Susie's running, that's all.'

He's right. The way I ran away from New York . . . after Brad.

'Right now, Susan wants a change, any change. She wants to be in motion, to keep moving. My guess is she'll get on a plane or a bus and head for someplace where she knows someone. Cape Cod or Maine or New Mexico. Isn't Buffie Harrington's in Taos? Pretty soon we'll get a postcard showing mountains or something and saying "*X* marks the spot where I climbed today."'

Roberta smiled in spite of herself. Jim really did make it seem less scary, but she was by no means confident. 'Jim, do you really mean that, or are you just trying to make me feel better?'

'Honest Injun. I have faith in Susan's intelligence, even if she has been behaving like a kid since Dad died. I don't really think it's Zack at all. I think Dad's death hit Susan very hard. She didn't realize how much security he

represented to her, and for that very same reason – Dad
– I'm not worried about her.'

'I don't follow you, Jim.'

'She wouldn't do anything really crazy – for *Dad's*
sake. Even though Dad's gone.'

Roberta was stung. 'And what about *my* sake?'

'Oh, come on, Mom! You know pop psychology. You
know all that stuff that's written about mothers and
daughters nowadays. They say the conflict's built in.'

'So you wouldn't do anything? But it's so *hard* just to
wait.'

'Sure it is, but we'll just have to sweat it out. If we
tried to trace her, or called Missing Persons or something,
it would just prove we don't think Susan can take care of
herself. The biggest compliment we can pay her is to
trust her. I have a hunch this will be her last, let's say,
escapade. I'll bet the next time you see her, she'll be all
grown-up.'

'Jim. What would I do without you?'

'It's mutual, Mom.'

Later, in bed, Roberta wondered how you knew when a
phase of your life *was* a phase. When it was over? *Only*
when it was over, receding into the past, she decided.
Before it was over, you had the illusion it was your on-
going life.

A phase of her life had just ended abruptly, as the
previous phase had. Less than a year ago she had taken
her happy marriage for granted. Less than a month ago,
she had believed in the possibility, almost the certainty,
of a second happy marriage.

Now Zack was gone . . . and Susan was gone.

Back to Square One.

She couldn't sleep. Square One was cold and empty.

She could not bear it. She couldn't face a blank future for a second time.

She didn't know she was crying until she felt hot tears on the pillow. Zack . . . she wept for Zack. She wanted him to take over, protect her, make everything right.

. . . Like a child, she slowly realized, as she cried herself out and her sobs diminished to sniffles. A lost child, like Susan. Susan who wouldn't face reality.

Reality. Roberta switched on the light, reached for the Kleenex and mopped her face. Staring at the ceiling, she thought about reality.

I'm feeling sorry for myself, Maybe I was too lucky for too long? All those good years with Brad. I took them all for granted. And now life is catching up with me – to balance things? Life isn't supposed to be easy, but mine was. Why should I be immune? Join the club. Live with it – whatever 'it' is.

Tomorrow I'll advertise the carriage house. I still need the rent money. But I'll ask Jim to show the place. How could I bear to set foot in it again, now?

Part II

It was summer. Nothing much happens in Greenwillow in summer. Nothing much happens in Manhattan either. Those who can't get away from the city mark time waiting for the escapees to get back. And the town empties on Friday afternoon, to make room for the tourists and day-trippers.

In Greenwillow, people don't take vacations. The weekenders bring their guests with them. The natives, after a rough winter, settle for backyard barbecues.

In the city, there is the hum of air conditioning. In the country, the drone of the tractor is heard in the land. There is an air of somnolence, the days are long and slow, life seems suspended.

But at a get-together which would be held a year in the future, the women present, comparing notes, would agree that this was the summer everything happened to them.

19

Three miles from Roberta Marston's house, Dr John Blair's wife felt the station wagon skid as she headed up their mile-long lane. The recent heavy summer rain had made the road treacherous.

'Don't forget the monster hole at the top, Mom,' warned Billy, her youngest.

The big pothole. She visualized it and all the other holes on this horrible, dangerous, impossible driveway, if you could call it a driveway. During the school year she struggled with it four times a day. First she took Billy and the twins to their private school, twenty-five miles away. Then she returned home. At three, she went back to the school to pick them up. Then she drove home again. That took up most of her day, not that her days were worth much.

She hit another pothole. 'Watch it, Ma!' the kids yelled. My whole life is a pothole, she thought, one endless bruising.

The gas tank is low, she noted. As usual, she had no cash. She just hoped she could make it back, so she could charge some gas at the local station.

She dropped her teenagers at the entrance to the Swim Club. Billy, just thirteen, pecked her on the cheek as he got out. The kids seem happy enough, she thought. They throve on the outdoor life they lived. They loved riding the tractor, and the horses John had bought them, without consulting her. Horses, but only one bathroom. Still, the children did not seem to mind the shabby household, not yet. Nor were they, as far as she could see, affected by her own chronic depression. Perhaps she concealed it better than she knew.

Of course, they had *one* fulfilled parent. Their father, heaven knew, was absorbed and happy in *his* life. He had plenty of ego gratification, his adoring patients. And the great respect in which he was held by the community probably rubbed off on his children, even if *Mrs* Blair was generally considered to be stand-offish.

No one knew how lost she felt, least of all her oblivious husband. Her daughter Midge, perhaps. Midge sensed her unhappiness, and she cared. But Midge was in college now, preparing for her own life. Mary Blair fervently hoped her daughter would not fall for a man whose true love was his work.

At the small country gas station near the turn off to her lane, Mary greeted the owner. 'Good morning, Mr Uznyzki. Would you fill it up, please? And would you check the oil?'

The man hesitated. He gave her a sharp look from under his oily peaked cap. Then he moved to the side of the car and unscrewed the gas cap. When he finished he said, 'That will be fourteen dollars and ninety cents, Mrs Blair.'

'Will you charge it, please, Mr Uznyzki?'

He stepped closer to the window of the car. 'Mrs Blair, I hate to bring this up, but your bill is over three hundred dollars. In fact' – he fished a folded paper from his overall pocket, as though he had prepared himself for this opportunity – 'it's three hundred forty-eight dollars and seventy cents. Ain't been paid in three months. Not countin' today's.'

Mary Blair felt her face flame with embarrassment. 'I'm – I'm sorry. If you'll just send the bill to my husband, I'm sure he'll – '

'I already done that, and I spoke to the doc last week.

He was right uppity. Said he'd have his office take care of it, but he ain't done it. Not yet. And that was a week ago.'

'I'm sorry,' Mary said again.

He looked at her with something like pity in his face. 'It ain't your fault, Mrs Blair. I know that.' But he was also resentful. 'You know, inflation is hitting a lot of us. Times are bad. I don't mind carrying folks on credit for a while, folks who're up against it. But when you know folks have plenty, like the doc, that's hard to take.'

Mary nodded mutely.

'I'm awful sorry, Mrs Blair. But I won't be able to give you any more gas until the arrears is paid. Nothing personal, Mrs Blair. Ain't got a choice.'

Mary nodded, started the motor, and pulled out. Blinded with tears, she turned into her lane, put her foot on the gas, and hit the big pothole with a jolting impact. The car was stalled at a lopsided angle. Mary put her head on the steering wheel and gave herself up to sobs.

Roberta wished it were not her Monday off. It was easier to work at the shop and not to think, or not think so much. Especially when her thoughts went in circles. Either Zack, Zack, or Susan, Susan. It was two weeks since Susan had left, but she'd sent no word. Worry ran through Roberta's mind like a dark underground stream. She imagined drugs, cults, communes. Jim would catch her at it and read her mind. 'Communes are out of style, Mother. Besides, Susan's not the type.'

There were other moments when she flamed with anger. Damn you, Susan. You don't know what you did to me. You ruined my dream. You killed my hope. You got in my *way*! And now you've made me sick with worry. You disappear without a word. Thoughtless! Childish! Selfish! Monstrous!

As fast as the anger flared up, it subsided, and the worry began again. Oh, Susan, are you all right?

As for Zack, she had lost him. She would never see him again. But every day, as she went through the mail at the shop, she looked for a letter. And every time the phone rang, she hoped desperately it was Zack. But I'm not making sense, she told herself. I asked him *not* to write, *not* to phone. I broke *off* the relationship. Still, something so close, so sweet, could not just end. Could it? He said he'd be back, but I shouldn't even be thinking of him, when I don't know where Susan is . . .

Exerting her will, Roberta tried to turn off her conflicting, inconsistent thoughts. Stop it! she told herself. All I can do is the hardest thing of all – nothing. It's out of my hands. Maybe there is something to be said for fatalism. Meantime, I must get through today.

She would work in her flower beds. She had discovered an odd truth about gardening. No matter what is going on in a gardener's life to provoke grief, worry, disappointment, anger – working with the earth and living green things provides an unfailing solace, even pleasure. It is as though pain and pleasure can coexist on parallel lines, each being no less real despite the contradiction.

A half-hour later, on her way to the garden center to pick up bamboo stakes, she passed the entrance to Dr John Blair's lane. Just past it, she slowed. Out of the corner of her eye, hadn't she seen a station wagon there, at an odd angle, and what appeared to be someone slumping over the wheel? Dear Lord, an accident.

She backed up and pulled into the lane. Seeing the condition of the road, she got out and ran toward the other car. From the back, it looked like Mary Blair. Motionless. Roberta's mind began to race. How fast could she get to a phone to call the first-aid squad? How fast would they come? Oh, let her not be badly hurt.

Her heart pounding, she opened the door of the Blair car. 'Mrs Blair? Mary?' Mary Blair turned her head. Her face was wet with tears, her eyes hopeless. Roberta felt shock. At the same time, she felt she shouldn't be seeing this. It was too private, too naked an image of suffering.

'Are you hurt?'

Mary Blair shook her head. Then she began to cry again.

Roberta considered. This was a deeply upset woman. How could she help? Obviously, she should just let her cry at the moment. Then what? She couldn't just walk away. Perhaps she could take Mary home with her, at least until she felt calmer. But she would not watch her cry. It was indecent. Roberta walked back to her car and picked up the Kleenex box. She went back and gently put it in Mary's lap. Then she returned to her own car. At length she saw Mary sit up and mop her eyes. The worst of the storm was over.

'Mary? Would you share some lunch with me? At my house?'

Mary tried to smile, but failed. 'Thank you. But I should really . . . I should get home.' Her voice was hoarse from weeping. A black and blue lump was developing on her forehead.

'Would you like me to call your husband?'

At the word *husband* Mary's face crumpled again.

Roberta decided what to do. There were times when troubled people *wanted* someone else to take over. From Mary's reaction a moment ago, it looked as though her husband were part of the problem, rather than a solution to it. She simply could not be left alone.

'Please come, Mary. I've got an empty day. I was wishing I had company. I'd love to have you.' At least she might get her past this low point. 'Come *along*,

Mary,' Roberta said firmly, like a mother speaking to a child.

'All right,' Mary replied.

Once she had Mary settled in the kitchen, Roberta carefully talked about nothing until Mary could get her bearings. As she brewed good strong coffee and made sandwiches, she chitchatted cheerfully about the weather, a tree that had fallen, double coupons at the A & P. Mary nodded, and said 'Yes' and 'No.' She seemed as shy and inarticulate as Roberta remembered her being that first night at the Fentons, the night she had needed a ride home because her husband and forgotten she was there.

Mary didn't touch the sandwiches, but she did drink the coffee gratefully. 'It's so nice and hot,' she said. 'I have been feeling so . . . cold. Cold,' she repeated. 'Inside. Icy. As though I'm frozen. Oh, Mrs Marston.' And then it came – a torrent of anguish pent-up for years, words rushing out as though a sluice had been opened. 'Oh, Mrs Marston, I can't *stand* it – my life – I'm miserable from morning to night – I feel so alone – John doesn't even know I'm there – he acts as though I don't exist – he's in another world – there's no room for me . . .'

Out it all came. How she had fallen deeply in love with John when she was still in college. How she had been dazzled by his brilliance, his idealism. How humble she had felt at being chosen by this man among men. She described the tough years of John's internship and residency, when she struggled with small children in a New York walk-up. And how she had been sustained by her faith that eventually, when John had his own practice, they would at last begin to share life.

But it had never happened. Even after they'd moved here, and John was well established, the closeness never developed. Never. John simply became more and more absorbed in his work. Now she felt she was at the breaking point. For the last eight years she'd been achingly lonely . . . isolated from everything, no social life, no adult companionship, no hope of altering things.

'But surely you have friends?' murmured Roberta.

'Only acquaintances. People I've met through the kids, or out shopping. When we first came people *did* make overtures – people from the hospital, other doctors and their wives, and neighbors in Greenwillow. Like the Fentons. But John has no interest in people except as *patients*. He *scorns* social life. He won't go anywhere except to a medical convention. Not that it matters, really. We couldn't entertain anyway. Our house is beyond the pale.'

For a split second Roberta wondered whether Mary Blair was mentally disturbed, suffering from delusions, or paranoid.

Mary caught Roberta's expression. She forced a wry little laugh. 'Oh, I know what you're thinking, Mrs Marston. You're wondering if I'm a little crazy. I don't blame you. Who ever heard of a doctor's family living in – well, I'm sure *you* would be shocked.' She looked wistfully around the shining kitchen, her eyes lingering on the huge stainless-steel restaurant stove. 'Incredible as I know it is, I cooked for five years on a couple of hot plates, and I lugged laundry for four children to the laundromat.'

'But how can that be? I don't understand . . .' Roberta was aghast.

'I didn't even see our house until after John bought it. Beat-up hardly describes it – you can't imagine. He said it could be restored, but it never was. We finally did get a kitchen and a washer-dryer. But otherwise . . .' She gave a defeated little shrug. 'Not what you'd call gracious

235

living. John doesn't even notice. He's *oblivious*. He's above *things*. And he forgets to pay bills.'

Roberta felt strongly that she should not be hearing all this. She didn't know Mary Blair well enough for such private disclosures. The fact that she also knew Mary's husband, if only as a member of his committee, made it all the more sticky. And yet, considering the state Mary was in, it would be unthinkable to deny her the relief of venting her feelings. Another kind of battered woman, she thought.

Roberta had an indignant urge to prod her. *Look here, Mary, you must assert yourself. If John's no good at money, insist on a separate checking account, with adequate cash for what you need* . . . But of course she could not say that. It would be presumptuous. Besides, she had a hunch that it was not only money that was bothering Mary. Shocking as that was, considering what Dr Blair's income must be. Clearly, it wasn't only overlooked bills. It was the overlooked woman.

'You know, Mary,' Roberta began slowly, feeling her way. 'Even when things are at their blackest, there are ways to let in a *little* light. I know that's terribly Pollyannaish. But that doesn't mean it isn't true.' She decided to use shock tactics. 'Have you ever thought of getting a job?'

Just as she expected, the idea was a shocking one to Mary. So much so, that for a moment she forgot her misery in sheer surprise.

'A *job*? Me? What could I do? Who would hire me? I'm *forty*!'

'I'm forty plus. And I got a job. It's a minor one, as careers go, but it's mine. And I enjoy it.'

'But I have no experience. I married right out of college.'

'Me, too. It's terribly scary, looking for a job, when

236

you've been home for years. But lots of women do it. Do you know lots of the farmers' wives have jobs? I was amazed. Middle-aged women.'

'Really? I had no idea.'

'Absolutely. Not that's it's easy. And of course when you're inexperienced you earn very little money, at least at first. But that's not the point.'

'Oh, I know I wouldn't earn much,' said Mary earnestly. 'It's the thought of earning *anything*.' She was turning the idea over as though it were extraordinary. Like Roberta before her, she had never related to the majority of women who work. 'But there are the kids . . .'

'How old is your youngest?'

'Thirteen.'

'That's old enough. You could manage.'

'You really think so? It's such an *unheard* of idea – for me I mean.' But she looked more animated, less defeated. 'You know, Mrs Marston, you almost make me believe I might be able to change things. For the first time in I don't know when, I feel maybe I'll . . . *live*.'

'I knew that all the time.' Roberta laughed. 'And please call me Roberta.'

'Thanks, I will. But is that really the time? I've been here for hours. I have to pick up the children.'

'Right. I'll drive you back to your place. By the way, can you maneuver your car out of that hole?'

'I've done it before. I'm sure I can.'

Roberta waited in Mary's lane until the station wagon was safely on solid ground.

Mary came to the window of Roberta's car. 'I don't know how to thank you, Roberta.'

'Please . . . I'm glad I happened along. And Mary' – how could she put this? – 'Mary, I hope you'll believe I'm a respecter of confidences.'

'Yes, I do.'

'Look. I'm alone a lot. I'd love to have you spend an evening with me. Would you call me when you're in the mood?'

'Would I!'

'Good. Until soon, then.'

Later, on her knees in the garden. Roberta wondered whether Mary really would call. She hoped so. She could use another woman friend right now, and she was drawn to Mary, who was obviously a well-bred, gentle woman. She knew Mary was bound to be embarrassed because she'd revealed so much to someone she hardly knew. That often happened. People poured out their troubles, and then avoided you, ashamed of their indiscretion.

And what an amazing glimpse into their private lives. Dr John Blair, that extraordinary man, devoid of ordinary feelings. Devoid of the ability to relate, apparently, except to his patients. But even the most compulsive workaholics – politicians running for office, merger-minded corporate types – usually wrapped their families in comfort, to make up for their lack of emotional commitment. Mary Blair's description of their home was hard to believe, but Roberta believed her.

As she put in the last stake, Roberta was startled to realize that she had not thought of Susan, or of Zack, for hours.

Other people's troubles. They did put your own into perspective. She wondered how many other hidden dramas were being played out behind Greenwillow's peaceful windows.

20

In Phoenix, Carole Harcourt was exhausted. Even unlocking her hotel-room door was an effort. She wanted to throw herself on the bed, clothes and all, and conk out. She had to force herself to carry out her bedtime ritual: off with the lashes, off with the makeup, on with the cleansing cream, into the tub. Lay out her clothes for tomorrow, reorganize her handbag, leave a call for six A.M.

What a day. She had been shooting a soft-drink commercial on the desert. God, no TV viewer would believe what went into sixty seconds on the tube. Broiling sun, huge crew, that know-nothing bitch representing the client, a couple of kid actors. Child professionals – the worst, next to trained animals.

Scarcely able to keep her eyes open, Carole got into bed. The phone rang. Let it ring. It had to be somebody from her crew, something about tomorrow's shoot. Let them think she was in the shower, or not yet back in the hotel. Anything. But a thought entered her drowsy mind. It *could* be The Man. The head of Carole's agency had a habit of calling his top people at odd hours, the bastard. Better answer.

It was her doctor in New York. 'Carole, are you sitting down? Carole, it's about Greg.' Massive heart attack. Intensive care. Columbia Presbyterian Hospital.

She tried to speak. Nothing came out.

'Carole?'

She managed a hoarse whisper. 'How bad is it Arthur?'

239

'Nip and tuck. I've called in Greene. The best, Carole. Everything's being done.'

'I'll get the first plane.' She hung up.

She willed herself to sleep on the plane. Carole Harcourt was practiced at self-discipline. She had to be. How else could she have fought her way from secretary to Creative Group Head in one of Manhattan's most aggressive ad agencies? She knew very well that some of the people she had passed on her way considered her a barracuda. Who gave a damn? You do what you have to do. Doesn't everybody? If you get hurt in the process, you didn't try hard enough, or you aren't jungle-smart.

Carole awakened as the plane approached Kennedy. She was always terrified by that sickening, dipping descent over crummy parts of Queens. She usually hid it by wise-cracking to the passenger in the next seat. But today she barely noticed. As her knuckles whitened on the arm-rests and her heart lurched, her terror was for Greg.

On the imterminable ride from the airport, Carole alternately prayed and tried to practice mind control. That was another of her survival techniques: Look on the bright side if it kills you. He'd said nip and tuck. That's fifty-fifty. Okay, the bottle is half-full, remember half-full. If I believe, it will be true.

At the hospital, Carole clung to the reception desk as she waited for Dr Magowan to answer the page. From across the lobby, as he stepped out of the elevator, Arthur Magowan signaled a cautious Okay sign.

'He's not? . . .' she asked as he reached her.

'So far, so good,' he replied. Her knees buckled.

He took her by the arm and propelled her firmly toward the coffee shop. 'We'll talk in here. You need black coffee.'

'Give it to me straight, Arthur.'

'Carole, we don't know. We won't know for seventy-two hours or so. If he gets through that, we'll be a lot more confident.'

'Seventy-two hours.'

'Carole, he has a chance, but it's a fighting chance. And we're fighting like hell.'

'I want the best, Arthur.'

Arthur Magowan looked at her. He'd known her for a long time, since she'd been married to her previous husband. He found her blind faith in money both touching and irritating. When in trouble, apply dollars.

'You've got it.'

'This cardiologist, Greene – you're sure?'

'Nobody better.'

'Round-the-clock nurses?' He nodded. 'Are they good?'

'Tops. He couldn't have better care if he were the President.'

'May I see him?'

'Tomorrow. Now go home and get some sleep. Take a sleeping pill.'

For the next several days, Carole spent long hours sitting in the visitors' lounge. It made no sense, she knew. She couldn't really *do* anything. But it was a compulsion. She had to do what she *could* do: *be* there, willing Greg to live; charm the nurses by giving each of them a bottle of Joy – 'I'm so grateful for what you're doing for my husband.' A little *schmeer* never hurt.

She was allowed to see Greg only a minute or two at a time, just glimpse him really. The first time, Mr Magowan led her down corridors heavy with the smell of antiseptic and the aura of anxiety. Just before he pushed open the heavy silent door marked Intensive Care Unit, he cautioned her.

'Be prepared, Carole. Greg doesn't look like himself.'

She nodded.

Outside Greg's room was a monitor. Very like a TV screen. Carole realized that those jagged lines were Greg's heartbeats. Arthur Magowan looked at them expressionlessly.

Inside, Greg lay in a tangle of metals, wires, intravenous needles and dangling bottles. His eyes were closed. His face was waxen. There were deep lines from his nose to his mouth, lines Carole had never seen before. He did not open his eyes. Dr Magowan motioned to Carole, and they tiptoed out.

Carole went back to the visitors' lounge and took out her needlepoint. It eased the waiting. The in-out, in-out of the needle was soothing, rhythmic. Like breathing, she suddenly realized. A symbolic way of helping Greg breathe. He had to live. She couldn't lose him. She needed him.

But why? Unbidden, the question arose from another part of her mind, almost from another Carole.

Who do I feel I'd be nothing without Greg?

It wasn't love. Or what she had thought was love. Carole had recognized for some time that her marriage to Greg had been a case of mistaken identity. Mistaken on her part. She had thought Greg was as powerful as he came across, a cando guy. He wasn't.

They'd met when she had been divorced for two years. She'd already played the field. Nothing much out there. Greg came on strong. He put on a big campaign: flowers, dinner, weekend trips. He was very good at it. Then, too, he was actually single, a nice quality in a man. Greg was divorced, unlike the standard models who acted single, but invariably turned out to be married and only *considering* divorce.

Another big asset to Greg, besides his lazy, sexy good

looks, was that his job was in a different field. She wouldn't dream of a man working her side of the street. Competing spouses could be murder. Greg was with Barton Publications, the slick magazine empire. So although they were both in media, he was Print and she was Video. No conflict.

When they were married, she thought they had everything going for them. He moved into her apartment, because it was so much bigger than his. Six months later, he threw up his job in an egotistical rage. The publisher had turned down a promotion plan he'd submitted. When Greg told her about it, Carole privately thought his plan sounded rather half-assed. But she didn't say so. She backed him up.

His next job was a step down. He held it a year. Then, over an expensive dinner, which he'd ordered with a flourish, making a big show with the maitre d' but which Carole would pay for, he'd told her that job, too, was a dead-end. Cut-backs. The economy. But she happened to know, from contacts of her own, that Greg's company was expanding, not cutting back. That was when she knew Greg was a goof-off. He came on strong, but he didn't deliver. He didn't do his homework. He was, in fact, a lazy bum. Whereas she worked like hell, sometimes putting in twelve-hour days on the cold concrete floors of production studios and editing rooms.

She came to terms with it. She wasn't, after all, looking for a meal ticket. She could provide her own, and his too, which was the way it turned out to be. Greg's current Micky Mouse job hardly kept him in clothes, cigarettes, and taxis. But to hear him tell it, he was 'in publishing.'

So why, she asked herself again, as she kept her vigil in the hospital, do I feel I'll die without Greg?

Because I can't stand being alone a single second. I go bananas.

And because I need a man for my image. To hell with Women's Lib. I have to have a man escort me to all those P.R. parties, and screenings, and to the theater, to stand in the rain getting a taxi, and to cope with the headwaiter when they claim there's no table. Even though I pay the credit card bills.

And how could I ever make it in the country? Coping with the people who take care of the heat and the pump and the pool. Not that Greg really knows what he's talking about with all that stuff either. He was all wet, it turned out, about glassing in the porch. Still, workmen screw you less when they deal with a man.

Carole thought of her friend Roberta Marston. How does she handle all that, alone in that huge house? How does she stand being alone, period? It doesn't seem to faze her a bit to go to a party on her own. Me, I'd feel like a fifth wheel.

Besides, I can't drive. Carole came close to indulging in a small hysterical giggle. She repressed it. She was in a hospital. But it was absurd. A born city-dweller, she had never learned to drive, and she had a hang-up about learning. Once in a while, when Greg's maddening air of male superiority got to her, she had a strong urge to throw him out. Then she invariably thought: But how would I get to the country? Crazy. Carole Harcourt, with considerable clout in her working world, felt helpless about the little mechanics of life.

She supposed that was why she clung to the status quo. And Greg could be great fun, when he wanted to be. She reversed her needlepoint. In, out, in, out. You've got to make it, Greg. You've got to.

Greg Harcourt pulled through. But three days before he was to come home, heads rolled at Carole's agency, hers included. Her firm merged with another. A power struggle between the newcomers and the entrenched had ensued. Everyone had to be in one camp or the other. Carole had been on the wrong side.

Now, in the middle of the afternoon, she sat in a dark bar with the other casualties. Everyone drank too much. Gallows humor abounded, as they tried to top each other with sick jokes. Inevitably, there were a couple of people who had backed the right side and survived. They were there to offer condolences, to say it was the double deal of the century, and to think better you than me. Everyone said, at least once, 'You can't win 'em all.'

It was the classic wake of highly-paid people who find themselves suddenly unemployed. Eventually they left, one by one, to catch trains to plush bedroom communities, or to stand in the street, groggily hailing taxis. And to break the news to wives or husbands and kids. And, the morning after, to face the loss of identity. The identity of power, of association with a prestigious firm, of status. And of the perquisites thereof: the open sesame to fashionable restaurants, hotels and bars: the smiles and bows of an army of flunkies; instant access to cars, airline tickets, and the services of top hairstylists, tailors, shirtmakers, and masseurs who make house calls. All the expense-account luxuries and credit card goodies. To say nothing of the privileged level of family living; the house, cars, boat, camps, colleges, country places, travel.

Tomorrow the dispossessed would wake up not only facing the loss of luxury, but worse, the loss of self. John or Jane Doe. V.P. in Charge of . . ., dies a little at reverting to John or Jane Doe, period.

Carole's head was swimming with the Scotch she had drunk. At the door of the ten-room West Side apartment she'd lived in for years, she rang the bell rather than fumble for her key.

Ada, who had been her housekeeper since before her first marriage, opened the door.

'Ada, I'm bombed. I'm going straight to bed.'

'Best thing to do, Mrs Harcourt, after all you've been through. Mr Harcourt so sick, and you practically living at the hospital. Do you good to take a little likker. Relax you.'

Ada lived in six days a week, and went home to her husband in Harlem on Sundays. She was used to drinking.

Five minutes later, she carried a tray of hot comsommé and plain biscuits into Carole's bedroom. 'This'll settle your stomach, Mrs Harcourt.'

'Sweet of you, Ada.. Thank you.' But after three sips, Carole put down the cup. Dizziness engulfed her as her head touched the pillow. I'll think about it tomorrow. Right now, to hell with it.

Carole, with Ada's help, brought Greg home from the hospital in a Carey limousine. He needed rest, quiet, and fairly soon a carefully planned program of exercise. But he must now be allowed to think of himself, Arthur Magowan had stressed, as an invalid.

Fifty-six was the prime of life, Dr Magowan said, and Greg could live as long and as well as a man who had had no heart attack, providing he used his head. He must give up smoking entirely, and for now, of course, drinking. Later he could take a social drink or two.

Carole and Ada put their heads together. All household chores were to come second to Mr Harcourt's comfort and well-being. Remember, Ada. Drop everything when Mr Harcourt wants something. Forget the kitchen cupboards. Forget the laundry. Forget cleaning. And don't leave the apartment for any reason at all. Right, Mrs Harcourt, nodded Ada.

But alone in the kitchen, Ada shook her head. How

could a woman like Mrs Harcourt knock herself out so for a man like Mr Harcourt? That was one mean man. How come Mrs Harcourt didn't catch on? Her husband had a cruel streak Ada could spot a mile away. Oh, he hid it, he was smart about that. And he picked on people who couldn't fight back. You wouldn't guess, to meet him, because he was good-looking and had that smile people fell for. But not Ada.

She'd seen Mr Harcourt needling Mrs Harcourt in front of guests too many times. Making little jokes that sounded okay, until you did a double take and realized they were nasty cracks. Then he'd get all sweet and ruffle Mrs Harcourt's hair and pretend he was just being affectionate. Affectionate my rear end.

He did it to Ada too. Every once in a while he'd call her 'Mammy' and talk according to his crazy idea of how Blacks talk. You could tell he enjoyed seeing how upset she got. Then he'd laugh and pinch her arm and say, 'Just kidding, Ada. You know we couldn't live without you.'

Well, she could live without him. More than once she had come close to quitting. But she couldn't do that to Mrs Harcourt. She'd been with her too long, and Mrs Harcourt had been too good to her. Like the time Ada had had acute appendicitis. Mrs Harcourt had ridden in the ambulance with her, called her own doctor, visited, sent flowers.

She couldn't walk out on a lady like that. But when was Mrs Harcourt going to wake up?

Greg returned to an apartment filled with fresh flowers, a stack of new books and magazines, and new tapes for the stereo. All had been carefully selected by Carole to match his taste and give him pleasure. And she had rashly bought him a handsome new dressing gown at Countess Mara.

'Now, make the most of it!' Carole said gaily as she settled Greg in his room. 'Right now, you're king of the hill. Enjoy! Because you're going to be back on your feet in no time.'

'Maybe,' said Greg dourly. 'I hope Magowan and Greene know what they're talking about.'

'Greg! Of course they do.'

'I forgot you invented optimism. Well, we'll see.' He shut his eyes.

Carole felt hurt and deflated. She had knocked herself out to be cheerful for Greg's sake. But tomorrow she must face the frightening fact that she was out of a job. And she must hide that fact from Greg. A man who had come so close to dying was in no shape to be told the breadwinner was out on her fanny. Tomorrow Carole was going to leave the apartment at the usual time. As far as Greg and Ada would know, she was going to the office as usual. Actually, she was going to the office of a casting agent who had offered her the use of a desk and phone. Well, she thought cynically, I've given him plenty of business. And when I connect, he knows I'll give him plenty more. I don't have to fall on my face with gratitude.

She had arranged with the office manager of her ex-agency, a woman whose job was safely outside the orbit of internal politics, to have all her calls switched to her ex-secretary. Betty would take her calls and relay them immediately. That would prevent Greg from being told 'Carole Harcourt is no longer with us.' And to ward of Greg's calls to the agency, Carole could call the apartment at regular intervals, which would look natural enough, under the circumstances.

But now, as she left Greg's room, she felt coldly alone. She went into the living room and sat down. Scary to be there in the middle of a weekday. Damn it, she admitted to herself. I want a shoulder to bawl on.

It was normal for a wife bounced out of her job to run to her husband. Under other circumstances, a husband would be bringing her flowers, building her ego, swearing this was the best thing that had ever happened, because she was bound to get an even *better* job.

Aching for a supporter, a defender, somebody on her side, Carole put her head down and cried, her shoulders shaking helplessly. It released the tension. But as soon as it was over, she was mad at herself for indulging in tears. *Who do you think you are, the Poor Little Match Girl? One of the 100 Neediest Cases? You've always made it. You'll make it again. Get with it.*

She got up and crossed to the desk. Then she made a list of her contacts in the advertising workd, in descending order of importance.

21

Just as her brother Jim had predicted, Susan Marston
rushed to New York, cashed in her CD's, and fled to the
West Coast.

She'd had a vague idea of joining a friend in Los
Angeles, but the friend turned out to be in Mexico. Susan
took a room in a motel, rented a car, and wandered
aimlessly around for a week. She decided she hated
California, the body worship and bean-sprout sandwiches
and the crazy speeds on the Freeway, and she was
frightened to discover that she had spent over a thousand
dollars of the three thousand she had brought in travelers'
checks.

So she flew back to New York, not intending to stay in
Manhattan but knowing the West Coast was definitely
not the answer. The man next to her tried to pick her up.
He was everything that turned Susan off. Too good-
looking, too expensively dressed. The new young fast-
track, bi-coastal type. She feigned sleep. 'An ice baby,
right?' murmured the man insolently. 'Who needs it?'

Behind closed eyes, Susan surrendered to what she
now considered her permanent *down*. A built-in ache, a
gnawing. Like that boy with the fox, or was it a wolf?
What she wanted was out of her reach, like the brass ring
on the merry-go-round. Unattainable, at least for her.
She thought of Zack. But already Zack was becoming
less of a reality, more of a symbol. Symbol of the forever-
not-for-you.

Why don't I just knock it off? Give it up? Forget love,

whatever it is, and . . . and just exist. On my own. See if I can.

Susan spent less than a week in New York. She stayed in the apartment she had shared with roommates. Luckily one was on vacation. She could have stayed, she knew, in Mingo Darcy's townhouse or with Mr and Mrs Paul Reston – both cushy places. And they would have fallen all over her, for her mother's sake. But she didn't want anything for her *mother's* sake. Anyway, she'd be moving on as fast as possible.

From an ad in the *Village Voice*, she bought an old Volkswagen bug from a man on West Twelfth Street. To do so, she endorsed another eight hundred dollars in travelers' checks. By the time she'd taken care of registration and insurance, it was late in the day. But she was too restless to spend another night in the city. She could wait until nine o'clock or so, when traffic had thinned, and then take off. . . for somewhere. Maybe drive all night. See where she landed.

She drove north, and then, on impulse, turned west into New York State. She didn't know a thing about upstate, but she had the impression it was quiet and absolutely nothing like Manhattan or L.A.

At one in the morning, Susan began to recognize signs of trouble with the car. It seemed to be losing power. She calculated she was about twenty-five miles from Ithaca, now her destination for the night. She was too drowsy to drive much farther anyway.

Luckily she was near an exit. She left the highway, crept along a side road, and turned into what seemed to be the main street of a small town. She just managed to make it to the curb when the bug stopped entirely.

Susan had a strong impulse to put her head on the steering wheel and howl, but she resisted it. She looked around. All the houses were dark, but down the street she could see a blue spruce faintly lighted by the glow from a window behind it. She walked to that house, a simple white clapboard, tall and skinny, and dark in front. She hesitated to knock. She visualized a taciturn old man more than annoyed at being awakened at this hour. Well, tough. I have no choice.

She knocked twice. Nothing happened for a full two minutes. Then she heard rapid footsteps and the door opened on a dark young man, naked to the waist and wearing jeans. Susan had been so braced for a cantankerous upstater that for a few seconds she only stared in surprise.

'Yeah?' said the young man.

'I'm really sorry to disturb you – I know it's very late – but my car is stuck. Could I possibly use your telephone?'

'Yeah. Come in.' He stepped aside and Susan entered a small hall with a steep staircase rising directly in front of the door.

'Phone's at the end of the hall. Under the staircase.'

'And could you tell me the name of the nearest garage?'

'Garage? At this hour? For gas, maybe, but not for service. Look, if you're not going too far, I could take you. But you'll have to wait awhile. I'm busy right now . . .'

Just then a strange sound came from the back of the house – part squeal, part squeak. 'Sit down,' said the young man, and sprinted from the room.

Susan sat in a rocker and looked around. Even though the young man was not what she had expected, the room was. Polished bare floor, braid rug, white curtains – a miscellany of modest old furniture. New England neat, New England homey. Upstate seemed to have a Yankee flavor. The only incongruous note was a pair of speakers, one placed at either end of the painted white bookshelves. Quite a lot of books.

There was a short sharp yelp from the back of the house, and more squeals. What in hell is going on? she thought. He said he was busy. Weird.

And he didn't fit in here. He looked Latin. Spanish, maybe? Italian? She wondered how many people were sleeping upstairs. She would give a lot to be sleeping herself. She was exhausted.

The young man came back into the room, grinning. 'That's about it,' he said. 'Five. Puppies. My dog just had five puppies.'

'Oh! Good!' said Susan inanely.

'Come on. I'll show you.'

But at the door of the kitchen, he suddenly stopped.

'You're not squeamish, are you?'

'Not really.'

He nodded and beckoned her to follow.

Lying on a blanket in a corner, a nondescript black-and-white dog lay licking a mass of wiggling, wet, surprisingly noisy small creatures. She saw what he meant about squeamishness. It was rather messy. But the dog was doing her best to clean them up. For a second she felt sick, but she conquered it.

The young man saw her expression. 'It's only natural,' he said, as if rebuking her.

He squatted down beside the dog and gently stroked her head. 'Nice going, Mabel. A good night's work.' The dog gave one tired thump of her tail and then went on with her job.

The young man rose and took a pan of milk from the stove. He poured it in a bowl and set it near the dog's head, so that she could easily drink without changing her position. The dog lapped thirstily, then sighed and closed her eyes.

'Get some sleep, Mabel,' said the young man. 'They'll all be here in the morning.' He nodded to Susan, and waited until she had gone through the door before switching off the light.

In the living room he said, 'Just a minute, while I put on a shirt. Where do you want to go?'

'Well, you see, I drove up from the city, just sort of . . . sightseeing. I thought I'd spend the night in Ithaca.'

'You mean you're not going anywhere in particular? Nobody's expecting you? Just Ithaca, period?'

'Sort of. You see, I – '

'Look,' said the young man. 'Ithaca's about twenty-two miles from here. Then you'd have to get back here tomorrow, for your car. You know what would make sense? It would make sense if you just sacked out upstairs. There's a spare room. Get some sleep. Then tomorrow you can call a garage.'

She hesitated. He looked impatient.

'It's either sleep here or out in your car. Right?'

'Right. Thank you. I'll stay, if it's okay. But will I be disturbing anybody?'

'There's nobody here but me and you won't disturb *me*. Come on.' He gestured toward the stairs and waited for her to precede him.

Upstairs, he opened the door of a small bedroom, switched on a lamp, and opened a window. 'Bathroom's down the hall and around the corner.'

'Thanks a lot,' said Susan. 'My name's Susan Marston.'

'Bob Giordano. Good night.'

Susan waited until she heard Bob Giordano leave the bathroom and then the closing of a door before she tiptoed down the hall, found the bathroom, and tiptoed back. She intended just to lie down on top of the bed in her clothes, but at the last minute she decided that was silly. She'd feel so crummy in the morning. Swiftly she peeled off her clothes, slipped between the clean white sheets, and was soon asleep.

Bright sunlight awakened her. It took her only seconds to remember where she was. From the brightness of the light, it must be well past nine, and she had thought she would be up at six.

She must have been really bushed. She went to the window. She could see the house next door, somebody's zinnias, part of the street, and, in the distance, a white church steeple. A calendar picture, she thought, but nice.

She dressed and wondered whether to strip the bed. In the end, she decided to remake it, taking care to square the corners as precisely as she found them.

At the bottom of the stairs she found a note.

'Sarah,' it began. Well, close enough. At least it began with an S. 'Here are the numbers of two garages. The first has the better mechanic, but he works alone and may not be able to come right away. The second is bigger, but farther away.

'Make yourself at home. Food in the kitchen. Help yourself.

'Try not to startle Mabel. She's not used to visitors. If you say her name a couple of times, she'll be okay. If her bowl is empty, please fill it.

'Thanks. Good luck. Bob G.,

The first garage was tied up for the next two days. The second said, 'That's pretty far. Couldn't make it to way out there before late afternoon. The tow truck's out right now.'

'But it's only a VW bug,' said Susan desperately. 'Couldn't you tow it with just an ordinary car? I'm stranded here.'

'Only got so many hands, lady. Do you want me to come or not? When I can?'

'Yes, please come. When you can.'

255

She went to the kitchen. The mother dog raised her head in alarm. 'Hello, Mabel. It's okay, Mabel.' She entered the kitchen slowly, so as not to frighten the dog. She found coffee on the stove, and a cup in the cupboard. She was very hungry, but she hesitated to open the refrigerator. Still, the note had said, 'Help yourself.' Finally, she did open the refrigerator, telling herself she would leave money for the food, with a note of thanks. She hoped he wouldn't be insulted.

She found eggs, scrambled them in the same pan Bob Giordano had evidently used, and made some toast. Then she washed and dried everything, including the pan.

She knelt down beside the dog, who was looking at her warily, and stroked her head until she relaxed. The puppies, who had all been sleeping peacefully, awoke in unison. Susan watched their blind, noisy scramble for the nipples. No problems for you, Mabel, are there? You're just fulfilling your destiny, right? How do you *manage* that?

By three o'clock, the tow truck hadn't shown up. Susan called the garage again. The man said they couldn't make it until five, maybe six. Susan began to panic. She couldn't just stay here, trapped in a stranger's house. Maybe she should just abandon the car, get a ride to a bus stop, go back to New York? But then what? Should she call Jim to come and get her? That would mean turning up at the farm for the second time. Dependent again. On her mother. Her self-sufficient mother, so cool *nothing* threw her. Damned if I will, she thought. If I did that, it would prove I can't fight my way out of a paper bag.

The tow truck and Bob Giordano arrived simultaneously. 'Look, I'm sorry,' said Susan. 'I waited all day.'

'No sweat,' said Bob Giordano. 'How are the puppies?' He headed straight into the house.

The garage man was shaking his head. 'Lady, didn't you put oil in this car? You've been running without oil.'

'Oil? But I only bought the car a couple of days ago. Isn't there oil in a car when you buy it?'

'Not this time, looks like. You ran dry and your engine seized.'

'Seized? What does that mean?'

'It means your engine's shot. Kaput. You need a new engine.'

'How long does that take? And how much does it cost?'

'Depends on how long it takes us to find a rebuilt engine. If we're lucky, maybe a couple of days.'

'And how much does it cost?'

'Depends. I'd say six hundred. At least.'

'Six *hundred*!'

Bob Giordano came out of the house. 'What's the story?'

'She was running without oil. Engine's shot.'

'Look,' said Susan. 'Is there a motel anywhere near your garage? Could you give me a ride to it?'

'Against the rules to carry a passenger.'

'I'll give you a ride,' said Bob Giordano.

'You will?'

'Make up your mind, lady,' the man said impatiently. 'I'm on overtime already.'

'Go ahead, take the car,' said Bob Girodano, making up Susan's mind for her. The garage man began to get out his cables. 'But let's eat first,' Bob said to Susan.

In the kitchen, she sat down. 'Listen, I know I'm putting you to a lot of trouble.'

'It's okay.'

'But I mean, taking in a total stranger. Not many people would . . .'

'Oh, I've got a crazy kid sister,' said Bob Giordano, as

if that explained everything. He was deftly slicing two beautiful purple eggplants.

Susan flushed. Did she come across as that unput-together?

'How old is your sister?'

'Seventeen.'

Susan flushed even more. He was telling her she was acting like a teenager. 'Oh. Well, can't I help with dinner?'

'Thought you'd never ask. Wash some salad stuff, will you. And be sure to get it good and dry. There's a spinner hanging over there.'

They ate in a corner of the kitchen. He poured two glasses of wine, without asking Susan whether she wanted any.

'Why, you're a good cook,' said Susan. 'The eggplant is great, so is the salad.'

'I'm not a Wop for nothing,' grinned Bob Giordano.

'Did you grow up around here?'

'Brooklyn.'

'Brooklyn!'

'Sure. Like in Toity-Toid. And Long-Guyland. Don't tell me you didn't notice?'

She had, just a little.

'I see you did. Well, you know what they say: "You can take the boy out of Brooklyn . . ." So how did I wind up here, right?'

'I was wondering.'

'I had an aunt who married a man from here. She left me this house. I came up to sell it. Then I decided I liked it here. So I stayed.'

So I stayed, thought Susan. He has no problem making decisions. But what would he do if he knew what he wanted and couldn't get it? She had the feeling he *would* get it, whatever it was.

Bob Giordano rose. 'I'll take Mabel out,' he said.

'I'll wash the dishes.'

'Good.' He put the leash on Mabel and left.

Maybe he'll offer to let me stay here until the car's fixed, she thought. 'But that's crazy. I'm a stranger. Why should he?

He didn't. When he came back he said, 'Be right with you. Have to make a quick phone call.'

She couldn't help hearing. 'Hi. Listen, I'm going to be a little late. I've got to give someone a ride. Broken-down car. I'll be there as soon as I can.'

Of course, she thought. He's got a date.

The motel was fifteen miles away. But he drove fast and they got there in minutes, or so it seemed to Susan. He waited to make sure there was a vacancy; then he said, 'Listen, you didn't ask, but if I were you and your car isn't ready tomorrow, I'd call my family, or somebody.'

'Right. Look, I don't know how to thank you.'

'No problem,' said Bob Giordano. 'Good luck. And don't forget to put oil in the car.' He waved, and was gone.

The next afternoon Susan sat in the motel room, staring at TV without seeing it. Should she walk to the diner for yet another cup of coffee? She had come back from the last one only an hour ago. She was going out of her mind from being cooped up. The garage had gotten hold of another engine, but it wouldn't be installed until tomorrow. No, they couldn't say what time.

Could she stand another twenty-four hours, even more? She went over her alternatives again. Get a taxi somehow, no matter what it cost, and get to a New York bus. No. Call the farm. No, Then decide what you're going to do when you *do* get the car, dummy! Right. Find a little town, maybe like the one she'd just been in. Rent a room in somebody's house – motel prices were out of sight. There must be a widow or a retired couple with a room to rent? Then a job. Not even a job – work. Clerking in a supermarket, anything. Just to prove she, Susan Marston, could survive on her own, without needing *anybody*. Then, if she got her head together – *when* she got her head together, she'd figure out how to get through this big problem called life.

There was a knock on the door. 'Telephone for you, Miss. At the front desk.' It had to be the garage. Was the car fixed already or had something else gone wrong with it?

'This is Bob,' said the voice. 'Giordano. Is your car ready?'

'Maybe tomorrow, they said.'

'Good. I mean, too bad. But maybe you could do me a favor.'

'Sure.'

'Something crazy has happened. I'm in the hospital.'

'The hospital! What happened?'

'Broken leg. Guy backed a van into a ladder. I was on the ladder.'

'That's *terrible*. I'm sorry.'

'Not so terrible. Doc says I'll be hopping around on crutches in a week, maybe. But listen. You're in no special rush, right?'

'That's right.'

'So would you consider staying at my place for a while?'

'To take care of Mabel and the pups, you mean? Sure.'

'Great. I'll have a friend of mine pick you up and take you back. Tom Gordon. He's here with me now. He'll give you the scoop.'

'Sure,' said Susan. 'Glad to.'

When she opened the door of Bob's house, with the key he had sent via his friend, Susan had a weird sense of coming home. After the blank walls of the motel room, she was ridiculously glad to see Bob Giordano's plain little house again, and Mabel and the pups.

She slept that night in the same prim little room. Drifting off, she was dreamily conscious that something had stopped hurting. For the short immediate future, at least, she knew what she was doing. She was needed. She fell into a deep, relaxed sleep.

22

As Roberta Marston had foreseen, Mary Blair did not call her. For the reason Roberta had also foreseen: embarrassment at having poured out her most private feelings to a woman she hardly knew.

But Roberta had planted an idea that Mary could not get out of her mind, the idea of getting a job. Could I? she wondered. Other women do. Roberta did. But Roberta seems so self-assured, so at ease with people, and I never see anybody but the children. No wonder I'm shy – at the age of forty. I couldn't believe it when Roberta said she was over forty. But she's so marvelous looking. Anyone would look at her twice. Imagine a husband ignoring *her*.

Mary went into her daughter Midge's room, the only room in the house with a full-length mirror. She forced herself to face her image. Dowdy. Colorless. Nothing. She was slim, but that was about all. Still it was a miracle, after four children. Genetic good luck that she'd never gained weight. As for the rest! Dark hair, no particular style. It grew the way it wanted; when it got too long, she lopped off the ends. Changeable eyes – blue, but sometimes green. Pretty good skin, but pale.

I'm so depressed-looking I must be depressing to look *at*. Who would want to hire me? *I* wouldn't! I can't even think about a job until I look different. But how?

Mary gazed hopelessly at the mirror, and her image looked hopelessly back. She had no instinct for clothes, and she knew it. As for makeup, she'd hardly ever even worn lipstick since college.

Staring at herself in the mirror, Mary Blair felt a flicker of anger. You're a *mess* – and you just take it. You're miserable – and you accept it. Why don't you fight back? Adapt or perish, isn't that what you learned in Anthropology I? Survival.

The flicker of anger grew to a flame. Mary felt rage at her life – at herself. You're a coward. You're married to a man who's married to his work. You live an empty monotonous life, and you *accept* it. Why? You've got a brain. You've got a will. Why don't you use them? Or is *this* good enough for you?

Shaken by the strength of her feelings. Mary was surprised to see a different image in the mirror. There was a light in her eye, a lift to her head. She looked down at her hands, to see if the mirror was lying. Yes, her hands were clenched. Fists, almost.

Maybe I've got some fight in me after all. Anyway, I've certainly got nothing to *lose*.

That evening she called Roberta. Listening to the ringing sound, she urgently hoped Roberta was home. Later she might lose her nerve. She had a strong now-or-never feeling.

Roberta did answer.

'Roberta? This is Mary Blair.'

'Mary! How nice to hear from you.'

'I've been thinking about what you said, about getting a job . . .'

'You have! Good!'

'But first I'd like to do something about my . . . my looks, what to wear. I was wondering. Could you possibly spare the time to give me some tips? You look so wonderful.'

'Why, thank you. Yes, of course. I'd love to, Mary. When would you . . . oh, listen,' Roberta broke off. 'I just thought of something. We're in luck! A friend of

mine is coming to spend Saturday night with me. Mingo
Darcy. She knows more about clothes than anybody.
She's the editor of *Cachet*. Come for lunch Sunday, and
we'll pick her brains.'

'The editor of *Cachet*! Oh, I couldn't. I didn't mean *that*
kind of look – that's so *chic*. Besides, I'd be intruding.'

'Nonsense! I'll expect you at one on Sunday . . . And
relax! Believe it or not, Mingo's as comfortable as an old
shoe.'

Mary hung up half-scared and all thrilled. An old shoe!
Ridiculous. But imagine the editor of *Cachet* personally
telling her how to dress. She hoped she wouldn't have a
fit of shyness and beg off at the last moment. No you
don't, she caught herself. None of that.

At first, Mary was intimidated by Mingo Darcy's aura of
glamour. As Mingo herself would put it, she did 'reek
chic.' But as Roberta had promised, Mingo's direct natural manner and breezy speech put Mary at ease.

Covertly, she studied Mingo. Her face, with its beaky
nose and scraped back hair, was what many people would
call homely, Mary thought with surprise. And she was
wearing a simple shirt, pants, and narrow leather pumps.
Yet you wanted to look at her. Why? A million women
wore pants and shirts and pumps. What was the difference? It must be the perfect fit, thought Mary, and the
way she wears them, the way she moves and holds her
head. And the look of perfect grooming – the gleam of
her hair, her flawless skin, her beautifully manicured
hands. Mary had an impulse to hide her own hands. She
simply clipped her nails, and let it go at that.

After lunch, Roberta said, 'Mingo, Mary has decided
to tackle the job market. But first she wants to change
her image a bit. I promised her the benefit of your
expertise.'

Mary felt sure Roberta had briefed Mingo ahead of time. What had she said? Had she described Mary as a down-trodden housewife, miserable with her lot? Mary didn't care. In any case, she was confident that whatever Roberta had said, she had said sympathetically.

'Hm,' said Mingo, narrowing her eyes and looking at Mary speculatively. 'I'll tell you one thing off the top, Mary. You don't have to be chic. Because you can be pretty. Much, much better, you lucky thing. And much less work.'

Mary glowed. Pretty!

For the next hour, Mingo gave Mary a crash course in clothes, colors, and makeup. She made rapid little sketches, to illustrate the silhouettes right for Mary. She dashed upstairs and brought down her own makeup kit, to demonstrate. 'Of course these colors are not right for you. You want blue tints, lipstick with a blueish cast, not bright but clear – brown mascara, not black. And you'd be a *fool* not to play up that green in your eyes – why, people choose contact lenses to get that shade!'

She wound up by saying, 'Hair first, of course. But you need someone really good for the first cut. Tell you what, do you ever get to New York?'

'No, but I could.'

'Let me make an appointment for you. Gustave, I think. Or Mr Richard. Neither one takes new people, but I can fix it. I'll call you.'

Mary rode home on a cloud of hope. Gustave. Even she had heard of Gustave. He probably charged a king's ransom. Where would she get the money? From the food money. John was due to give her the month's food budget tomorrow. She'd spend it first and tell him later. She'd point out that it was *nothing* compared to the *years* of weekly beauty salon visits most women enjoyed. She'd tell him to replace the food money or the kids wouldn't eat.

On Wednesday evening Mary's youngest answered the phone. 'Mother, it's for you. Lady with a funny voice,' he stage-whispered.

Mingo's clipped, upper-echelon tones came over the wire. 'Mary? Mingo Darcy. I was just going to call you about your booking with Gustave, but something else has come up. Tell me, are you photogenic?'

Photogenic? 'I've been told I am.' Mary was bewildered, but photos always did seem to flatter her.

'Good. Then maybe you could do me a favor. A friend of mine, Ginny Morrow, is Beauty Editor of *Home Woman*. She's doing a makeover feature. A before-and-after on real people, not models. One of her subjects has dropped out at the last moment. She called in a tizzy to see if I could think of an honest-to-goodness homemaker who could do it. Of course I thought of you.'

'Me? But what . . .'

'When will I learn to begin at the beginning?' Mingo laughed. 'I want to know if you will pose for your photograph, and then pose again after a new hairdo and makeup?'

Pose for a magazine? She must be dreaming. 'I'd be thrilled. Of *course*. But I'm not sure. I've never – I mean, what would I have to *do*?'

'Nothing. Just let yourself be done *unto*. And Mary, the hairdresser is Gustave. I had already lined him up for you. But this is better, because of course it's a freebie – free, I mean. And Ron Leco is one of the best makeup men in the business. You'll come home with some loot too – all the cosmetics they choose for you, on the house. Will you do it?'

'Oh, *Mingo*! Will I! I'd be thrilled.'

'Good. It's next Tuesday. Ten in the morning. At Mark

Drew's studio.' Mingo gave an address in the East Sixties. 'Just ask for Ginny Morrow at the desk.'

'Will you be there?'

'Afraid not. I'll be on the West Coast. No rest for the weary. And, Mary, just wear a skirt and top. Or jeans.'

'Jeans!'

'That's what lots of models wear. I'm so glad you can make it, Mary. I know Ginny will be delighted with you.'

Mary had an impulse to turn and run. The very look of the small elegant nameplate was intimidating. Just Mark Drew engraved on copper. She should never have agreed to come. They would never want to photograph her, not once they saw her. And everyone inside would be as spectacular as Mingo, but probably not as friendly. Still, she had promised. She pressed the bell with a finger which trembled. Immediately there was a buzz, and she pushed open the door.

She stepped into the white marble reception hall of a converted townhouse, green with tall potted trees and throbbing with rock music. The young woman at the desk cradled a phone on her shoulder as she flipped through a Rolodex with one hand and furiously scribbled with the other.

She's got that New York look too, thought Mary.

The girl hung up and said, 'Yes?'

'I'm Mary Blair. I'm to see Miss Morrow.'

The girl pushed buttons, said into the intercom, 'Your ten o'clock is here,' and hung up.

'She'll be right down.'

Ginny Morrow rushed down the stairs. 'So good of you to rescue us, Mrs Blair,' she said and rapidly led Mary upstairs. She pushed open the door to a huge room, empty except for a thicket of cameras and lighting equipment and a tangle of electrical cables snaking across the floor.

'Do watch the cables, Mrs Blair. Don't trip,' said Miss Morrow. 'Mark! Our brunette is here.'

A man in a rather mangy sweatshirt, running pants, and Nikes approached. 'Hi, hon. Let's take a look at you.'

To Mary the next few hours were like an exciting, speeded-up movie. People rushed in and out of the studio: young men in jeans and beards, others in business suits, young women in smart summer dresses or T-shirts and pants. People dashed around with clipboards and boxes of props – belts, costume jewelry, scarves. A boy pried open cartons with Germaine Monteil or Estee Lauder stamped on them. A girl with a tray offered Mary coffee, Danish, or Coke. Refreshment was in constant circulation, white styrofoam cups and Tab cans were parked everywhere.

An assistant took Mary into a dressing room, one of a line of cubicles against a wall. In passing Mary glimpsed a very thin girl in a bra and bikini underpants. 'That's Mingo Darcy's favorite model,' whispered the assistant. Mary was amazed. The girl looked gaunt, and her shoulder blades stuck out.

Then there was her surprise at Gustave. When Ginny Morrow introduced him, Mary took him for an executive. A hairdresser? He looked like a well-tailored broker, right down to the attaché case.

'Oh, goody,' said Gustave, running his fingers through Mary's hair. 'Virgin.'

'He means you've never had it stripped or tinted,' explained the beauty editor.

'Sweetie,' said Gustave to Mary. 'You have very good hair, great body, but much too much of it – really *much* too much. It's gotta *go*.'

Ginny Morrow and Gustave circled Mary, looking at

her from all angles, quite impersonally, as if she were an inanimate object.

'You see,' said Gustave, flipping his comb through Mary's hair, 'there's this tilt to her eyes. I want to bring that out. And look' – he grabbed all of Mary's hair and held it high abover her head – 'look at the line of her nose. It's classic. I want to play that up.'

'Now, Gussie,' said Ginny Morrow, 'nothing too far out. Restrain yourself. This isn't one of Mingo's covers, remember. This is *Home Woman*. I want it attractive, but middle of the road.'

'Right. Well, look. I think lifted here, clinging *there*, with just a whisper of bang. That's the way *I* see it, Ginny.'

'Good.' Ginny Morrow looked at her watch. 'Ron is scheduled for her makeup in fifty minutes. Let's go.'

As Gustave's scissors snipped, Mary watched her own face take shape. Skillfully Gustave revealed the curve from ear to chin, framed her eyes so that the tilt was pronounced, made it clear that her nose traced a pure line from bridge to tip.

Gustave saw the expression in Mary's eyes. 'Like it, sweetie?' he asked her reflection in the mirror.

'Oh, *yes*,' said Mary humbly. 'I – I can't believe it.'

Gustave laughed, secure in his talent. He stepped back and looked at her critically from all angles. 'Yes, that's it. Definitely patrician, you know, but a hint of *gamine*.'

By the time Ron Leco began her makeup, Mary had lost some of her self-consciousness to fascination with the people around her. How hard everybody worked. How intent they all were on a common objective: Ginny Morrow's beauty feature. She envied everyone, down to the girl with the coffee tray. She thought of her life in Greenwillow. Another planet.

Ron Leco looked like a jockey or a member of a street

gang. He was wearing a green silk shirt, and his bald head was circled by carrot red curls. When he opened his mouth, he had a Cockney accent.

Like Gustave, he gave Mary a merciless scrutiny. He peered at her skin under a magnifying glass. 'Sensitive skin, 'aven't you, luv?' He asked her to raise her brows and suck in her cheeks. He smeared color from little pots onto the back of her wrist.

'Lot's of blue,' he murmured, 'with green in it.' He turned to his assistant. 'Bring me Numbers twelve, thirteen, and seventeen and the green undertoner.'

Ron Leco carefully protected Gustave's handiwork under a gauze headband. Then, working with a variety of brushes and palettes and little tubes, he defined her eyes, highlighted her cheekbones, ran a tiny white line down the center of her nose.

While he worked, he kept up a running commentary on what he was doing and why. Ginny Morrow's associate noted it all down. 'This is for the copywriter, Mrs Blair,' she explained to Mary, 'so she'll have all the facts for the story. And in the back of the book – that is, the back of the magazine – there will be a step-by-step instructions on how a woman can do this at home. We'll send you a Xerox of the copy, so you won't have to wait three months until the magazine comes out.'

'Thank you,' said Mary. 'But I'm sure I could never – '

'Yes, you *could*, luv,' Ron Leco insisted. 'Women make such a mistake. They think they must be experts, so they give up. But you only 'ave to be expert for *one* face – your *own*, luv. I'm laying this all out for you, exactly what to do. All you need is practice. There!' He gave a final fingertip smoothing to Mary's eyebrows, removed the headband, and gestured toward the mirror. ''Ave a look.'

A strikingly pretty woman looked back at Mary from

the glass. Delicate features, creamy skin, tip-tilted eyes of a turquoise Mary had not seen before, smoky lashes. In a way, the woman in the mirror was a stranger. In another way, she recognized the Mary who had been concealed for so long.

By the time she was back in the studio for the 'After' picture – the *point* of all this effort – Mary's heart was soaring. She felt as though she had been there forever, she felt like an old hand. And she very much wanted the photos to be good, for Mingo Darcy's sake, for Ginny Morrow's sake, for Gustave's and Ron Leco's sakes. I'll never open a magazine the same way again, she thought. How hard these people work for just one photo.

When Mark Drew, seeing her for the first time since her transformation, said 'Very nice,' she was able to believe him. And when he posed her under the lights and gave her instructions – 'Wet your lips . . . that's it . . . now smile . . . raise your eyes . . . fabulous. Once more . . . super . . . tilt your head . . .' – she was amazed at how relaxed she felt and how easily she followed his instructions.

Ginny Morrow seemed very pleased. Peering into the camera, she said, 'Mark, this *could* be our opening spread.'

Mark nodded, clicked a final shot. 'That's it. I've got it.'

As she walked down Park Avenue to her car, two men gave Mary second looks, and a woman, waiting for the light to change, openly sized her up. It was hard to get used to the attention. Am I really a woman people *look* at?

As she neared Greenwillow, Mary found herself more and more reluctant to go home. She was far too exhilarated to face another evening in an endless string of evenings with the kids.

She stopped at a phone booth and dialed her husband's office.

John's receptionist had to ask who was calling. She called so seldom, her voice was not recognized.

John came on the line, sounding hurried.

'What's wrong, Mary?'

'Nothing's wrong . . . but I have a sort of surprise for you. John, let's go out to dinner tonight, maybe that place on the river? I could meet you . . .'

'Out? Tonight? Impossible. My waiting room's jammed. I've got two patients coming after eight.'

'Could you switch their appointments?'

'Of course not. Mary, this isn't like you.'

'Just a thought, John.' She hung up.

But it *is* like me.

She sat motionless at the wheel of her car for a moment. Then she drove to the restaurant on the river. It was early for dining, and the place was still empty. When the waiter asked if she was meeting someone, she looked him in the eye and said no, she was alone.

She ordered a drink and lobster. She wasn't sure she had enough money to pay for it, but she didn't care.

When the check came, she asked the waiter to call the manager. She smiled at the manager and said: 'I'm Dr John Blair's wife, and I've done the silliest thing. I was in the city all day, and I didn't realize I was running so low on cash. May I sign, please, and will you send the bill to Dr Blair?'

The manager scrutinized her and decided she looked and talked like a doctor's wife. Spoiled, all of them, but good for the bill, certainly.

Mary drove home feeling she had crossed a line. She had not enjoyed dinner. She had hated sitting alone in a public place. But she had proved something to herself.

23

'Mom, isn't the head of that committee of yours Dr John Blair?'

'Yes, Jim. Why?'

'Well, guess what. He's my girl's father.'

'He is? She's Mary and John Blair's daughter? I had no idea.' Roberta didn't know why she was so surprised. After all, Greenwillow was a very small place.

'Midge says you know her mother, too. Wait 'til you meet Midge, Mom.'

'I'm eager to meet her, Jim. When will I?'

'The problem is she has a summer job and works six days a week. But maybe Sunday. Will you be home?'

'I'll *definitely* be home.' Roberta smiled fondly at her lovable son.

Now, on Sunday afternoon, Roberta put aside her book in the garden as Jim's car pulled in with a girl at his side.

'Mother, I'd like you to meet Midge Blair.'

'I'm so happy to meet you, Midge. Do sit down.' Lovely girl. This is how Mary must have looked at twenty. 'My goodness, you're the image of your mother. How *is* your mother?'

'She's great, Mrs Marston, thank you. She's job hunting. No luck so far, but she's trying. She joined a women's reentry group. They help women get into the job market, after years at home.'

'That's *wonderful*.' Roberta thought of the sobbing woman she had met in the Blairs' lane.

'She swears she owes it all to you, Mrs Marston. That

273

magazine feature, through that friend of yours. It gave Mother such a lift. She needed it, she's been stuck with us kids for so long.'

A devoted daughter, thought Roberta. Does Mary Blair great credit. Whereas Susan . . . there had been no word from Susan. It had been almost a month. Controlling the worry that was always lying in wait, Roberta had to force her attention back to the present moment.

'What wonderful trees and shrubs you have,' Midge was saying, looking across the sweep of lawn. 'Magnificent specimens.'

'Mom, I want you to know that's from the horse's mouth,' kidded Jim. 'Midge knows a good tree when she sees one. She's taking her degree in Botany.'

'Really? I'm impressed. I've never met a botanist. How did you come to choose that field?'

Midge laughed. 'I know it sounds weird, Mrs Marston, but I was taken to the Brooklyn Botanical Gardens when I was twelve – and that was it. I fell in love with plants, I guess.'

'But how do you apply botany – in a career, I mean?'

'I'm hoping to be a landscape architect. You see, to me, it's a terrific combination of science and art. The science is knowing how plants grow and where and why – you wouldn't *believe* Mother Nature. But the art part is creating beauty, using living materials. It's like painting and sculpturing with growing things.'

Midge broke off, embarrassed. 'Heavens, I'm afraid I'm being carried away.'

Both Roberta and Jim had been looking appreciatively at Midge's enthusiastic face.

'Hey, you're turning me on too,' said Jim. 'Tell us more!'

But Midge, afraid of talking about herself too much,

politely turned the conversation back to her hostess. 'How beautiful your fanlight is. Is that the original glass?'

A few minutes later, Jim said, 'Come on, Midge, I want to show you the view from the back forty. Come for a walk, Mother?'

Roberta had the good sense to refuse.

As she watched the two young people head toward the meadow, Jim reached out his hand to Midge, and Midge took it. Swinging their arms in unison, they disappeared from sight.

For the first time Roberta realized that when Jim left for law school, he would never, in a sense, be back. Once he launched his career, he would launch his own life . . . and marry . . . and leave.

A wave of longing for Zack hit Roberta so unexpectedly that she caught her breath.

Zack. She had never really resolved the issue of the ten years between them. She had never had the *chance* to think it through, because of Susan. Would she have married him, had the problem with Susan never arisen?

She still wasn't sure. Trying to balance her longing for Zack against her nagging sense that there were pitfalls in such a marriage, she wound up with the original question mark.

Anyway, what was the point? *She* had cut the bond between them. Zack had sworn he would be back, but would he? Any why should he? A man like Zack was bound to meet platoons of women who would love him without reservation, women his own age. Women without family complications. Women who were free.

Roberta felt a surge of jealousy, and a rush of prior rights. He's mine! He loved me first!

Then, beyond her control, her thoughts wrenched toward Susan. I don't know where my daughter is. I

don't know if she's safe. I shouldn't even be thinking of
Zack.

She knew it was irrational, but she felt she must make
a deal: I'll forget Zack, life, if you'll let me hear from my
daughter.

In Tokyo, Zack Owen was grateful for a Sunday alone.
Thank God he had managed to duck the Japanese invitation for today. He'd had enough of wining and dining.
Besides, he'd been in a pressure cooker of meetings,
tours of outlying plants, negotiations, reports to the home
office. He needed to unwind, and he wanted time to
think about the overriding concern of his life – the
obstacle between him and the woman he loved.

Downstairs he directed his driver to take him to Kak-
amura. As good a place as any to mark time, Zack
figured, a beauty spot with shrines and temples. But in
the garden of Zuisen-ji, with a Zen temple on a tranquil
hillside and a glimpse of the sea below, he barely saw the
beauty. Beyond thinking 'Roberta would appreciate this,'
he paced the winding paths unseeingly.

Not a day had gone by that he had not fought the
impulse to call her. But the chances were two out of
three that one of the kids, Susan or Jim, would pick up
the phone, leaving Roberta with explanations to make.

Even so, he had twice put through calls to her at the
shop. The first time the damned circuits were busy. The
second time he forced himself to cancel. Too rough on
her. If the situation with Susan was as bad as it had been,
hearing his voice would cause Roberta fresh pain. He felt
sure if the situation with Susan *had* resolved itself,
Roberta would have called or written.

A man who had sustained the brutal loss of his wife
and child, Zack Owen was a fatalist. He believed that
when irresistible forces – the fates, if you will – altered

events, to fight them was to spin your wheels. Only when the altered reality was clear could you exert *your* force to get what you wanted. But your timing had to be right.

It was simple, really. He and Roberta loved each other, they belonged together, they would be together. He was convinced of that. But sometimes you had to outwait circumstances, so he would. He'd bide his time, until he could reach her with the discretion the situation demanded. Somehow he'd know when the moment was right.

Meantime, that phony letter he had written Roberta – the tenant-landlady letter – had come true. He would not be going back to New Jersey, at least not immediately. Randall himself had called. They wanted him in Dallas. A possible acquisition, they wanted his input. If it looks promising, Randall said, be prepared to stick around awhile. That could mean weeks, even months. Still, it would sure as hell be easier to get to Roberta from Dallas than from Tokyo.

Zack took a last look at the temple and then headed down the steps to the waiting car. In two weeks I'll be on the same continent with her.

'So after you graduated from Brooklyn College, then what?'

'I got a job with Chase Manhattan. The pits.' Bob Giordano shifted the position of his plaster cast on the sofa.

'So you simply decided to be a carpenter, and live here?' Susan couldn't believe it was that easy.

'Not exactly. First I got the house, then I decided to stay awhile and look over the territory. I took the first job I could get, helper to an old German carpenter – a real nitpicker. Everything had to be perfect. I liked it, he had real pride in workmanship. Everything solid – and

277

accurate. When he retired, I just kept going on my own. Not that I'm half as good as he was – that takes years.'

'And that's it? You've found your thing?'

'What I really want to do is design and make furniture. There's a guy in Massachusetts who makes Shaker reproductions. Beautiful stuff – an art form. My partner and I have a little workshop. We work on cabinetry between paying jobs.'

'Lucky you, doing what you like to do.'

'You don't?'

Susan shrugged. 'I worked at NBC. Beginners' job – news department. I thought the greatest thing you could be was a newscaster. I even would have settled for weather person.'

'What happened?'

'My father died, suddenly, and my mother gave up our apartment . . . suddenly. She moved to the country.' She trailed off.

'And?'

'I don't know. Everything went flat. Dull. Null.'

'I get it. But you have to snap out of it, right?'

'Sure.' Susan jumped up. She didn't want to talk about this. Too close to the bone. 'I'd better get these dishes done.' She picked up the tray on which she had served Bob his dinner. 'Hey! Not bad!' he had said of the first meal she'd served him, the day he came home from the hospital. She had flushed with pleasure. Lucky that cooking was something she still got a kick out of.

'But listen,' Bob had protested. 'I don't want you to *wait* on me. It was just the problem of taking Mabel out . . .'

'Don't be silly,' Susan said. 'I'm living in your house. I owe you. *Quid pro quo*.' They had a deal: Susan would stay until Bob's cast came off.

Cleaning up the kitchen, she was glad she had cut off

the conversation about herself and her life. Why probe the sore spots? Things were okay, for now. Even better than okay, actually. It was kind of weird, but kind of nice, to share everyday stuff with someone else, without any kind of *personal* intensity. Someone different enough from yourself to be interesting but someone in whom you could discover some likenesses.

Last Sunday they had laughed when they had simultaneously reached for the *Times* crossword. And he liked music. He had a lot of Mozart and Puccini, as well as a lot of rock. He said his father was a opera buff, used to buy standing room at the old Met at Thirty-ninth Street. His father still missed all that gilt and red velvet, Bob said. Lincoln Center didn't do it for him.

Susan hung up the dish towel – no dishwasher – and snapped on Mabel's leash for her bedtime walk. There had been a bad moment, when Bob had asked her to put on *Don Giovanni*. She'd been transported back to the barn, had heard a stranger whistle – a stranger who turned out to be Zack. Zack? He didn't seem real anymore. More a mirage than a man. Some kind of never-never land symbol of happily-ever-after. There is no such thing, of course. She must have been crazy. Meantime, she was feeling no pain. She cleaned the house, ran errands, shopped for food – not forgetting Bob's Oreos, a habit he said he couldn't kick – and stayed close behind him, ready to grab, as he negotiated the stairs on his crutches.

As she brought Mabel in through the back door, the place felt kind of homey. In the living room she asked Bob, 'Want to see the ten o'clock news?'

'No thanks, not unless you do.'

'Not especially.' Susan picked up her book.

'Listen,' said Bob, 'I've been thinking – about what

you told me . . . about losing your father. How is your mother doing?'

'Doing? All right, I guess. My brother's with her.'

'But doesn't she *need* you?'

'What do you mean?'

'What do I *mean*?' His look said *I can't believe this*. 'I mean at a time like this – she's a *widow*, isn't she? It must be hard on her . . .'

'My mother is very self-sufficient.'

'You probably mean she has guts. But even so, what does she think of your wandering around like this?'

'I don't know. She doesn't know where I am.'

'You just took off without telling her? You haven't been in touch with her? Your *mother*?' Bob's Italian face was outraged.

'I'm twenty-three. I'm not accountable.'

'But don't you care that your mother is sick with worry? She must be. *Wow*.'

Susan said nothing.

'Sorry. None of my business. I got carried away. It's just that when I think of *my* mother . . . well, forget it. Will you give me a hand up the stairs?'

Susan lay in bed, feeling the hot sting of rebuff. Bob had looked so *disapproving* – so *condemning* – as if she were some sort of inhuman specimen. You didn't call your *mother* – your MOTHER – your *MOTHER*? You pull wings off *flies*? *Mamma mia*!

But the truth was, she hadn't thought about her mother. It wasn't that she'd *tried* to hurt her mother – had she? – but she'd hurt so much herself, she hadn't thought of anyone else. Besides, in her experience, grownups helped *you*. You didn't help *them*.

But *you're* supposed to be grownup, Susan. As you just told Bob, you're twenty-three. He thinks you're a *shit*.

Am I a shit? Shame spread through Susan like a stain. I am. I am a shit. Of course Mother's worried to death – and Jim is too. I'm a monster. I thought Mother was so cold and indifferent after Daddy's death, but maybe it was her way of coping. Bob said she must have guts. I never *thought* of that . . .

Susan got up, put on a robe and slippers, and tiptoed downstairs. She hated to call collect, but it was not her phone.

Roberta's hand shook as she picked up the phone. She felt fear every time it rang nowadays, and at this hour . . . 'Hello?'

'Will you accept a collect call from Susan Marston?'

'Yes, yes, of course . . .' Roberta gripped the receiver. 'Mother . . .'

'Susan! Oh, *Susan*, where are you? Are you all right?'

'Mother. I'm fine. I'm in upstate New York. I'm okay . . .'

Roberta burst into tears. The relief was so great it overwhelmed her. She sobbed helplessly, while Susan's voice came remotely through the phone. 'Mother, Mother, it's okay, don't cry . . .'

Roberta reached for a Kleenex and mopped her eyes. 'Oh, Susan, I'm so *relieved* . . .' Her voice was shaky. 'You can't know . . .'

'I guess I can't, Mother.' Susan's own voice sounded tearful. 'I'm so *sorry* to have put you through this . . . I've been a beast.'

'But *exactly* where are you? You said upstate?'

'I'm staying with a friend. He has a broken leg. I'm sort of taking care of things until he's on his feet again.'

'But what's the phone number? Where can I reach you?' Roberta's anxiety rose again. She was afraid Susan would hang up without giving her exact whereabouts.

'His name is Bob Giordano, Mother. G-i-o-r-d-a-n-o. The number is . . .' Susan gave the phone number and address, complete with Zip code. Roberta felt better with each piece of information.

'But after your friend is walking again, what then, Susan? Where will you be?'

'I don't know exactly. I'm still . . . floundering, I guess you could call it. I like it up here. I thought I'd stay awhile, but I won't go anywhere until I let you know first . . . Promise.'

'I'll count on you to do that, Susan. Have you money?'

'Some. Enough for a while yet. I cashed some of the money Grandpa gave me. Is Jim there?'

'He's out with his girl.'

'Give him my love . . . and Mother, I'm truly sorry. I hope I can make up for it. I mustn't run up your phone bill. I'll write you.'

'Please see that you *do*, Susan.' Roberta's voice suddenly had asperity in it. 'Good night.'

Only now that her anxiety had diminished could Roberta gauge just how severe it had been. And, consequently, feel anger at having been subjected to it. When the opportunity arose she would let Susan know, in no uncertain terms, just how thoughtless of her family she had been.

Meantime, she thanked God that her daughter was safe.

The next morning Susan said, 'By the way, I called my mother last night.'

'Yeah?' was all Bob Giordano said. But he smiled.

24

Mary Blair was early for her job interview in Somerville. She sat parked in front of a small glass and redwood building. A discreet sign read: Richard West & Associates, Advertising.

She nervously checked her watch again. Yes, she had a few minutes to build up her courage, and to remind herself that her letter of application claimed she'd had two years of general office experience, which she hadn't.

At the reentry group rap sessions she had attended, one woman had fiercely said, 'Look, if you have no experience at all, *fake* it. If you think you can get away with it, that is, and if you're sure you can do what you claim you've done.'

So Mary entered on her brief résumé the name of her father's firm in Philadelphia. The support group also urged: 'Polish your skills.' Mary hadn't typed since college, so she'd spent hours practicing on Midge's portable. Then she realized she had never used an electric typewriter. She rented one for a week. Now she was only moderately fast, but accurate, at least.

She checked her makeup in the rear-view mirror. She looked nice – she had made herself up exactly as Ron Leco had taught her – but she looked scared. 'You must look *confident*,' the group had stressed. Up. Head up. Corners of mouth up. Mary took a deep breath. After all, she told herself, you answered their ad, and they *called* you. You have an appointment.

She got out of the car. Squaring her shoulders in her new dress-for-success suit, she walked to the entrance.

The desk in the small reception room was empty. She stood there for a couple of minutes. A man in a hurry came through an inner door, started down the corridor, then backed up.

'May I help you?'

'I have an appointment with Mr West.'

'He'll be with you in a minute. Have a seat.' He was halfway down the hall as he smiled over his shoulder. 'We're shorthanded today.'

His informality was reassuring. This wasn't an intimidatingly gigantic corporation, and if they were shorthanded, they needed help. Mary felt a small glow of hope.

Fifteen minutes later Richard West apologized for keeping her waiting, and ushered her into his office. He glanced at a paper on his desk, then looked at her.

'Tell me, Miss Brody, what did you do at Kenyon & Eckhardt?'

Miss Brody? Mary could only stare at him a second. Then she said, 'My name is Blair. Mary Blair.'

He looked at the paper again. 'You're not Marilyn Brody? You didn't work at Kenyon & Eckhardt?' He seemed to be accusing her of assuming a false identity.

'I'm afraid not, Mr West.'

He looked at her incredulously. Then he burst into laughter. 'Kids today,' he said between gasps. 'In their twenties . . . Can't spell, can't punctuate, can't add, can't follow directions. The age of the goof-off.'

He pulled a handkerchief from his pocket and mopped his eyes. 'Forgive me. It's not at all funny, really. But it's such a perfect example . . . Tell, me, Miss – Mrs . . .'

'Blair.'

'. . . Mrs Blair. Have you noticed the use of the word "whatever" nowadays? You tell a child two and two don't make five, they make four, and the child shrugs and says "whatever."'

Mary smiled. 'I have noticed.'

'Well, that's the basis of this mix-up. I owe you an explanation, Mrs Blair. This place is held together by a wonderful woman, Kay Jones. A dynamo. Three months ago she said she had to have some help, which God knows she did. We hired an assistant for her, Janie. Just after Kay left for vacation, Janie gave us a week's notice. Something about her boyfriend wanting to move back to the city. Janie's last assignment was to set up appointments for her replacement. Obviously, she goofed. Marilyn Brody, Mary Blair. Close enough. Whatever. You see?'

Mary nodded.

'I'm sorry for this foul-up. I apologize for wasting your time, Mrs Blair.'

He smiled at her. He expected her to get up and leave. It had been a mistake, they had never meant to interview her. Should she say 'That's all right' and leave? No. She was here. She'd spent time getting here. Sell yourself, reentry stressed. Assert yourself.

'Mr West, I'm an applicant for this job, too. Your office did make this appointment for me. You felt you owed me an explanation. I think you owe me an interview.'

He looked startled. 'Yes, I see your point. But you see, we were hoping for someone with agency experience. I'm afraid – '

'I understand. But you were just let down by a . . . a "whatever."' She smiled. Once you got started, it got easier. 'By an irresponsible young girl. I'm a responsible *adult*.'

She had his serious attention now, she could see it. She

285

pressed her advantage. 'Won't you tell me what this job requires, Mr West?'

'We're a small shop – sixteen people. Mostly defectors from New York agencies. We have a good creative team, we're growing, and we believe there's a "felt need" in New Jersey. But we haven't licked the organizational nuts and bolts yet – the work flow. Kay Jones is a marvel, but she can't do everything. The job is really to do anything *she* needs doing. Ordinarily, of course, she'd be doing the interviewing. I wish she were, she knows more about it than I do. But in broad terms I suppose it's typing and filing, and keeping track of deadlines and not letting stuff get lost. Follow-through.'

'General office work, then?'

'Yes, but very diversified. A lot of balls in the air at the same time. In a large agency there are specialized departments, but Kay's office handles everything. So she needs someone to grasp what needs doing *first*, without being told. A sense of priorities, if you will. Otherwise known as common sense.'

'Mr West, I could handle that job.'

'You've done it?'

She took the plunge. 'Mr West, I haven't worked in some time, as an employee, that is. But you mentioned keeping track of things. I've been raising four kids. That requires keeping track – which one has the music lesson, which one has the dentist's appointment. I'm experienced at juggling, coordinating, doing two different things at the same time. You also mentioned common sense, responsibility, a sense of first things first. I think I have those qualities. I *know* I have.'

'Go on, Mrs Blair.'

'I'm an accurate typist. Only medium fast, but neat. I'm an excellent speller, and I know how to punctuate.'

'You're also a very good salesperson, Mrs Blair, did you know that?'

Maybe I *am*. Mary was amazed at herself.

'And I must say I'd never take you for a mother of four. But wouldn't that be a problem? I have three kids myself. They get sick, they fall out of trees – there are crises. And sometime we work overtime here.'

'My youngest is almost fourteen. There'd be someone there when they got home from school. No, that wouldn't be a problem.'

'Another thing, Mrs Blair. As a young firm – we've only been in business three years – we don't pay much. Later, as we grow, we hope to do better. Right now, the job pays twelve thousand. Would you accept that?'

Twelve thousand. It sounded enormous to Mary.

'I'd be happy to accept that, Mr West,' she said with considerable dignity. 'I realize this is an entry-level job.' That's what they called it at her group.

He gave her a long, speculative look, visibly trying to make up his mind. Mary gazed steadily back.

'Mrs Blair, you've got it. You're hired. Of course Kay Jones has to be happy, too, but I have a hunch she will be. She'll be back on Monday. Can you be here at nine?'

'Yes. Monday at nine.'

He stood up, offered his hand, shook hers warmly. 'Welcome aboard, Mrs Blair.'

She pulled onto Route 22 almost dizzy with elation. She had a job. She was a member of the 'work force.' She was Mary Blair, employee of Richard West & Associates. She was a *person*!

Now she had to go like the wind to arrange things: line up Mrs Kracowis to be home for the kids, pick up one more work outfit and a couple of tops, she couldn't wear this suit every day. She'd raid the food money again, and pay it back out of her paycheck. Her paycheck! And she'd have to figure out how to get the kids to school in the fall, but she's tackle that later.

Right now she had to *tell* someone, share this high – celebrate. It was twelve-thirty. Maybe Roberta Marston had not yet had lunch?

Roberta hadn't. They left the shop and went to the hotel in Frenchtown. Each woman ordered a drink. 'Congratulations!' Roberta raised her glass. 'To your new job, Mary.'

'I owe it to you, Roberta. Your encouragement and your introduction to Mingo Darcy.'

'Nonsense. You impressed the man, and he's lucky to get you. Incidentally, you look smashing, Mary.'

On the way home, Mary thought that Roberta had seemed a little down. She had rejoiced in Mary's news, certainly. But aside from that, she had struck Mary as subdued. Sympathetically, Mary wondered what could be troubling Roberta – a woman like that.

Then she turned her thoughts to next Monday. Mary Blair? She works in advertising.

25

Midge Blair and Jim Marston lay in the sunny hollow in the Marston's far meadow. They had made love. Their shorts and T-shirts lay in a little heap. Midge's head was on Jim's shoulder, her long dark hair strewn across his chest. They were concealed from sight, unless a helicopter flew over. They would not have cared if it had.

Jim stared thoughtfully at the sky. He was wrestling with a problem he hadn't known he had. With less than three weeks before he was to leave for law school, he had doubts about his chosen profession.

He gave Midge's hair a gentle tug.

'Asleep?'

'Awake.'

'Hey, I want to talk.'

'Sure.' Midge sat up, and reached for her shirt. 'Listen, we'll be burned to a crisp in this sun. Let's talk down by the creek.'

Unselfconscious as puppies, they dressed. On the bank of the creek, they sat under a willow and stuck their bare feet in the rippling water.

Midge planted a kiss on Jim's cheek. 'So what are we going to talk about?'

'About me. Well, about you and me, of course. But really about law school. Midge, I'm beginning to realize I haven't got such great vibes about it.'

'No kidding! How come?'

'Well, I've been trying to figure out what kind of law I'd actually want to practice. Most of the guys I know are gung ho about corporate law or labor law. That's where the big bucks are. But I'm not so sure. Corporate lawyers help big companies swallow little companies – you know, takeovers – or they lobby so that chemical companies can pollute.'

'Ugh.'

'Right. And labor law isn't so pure either. It's pretty much the flip side of big business.'

'Like holding out for contracts that put people out of work?'

'That's what happens.' Jim had been frowning at the rushing water, thinking aloud as he tried to analyze the problem. Now he turned to face her. 'Listen, Midge, do you care about money?'

'Yes. Definitely. Not obscene amounts. But enough to live nicely. Like your mother.'

He laughed. 'Actually, my mother happens to be hard up for cash, but I know what you mean. Until my father died, it was pretty nice.'

'Well, you've been in our house, Jim. You know how we live. Not so great. It's been rough on my mother. My father – well, he's sort of like an absent-minded professor. I think he earns quite a lot of money actually. But he just doesn't notice stuff like furniture, or having enough bathrooms. He's a terrific doctor, though,' she added hastily.

Jim squeezed her shoulder. He *had* been a little surprised at Dr and Mrs Blair's home. 'I know. I heard two women raving about your father in a store the other day. A third woman came up and said, "You must be talking about Dr Blair!"'

'That's my Pop all right. But back to you, Jim. Corporate lawyer, labor lawyer, Indian chief. Why can't you just be a general, independent lawyer, hang out your shingle, maybe next to my landscape architect shingle. Sounds good to me! What's wrong with that?'

'Nothing.' Jim hesitated, because this was the first time

290

he was facing his deepest feelings. 'Midge, I guess the bottom line is that I'm not sure I want to be a lawyer at *all*.'

'Jim! That's a pretty big switch!'

'I know. It is. But I'm sort of . . . turning off. Or maybe I'm turning *on* – to something else.'

'Like what?'

'It seems I've developed this urge to work on the land – outdoors, not caged in an office – doing something I could put my back *and* brain into.'

'You mean farming?'

'Not exactly. At least not like the farmers around here. But I've got this gut feeling something productive could be made out of this place. It bugs me that all these acres are just sitting here and going to waste. Anyway, how would you feel about it if I gave up law? Would it make a difference to you?'

'Jim! Are you out of your mind? Of course I'd want you to do what you want to do.'

'That's what I thought you'd say. Come here.' He kissed her.

'But, Jim, you don't mean you're not going to Georgetown at *all*?'

'No, Midge, of course not. I *have* to go. I owe it to my family, and I suppose to myself, at least for a year.'

'You might go for it after all. You might eat it up, once you're into it.'

'Maybe. Anyway, I'll give it my best shot. But by the end of a year I should know whether it's for me or not. I wanted you to know what's on my mind, Midge.'

'Got it!' said Midge.

On the same hot August day that young Jim Marston was debating his future, Carole Harcourt was beginning to

291

panic over hers. In her borrowed Manhattan office, she made yet another phone call.

'Tom Robson, please.'

'Who's calling?'

'Carole Harcourt.'

'Of where?'

Of where! Good question. Of nowhere, that's where. But wasn't her name enough? Hadn't this dumb bitch ever seen it in *Advertising Age*? In the *New York Times* ad column? Control yourself, Carole.

'It's a personal call,' she said.

'One moment.'

She was kept waiting. Then the indifferent, couldn't-care-less young voice said: 'Mr Robson's in a meeting. He'll get back to you.'

Carole hung up and stared at the phone. He'll get back to you. She'd *hired* Tom Robson, she'd given him his first break. She'd *trained* him. Bastard. They were all bastards.

Fear gripped her. For two weeks she'd pulled every conceivable string, tried every contact. She'd gotten either 'He'll get back to you' or 'Carole, baby, there's no one I'd rather work with, you know that. But right now – more or less zilch, what can I tell you?'

Oh, she'd been offered jobs – word gets around fast – but nothing she'd touch with a ten-foot pole. Cockamamie jobs far below her level. Take a step down and you never live it down. She'd be damned if she would.

But hiding the fact that she'd lost her job was an impossible strain. How long could she keep up this pretense with Greg? He was turning out to be a rotten convalescent, demanding and hard to please. And he put her down in such subtle, sneaky ways. All those remarks about 'Girl-Producer' and 'Alice in Ad Land.' His way of venting his own frustrations. But it was getting hard to take.

She looked at her watch. Three o'clock. Too early to show up at home. And there wasn't a single other call she could make. She had already gone through her B list.

She went to a movie, arriving in the middle. It didn't matter, because she neither saw nor heard it. In the anonymous air-conditioned dark, with empty seats around her, she put her tough survivor's mind to work.

Step One: Send Greg, with Ada to care for him, to the country. Get out from under the strain at home. Free herself to tackle the job problem full force.

Step Two: Set a deadline to make a decent connection. Say October first. Then, if she kept running into stone walls, go into business for herself. Set up as an independent and compete on her own, with everything she had.

Step Three: Go through with her big Labor Day weekend party in spite of everything.

She left the theater and walked the forty blocks home, thinking hard. Greg would willingly go to the country, she was sure. He liked the place, and he loved being lord of the manor. But she wouldn't consider it, even with someone as reliable as Ada, without the reassuring presence of her Greenwillow friends. Roberta Marston in particular. Wonderful friend that she was, Roberta would knock herself out to be helpful in keeping an eye on Greg. Terry and Tim Fenton would too. Such sweeties. They'd drop in on Greg, keep him amused, offer to run errands. So would Sarah Smith and Luther Hodges, she was sure, if she alerted them to the situation. Greg would probably wind up having a ball. Maybe he'd even be able to swim in the pool a little, subject to Dr Magowan's approval, of course.

Her mind turned to the scary idea of starting her own firm. There weren't any independent women producers as far as she knew. But why the hell not? She knew she could handle it. It was a question of getting started.

She'd need a small office, one good assistant. Her hefty severance pay and the proceeds from her profit-sharing would carry her for a year or so, but she'd have to land one decent account long before that. And if she didn't? But she *would*. Think positive.

As for her big party, that was crazy, she knew. Out-of-her-mind expensive for a hostess out of a job. And she even had a perfect excuse to call it off – Greg's recuperation.

But damned if she would. She'd invited everyone she knew weeks ago, before the roof had fallen in. Sixty people had accepted, and she had already booked a small dance band and arranged to rent a dance platform and a tent. Besides, if you think poor and act poor, you'll *be* poor. Not me.

She turned in under the canopy of her apartment house on Central Park West, a small perky redhead in an Adolfo dress. The doorman rushed to open the door, beaming. Carole was one of the better tippers in the building. 'How are you, Mrs Harcourt?'

'Can't complain, Mike. How's with you?'

In upstate New York, Bob Giordano's leg cast had been off for a week. He was still limping, but he could navigate. It was time for Susan Marston to move on. Her bag stood at the front door. The VW, with a full tank and checked for oil, was ready to go. Bob and Susan were having a final breakfast.

'You're sure you're okay?' Susan asked.

'Sure. I won't be climbing any ladders for a while, but I'll be okay in the shop. Are you sure *you're* okay?'

'I told you, I'm going to Ithaca. I'm going to check out Cornell. Maybe there's an opening in the registrar's office or the library or something, or maybe I can grade papers for a prof. I might just luck into something.'

'Yeah, maybe.' He frowned. 'I hope so.'

'Well, time to get the show on the road. But I have to say goodbye to Mabel.'

She went out the kitchen door into the backyard and Bob followed. Mabel and the pups, now much larger, rollicked toward her, tails wagging. Susan knelt down, gathered the pups in her arms, and stroked each in turn. Then she put an arm around Mabel's neck and laid her cheek against the dog's head. 'Goodbye, Mabel,' she whispered. 'I'm going to miss you, Mabel.'

Watching, Bob saw a tear escape. Susan brushed it away, looked up, and met Bob's gaze. They looked at each other over Mabel's head for a long moment, the puppies yelping around them. Then Bob held out a hand to her and pulled her to her feet.

'Susan.' It was a voice she had not heard before. 'Susan, I don't want you to go. Hang around for a while? Don't leave.' He put his arms around her. 'You could commute to Ithaca if you had to, right? Stay, Susan?'

'Yes,' she said.

In Bob's big double bed Susan said, 'But you never . . . how was I to know?'

'I didn't know myself, until out there with Mabel when I realized you were really going. But even if I had known, you don't think I would have made passes, do you? Under the circumstances?'

'No, I don't. You're such a gent.' She tightened her arm around his neck, buried her face in his shoulder.

'Baby.' He stroked her hair. 'I think this is going to work.'

'Me, too.'

26

Carole Harcourt got out of bed and went straight to the window. Good! A gorgeous day for her big party. She intended to make it a blockbuster, and the weather was on her side.

For this weekend, anyway, screw job hunting. Screw problems. How's that for whistling in the dark? She was operating on nerves, and she knew it. She'd had some sleepless nights; she carried Valium in her handbag.

Today, though, she was going to have fun, especially since she'd invited such a wild mix of people. Besides their New York and Greenwillow friends, and a large contingent of TV types from the advertising world – actors, models, art directors – she'd also asked a few of the neighboring farmers and their wives, just for the hell of it. 'Wait until those two crews meet each other,' she thought gleefully. 'The Manhattan swingers and the local yokels!' She figured each group would get a kick out of the other.

Better get dressed. She glanced at Greg, asleep in the other bed. You'd never know he'd been so ill. He looked as handsome as ever, his long body somehow arrogant even in sleep. He'd made a remarkable recovery, but why wouldn't he, considering all the pampering? Roberta and the Fentons and Sarah and Lucas had all made a fuss over him, as she had known they would.

Well, let him sleep. Later, she knew, Greg would play the role of host to the hilt, every inch the country squire. Somehow he exuded an air of proprietorship. Anyone would assume that the house, the grounds, the pool were

296

all *his* doing, especially since he always said *my*: 'When I was having *my* fireplace restored,' 'When I decided where to put *my* pool.' Sometimes it bugged her. Today, it wouldn't. She was too grateful he was alive. But she couldn't help thinking how shocked the farmers would be if they knew the facts. Locked into the idea, as they were, that the man provides, she could just hear them say: 'You mean the *missus* pays for everything?'

She pulled the shades against the bright sunlight, so Greg could sleep as long as possible. Then she ran downstairs, eager to check on party preparations.

Tim Fenton carried grocery bags onto the porch of the house where he'd grown up. He rapped on the door three times, a prearranged signal so that Aunt Martha would know who it was. These days she was growing fearful.

The old woman opened the door and said, as she always did, 'It certainly is good of you to do my storing for me, Timothy.'

And he said, as always, 'Happy to do it, Aunt Martha. That's what families are for.'

He meant it. He had been brought up with a strong sense of Christian duty. You helped those weaker than you. Terry had the same sense of family obligation. Between them, they had several elderly relatives they drove to doctors and dentists, and for whom they ran errands. And both gave a night a week to volunteer work.

Tim followed his aunt's frail shoulders down the hall to the kitchen. 'Coffee's ready,' she said. 'And I made blueberry muffins.'

They sat at the kitchen table chatting. Other than the refrigerator which had replaced the old oak icebox, the room was unchanged since Tim was a boy. They had eaten all meals here, leaving the dining room untouched except when there was company and for holidays and funerals.

'You look more like your mother every day, Timothy. She had the looks, you know. You're a handsome man.'

'You're just prejudiced, Aunt Martha.'

'I don't know why she was took so early, Timothy. Your father, too. Seems like it should have been me. I was the oldest.'

'The Lord giveth and the Lord taketh away, Aunt Mattie.'

'Yes. Ours not to questions why. But it does seem queer to be the only one left. Why, when you young ones were growing up, it was all a body could do to find a quiet spot in this house.'

Tim remembered. Aunt Martha had lived with them, and so had Grandma and Grandpa. Uncle Albert had too, whenever he was out of work. And of course there had been Tim's brother Chuck and his sister Maribel. But he had never been close to his brother and sister. Chuck lived for football, and Maribel was prissy. She cared what the neighbors thought and put her hair up in curlers. His parents had been simple people, modest but proud folk who worked hard and owed no man. Tim never doubted they'd loved him in their undemonstrative way, but he knew he puzzled them, as he puzzled himself. Like Terry, he knew he didn't fit. But he didn't know why.

'Timothy, before you go, I need more canning jars. Would you bring them down from the attic – two dozen?'

On his way down from the attic, Tim passed the open door of his old room. He stopped and looked in. Here he had spent hours alone, dreaming: dreaming of taking piano lessons, singing lessons, dancing lessons. Secretly fantasizing a future he had never confessed to anyone:

298

that of being an entertainer, a pianist and singer, a public performer. Here, too, he had dreamed of his high-school music teacher.

Mr Latham was the only teacher who had not seemed to disapprove of Tim. Mr Latham had said he had a good voice, and had urged him to join the Glee Club. And once, when Mr Latham had asked him to stay late to help with the sheet music, Mr Latham had kissed him. Tim had known he was going to. Tim had known he wanted him to. At the same time, Tim had never heard of such a thing. He had worried about it ever since.

In the end, Tim had had no chance to study anything, let alone piano and voice. His father had died, and Tim had just managed to graduate from high school before he'd had to take a job – the job he still had, in the office of a plant near Allentown. He did sing in the church choir, and he did teach himself to play the piano by ear, on the old upright in the front parlor. But no one had ever heard him play. He practiced only when he was alone. Even Terry hadn't known he could play until she'd accidentally heard him on the secondhand spinet they'd bought for their daughters' lessons.

'Timothy? Did you find them?' Aunt Martha called from downstairs.

How long had he been standing here dreaming? Terry was waiting for him. He had to get home and dress for the Harcourts' party.

At the last minute, Tim panicked. They were ready to leave, Terry in the lovely dress she'd made from a *Vogue* pattern, Tim in the jacket he'd felt guilty about buying, even on sale. Tim felt a tight knot in his stomach. The Harcourts' guests, he knew, would be exciting, successful people like Greg and Carole – the kind of people he'd longed to know all his life. But he couldn't face them,

299

couldn't go through a lot of introductions to strangers who would wonder where the Harcourts had dug *him* up.

'Terry. I don't feel so hot. I think I'd better not go. You go ahead. Maybe I'm coming down with something . . .'

'Tim! Stop that! You've just got stage fright. I know you so well. They're just *people*. Even if they're big shots, remember what Grandpa Wilks used to say? "Don't think their shit don't stink, like everyone else's."' Terry could be earthy on occasion, a heritage from pious folk who nevertheless used barnyard expressions to drive home a point.

'Terry! What language!'

'Well, I've got to shake you up *somehow*. Come on let's go. And you look smashing,' she added loyally. If only her sweet, decent, sensitive husband would stop putting himself down. Terry was made of sterner stuff.

'My fan club of one,' said Tim. 'All right, let's go.'

At the Blairs' house, another husband was backing out of the party. Mary Blair had been surprised and delighted when John had agreed to go. Could it be that he had a new respect for her, now that she had shown some independence? Or did he merely feel that, for once, he owed it to his committee members to socialize a little?

Whatever his reason, Mary looked forward to the party. John was Somebody, after all. It was a long time since she'd made an entrance on his arm.

The phone rang. John answered. He listened, frowned, looked at his watch, said 'Twenty minutes.' Mary didn't need to be told it was the hospital.

He hung up. 'Mary, they need me.'

'John, you're not on call today. Randall's on call.'

'Yes, but – '

'Even so, you were at the hospital this *morning*.'

'You don't understand.'

'Why don't they call Randall, off the golf links? *You're* not available. You have a social commitment, with your wife.'

'I'm sorry, Mary. The patient is asking for me.' He was halfway down the stairs. 'Have a good time,' he called over his shoulder.

Mary didn't answer. She picked up her mascara brush, and finished her makeup, as Ron Leco had taught her. She was getting good at it. She managed it in six minutes flat every morning before work. Now she added a touch more color for the party, at which her absentee husband had suggested she have a good time. She intended to.

Roberta turned onto the Harcourts' lane just as the Fentons were getting out of their car. Parked automobiles stretched far up the road, some pulled onto the grassy bank.

'First traffic jam I've ever seen in Greenwillow,' Tim greeted Roberta.

'Looks like a bash,' said Terry happily.

A bash it was. A five-man combo with amplifiers played on the loading platform of the barn. A babble of voices rose from clusters of people attired in a wild variety of clothes, tennis shorts to elegant silk or linen designer fashions. Ada presided smilingly over a long buffet table; Ada's husband Elwood, imported from Harlem for the occasion, manned the bar. From the pool came shrieks, laughter, and splashes as gleaming bodies in bikinis disported like leaping fish.

'Isn't it mad?' Carole greeted them gaily. 'Did you ever see such a mishmash? And lots more coming. I told everyone any time from two on. That means people will still be showing up at *sunset*, can you bear it?'

She turned to greet more arrivals: a man with chin

whiskers; a soignée, silver-haired woman carrying a toy poodle; a young man with a shaved head; two girls in garden-party dresses with wide-brimmed straw hats. The older woman and the two girls looked oddly familiar.

'Soap opera,' whispered Terry to Roberta. '"Life Is Like That." One plays the mother, and the girls are the daughters.'

All five newcomers greeted Carole with 'darling,' all kissed her, and all said 'fantastic' at some point. Fantastic house. Fantastic country. You look fantastic! All pronounced it with the very short *a* cultivated by speech coaches.

'See?' Carole laughed. 'I told you New Jersey isn't all Secaucus.' She made the introductions. 'Now go and mingle, everybody. I have to stay here on gate duty, so I'll just point you in the right direction. Pool house over there . . . bar under those trees . . . powder rooms in the house, upstairs and down. And Greg's out there somewhere. Circulate!'

They moved off in a group, just as Mr and Mrs Herman Krantzen owners of the dairy farm big enough to boast its own small hangar and landing strip, arrived in their old but impeccably kept Lincoln. 'Herm! Minnie!' cried Carole. 'Darlings!' Roberta turned in time to see Carole plant her social kiss on Herman Krantzen's beefy cheek, and to see Herm manfully peck back.

Roberta smiled at Carole's exuberance. What a zest for living. A party is her natural element, she thought. But didn't Carole seem a little wound up, a touch hyper? It couldn't be the party; Carole was a relaxed hostess. It must be Greg. She's still anxious about his health. What spirit, to go through with this mob scene after all she'd been through.

The young man with the shaved head was saying, 'Come on. Let's get a drink.' He took her elbow and

302

steered her toward the bar. 'If you're wondering about my bald pate, it's that damned wig I wear on the show. They couldn't get it to sit right, so finally I said to Antonio, 'Oh, go ahead, Tony, just take it off, *all* of it." You know?'

Roberta had not realized that Carole and Greg knew so many show business people. But there was a strong show-biz flavor to the snatches of conversation she picked up as she moved from group to group. Here someone was talking about making a 'demo,' there someone said 'his reviews were lou-say,' and elsewhere she heard 'They're taking it into the Kennedy Center.'

She spotted Mary Blair, looking slim as a blade of grass in cool green.

'Mary! You could be Midge's sister!'

Mary laughed happily. 'Oh, Roberta, isn't this fun?'

'Isn't it! How's the job going?'

'I *love* it. I can't wait to get there in the morning, and . . .'

An attractive man came up, bearing two plates of food, one for Mary. Roberta moved on. Do her ego good, she thought, a little male attention.

Greg approached with an older woman whose face still showed signs of great beauty. 'I want two of my favorite women to meet,' he said, turning on the charm and draping an arm over each woman's shoulder. 'Paula Phillips, Roberta Marston.' Roberta had recognized the face before she heard the name. Paula Phillips had been a film superstar in the fifties. Before Roberta had a chance to respond, someone called Greg to the pool.

'Excuse me, girls,' he said. 'I'll be right back.'

'Not if I see you first,' muttered Paula Phillips.

Seeing Roberta's astonishment, she shrugged. 'I can't stand him. No, I'm not being unforgivably rude to my

303

host. I consider myself *Carole's* guest. Love her, *loathe* him.'

Looking at the once-famous eyes, Roberta saw that Paula Phillips had had too much to drink.

Just as Carole had anticipated the Greenwillow guests were fascinated by the New Yorkers, and vice versa. She heard Herman Krantzen offer the two young things in straw hats a ride on the tractor. She saw Terry Fenton in rapt conversation with an art director who was saying, 'But I can't believe you were *born* here.' Meanwhile a gilt-haired actor in stark white asked Tim Fenton, 'Do you come here often?' as he offered Tim a bite of his chicken leg. And she heard Anton Browne, one of the better scriptwriters, say to Roberta Marston, 'Oh, *there* you are. I've been looking for you . . .'

Off and running, thought Carole. Good. Because this *could* be my last hurrah.

Mary Blair left the Harcourts' at about seven o'clock. She left reluctantly. The party was going full blast, and she was having a marvelous time. Why wouldn't she, with a fascinating man singling her out all afternoon, making her feel like a . . . a sex object? Heady stuff, after years of not feeling female at all. Naturally, she realized it was just an afternoon's diversion, but it definitely lifted her confidence, by several degrees. And sparked her need for more attention.

John was home, his car was there. Mary parked and sat thinking. Everything in her protested against going into the house. She couldn't face another empty evening with a man whose heart and mind were elsewhere. She realized that when an isolated occasion like the Harcourts' party could be such a red-letter day for her, she must be starved for human contact.

She loved her new job. But even after this very short

time, it was not enough. she needed more. She wanted real connections with people, a social life in her own right. She wanted to be wanted, for herself, and she would never get that from John.

Never.

The word sank into her mind like a stone, heavy and final.

Hardly conscious of her own intention, Mary went into the house. The kids weren't home yet, and John wasn't downstairs. She found him in the little upstairs room he used as a makeshift study. He was sitting at his desk, absorbed in some papers.

She stood in the doorway. 'John,' she said to his back.

He turned his head slightly, but didn't raise his eyes from his reading.

Mary grabbed a medical journal from the tottering stack in the corner, yelled 'Dr Blair!' at the top of her voice, and smacked him on the head.

He swung around and stared at her. Even so, it took a few seconds for his mind to come back from the medical paper he'd been reading.

'Are you crazy?'

'Just trying to get your attention. You only answer to *Doctor* Blair.'

'I see.'

'John, I want a divorce.'

'What?'

'I want a divorce.'

His eyes instantly took on that intent, penetrating physician's look. 'Are you feeling all right? Light-headed? Are you premenstrual?'

'I've never been healthier, John.'

'Then you're being absurd.' He looked annoyed.

'John, listen to me.' She spoke quietly and slowly. 'I am completely serious. I am going to leave you.'

'That's ridiculous. Why would you want to leave me?'

'Why wouldn't I, John? Tell me.'

'Because I'm your husband.'

'Yes. But what does that mean – *husband*? Do you *husband* me, in the sense of cherishing something you care about? Do we share, John? Do we laugh together and cry together and value the same things? Are we parents together? Companions? Do we *live* together on a daily basis, do we touch each other at any point?

'Do you mean sex?'

She looked at him. Brilliant man, idealistic man, in so many ways. But he genuinely did not comprehend. There was a blank space in his psyche – the space which should have held his capacity for relatedness. It reminded her of what she had read of certain reading disabilities. There were people who could read everything but verbs or everything but nouns due to a blankness in the relevant brain cells. They were hardly responsible for the blank spots, and perhaps John wasn't, either.

'No, I don't mean sex.'

'I don't understand.'

'I know you don't, John.'

'But I thought you loved me?'

'I did, John. I did. With all my heart.'

'But that can't end, can it? Overnight?'

Overnight! She felt the old bitterness.

'Overnight. No, hardly that. It takes a long, long time to kill love. Years. Years of hoping, Years of waiting. Years of medical school, when you had no time or energy for anything but study. Years of your residency, when I was tied hand and foot with small children. Years after we moved into this house . . .'

She broke off. Her voice had been rising. No. She would not recount all the deprivations and the hopeless yearning for closeness between them.

'John,' she said quietly, 'I have waited twenty years for you to join me . . . and you never have.'

John was silent. So was Mary.

'What about the children?' he said finally.

'They'll weather it. After all, they can't miss what they never had, can they? The school plays and Little League and PTA you were too busy for.' No, no. Stop it. Her feelings were getting the better of her again.

'And John . . .'

'Yes?'

'It's only fair to tell you that I intend to raise our standard of living. The children's and mine. It took me a long time to realize that the way we live is preposterous in view of your income. I know *you're* above material things, but I'm not, not anymore. I'm going to sue for enough support for us to live the way we should *always* have lived.'

'You're going to *sue* me?'

'If I have to. When I file for divorce. I'll have to consult a lawyer, of course, and I suppose you will, too. We can settle things through them.'

Only then did he look as though he at last realized this was actually happening. But he ignored the subject of money. As usual, it was unimportant to him.

'But Mary . . . *Mary*. What do you intend to do? How will you live?'

'I don't know,' she said slowly. 'Go on with the job I have, to see if something can be made of it. But mostly, I'll try to find out if there isn't a life open to me, other than the one I've been living – or rather, *not* living.'

'Don't leave, Mary. Please don't leave. We'll do better. I'll do better . . .'

'It's too late, John.'

He saw that she meant it.

'But what will *I* do, Mary. How will I live?'

'Exactly as you have been, John. You are fortunate. You have an absorbing, ever-fascinating love. Medicine. You will never be bored. And you don't really *need* anyone. You've got your work to keep you warm.'

She went to him, kissed him on the cheek. 'I wish you well, John. Good night.'

He sat, staring blindly at the journal on his desk. After a long time, he picked it up and began to read where he had left off.

Alone in the bedroom, Mary wept for the boy she had loved, for the girl she had been, and for all the dreams which had come to this cold, ashen moment.

It was not until she was drifting sadly into sleep that she realized that John had not once asked her whether she was in love with someone else. So devoid was he of the very concept of love, it had simply not occurred to him.

27

By midnight at the Harcourts', the diehards were still whooping it up. There were about a dozen people left, all at that stage where there is a collective urge to keep going. Tim and Terry Fenton wanted the party never to end. Both felt, to their amazement, that they had been hits. These incredibly worldly people had actually seemed interested in them.

'What did I tell you?' Carole had whispered to Greg, as she'd watched two of her male guests compete for Terry's attention. Tim, glad to be sought out, was also proud that his wife could hold her own with any woman in the group. And she made that dress herself, he thought. What would they say to *that*?

Passing Terry now, sitting on a porch swing with that tall man with the British accent, Tim gave her a little salute, and she smiled back. She's having the time of her life, he thought, and so am I. He made his way a trifle unsteadily up the stairs, in search of a bathroom. He had had a lot to drink, but so had everyone else.

Downstairs again, Tim made a wrong turn. He found himself in the doorway of the Harcourts' Victorian back parlor. He stood admiring the room, especially the piano gleaming in the far corner. A grand piano. He had never touched one. He wondered what it would be like to play. He walked across the room and very softly struck a chord, then another. He slid onto the bench, and very lightly began to play Cole Porter.

Stop, he told himself. Don't make a fool of yourself. But his long bottled-up urge to express himself musically was too strong. Why shouldn't I? It's a *party*. Why am I so afraid of what people think? His foot pressed the pedal.

In two minutes the others were crowding into the room.

'Tim!' cried Carole Harcourt. 'You never told us you could play! What's the idea of holding out?'

'Goody!' said someone else. 'Golden oldies! Now let's have "That Old Black Magic."'

'Gershwin first! "Someone to Watch over Me".'

For the next hour Tim Fenton had the intoxicating experience of being what he had never been before, the center of attention. In usual around-the-piano style, the others competed for their favorites, plied him with requests, sang along. Eventually, Tim dared to sing. He had a pleasant untrained baritone, but a natural sense of phrasing. When he segued into the verse of 'My Funny Valentine,' everyone else held back, then joined him in the chorus.

He ended with an old Noel Coward patter song, 'Alice Is at It Again,' to rousing applause.

'You're good, you know?' said David Warren, the gilt-haired actor. 'You should be in a piano bar on the East Side. Bobby Short, eat your heart out.'

Tim flushed with pleasure. He knew who Bobby Short was. He and Terry read *New York Magazine*.

'Listen, everybody.' It was David Warren again. 'I'm starved. Isn't it crazy, after all that food? Let's go to a diner or something. Bagels. I want a bagel, and scrambled eggs.'

'Let's!' said Carole, now at the top of her form. Thank God she'd gotten Greg safely into bed at midnight. Doctor's orders. But no reason why she shouldn't make a night of it. 'Come on, everybody, who's for the Blue Bird Diner?'

310

Everyone was game except the young dancer who had come with David Warren. 'David,' he said plaintively, 'you know we told Mark and Carlos we'd be in New Hope by midnight at the *latest*, and now it's two.'

'It hardly matters, does it?' said David. 'Unless you want to go on ahead?'

'Don't be *silly*. But you know I hate diners. I'll wait here.'

Carole gave directions. Ten people crowded into two cars and roared off. Tim was the last to come out of the house. He found David Warren waiting for him. On the way to Route 22, David said, 'Ooh, look at that *tacky* bar. Let's have a drink – a quickie. Don't you love those lurid Schlitz signs?'

At the diner the group noisily pulled two tables together. As they waited for their orders, one of the men began to tell jokes, deadpan. He was very funny. The group broke up. Terry laughed until tears streamed down her face.

It wasn't until an hour later, when they were waiting for the check, that Terry realized Tim and that blond man – what was his name – hadn't shown up. For a moment she was worried. Then she told herself not to be uptight among these free-and-easy people. So she said casually. 'Wonder where my husband got to?'

'Don't worry, darling,' said someone. 'Knowing David, he probably decided he wasn't hungry after all, after rounding up everyone else, of course. That's David for you. My guess is he's probably got your husband back at the piano, wearing his fingers to the nub.'

But Carole, who had also noticed the absense of Tim and David, felt alarm, God, David of all people. That *alley* cat.

It was four in the morning when they got back to the Harcourts'. Tim's car was not there. 'Maybe they went to

311

your house,' Carole said to Terry. 'Come on, Peter. You and I will drive Terry home.'

Tim's car was not in the Fenton's driveway. Now Terry began to panic. 'Oh, Carole, I'm really worried. Tim isn't used to drinking so much. Do you think I should call the police?'

Carole took charge. 'Peter, you go back to our house, and stay awake, please. Call us here the instant they show up.' She scribbled the Fentons' number and gave it to him. 'I'll stay here with Terry. Please don't worry, Terry. Just some of David's hijinks, probably,' she said, but inwardly she was sick with anxiety.

Terry was worried about an accident. However, that wasn't what Carole was worried about. 'Queer as a three-dollar-bill,' Greg had pronounced in his know-it-all way when they'd first met Tim, and Carole had to admit that was her initial impression too. But the Fentons had a working marriage, whatever its private nature. They loved their kids, and Tim was certainly a more devoted husband than Greg would ever be. Then they were both so sweet, so damned guileless, and they'd been so helpful, while Greg was recuperating.

Now she felt guilty. She should have known better than to expose an innocent like Tim to the likes of David Warren. Amusing as he was, talented as he was, he was a total hedonist. If worse comes to worst, she prayed, let it be just an . . . incident. Let Terry never find out, and let it not hurt Tim.

It was seven in the morning when Tim Fenton opened his eyes. He was facing a blank, pale-green wall. His head pounded. He felt nauseous. He struggled to sit up. Opposite, were a made-up twin bed, a chest of drawers, a night table. All of a pale, anonymous fake wood. And there was a blank anonymous door.

Then he remembered. Horror hit him with such impact that he fell back on the pillow, as though knocked there. Remembering was unbearable, but memory trod heavily, mercilessly, into his mind, detail by detail.

Tim Fenton felt he faced the gates of hell. He had sinned. He had committed the vile, the unspeakable. His strict, fundamentalist upbringing would not allow him a shred of self-justification. Yes, he had been drunk, but that was his own fault. And yes, he had been carried away by flattery. 'You're wasting yourself, you know? You belong in the Big Apple. I know a talent scout . . .' But he had *listened* to the blandishments of Satan. Worse, he had *wanted* to.

Tim Fenton lay motionless, suffering.

At length, he struggled out of bed. He could hardly bear to put on his clothes, remembering, as he did, how he had taken them off. Sackcloth, he thought. A scrap of paper was propped on the chest, with a New York phone number printed in bold ink. Tim stared at the seven in the number. It had the extra horizontal stroke of the European seven. Sodom and Gomorrah, and the trappings thereof. He tore the paper into shreds, dropped it into the toilet, and was sick.

He hardly dared show himself outside, but he forced himself to open the door. His car was parked a few yards away. There was an early Sunday-morning silence. No one was in sight. It took a few minutes to get his bearings. Then he recognized the motel. The Cedar Hill, with individual cabins. He was less that fifteen miles from Greenwillow. Now he knew what to do.

The car key, thank heaven, was in his pocket. Shakily he started the car, and pulled onto the empty highway. But almost immediately he turned off onto a back road. It was lucky that, having lived in the area all his life, he knew the back roads so well.

Tears in his eyes, he thought of Terry, and of his two little daughters. He was not fit to live. He had spent the night in the arms of another man. And vile as he was, how did he know that he would not do it *again*?

Approaching a mile-long level stretch where he knew there was nothing but open field on both sides, Tim set his eyes on a large roadside sycamore. He pressed his foot on the accelerator, and aimed straight for the tree.

'You bitch,' David Warren's roommate had said, as he'd pulled up at the spot on the highway David had named over the phone at six-thirty A.M. 'I sat in that damned chair all night, waiting for you. This is *it*. I'm through.'

'Oh, come off it, Christopher,' said David, running a gold comb through his gilt hair. 'You know what we agreed. Fun-and-games, right? Besides, you know I can't resist a conversion, especially when it's sitting up and begging.'

The MG roared off toward New Hope.

It was nearly nine o'clock when the police called an ashen-faced Terry Fenton. Her husband had been in an automobile accident. He was seriously injured, but he was alive. He was at Memorial Hospital.

On a Saturday morning two weeks later, Terry Fenton vigorously attacked her housework, trying to finish by noon. She'd make lunch for the kids before she left for the hospital to see Tim.

Since Tim's accident she had daily thanked God for sparing his life. The quiet life she and Tim had lived, the one they'd considered so narrow and hickish, now seemed heaven to her. She lived only for the moment when Tim would be at home again.

A voice at the screen door startled her. 'May I come

in?' Greg Harcourt, handsome and rangy, loomed in the doorway.

'Greg.' The long days of anxiety over Tim had wiped out her previous thrill at knowing the worldly Harcourts and their glamorous friends. She had even wondered if she and Tim were not being punished for being dissatisfied with their simple lives and hankering for glitter. Now Greg's city aura meant nothing to her, and she greeted him simply as a friend.

'Come on in. Care for a cup of coffee?'

'Fine,' said Greg. dropping into a chair. 'But I really came to see how you're bearing up. Is there anything I can do to help?'

'How nice of you, Greg, but everything is fine, really. Tim is progressing slowly. The kids are all right. We're managing.'

'I didn't quite mean that, dear.' Terry knew by now that everyone was 'dear' to Greg. 'I mean how are you, *personally*, bearing up under the shock of what happened? The circumstances?'

'The circumstances? You mean that Tim was drunk? Oh, Greg, that happens, doesn't it, at a huge party? It's so easy to drink too much, without even realizing . . .'

Greg smiled and leaned over and patted Terry's hand. 'Such a loyal little wife. No, I didn't mean the drinking. I mean what rocked poor Tim so much that he was driven to try to kill himself.'

'Kill himself!' Terry went white. 'What are you talking about, Greg?'

Greg's handsome brows knitted in a look of deep concern. 'Oh Terry, I'm so sorry. You didn't *know*? But I thought you did. I thought you knew about the police report. I talked to them. They said the tire marks showed the car was aiming straight for that tree, at high speed. At the very last moment it swerved and turned over sideways. That's what saved him, thank God. The chief said . . .' He broke off.

Terry's hand shook as she put down her cup. 'He was drunk. He lost control.'

Greg looked at her. 'All right, Terry,' he said gently. He was silent while he lit a cigarette. Then, with the air of someone willing to try again, for the other person's sake, he veered in a new direction.

'You know, Terry,' he said soberly, 'I blame myself, and I blame Carole. We should never have mixed someone of David Warren's *proclivities* with someone of Tim's . . . susceptibilities. I feel we're responsible. That's why I want to help.'

Was she having a nightmare? Terry tried to blot out Greg's words – proclivities, susceptibilities – tried to hold them back before they reached full consciousness in her mind.

'Help?' she repeated mechanically.

'People can't bear shocks like this alone, Terry. You have to vent them, take the pressure off, share them.' Again Greg's face reflected concern, compassion. 'Perhaps I *can* help. Perhaps I could give you a little perspective. These things don't hurt so much then you see them in a broader context. Tim can't help himself, you know. Don't – please don't, Terry – feel he has been disloyal to you. He's devoted to you, that's obvious. It's just that he's trapped in his own nature, poor guy.'

Terry could barely speak. 'Please . . .'

Now Greg's expression was one of horrified contrition. 'Terry, but you knew *that* didn't you? This isn't news to you, is it? You did know, didn't you? . . .' his voice was almost pleading. He was begging her to relieve him of the responsibility of breaking it to her. 'Terry, surely you know Tim is gay?'

Terry stood up. 'Please leave,' she said.

Greg rose too. 'I'm sorry as hell, Terry. I thought you knew. Everyone else does. But now that you do know, let me help. It must be hell for you. You're damned sexy, you know. How do you stand the frustration? If ever I saw a woman who needed a *man*, it's you.'

In a split second Greg had pulled Terry to him, slipped a hand inside her blouse, and crushed his mouth to hers.

Terry hadn't known she was so strong. With one instinctive twist of her body she broke free, swung her arm wide, and slapped Greg with all her force.

The sound of the slap rang in the room.

Greg smiled, slowly, confidently, with lazy amusement. At the door he turned back. 'I only wanted to help, dear. Another way of helping.'

Terry saw triumph in his eyes as he left. She realized, with sickening certainty, that Greg Harcourt was sadistic. He had deliberately set up this little psycho-drama for kicks. Under the mask of compassionate concern, he had tested her reactions for the sheer sport of witnessing them. An image of a caged animal goaded with a stick by a detached observer crossed her mind. As for the pass he had made at her, that was part of the sport. For him, fun came from inflicting pain.

Terry just made it to the bathroom to throw up.

Then, feeling weak and dizzy and somehow dirtied, she got into the shower. With the water drumming full steam on her head and body, she forcibly dismissed Greg Harcourt from her mind. Except to think, fleetingly, *poor Carole*.

Tim. Tim was the important thing. As for Tim's trying to kill himself, she did not believe it. That was a vicious lie. Tim was too decent, too responsible, he would never do that to his kids and to her. And he was too God-fearing.

'But surely you know Tim is gay?' She clenched her

317

hands under the pounding water. Of course she hadn't known . . . not for sure. No, that wasn't totally honest. She hadn't *known*, but she had suspected, in the deepest recesses of her unconscious. Yet she hadn't let herself know that she'd suspected . . . from the beginning, she now forced herself to admit. She remembered being attracted to Tim because he was *not* macho like her father. But she also remembered that Tim was twenty-nine when they'd met, old to be single in this part of the world, and still living with his parents. And confiding that he never intended to marry.

Face it, Terry, she whispered to herself. Didn't you kind of maneuver him? Didn't you egg him on? Promote the idea that together, you two sensitive oddballs could thumb your nose at small-town ideas? And didn't you secretly feel that you were strong enough for two, that you could make up for whatever Tim lacked in masculinity?

Yes, Terry admitted to herself. Yes, I did.

And didn't you more or less lead the way in your sex life? Weren't you, more often than not, the initiator? And didn't you feel that *you* could overcome anything, that you could make marriage and sex so satisfying, that it would wipe out any 'susceptibilities' Tim might have?

Was I wrong? Was I too egotistical about my own powers? Did I do Tim harm?

She heard the kids come in and call from downstairs. 'We'll have lunch in a few minutes,' she called back, amazed that her voice sounded so normal. 'I'm getting ready to go and see Daddy.'

If Tim was torn by conflicting drives, where did that leave their marriage? There were other aspects to marriage besides sex, weren't there? Compatibility and shared goals, love for children, and courtesy, sensitivity and mutual respect. She and Tim had all that. She thought of the many couples they knew whose sex life had gone stale. Left without these other sustaining qualities, there was barbed hostility between them. She and Tim had never been hostile, because neither had struggled for power. Rather, they'd been united against what they saw as a rough world.

And if, at some time in the future, Tim really wanted something else, they'd cross that bridge when they came to it. But they'd cross it together.

Tim's eyes were closed when Terry tiptoed into his room at the hospital. But he did not look peacefully asleep. His face was drawn into a look of suffering. Terry moved close to the bed and took his hand.

She had never seen such depths of misery as when he opened his eyes. He withdrew his hand from hers, 'Don't touch me until you hear what I have to say. You might not want to, afterwards.'

'Tim, dear – '

'Terry, listen. I can't stand this agony any longer.' He closed his eyes and then opened them, looking directly at her.

'Terry, I think I'm . . . gay.'

'So what?' said Terry.

He closed his eyes again, but not before she saw profound relief and gratitude and love in them.

He grasped for her hand. She gripped his. A tear rolled down Tim's cheek, and they stayed that way, silently, for uncounted minutes.

28

The clock chiming six roused Roberta Marston from her reverie. How long had she been standing here on the stair landing, looking toward the carriage house, remembering Zack?

Stop it, she told herself, and went downstaits to make her morning coffee. She had been awakening very early ever since Jim had left for Georgetown. She missed him, after having him at home all summer. And she missed Midge Blair too, for that matter. Midge had been in and out almost daily these last few weeks.

I suppose it's the transition to being alone again, Roberta thought, taking a single cup from the shelf, slicing only one peach. But it's easier than it was last year – I've had some practice.

She picked up Susan's last letter from the counter and sat down to reread it. Susan wrote that she was working at Cornell and still living at the same address, with her friend Bob Giordano. She would be home for Christmas. She added, 'Mother, I know I behaved hideously. Super Brat. I'm truly sorry. But I'm getting my head together now, I really am. You'll see. I hope.'

Roberta wondered whether Susan was living with this unknown Bob Giordano, or simply living under his roof. She had learned from Jim that it was out-of-date to assume that because people shared premises, they shared a bed. Not at all. The young were free to enjoy sex at will, but they were also free *not* to. There was such a thing as being good friends, mutual support systems.

In any case, Susie's letter did sound more stable.

Roberta was deeply grateful for that. But she had no way of knowing whether Susan had gotten over her infatuation with Zack. Was she still suffering? Perhaps Bob Giordano was just a consoling pal?

As for Zack and herself, Roberta felt an aching regret that something which had promised so much had come to nothing. How *begrudging* of life that now, when there was not a soul around and they would have had freedom to be together, it was over. Was it over? It must be. The date for his return had passed. She had not heard from him.

She was glad. now, that she had not completed that phone call to his office last week. Something had come over her. She had felt a compelling need, at *least* to know whether he was back. But fear and uncertainty and self-doubt had made her hang up just as the connection was made. Suppose he *were* back and hadn't called? Suppose, from the perspective of absence and distance, he had decided it had been merely an – incident. Suppose he had met somebody else?

Roberta got up, determined to cut off this line of thought. It was useless conjecture. And in any event, the troubling age difference remained. *That* had not changed.

She threw on a sweater and went out into the garden, now beginning to wane. The earth was preparing for its long sleep. She shivered in the September chill. Even her local social life was dormant. Tim Fenton, poor man, was still in the hospital. The Harcourts had returned to the city. They would not be back in the country until the holidays.

She looked at her watch. Not quite seven. But she might as well to get to work early. She had next week off, and there was a lot of paperwork to get out of the way beforehand.

As she pulled up to the shop, Roberta realized that it

was a year ago, almost to the day, that she had driven down this village street and had stumbled on Jane Whitford's. The cheese sign had caught her eye, she remembered. Only a year? It seemed like a couple of lifetimes ago.

Jane was already there. 'Oh, Robbie, bless you for being so early. Perfect timing, too. I have something I want to talk over with you before we get busy. Come on in the back room, coffee's on.'

'Look, Roberta,' said Jane, getting straight to the point. 'I want to plant a seed in your mind and I'm hoping like hell it will sprout. I'll give you the bottom line first: I think we should expand and that we should be partners.'

'No, wait.' She waved her hand as Roberta opened her mouth. 'Hear me out. We're doing well here, right?' – They were. And Roberta had had a raise – 'But I think we're reaching the saturation point for this location. You know I've been muttering about a second shop for some time. Well, I've found the perfect shop. Near Flemington. Everything's right, Roberta – size, access, parking. Oh, I can just *see* it. The front has big old-fashioned display windows.' Roberta had to smile. Jane had a visionary gleam in her eye; she was already dressing those windows.

'Well,' Jane went on, 'I want us to buy it. The whole damned building. An investment in itself, actually, outside of the business. We could rent the top floor, to help pay the taxes.'

'Jane, it sounds – '

'Now, here's where you come in, Roberta. Point one, it's ridiculous for you to be working as an employee. You should be in business for yourself, as I am. Point two, you should be making more money. Point three, we work well together. I know more about buying than you do, but you'll learn. And you've got it all over me on display

322

and ambiance. You have a feel for trends. If you took over this shop, and I opened the new one, I'm convinced we could have a good thing going for us.'

'So what's the catch?' asked Roberta, matching Jane's own cut-through-the-fat manner.

'The catch. Well you may ask.' Jane put down her cup, and lit a cigarette. 'The catch is money, of course. Capital. I'd sell you half-interest in this shop. And together we'd invest in the new one. You'd need at least one hundred thousand.'

'Jane, I hardly have one hundred thousand *cents*.'

'I know, I know. Who has, lying around to hand? But there are ways of raising cash.'

'You mean borrowing?'

'Sure. It's called OPM – Other People's Money. You rent money to make money.'

'Jane, I'm flattered. But, my God, I'm no business-woman. I don't know the first thing about investment.'

'You could learn, if you were interested. Look, Roberta, the property I'm talking about isn't even up for sale yet, but I happen to know it's going to be, probably some time during the next six months. As I said, I just wanted to plant the idea. So put it on the back burner and see if it perks.'

'I will. It's just that it's such an unheard-of idea, for me, I mean.'

'Well, you've heard of it now.' Jane stood up. 'By the way, have you decided where you're going on your week off?'

'New York. I'm going to stay with my friend Mingo Darcy.'

'Terrific. Best time of the year in Manhattan. Take a big bite of the Big Apple, and enjoy.'

* * *

'A week off and you don't know what to do with it?' Mingo had said over the phone. 'Easy, silly. Come to town and spend it with me. Oh, Robbie, it's ages since we've been together in the city. Come on, we'll live it up or slop around, just as we choose. And after what I went through at the Paris openings, I *deserve* some pleasure. And so do you, God knows. I won't take "no" for an answer.'

'In that case, *yes*.' Roberta laughed. 'I'd love it.'

'That's settled, then. I'll line up some gents to take us to the theater – there are a couple of good openings coming up – and a private art showing, full tiara, my dear, might be amusing. Then there's a fashion luncheon – '

'My God, Mingo, you can't do all that in a week . . .'

'You'd be surprised. Of course, I'll be tied up at the salt mines all day, but you'll find plenty to do – stay in bed until noon if you like, cruise the boutiques, see some of your old friends. By the way, did I tell you I ran into Paul Reston in Paris? He made a huge point of asking about you.'

'Paul Reston? Oh, Mingo, I feel so guilty. I haven't even *thought* of Paul in ages, and he was so terribly kind when Brad died. He knocked himself out to be helpful. Really, I'm an ingrate.'

'He *did* seem very concerned about you. "A woman like that," he said, and I quote, "shouldn't be alone in the middle of nowhere." He came on very stern, I must say.'

'Oh, dear. He tried so hard to talk me out of moving to the farm. He seemed to feel he owed it to Brad. Well, I certainly owe it to him to call him. How was Alicia?'

'Alicia wasn't with him.'

When his secretary said 'Mrs Marston on Three,' Paul Reston had to wait several pounding heartbeats before he picked up the phone. When he could trust his voice, he said, 'Roberta, will you believe I was just thinking of you?' *Now and ever since I last saw you*?

'Paul, it's good to hear your voice. It's been so long.'

'Much too long. As it happens, I was going to call you this week about the disposition of your apartment.' Damn it, why did he have to sound like a judge in chambers? And how hellish that he needed an *excuse* to call. 'Besides looking forward to seeing you, Roberta, we must discuss whether you'll sell your place on Seventy-ninth Street. The Erskines' term is nearly up. They are eager to know your decision.'

'Paul, I do want to sell. I always intended to.'

'You're happy staying in the country then, Roberta?'

'I feel I'm committed to it, yes, Paul.'

'Very well,' he said reluctantly. 'I'll put things in motion. Can you come into town? I'll need you here for some of the formalities.'

'Paul we're in luck. I'll be in the city all next week. I'll be staying with Mingo.'

'Oh, Roberta, that *is* luck.' What he could do with that week, if he were free. 'Look, what about Tuesday, the twenty-first, at my office. Would that suit you? Ten-thirty? And you'll let me take you to lunch afterward?'

'Of course, Paul. I'd like that very much. Tuesday, the twenty-first.'

Paul hung up and sat staring at the phone. The summer in Europe hadn't helped. He had made up his mind to settle Roberta's remaining business and then try to forget her. It hadn't worked.

Was he a quixotic fool? Another man wouldn't hesitate. If another man wanted Roberta, he'd tell her so. And if some other man's venomous wife threatened to tell Roberta of her dead husband's infidelity, that man would have ego enough to feel he could overcome Roberta's shock with the strength of his love.

Well, there was no question about the strength of *his* love. He'd risk absolutely nothing in leaving Alicia and declaring himself to Roberta. It was *Roberta* he'd be putting at risk. That was the catch.

The pencil Paul was holding snapped in two. He flung the pieces on the desk and got up and paced the floor.

That *was* the catch. What *would* it do to Roberta if Alicia carried out her blackmail threat, as he was dead certain she would? Would it be so devastating a blow that she'd never recover from it? Not, as Alicia had so contemptuously suggested, that it would 'rock her reason.' But it might disillusion her, strip away her faith in life, to say nothing of love. Anyway, it would hurt her hideously. It was his inability to hurt Roberta, even indirectly, which had kept Paul immobilized.

But he would have to resolve this one way or another. It had been rough enough to hide his love while Brad was alive. Now that Brad had been dead more than a year, Paul couldn't stand it any longer.

He made a decision. He would choose his course when he saw Roberta next week. He would let instinct be his guide. If he sensed that after a year alone Roberta was a woman receptive to a new love and if he sensed that a new love could heal the wound from Alicia's poisoned arrow, he'd declare himself. But if he picked up vibrations that Roberta was still largely sustained by memories of a happy marriage, still cherishing Brad's image and unable to really see any other man, then he'd protect those memories for her sake and bow out for good, ending this brutal dilemma.

Paul Reston wished he could speed up time, so that the moment of decision would come sooner.

Mingo's white limestone townhouse in the East Sixties was a surprising contrast to Mingo herself. Whereas Mingo was linear and contemporary, her house was Nineteenth Century, all curves and cushions and comfiness, if you could use such a word in connection with Mingo. Mingo's rooms were filled with plump sofas and patterned fabrics, photographs in silver frames and sterling tea services and fresh flowers and footstools covered in needlepoint. Her bathrooms had claw-foot tubs and French soaps and towel warmers, as in English country houses. Her second-floor sitting room, jutting out of the back of the house, had a curved bay window with a window seat that overlooked the garden.

'Oh, Mingo, I'd forgotten. Coming into this house is like being *hugged*, it's so welcoming,' Roberta said when she arrived Saturday night.

'By somebody motherly? Wearing an apron?' joked Mingo, indeed hugging her. 'If that's what you mean, that's just the effect I aim for. Oh, Robbie, I'm so glad you're here. Come on upstairs and get comfortable.'

She picked up Roberta's bag and led the way to her little gilded-cage elevator. 'Listen, Robbie dear, I've got a full week planned. There's a party we can go to later tonight, if you like. But *I* thought, since you've just put in a hard day at the shop and traveled up from the country on top of it, it might be fun just to stay home tonight. Sit in front of the fire, and put our feet up. Suit you?'

'Absolutely perfect.'

'Good. Later, we can even make *fudge* if we feel like it.'

It was a reference to their school days. Roberta giggled. 'We could never get it smooth. It always turned out grainy.'

'Like so many things,' said Mingo. 'Here, Robbie, I've put you in the Blue Onion room.'

'My favorite.' They chatted like girls in a dormitory while Roberta unpacked. Then they chattered downstairs, sipping drinks before the fire, while Mingo outlined what she'd cooked up for amusement: everything from Sunday brunch in a Tribeca cast-iron landmark building to dinner at an international banker's stupendous apartment crammed with treasures from his various French châteaux to a private party in the latest disco.

They were still chattering at two in the morning.

Paul Reston had had plenty of time to prepare himself for his appointment with Roberta. Indeed, the day and hour had burned itself into his mind. But he could not control the quickening of his pulse as she was shown into his office. For him, it was D-Day. Now . . . or never.

'Roberta. You are beautiful.'

'Paul, it's good to see you.' He had intended only to shake hands, but she leaned across the desk and kissed him on the cheek.

A family-friend kiss, of course. This woman he had loved so long had no inkling of his feelings. Careful, he warned himself. Feel your way.

He asked about Susan and Jim. She asked about Alicia. He said he hadn't seen much of Alicia, she'd spent the summer in Taos. Then he picked up Roberta's file.

At the end of an hour, he had laid out all the details of the proposed transaction, and she had accepted them.

'It *is* a good price,' he said in conclusion. 'And it's a considerable chunk of money. On the other hand, there'll be capital gains, and you'll be losing the income you got by renting to the Erskines. Of course you must invest the proceeds. I hope you'll let me advise you?'

'Gratefully, Paul.'

'Good. Then if you'll sign these papers, I'll set up the closing. We'll have to plan on vacating the apartment, too. What about your furniture?'

'I want to ship the family pieces, the things from Brad's family and mine, to the farm, to keep for the kids. I have acres of room in the attic, to say nothing of the barn. I'd like to sell everything else.'

He nodded. 'I can take care of that, Roberta. I have an inventory in the file, and if you'll just check what you want shipped, I'll see that it's done. I'll call in one of the auction houses for the rest.'

'Thanks, Paul, but I really can't let you do *all* my chores. Anyway, I think I'd like to go over the things personally.'

He hesitated. 'But won't it be painful for you, Roberta?'

She thought for a moment. Thirteen months ago, when she had clicked the door of the apartment shut, bitter over Brad, she had never wanted to set foot in it again. But since that dreamlike meeting with the pathetic woman Brad had felt responsible for, her perspective had shifted.

'Perhaps it will be painful, Paul. But I'd like to see the place again, I think.'

Paul's hopes soared. If it wouldn't hurt too much to visit what lawyers call 'the marital home,' surely that was a good sign? Maybe today *could* be the day to tell her he loved her. Perhaps over luncheon?

'Then I'll go with you,' he said decisively. 'If I can get Myra Erskine on the phone, perhaps we can go right now.'

It is an eerie thing to revisit the heart-place of an earlier life. Not only is there the sense of two times, past and present, in unsettling juxtaposition; there is the even more disorienting sense of two selves: the one you used to be, the one you are now.

It began, for Roberta, at the canopy. Then the lobby, the elevator, the familiar turn to the right, the door – 24B. As she waited for Paul to take out the key, she was grateful that Myra Erskine had tactfully absented herself and that the maid was out. When she stepped into the foyer, memory ignited so vividly she forgot Paul's presence.

She stood in the living room and remembered where the Christmas tree had touched the ceiling, remembered the children flat on the floor, reading comics. In Susan's room she remembered Susan's first bra . . . and a lost doll. In Jim's room, she saw again his kicked-off covers, and his gerbils. In the master bedroom, the corner one which had been hers and Brad's, she remembered everything . . . and the last residual bitterness melted away. It *had* been a happy marriage, for twenty-five fulfilling years. Nothing could change that.

Paul realized that Roberta, absorbed as she was, had forgotten he was there. But he saw every nuance of her expressive, remembering face. He saw tenderness and regret, sadness and relived moments. He saw her hand linger on the back of the chair he knew had been Brad's favorite. He saw the brightness of unshed tears when she came out of the bedroom.

And he knew his hopes had been false. He had been right all along. Of *course* Roberta found security in the memory of a happy marriage. To allow her to be disillusioned, posthumously, was unthinkable. It would rip away her past, devastate her present.

He would not let that happen. He could not think of a man who would not say he was a fool, but he loved her too much to put his own feelings above hers. If his own chance for happiness was thereby destroyed, that was the reality of it.

But he didn't know how he could get through lunch with Roberta so near . . . and so beyond reach.

At the quiet, elegant restaurant where he had made a reservation, with such anticipation, Paul was of course the attentive host. But he stuck carefully to impersonal subjects: the new theater season, the mayor's latest sally, the new buildings going up all over Manhattan.

Roberta was a trifle surprised when, directly after coffee, although it was not yet two o'clock, Paul glanced at his watch. 'Roberta, forgive me, but I have another appointment. I hate to rush, but . . .'

She reached for her handbag. 'Not at all, Paul. And thank you for a superb lunch.'

Of course, she thought. He's a busy and important lawyer. He has other things to do than attend to my piddling affairs. On the way out, she saw two women eyeing him. And he's so handsome. I wonder why Alicia is away so much nowadays?

Outside on the street, he offered her his waiting car and driver.

'Of course not, Paul. You're in a hurry. Anyway, I'm only going to Fifty-seventh Street.'

'Then goodbye, Roberta. And keep well.' He hesitated, then he kissed her lightly on the lips. 'Keep well,' he repeated, and got into the car.

How funny, thought Roberta. He said that almost as though he never expected to see me again.

I may never see her again, thought Paul, nails digging into his palms. He dismissed the car two blocks away. Her perfume lingered within it.

Late that afternoon, in Mingo's third-floor beauty spa, Roberta lay relaxed in the sauna. Too bad she hadn't had a chance to tell Paul about Jane Whitford's offer of a partnership and about the building Jane wanted to buy. Not that she couldn't guess Paul's reaction, he'd probably be horrified.

Then she forgot about Paul as she went down to her own room to dress for the evening. A cosmetic king and a biochemist were to be their escorts tonight, Mingo had said. A dinner pary to honor this year's novelist. Dabbing perfume at the pulse points – inside the elbow and knees, at the base of the throat, behind the ears – slipping into the kind of little-nothing dress which added up to everything (Mingo had gotten it wholesale) – Roberta thought of Zack. How wonderful to be dressing for *him*. Probably the very sexiness of the dress, the perfume, made him suddenly so vivid in her mind. But such thoughts were pointless.

She went downstairs to meet the cosmetic king and the biochemist.

29

Roberta looked forward to her New York luncheon date with Carole Harcourt. It would be fun to see Carole out of context. Roberta knew her only in her country-weekend setting. Now she'd get a glimpse of the Manhattan career woman. A bit different, she suspected, if Carole was the high-powered executive she believed her to be.

Carole called at eleven. 'Roberta . . .' her voice sounded strained, unnatural. 'I'm sorry, I can't make it. I . . .' The words were so choked Roberta could not make them out.

Alarmed, she said, 'Carole, what's wrong?'

'Everything. Just everything.' Carole was sobbing now. 'I'm in pieces. I'm home.'

'Then I'll come to you. May I?'

'*Would* you? I need . . . I need *somebody*.' Carole sounded pathetically grateful. 'Could you come right now?'

'I'm on my way, Carole.'

A grim-looking Ada admitted Roberta. 'Oh, Mrs Marston. I'm glad you're here. Mrs Harcourt . . . she's very upset.'

'Is she ill, Ada?'

'No, she . . .' Ada looked as though she could say a mouthful, but she restrained herself. 'This way, please, Mrs Marston.'

Carole had huddled in a chair in the living room. For a second Roberta barely recognized her. Without makeup and her ubiquitous fake lashes, Carole looked both older and younger: older, because weeping had emphasized every line; younger, because her woebegone expression made her look like a lost child.

She made an attempt to smile. 'Thanks for coming, Roberta. I know this is your vacation and the last thing you need is . . .' Then she burst into tears again. 'Oh, *hell*,' she sobbed. 'Sorry, this will be over in a minute.'

Roberta sat down and looked the other way. She thought of the day she had found Mary Blair sobbing. No two women could be more different than Carole and Mary, but they had tears in common. Can no woman escape weeping? Weeping over a man . . . or a child. But Carole had no children.

Now Carole sat up, mopped her eyes. 'There! That ought to hold me for a while. I hope.' She tried to smile again.

'Can I help, Carole?'

'Will you read this?' She picked up a letter from the coffee table and handed it to Roberta.

The first thing Roberta saw was the signature – a huge, scrawled 'Greg.' She hesitated. A letter from a husband was surely too personal. 'Carole, I shouldn't read this . . .'

'Roberta, there's no need to be delicate. *He* isn't . . . as you'll see. Please read it.'

The letter was datelined Jamaica.

Carole:

I won't be back I have found a woman who loves me. A *womanly* woman. Not a castrating female. Draw your own inference, dear.

Anyway, under existing economic conditions, won't it really be easier for you? I'm sure with your aggressive drives you'll claw your way back to the driver's seat.

Don't bother about a divorce, if you don't want to. We'll handle it. Love and kisses.

Greg.

'Look at the photo,' said Carole.

There was a colored photo attached to the note. It showed Greg in bathing trunks, stretched out indolently on a chaise next to a large swimming pool in a lush tropical setting. He was wearing sunglasses, and there was a faint smile on his lips. In the background was a large, elegant, pale pink villa.

Roberta was bewildered. 'I don't understand.'

'Greg's found another . . . another sugar mama,' Carole said bitterly.

'Sugar mama?'

'Someone to keep him in the style he enjoys. The difference is I work for my money – work my *rump* off. *She* undoubtedly inherited from her last husband. The other difference is that now I'm not earning *anything*. I'm unemployed, Roberta.'

'You're out of a job?'

'Since before Greg had his heart attack. I kept it from him. I wanted to spare him worry while he was recovering . . .'

'You mean you've been bearing all this by yourself? And you gave that huge party with this on your mind? Carole, you're a heroine.'

'Fool is more like it. I finally told Greg about it when we came back to town. He was almost back to normal – the doctor even said he could go back to work – and it was getting so hard to conceal it, pretending to go to the office. Anyway, I was hoping Greg would give *me* some moral support, buck me up . . .'

'Not much for a wife to expect,' said Roberta indignantly. 'But what about Greg's work? Couldn't he . . .?'

'Take over? Oh, Roberta, of course none of this makes sense to you without your knowing the facts.' Rapidly Carole sketched the story of their marriage: how it early became obvious that Greg would hold only minor jobs,

335

how Carole had supported them both, carefully preserving Greg's ego, how the jobs he did hold for a time were mostly for his charm and looks. He was a good man on a publicity junket. 'In fact,' she concluded, 'that's how he got to Jamaica. A P.R. freebie. As good a place as any to jump ship, I suppose. Especially a *sinking* ship.'

'Carole,' said Roberta firmly, 'if there is any woman who is not a sinking ship, it's *you*. I know, it, I'm sure of it, I guarantee it.'

Carole looked so hopeful at this vote of confidence, that Roberta knew she was on the right track.

'Look, Carole, you've had two kicks at once. Your man and your job. Let's tackle them one at a time. Do you love Greg?'

Carole looked confused. 'I don't know. I've hated him sometimes, times when he put me down. He was always putting me down in sneaky, subtle ways, ways he could always claim were just kidding. Like when he called me Girl Producer. Or Mz Ad Biz. And right now, when he's sent me that brutal note and that sadistic photo, I know he's a bastard. I loathe him. And yet, I've always felt I needed him, that I couldn't survive without him.'

'But why? You've been the provider of both financial and moral support. What do you need him for?'

'To drive me to the country.' Carole began to laugh. 'Oh, Roberta, isn't that hysterical.' *She* was a little hysterical, Roberta saw, but laughing was better than crying.

'And to be a host,' Carole went on. 'Make drinks. All that.'

'That's ridiculous.'

'Yes, it is. Ridiculous. But I'm stuck with it.'

'No, you're not. You know, Carole, I think a lot of women our age still have that hang-up. We got it from our mothers. A woman is nothing without a man. But a woman obviously is whatever she is – with or without. A really good marriage, of course . . . well, who wouldn't want that? But how many do you know?'

Carole thought. 'Give me twenty-four hours, I may think of one.'

'Exactly. At this late date, Carole, I'm just catching on. Lots of marriages are shams – based on that famous quiet desperation.' She thought of the Blairs. 'Did you know Mary Blair is divorcing her husband?'

Carole sat up. 'Honestly? That terrific guy?'

'Not so terrific as a husband, apparently.'

'But I wouldn't think she'd have the nerve to be alone.'

'She found the nerve. She's moving into a place of her own, and she's only been working a few months, you know. Practically a beginner.'

'Gee, Roberta, you're making me feel like a coward.'

'I'm only trying to convince you that being alone is not the end of the world. Fear of being alone is worse than being alone. I found that out. Once you get over the panic, you may even find some fringe benefits.'

'Really?' Carole looked as though she'd like to believe it, but couldn't quite.

Ada appeared in the doorway. 'Luncheon is served, Mrs Harcourt.'

'What an enormous apartment, Carole,' Roberta said as they entered the dining room.

'That's what Greg said, when he first saw it. I've had it for years, Roberta. But now I'll probably have to give it up.' Carole was looking frightened again.

While they lunched, she told Roberta how panicky she was becoming over money, and how she'd been struggling to set up her own business, with only one small account so far.

'I've got very solid experience, especially in drugs and cosmetics. But of course I've always had a powerhouse agency behind me. On my own, I can't even get my foot in the door to make a pitch. I know I could make it, Roberta, if I had a little time, but I don't think my cash will hold out. Now Greg's bowing out has clobbered me so . . . I haven't much fight left.'

'Listen to me, Carole. I don't know a thing about your field, of course, but I did learn something about making do with less cash. Could you buy time by cutting down on expenses? Live on less, so you'd have more time to get your business going?'

'Like how?'

'Well, how about renting this apartment? To a diplomat or something? With rents what they are you'd probably get twice what you pay, wouldn't you?'

Carole looked amazed. 'You know, Roberta, I can estimate the cost of a TV commercial within a couple of hundred bucks, but I'm a *dope* about money. Personal money, I mean – would you believe it? I've always handed my income over to my accountant. He pays the bills, and screams when I go overboard. It would never have dawned on me that I could rent this place and still hang on to it.'

'Well, you can. I did it with mine. Providing there's no red tape to prevent doing it, of course.'

'Don't worry about that.' Carole suddenly had a pugnacious tilt to her chin. 'I'm a great finagler when I have to be.'

'That's the spirit. Then you could rent your country place, also for quite a lot, I should think. Plus, you could mortgage it, couldn't you? Pay the mortgage with the rent, and keep the difference?'

Carole stared at her in disbelief. 'Roberta, you're a regular Hetty Green, for God's sake.'

Roberta laughed. 'I'm a fraud, that's what I am. Don't be deceived, Carole. I never knew a thing about money either. My husband handled everything – I never even balanced a checkbook. And I suddenly found myself short of cash too. But I've got a very smart boss. She's the one who knows about turning assets into ready money. It's all new to me too, so don't be impressed.'

'Well, I *am* impressed. You've opened by eyes. Maybe I *could* swing it, that way.' Carole's eyes were alive now, and she looked more like her vivacious self. 'I'll get hold of my accountant and see what he says. Maybe I could get a smaller place that I could also use as an office, a combination. Then, with any luck at all . . .'

She jumped up and hugged Roberta. 'Roberta, I didn't think anything could cheer me up today, but you have . . . and then some.'

Riding back to the East Side through the park, thinking about Carole, Roberta made a mental connection. Carole had said she had heavy cosmetic experience. One of the men who had escorted Mingo and Roberta the other night was the president of a cosmetic company – Lure, Inc, no less. Would a word from Mingo open the door Carole 'couldn't get her foot into?'

How wild – and how wonderful – if it did. Mingo didn't even know Carole Harcourt, but she hadn't known Mary Blair either. Yet that photo session for *Home Woman* had been a turning point in Mary's life. Which made Mingo a sort of unwilling *deus ex machina* . . . and Roberta another, since she was the connecting link.

What a jigsaw life is, Roberta thought. Almost anybody can drop a piece into your private puzzle and complete the picture.

As it turned out, Mingo's word did open the door for Carole, and Carole's talents did the rest. Her work for Lure, Inc, became the keystone of Carole's organization . . . but that came later.

30

Mingo gave a dinner party on Friday, Roberta's last night in town. Over Mingo's protests, Roberta planned to leave the next day because, she said, she would have to overcome the equivalent to jet lag. 'Ming, the East Sixties may be an hour and a half from Greenwillow, but it's light years away in ambiance. I've got to get over the culture shock, you know. I can't just step from all this *luxe* back to the checkout line at the A & P. I need a little buffer – to get back to reality.'

'Well, I do know what you mean. After a trip I'm always two feet off the ground for a while. But I'm going to miss you so.'

'It's been a wonderful week, Ming. Seven days in Manhattan is like six months anywhere else. What do you think of this eye shadow?'

'Ravishing. And my God, Roberta, you in that dress!'

The two women were in Mingo's dressing room, companionably, making up before Mingo's big mirror with the professional lights.

The phone rang at Mingo's elbow. 'Oh, sweetie, of *course*,' she said to the caller, '*bring* him – the more the merrier.'

'Good, another extra man,' she said as she hung up. 'That was Antionette O'Rourke, remember her? Used to be our Features Editor. She married a Texas oil man. He's got some sort of pal in town and wants to bring him along. Don't be surprised if he turns up in a ten-gallon hat.'

The extra man was Zack Owen.

Roberta saw him before he saw her. During the moments when the O'Rourkes were presenting him to Mingo, Roberta felt shock, then joy, then that strange impulse which makes people pretend in public not to recognize someone they have known intimately. I've never seen him in a dinner jacket, she thought crazily.

As Zack turned to be presented to Roberta, she saw *his* shock. Then he recovered, took both her hands. 'Roberta!'

'How nice to see you again,' she said weakly. Then, realizing their eyes were locked together, she forced a smile she was sure was ghastly.

'You know each other?' said Mingo.

'Yes,' said Zack.

'From the country,' said Roberta.

It was impossible for them to speak further. The O'Rourkes carried Zack off, introducing him around the room, and Mingo was bringing people up to Roberta as new guests were arriving. Through the babble of voices and the clink of glasses and the mingled perfumes in the air, Roberta could feel Zack's presence as tangibly as a flame against her skin.

Dinner was served at tables for eight. Zack and Roberta were not at the same table – that would have been an impossible situation – but their eyes met across the room. She had no idea what she and her dinner partner were talking about.

Not until the party moved back into the living room did she and Zack speak again. Roberta was sitting with a man who was telling her about his collection of antique cars. Zack approached, said, 'May I?' and appropriated Roberta. 'Forgive me,' he said to the other man, 'but we're former neighbors – lots of catching up to do.' The other man took the hint and moved on.

'Darling.' His voice was low and urgent. 'I was in

Greenwillow this morning, looking for you. I called the shop . . .'

She could only say, 'Zack.'

'How soon can you get away from here?'

'I can't. The party's for me. I'm Mingo's houseguest.'

'When are you leaving?'

'Tomorrow afternoon.'

'That's too long. Meet me tomorrow morning. Seven. St Regis. Will you?'

'Yes. I will, Zack.'

'I'm not going to let you get away, Mrs M.'

'Oh, Zack, I . . .'

Another couple joined them.

At five-thirty the next morning Roberta awakened – if, indeed, she had slept at all. She had drifted into half-dream, mind and body thrumming to the sense of Zack only a few blocks away.

At six she dialed the St Regis. He answered immediately. 'You're awake, Zack?'

'Did you think I could sleep?'

'Should I come now?'

'Yes, darling, now. I'll meet you downstairs.'

She wrote a note to Mingo. 'Felt like a walk. Back by one.' Then she tiptoed into Mingo's darkened room and left the note on her night table. Mingo would sleep until noon, after last night's party.

Twenty minutes later her taxi pulled up in front of the St Regis. Zack was there, helped her out, paid the cab.

Three minutes later, just inside the door of his suite, he took her in his arms. Her desire flamed instantly, matching his. He held her off, to look at her. 'Roberta, my dearest . . . there's so much to say, to ask . . . but I want you so much . . .'

'Yes, Zack, yes . . . me too.' She unknotted his tie.

He picked her up and carried her into the bedroom. It was as though their souls left their bodies.

Roberta awakened first. She moved closer to Zack. In sleep, his arms tightened around her. She closed her eyes. She was where she belonged. When she opened them again, he was awake.

'My beloved.'

'I missed you so.'

'It was hell for me, Roberta. Tokyo. Then being side-tracked to Dallas. I called you from Tokyo; then I canceled it. I was afraid I'd complicate things for you. I called you again from the airport in San Francisco. No answer.'

'Ah, Zack, if I had only known. I wanted to write you, in fact I did – in my head, endlessly. But I wasn't sure how you felt by that time.'

'Fool.' He lifted her arm, and kissed the warm spot inside her elbow. 'When I hit New York yesterday, I drove straight from Kennedy to Greenwillow. I hung around Creek Road like a suspicious character, trying to size up the situation. Then I called the shop. They said you were on vacation. They didn't say where.'

'Here.'

'Yes, here.' He pulled her to him, and they made love again.

An hour later she said, 'Zack, I would stay here forever and die happy, but I must ask: What time is it?'

He picked up his watch. 'Twelve-fifteen.'

'I must get back to Mingo's.'

'Call her.'

'Zack. I have to thank her for my visit.'

'Right. But I begrudge the time. Look, I'll pick you up at three and drive you to the farm. We'll improvise from there.'

'I'll be ready.'

'But one question, before you go.' He hated even to mention Susan's name. 'Roberta, how is the . . . situation?'

'Better . . . I *think*.' Quickly she told him how Susan had disappeared for weeks and had eventually called from some tiny place in New York State; that she was living with a friend and working at Cornell.

'The friend . . . male?'

'Yes, but – '

'How can there be a "but"? That's the best news in – '

'He may be just a buddy,' she said cautiously.

'But it's a big step in the right direction. Anyway, Susan's okay for the moment . . . and you're alone at the farm?'

She nodded.

'Then come on, Mrs M. dear, I'll put you in a cab. The quicker you get there, the faster I'll have you back.'

Mingo was just coming out of her room as Roberta stepped out of the elevator. 'My God, Roberta, you look like a handful of shooting stars. Have you actually been out? I didn't *believe* that note.' She took another look. 'Why, Robbie, I could swear you've just come from a rendezvous. Don't tell me you sneaked out after the party?'

'Oh, no. I woke up very early and I couldn't get back to sleep, so . . .'

Mingo began to laugh. 'Oh, Robbie, we all know about the famous *cinq à sept*, but that's afternoon. I never heard of one in the early morning.'

'*Now* you have.' Roberta felt so bubbly with joy she wanted to spill it all out. She had never said a word about her affair with Zack, not even to Mingo. Now she had the very feminine urge to share it with her closest friend.

'Well, if it makes you look like *that*, I'm all for it. Anyone I know?'

'Zack Owen. The man who came with the O'Rourkes.'

'That *divine* young man? Nice *going*. *Tell* me about it.'

'Mingo, I'm dying to.'

'Tell you what, I'll have Mrs MacCochrane bring us trays in the back sitting room. Are you hungry?'

'Starved.'

Mingo laughed. 'I've *heard* it has that effect.'

Over black coffee and vitamins for Mingo and a hefty brunch for Roberta, the woman in love told the woman who had never experienced it about her romance.

'And he asked you to marry him way back then? Last spring?'

'Yes. The day you took me to lunch on my birthday.'

'Then what's the hitch?'

'Susan got a giant crush on him. Of course she didn't know about us – Zack and me. She was head over heels, and told him so. When he said he was involved – elsewhere – she went to pieces.'

'And that ended it?'

'I had no choice. Don't you see, Mingo? My daughter falling apart over a man and my marrying that same man?'

'God, yes. I do see. Sometimes,' said Mingo grimly, 'being childless isn't all bad, is it? But Susan's okay now, isn't she?'

'Well, I'm not sure. I think so. I *hope* so.'

'And if Susan is over her infatuation – better yet, in love with someone else – what then?'

'Well, there'd be nothing to stop me, I suppose, except . . .'

'Except?'

'He's almost ten years younger than I am, or I'm ten years older than he is. I don't know which way to put it.

Mingo, give it to me straight. How bad do you think it is?'

Mingo thought about it before she replied. She was too devoted to Roberta to give her easy answers. 'I don't know, Robbie,' she said slowly. 'In some cases I think it needn't matter a damn. It can be irrelevant. On the other hand, the world is too much with us – raised eyebrows department. It's still a youth society, although that's supposed to be changing, thank God. I guess it depends on how really indifferent you are . . . to other people's values.'

'I don't *think* I care too much about that. What concerns me is how he – Zack – would feel ten years from now.'

'You'll never know, Roberta, unless you have the courage to risk it. It's a risk, I agree, but what the hell isn't? And anyway, in a "worst case scenario," to use the awful jargon, what could happen? Suppose, ten years from now, it started fraying at the edges? You'd have had ten good years. That ain't chopped liver, you know, not to someone who's never had ten good *days*.'

Suddenly Mingo's eyes misted with tears. Feeling guilty, as though she'd been displaying a closetful of shoes to a barefoot woman, Roberta jumped up and hugged her friend. 'Oh, Mingo, how gross of me, to go on and on when you . . . Listen, Mingo, it may happen to you too, you know. It could take you by surprise.'

Mingo wiped her eyes and smiled. 'At this late date? Just a rush of hearts and flowers, Robbie. Think nothing of it. Anyway, my considered opinion is: If you love him, marry him . . . with my blessing.' She made a mock benediction. 'Provided I'm best woman.'

'Oh, Mingo, who else? And thanks for the advice. Listen, Ming, would you forgive me if I left a little earlier

346

than planned? Zack's going to drive me back to the farm . . .'

'And then?'

'We'll see.' Roberta's eyes left no doubt in Mingo's mind.

Mingo played dumb when Zack arrived. Her manner suggested only that she was *so* pleased Roberta would be driven to her door. Such *luck* that Mr Owen happened to be going in the same direction at the same time.

As Zack stowed Roberta's bag in the car, Mingo stood in the doorway and blew a kiss to Roberta, followed by an A-O.K. sign. Then, to make it even more clear, she nodded affirmatively.

Zack saw none of this pantomime, but as he pulled onto Park Avenue, she said, 'Quite a woman. She knows all about us, doesn't she?'

'Yes. She's my best friend. I told her. But how did you know?'

'Oh, I picked it up out of the air.'

Roberta laughed delightedly. What could possibly go wrong with a man as perceptive as Zack Owen?

She leaned back against the seat and tried to realize that although twenty-four hours ago she had been convinced she would never see Zack again, his shoulder was actually touching hers.

31

For the next two weeks, Roberta and Zack lived together at the farm. Long afterward, they both remembered that time as perfect.

When they arrived from Mingo's late Saturday afternoon, Zack parked the car and said, 'Home.' He sat looking up the lane toward the carriage house. 'If you knew how often I dreamed of this place.' He got out and went around to open her door. 'Come on, Mrs M, I've got an uncontrollable urge to make sure it's all still here. Let's walk through the back forty before it gets dark.'

Laughing, they walked up the lane hand in hand. As they rounded the curve toward the carriage house, Zack said, 'I hate your new tenant, on principle. Whoever he is.'

'It's a she. But do you know, Zack, I've never been inside the place since you left? I couldn't bear it. I had Jim handle the rental.'

When they got to the spot where they had met on that snowy Sunday, Zack drew her to the big rock they had sat on. 'Remember? I was sitting here, and *you* came along . . . in your boots and fur hat, with snow on your lashes.'

'You walked me to my door.'

'I hated like hell to leave you.'

'I wanted to invite you in for a drink, but I wasn't sure of the protocol. Landlady, you know.'

'Ah, Mrs M . . .' He took her in his arms.

When they got back to the house, Zack asked where

Roberta would like to have dinner. 'Golden Pheasant? One of our old places?'

'I'd rather fix something here, but I cleaned out the fridge before I left . . .'

'Then I'll go out and bring some food back. I'd rather stay here too – *much* nicer. I can kiss you here, I can't in the Golden Pheasant.'

When he left, Roberta stood for a moment, wondering if this were really happening. It was almost scary to be so happy.

But there was one nagging anxiety she had to confront. Susan. She had to find out how things really stood with her daughter. She went to the phone and dialed the number Susan had given her. She felt herself growing tense as she listened to the distant ringing.

A masculine voice answered. When she asked for Susan, she heard the voice call, 'Sue – for you.' There was something relaxed and easy about the sound of it, something domestic.

'Susan, it's Mother.'

'Mummy!' Susan's voice sounded spontaneously glad, and her reverting back to the affectionate childhood name was a good sign. Then, her tone turned anxious. 'Is anything wrong?'

'No, darling, nothing at all. I just wanted to know how you are, what you're doing . . .'

'Pretty good, Mother. Really good, in fact. I like the job at Cornell, and I've been able to fit in a couple of credits toward my Master's. I thought maybe I'd go in for teaching, eventually. And it's so beautiful up here in the fall. Bob and I can't wait for the ski season to begin.'

Bob and I. She'd said it as one word – Bob-and-I – with the ring of a team, a couple. Roberta wanted to ask: Do you love him, does he love you, are you serious

349

about each other? But that would have to wait until Susan herself offered the confidence.

'But, Mother, How are *you*? How's the farm? How's the shop?'

'I've just had a week's vacation. I was in town, at Mingo's.'

'Was it fun?'

'Great fun.' *Now*. 'And you'll never guess whom I ran into.'

'Who?'

'Zack Owen.' Roberta could feel her heart beating faster.

There was a split second of silence. Then Roberta heard Susan's peal of laughter. 'Oh, wow, *really*? Oh, Mother, remember how off-the-wall I was about him? Talk about having a *thing* for someone . . . I really thought it was the end of the *world*. He's a nice man, though.'

'Yes, he is,' Roberta said weakly. 'As a matter of fact, he's coming for dinner tonight.'

'Really? That's nice. Say "Hi" for me, will you?'

Roberta hung up, flooded with relief and stunned at the resilience of the young. Remember how off-the-wall I was, indeed. But, thank heaven, Susan was well and content. She hoped that whatever role this unknown Bob now played in Susan's life, her daughter would eventually find a woman's happiness . . . like her own.

Zack came back laden with groceries. He had bought out the store. While Roberta broiled the steaks, Zack mixed drinks and laid a fire in the dining room. She was reaching for china from the shelf when she felt his kiss on the back of her neck. He turned her toward him.

'Roberta. I was going to wait for the perfect moment, but I can't wait. Roberta, will you marry me?'

She saw the love in his eyes, and she had no need to think. 'Yes, Zack, Oh, Zack, *yes.*'

He gathered her in, and she wept against his chest.

They dined by candlelight, in peace and privacy, enclosed in a world for two. Oddly, they did not speak much. Just sharing fragments of thoughts aloud, memories . . . reading each other's minds.

'That day I brought you the firewood and we talked music, that's when I knew.'

'For me, it was the carriage house. That first night . . .'

'Ah.' In the silence, they both remembered.

'But how could you think I wouldn't be back?'

'I knew you would be, but I didn't believe it.'

'We must make plans, Mrs M.'

'Yes. Tomorrow. For now, let's just . . .'

'Bask.'

They sat for another hour, watching the embers die.

Then Roberta led him upstairs. They slept in each other's arms in the big front guest room.

On Sunday, Zack told Roberta about the direction his job was taking. He said he was increasingly involved in acquisitions for PetroFax. And that meant never really having a home base for very long. He was subject to sudden shifts from place to place, even country to country.

'How would you feel about that, Roberta? Pillar to post – could you live with it?'

'Of course. I'd be living with *you*, not it.'

Roberta felt reckless, ready for anything. All out for love. Whither thou goest . . .

His arm around her, her head on his shoulder, he went on. 'I'll be in the New York office for the next two weeks; then its back to Dallas. But the good news is that

January second I'll be back in New Jersey. Right in Clinton, for at least six months.'

She sat up. 'In Clinton? That's wonderful. Then we could stay right here.'

'I think I'm as attached to your farm as you are, Mrs M. Soon' – he kissed her ear – 'to be Mrs O. The problem is *I* want to provide the roof over *my* wife's head.'

'Zack, you know I love your feeling that way . . . but for six months? Anyway, I'd like to know this was here as a permanent home place, wouldn't you? A place to come back to whenever we can?'

'Absolutely. But we'd have to look for a couple to take care of it.'

'They could live in the carriage house.'

'Second-best use for the carriage house. Have you ever been to Portugal?'

'Never.'

'I'll take you there for our honeymoon.'

Zack was all for marrying immediately. But Roberta persuaded him that she needed a little time to get Susan and Jim used to the idea. Zack conceded the point.

They finally settled on the Christmas holidays for their wedding. It would be the most convenient time for all concerned: Roberta's kids, Roberta's father, and Zack's brothers and their wives. It would be a home wedding, very simple, with Mingo standing up for Roberta, and Zack's eldest brother for him. They wanted to commit themselves to each other in the presence of those dearest to them.

After settling their wedding plans, they drove along the Delaware into the Poconos for dinner. When they got back, Zack raised the question of his staying in her house. 'Look darling, of course I'll drive back here every night from New York until I leave for Dallas. But don't you think my being . . . in residence . . . might be a bit much? For you, I mean. Suppose some of your friends drop in?'

'What will people think? Whatever they please.'

That settled it. They went to bed early. They both had to get to work the next morning. And they both lived through Monday counting the minutes until they would be together again.

On Thursday Roberta met Zack in New York for a dinner with his associates from PetroFax. 'I'm afraid it's rather obligatory,' he told her, 'hard to duck. And, of course, I have an ulterior motive. I want to show you off.'

On Sunday, they drove to Connecticut, to meet Zack's brother Alan and his family. Roberta liked Alan and Wendy Owen at once. In their mid-thirties, they were as warm, relaxed and informal as their contemporary house, which was designed for easy care and children. At the door, the children hurled themselves at Zack. He swooped his niece onto his shoulder and put his arm around his nephew.

'Roberta, my favorite kids. This is special Betsey. And my namesake, Zackary.'

'I can't imagine *why*,' smiled Roberta. The little boy was a carbon copy of Zack: same mischievous eyes and quirky brows, same squared-off shoulders with the same graceful swing. She could hardly take her eyes off him.

It was a thoroughly pleasant day. By previous agreement, Zack did not mention their marriage plans. They had decided not to tell anyone until a month beforehand; meanwhile they would let family members know they were 'seeing' each other. Roberta could sense that, naturally enough, Alan and Wendy were curious about her place in Zack's life. Their devotion to Zack was obvious, and Roberta guessed that whatever would make Zack happy, would make them happy. She was going to like

353

her in-laws. Then the idea of new in-laws suddenly seemed unbelievable. At moments, she still felt she was dreaming.

Paradoxically, their two weeks together seemed to pass both slowly and rapidly. Slowly, because never having had so much time together – kissing each other goodbye every morning, meeting again every night, sharing daily living – their minutes and hours were packed with meaning. They had time to make endless new discoveries about each other, to share past history, to learn each other's special tastes and hang-ups, to plan the future – and, of course, to revel in the present. Those weeks seemed like a year's worth of closeness.

But when they day came for Zack to leave, they both felt the time had flown by too rapidly. She drove Zack to the airport. 'I'll call you every night at eleven, darling,' he said. 'And I'll be back weekend after next.' 'Zack, such a long trip for only twenty-four hours?' 'Yes, but *what* a twenty-four hours.' His farewell kiss was so lingering, he almost missed the plane.

Roberta drove back to Greenwillow in a bemused state of mind. Everything had happened so fast, from her first heart-stopping sight of him at Mingo's to his embrace just now, she'd felt a sense of unreality. She had a feeling she'd wake up any minute. But there was Zack's sweater on the sofa. And upstairs, on her pillow, Zack had left a note. Loving, funny, and blush-provoking.

Much as she missed him – already, in less than two hours – she was almost glad he was gone. His physical presence was so electric that she had been living on an emotional high. Now she could calm down, come back to earth, and think rationally about the tremendous change in her life.

In the following days, visualizing the future, she was increasingly glad she and Zack would begin married life in familiar surroundings. They would have far more private time together without the impact of new places and new people. She was glad, too, that she could keep her job. She would readily have given up ten jobs for Zack, but she enjoyed her work at the shop, felt involved in its success, and was very fond of Jane. Of course she owed Jane plenty of advance notice. She would tell Jane of her plans in November, and would stick with her through the first six months of the new year. Then she would knock herself out to help Jane find and train a replacement.

She thought fleetingly of Jane's proposition, the new shop. Would she ever have considered such a venture seriously? The answer was a very doubtful maybe. At any rate, she hoped Jane would find a way to realize her dream of expansion.

Zack flew back from Dallas for a six P.M. Saturday to ten P.M. Sunday visit. Every moment was perfect. She went to bed Sunday night feeling cherished and secure.

Why, then, did she wake up the next morning with a sense of anxiety? It was as though a crack had appeared overnight in the walls of her security. A hairline crack, but there. And she felt a sense of *warning*. Danger. Be careful. You are about to make a mistake.

A *mistake*? How could that be? Baffled and disturbed, Roberta tried to laugh off the feeling as the common human fear that when things are wonderful, something must be wrong. Too good to be true. I'm having a fit of nerves, because I can't trust my own happiness.

It was Monday, her day off. She had planned to shop for slipcover fabrics. She was going to redo the bedroom she and Zack would make their permanent room, was going to change the living-room color scheme as well. It was a symbolic gesture: a new look to celebrate a new

355

alliance. And what a joy it was to make a home beautiful and comfortable for a man she loved.

But when she put the key in the ignition, her hand trembled. She sat for a moment. She felt much too shaky to shop for fabrics today. She could not possibly concentrate. She went back into the house and sat down.

What's come over me? Struggling to keep calm, Roberta closed her eyes and tried to think. Anxiety like this doesn't spring up overnight. It may *surface* overnight, but it's been there, hidden, all along. What is its source? When did it begin?

She tried to cast her thought back over the time she and Zack had spent together since they'd been reunited. Had it begun when they'd dined in New York with that senior PetroFax executive and his wife? They were a handsome couple in their sixties, and graciousness itself. But when the women had refreshed their makeup in the powder room, the wife had skillfully made small talk. 'Zack tells us you are a widow, Mrs Marston. Do you have children?' 'A daughter and a son. Susan's working at Cornell and Jim's in law school.' A flicker of surprise had appeared on the woman's face, quickly controlled but conveying: Really? Children that old?

Yes, that had bothered her, Roberta realized. But only a little, only for a moment. She had pushed it to the back of her mind and had forgotten it. Not entirely, apparently.

Or had this disturbing sense of uneasiness begun when she'd watched Zack's face as he'd greeted his brother's kids? She could see his look now. Wistful. Almost hungry. Especially with the little boy who was the image of himself. Witnessing it, Roberta's spontaneous thought had been: he's a man who should have children. But that too, she had pushed away and, in the warmth of the visit, forgotten.

Now another small incident came back to her. Last

week . . . She had been brushing her hair, and had seen, for the first time, a silver streak. It was not visible under her hairdo, but there it was revealed. It was a glamorous streak, actually, the kind some women have their hairdressers create, and she knew Mingo would say 'Lucky you! *Exploit* it!' But Roberta had stared at the mirror, feeling chilled.

Could anything be more clear? The ten years between Zack and herself, the age difference which had worried her from the beginning, was still worrying her. Although she'd thought she had conquered it for good, it was not only alive but virulent. Strong enough to wake her up this morning, to make her so uncertain that her hands shook. The truth was that she was thinking the unthinkable: this marriage may be a mistake.

For the rest of that tormented week, Roberta was battered by the opposing forces of her heart and mind. Her protesting heart cried out: Give up this love, this life, I've found? Never! Besides, we thrashed it out. Zack and I. He said ages were just numbers, irrelevant. But her objective mind countered: *He* said! What do *you* say? You don't really believe it. If you did, you wouldn't have this conflict, would you? Things are different now, yes. But think of *later*. Later! Later!

Later . . .

She awoke from a restless dream that had been centered on a calendar. The date was ten years in the future, in red letters. Red for danger.

Suddenly she knew, with an icy certainty, that she should not and would not marry Zack.

And she knew why.

It was not the difference in their ages, per se. Zack was right about that. It was not that they might encounter, here and there, a raised eyebrow. Realistically, that might sting, in some circumstances, but they were both strong enough to ignore it.

No, the real danger was that she and he were at very different stages of life experience. She had had a long marriage, and the fulfillment of children. He had had a cruelly brief marriage, and had lost his only child. That would make *their* marriage unbalanced. Lopsided things topple.

Ten years from now she would be sixty, older for a woman. But he would be fifty, prime for a man. And bound to feel cheated, she was convinced, of having a family. Likely, much as he would try to hide it, to regret his choice. Or even resent his choice. It was a marriage, bright with promise as it seemed, which would prove disillusioning, if not disastrous.

But how could she tell him? How could she bear to? She loved him.

Zack was scheduled to spend the weekend after the next in Greenwillow. It would be cruel and unfair to let him make the trip, considering what she had to tell him. Steeling herself for the most painful act of her life, Roberta flew to Dallas early Sunday morning.

There, in the airport restaurant where an alarmed Zack met her, she told him she could not marry him. First he was stunned and incredulous. Then he was gentle and reassuring – she was just suffering a case of jitters. In the end, he was furious.

'What were you doing, Roberta? Playing a game?' His eyes were hot with pain and anger.

'Zack, Zack, you know better than that. I love you and I know you love me. Don't you see this is tearing me apart?'

'No. I see you deliberately tearing apart something I thought was . . . close to sacred.'

If only she could make him understand, not feel so betrayed.

'Zack – dearest Zack – we haven't been facing reality. The age difference between us *does* make a difference.'

'I thought we laid that bugaboo to rest a long time ago. And I thought you were above such stupid conventions.'

It hurt to have him imply she was frivolous, fickle, superficial.

'We did lay it to rest, Zack, and I agree with you about convention. But there's something more vital . . .'

'And that is?'

'Oh, Zack, I can't forget the way you looked with little Zack, your brother's child, in Connecticut. The love in your eyes . . . and the yearning. Zack, dear Zack, I think – I'm convinced – that ten years from now you'll bitterly regret not having a family. I think you'll feel cheated. I couldn't bear your feeling that way because of me.'

'I lost my child. I don't want another.'

'I know you think that now. But Zack, you're a man with so much love to give . . . just a wife wouldn't be enough. Eventually you'll need much more, a circle around you . . . your own flesh and blood to need you . . . and love you.'

'Are you telling me that you're sacrificing what we have – what we *had*' – he amended harshly – 'for *my* sake?'

'No. I'm saying it would be a mistake for both of us.' If he knew how much she wanted to throw herself into his arms. 'For me too, Zack. I don't think I'd be happy married to you, either.'

That was the hardest thing she had to say. She didn't even believe it.

He looked at her with a look she'd never seen before – hostility.

'Then there's no more to be said, is there?'

'I suppose not.'

She knew she should leave it at that. Say no more. End it. But she couldn't.

'Zack, you have given me one of the most beautiful experiences of my life. I'll live on its memory. I'll always cherish the thought of you – the fact of you. I hope you'll believe that?'

'Don't you think that's too much to ask?'

She saw it was no use. She had actually thought she could leave him without destroying the warm mutual bonds of affection between them. That was a foolish hope. She had shocked him and hurt him. She had wounded his ego. From his point of view, he had been brutally rejected, by a woman he thought was going to be his wife.

'Ah, Zack, of course you don't believe me. You can't. But I hope, someday, you will.'

'What time does your plane leave?'

'In forty-five minutes.'

'I'll wait and see you to the gate,' he said stiffly. That inborn chivalry which had made her feel so protected.

'No. Zack. Thank you, but you really needn't – '

'Very well.' He stood up. 'Goodbye, Roberta. I hope you find what you want . . . whatever it is.' He turned and walked away.

He was halfway across the waiting room when she was out of her seat and running after him. She caught him by the arm, he stopped and turned, she kissed him on the cheek. 'A proper goodbye, Zack.' He looked at her and then, indifferent to passers-by, took her in his arms and kissed her on the lips. A hard, accusing, bruising, furious final kiss. Then he released her and walked away.

On the plane back, the passenger next to Roberta wondered why the woman in the sunglasses kept dabbing at her eyes, and why her hand clenched and unclenched a sodden handkerchief.

Bereaved, thought the passenger sympathetically.

Bereaved, wept Roberta behind the glasses.

Bereaved, indeed, and by her own hand.

Part III

32

October was a terrible month for Roberta. Having gone through the anxiety and pain of giving up Zack, she was now half-convinced she had been crazy to do so. She had been a fool to reject love, a coward not to take a chance. Who was *she* to decide for both of them what the future would be? She had been playing God, deliberately destroying a rare bond between two people. How Zack must despise her . . . and with good reason.

She had a strong urge to call him, to tell him that she loved him. To ask him, humbly, if he would forgive her foolish fears and if they could go on as before. Most of all she wanted to convince him that she had not meant it when she'd said she would not be happy with him. It was unbearable to think that Zack believed her commitment had been false when, in fact, she had loved him – and still did.

Driven by an urgent need to hear his voice, she went to the phone. She dialed the Dallas area code, her heart racing. Then she dialed the exchange. Suddenly she pressed down the receiver. Wait. What are you doing? You're acting like a madwoman.

She sat, staring at the phone. Then she called Mingo and poured out the whole story. 'Oh, Mingo, was I right the first time or am I right now? Tell me what you think – I'm going out of my mind.'

'Robbie, Robbie, take a deep breath and try to relax. Now, let's go over it again. Was it just the age difference that made you give him up?'

'No. Not really. It bothered me, but I thought we

could . . . well, tough it out. Remember? You and I discussed it.'

'Of course I remember. What was it, then?'

'It's hard to explain,' Roberta said slowly. 'But I somehow felt our lives were at such different points that they wouldn't fit. Our histories were too different . . .'

'Histories?'

'Zack lost his wife and child – a little girl. I've had a long marriage and have two grown-up kids. It seemed . . . uneven. I thought he'd regret not having a family – later.'

'Hmm.' There was silence while Mingo thought it over. Then she said, 'Yes, I see your point. I didn't realize he'd been married. If he's the kind of man who marries young and immediately starts a family – apparently he *is* – then yes, I think that could have caused pain eventually. For both of you, Robbie, I think you were right the first time.'

'You do?'

'Absolutely. For the sound reason you yourself just gave.'

'You think it wouldn't have worked in the end?'

'I think you sensed a risk too great to take, and I think you're quite a dame. That took guts, Robbie.'

'Not such gutsy guts apparently, or I wouldn't be falling apart now.'

'Natural reaction. You're just experiencing the kick-back. You don't think you can give up a heavenly love affair and get over it just like that, do you?'

'I suppose not. But oh, Mingo, what do I do now?'

'You'll think of something, Robbie dear.'

Roberta hung up feeling a little better. *You'll think of something*. The very flipness of Mingo's remark was meant, she knew, as a tribute. It was Mingo's way of

366

saying: You'll live, you'll be fine, I'm not worried about *you*.

The first paroxysm of reaction being over, Roberta felt a sure, but sad, confirmation of her decision. She had been right to give up Zack, for both their sakes.

Still, that awareness didn't keep her from missing him intensely or from reliving every moment of the idyll they had shared while he was at the farm. She missed him physically too, Her senses having so recently reawakened, she struggled with unfulfilled sexual desire. Once, standing in line at the bank, thinking of Zack, she was hit by a wave of physical longing so strong she felt her face grow hot and she imagined that the teller was looking at her strangely.

Reverting to her working-woman-on-her-own routine didn't help either. The days were growing shorter and the nights longer. It was dark when she came home from work. Putting her key in the lock, she wondered how many times a woman could adjust to the mechanics of solitude. This was her third go at it. Upstairs to change her clothes. Downstairs to the kitchen, to start dinner for one. Sometimes preceded by a drink, sometimes not. The seven o'clock news. Then dinner, with a book propped before her. And when she had finished, it was still only nine o'clock.

She invited Luther Hodges and Sarah Smith to dinner. She invited Mary Blair and her kids to spend Sunday. She visited the Fentons. She enrolled in an adult education course to brush up on her French – What for? she wondered. But she still had too many empty evenings.

Toward the end of October, wandering restlessly through the empty house, having completed every chore she could think of – books rearranged on the shelves, closets weeded out, drawers reorganized – she wondered, for the first time, if she should give up the farm.

It was ridiculously large for one person. Jim was no longer a half-hour away, in case of an emergency. Jim was out of reach in Washington. Winter was coming. Anything could happen – blizzards, power failures, frozen pipes. Ninety-nine out of a hundred people would say it was absurd for a woman to live alone in the country. Paul Reston had tried so hard to convince her of that.

But I got through last winter, she thought. Ah, yes because Zack was in the carriage house. She'd felt a sense of security from his mere presence, even before . . . No, don't think about him.

Back to the question. Does it make sense to stay at the farm? Thinking about it, she decided that she *could* cope with the operation of the place – somehow. In an emergency, Luther Hodges, Sarah Smith, or the Fentons would help her.

The real issue was loneliness. It was strange that she felt a more acute sense of loneliness now than when she'd first come to Greenwillow. At the moment, she saw herself as a middle-aged woman with a minor job – though she enjoyed it – facing an infinite wasteland of empty nights and weekends.

Should she go back to New York? With the proceeds from the sale of her apartment and the sale of the farm, she could buy an appropriately small co-op and have a comfortable income. She could reestablish contact with her old friends, maybe get another job. Substitute the stimulation of Manhattan's many excitements for the stimulation of a shared life. Thousands of widows and divorcees lived that way in New York. Wasn't it a logical choice for her?

Yes, it was. But looking around the big comfortable living room with its mellowed wood and deep windows, Roberta realized it would be a wrenching experience to give up her beloved house. And not just the house. The creek, the garden, the hills, and the ever-changing views. The ties she had established with Greenwillow. She *had* put down roots here. It would hurt to pull them up . . . but maybe she would have to.

Pondering, she warned herself not to do anything hasty. She had fled New York on blind impulse. She must not flee back blindly. She must take her time and think things through, but she would consider giving up the farm a real option.

She went upstairs at ten and lay awake, wondering if next year at this time she would be in one of New York's honeycombed apartment buildings, hearing the sound of slamming taxi doors instead of the murmur of the creek. The decision, she felt, would slowly make itself.

Early in November, Roberta received a call from Paul Reston's office. His secretary said she had been asked to tell Mrs Marston that the closing for the sale of her apartment would be held on the following Monday. Mr Reston had especially chosen that day because he knew it would be most convenient for Mrs Marston, but Mr Reston very much regretted that he himself could not be present. Unfortunately, he would be out of town that day. He had arranged for one of his partners to represent Mrs Marston. Was that satisfactory to Mrs Marston, and could she be at the office at eleven? Roberta's response was yes, certainly, and thank you so much.

She hung up, regretting that Paul would not be there. Feeling isolated as she did nowadays, she would have welcomed Paul's warm, solicitous presence. Even so, I should be damned grateful for all his help, she thought. I *must* do something for the Restons soon. Invite them for a weekend. It's disgraceful how I've neglected them.

* * *

369

She left the offices of Reston, Whitefield, and Moore considerably richer. Paul's associate explained that the huge check made out in her name would be immediately placed, with her permission, in a short-term safe investment. Mr Reston would make recommendations for more permanent investment as soon as possible.

Myra and Richard Erskine took her uptown to lunch. They drank to the Erkines' new ownership of the Seventy-ninth Street apartment. Then Richard Erskine said, 'And I have another toast: To Roberta's speedy return to Manhattan, where she belongs.'

'I'll drink to that,' said Myra warmly. 'Roberta, we *miss* you. What are you *thinking* of, buried off there in the hinterland? Surely you're planning to come back to the city?'

'As a matter of fact, I *am* considering it,' said Roberta. And looked around the elegant restaurant, with its fashionable patrons, and sensing the heartbeat of a city where everything happened. Roberta felt a distinct tug toward the one and only New York, New York.

But when she got back to the farm, that tugged at her, too.

The following Saturday evening Roberta went to the movies in Easton, alone. As far as she could remember, she had never been to a movie alone in her life. But none of her Greenwillow friends was free that night. She had called them all. If you want to see the film – *go*, she told herself. Still, she hated standing in line and saying, 'One, please' at the ticket booth. Inside, she couldn't shake the feeling that she was the only person in the theater who was sitting alone. On the way home she felt desperate. I've got to do something about this, she realized. But what?

The phone was ringing as she entered the house. It was

Jane Whitford. 'Robbie!' Jane's voice was excited. 'I've been calling you every hour on the hour. Listen, Robbie, I got a call tonight about that property. It's coming up for sale any minute now, and . . .'

For a moment Roberta didn't know what she was talking about. Then she remembered. Of course. The second shop Jane wanted to buy. The truth was, Roberta had all but forgotten it. Under the impact of parting with Zack, Jane's proposal had gone out of her mind.

'The thing is,' Jane was saying, 'you've got to be able to grab a place like that, if it's any good at all. Look, I've talked them into letting me see the place tomorrow, even though it's not officially for sale. Could you go with me tomorrow, to look it over and see what you think? Then we could come back to my place, so I can lay out the whole scenario for you.'

'Of course, Jane. What time?'

'Listen, Robbie, I've got such a tremendous hunch that this is *it* – for both of us – that I'd like to go this minute. But how about nine-thirty? Okay with you?'

'Fine, Jane. I'll be there.'

33

Jane Whitford pulled up in front of a sturdy old wooden building and said, 'There! Future home of Whitford & Marston, I hope!'

'Why, it looks just like those old photos of a 1910 General Store.'

'Exactly right. It *was* a general store in 1903. Look, Roberta, don't you love that long porch front and the old square columns and the wide steps leading up to it? Can't you see the old-timers lined up, rocking away for dear life?'

'Yes, and the apple barrel and the pickle barrel – '

'And the hitching post. Look, it's still there, iron ring and all. Oh, come on, I can't wait to see the inside. Robbie, I've had my eye on this place for ages. It's just been sitting here empty, *wasted*.'

Inside, the original stamped metal ceiling had a fleur-de-lis pattern, the floors were oak, and one old wooden display cabinet remained. There was a faint fragrance of spices.

'It's bigger than I thought,' said Jane happily. 'And look, two back doors leading outside. That's a break – puts us on the right side of the fire codes. Listen, Robbie, off the top of your head, where would you put the cheese?'

'Right *there*,' said Roberta promptly. 'In that sort of recess, with the window behind it . . .'

'Just what *I* thought. With the kitchen stuff in front of the other window . . . and the little impulse items where you can't miss them, against this wall.'

The two women spent the rest of the morning measuring the space, taking notes, and discussing renovations. Jane masterminded their survey with talk of cost per square foot and building contracts. Roberta followed her lead, half carried away by visions of a new shop, and half wondering what she was doing there. Invest in a business? Roberta Marston, with a total of one year of working experience? It struck her as downright *bizarre*. At the same time, she felt a spark of exhilaration, Wild as it seemed – for *her* – it was an exciting idea.

When they left the place Roberta said, 'But Jane, look at this road. There's almost no traffic.'

'I know. I've given that a lot of thought, Robbie. Of course today's Sunday, but I admit even on weekdays there's not much action. Still, in five more minutes you're in Flemington, right at the entrance to Turntable Junction. That's what I'm banking on, luring people from Flemington. Meantime, we cash in on our "true country setting," which God knows it is. After all, it's sitting in five acres of meadow.'

On the way back to Jane's house, Jane said, 'Talk about putting the cart before the horse! Listen, Roberta, you haven't even said whether you're interested. I know there are a million things to be considered first, but if it *did* look favorable, *would* you be interested?'

The blunt question deserved a direct answer. 'The truth is . . . I don't know. It's an exciting idea. I can close my eyes and visualize that place, oozing with charm and beckoning customers . . .'

'See? I *knew* it!' Jane cried triumphantly.

'. . . but I should tell you I've been thinking about leaving Greenwillow altogether.'

'You *have*!' Jane was shocked.

'Oh, not immediately. I wouldn't do anything hasty. And of course, Jane, I wouldn't dream of leaving you in

373

the lurch. I'd give you lots of notice, and I'd stay until you found a replacement. I owe you that – you've been marvelous to me. But with Jim and Susan more or less off on their own, the place seems so big and empty.'

'And the nights seem so long, and Saturdays are a big drag, right?'

'Right.'

'Loneliness,' diagnosed Jane. 'Tell me about it! Listen, Robbie, when I first landed in this neck of the woods, I don't know how many times I wanted to turn tail and run. You wouldn't believe the misery. One Sunday I couldn't stand it another minute. I jumped in the car and rushed to New York. I called everybody I knew. Naturally everyone was out. So then I walked from Murray Hill and Yorkville, and back. I guess it's a natural impulse when you're lonely. You feel if you could just go somewhere *else* – anywhere – everything would be better.'

'Exactly.'

'But take it from the voice of experience, your loneliness goes with you. It isn't the place, it's you. Oneself, I mean.'

'I suppose that's true.'

'And the cure is . . .' Jane paused, as though she were opening an Academy Award envelope.

'. . . Is?'

'Working your ass off . . . in something you believe in, of course. And preferably something you own.'

'It certainly seems to have worked for you, Jane.'

'You bet. In spades. But forgive me, Roberta, for sounding off like this. Who do I think I am – Madame Oracle, dishing out the secrets of life? Sorry, Roberta, I'm afraid I was getting much too personal.'

'Jane, don't be silly. You're doing me *good*.'

'Okay, then. Back to business. Look, investing in a business takes a helluva lot of consideration. You're not even sure you want to stay in New Jersey, but now that you've seen the property, I'd like to lay out the possibilities for you, as I see them, anyway. After that, of course, it's up to you. Deal?'

'Deal.'

At Jane's house she said. 'How about a quickie lunch? I'm starved.'

As they enjoyed the savory stew Jane had simmering in a Crock Pot, Jane began to talk business. 'Roberta, before we get down to the nuts and bolts, let me give you an idea of what my *long*-range plans are, or maybe I should say my long-range *dreams*.'

'You mean a second shop *isn't* your long-range plan?'

'Hell, no. A second shop is only a stepping stone. I'm aiming higher than that.'

'A third shop. A chain of shops?'

'No. What I have in mind, Robbie, may be a castle in the air, but not entirely. It *could* happen. It's mail order.'

'Mail order! I thought that was tacky?'

'Not the kind I mean. Wait, I'll show you.' She jumped up and came back with a stack of shining, expensive-looking catalogues. 'Here, just riffle through these.'

Roberta turned the pages. They were beautifully executed on heavy glossy stock, and the merchandise was obviously quality: jade and Imari from one house, exquisite linens from another, special blends of coffees and spices from a third. Others offered costly soapstone wood stoves, exotic water plants for one's lily pond, park benches, sickroom comforts, 'nothing but cookbooks.'

'My word, Jane, I had no idea people bought so much stuff by mail. And such high-priced stuff, too.'

'You see? It's not just Sears and Montgomery Ward anymore. Now look at this.'

She handed Roberta a page from the *New York Times Business Section*. There was a long article about a woman who'd believed she could sell fine garden tools and accessories by mail. She'd struggled for financial backing, persevered, and made it. It was a success story, and the point was that the woman had just sold her business for more than a million.

'If she can do it, why can't we?' said Jane. 'You see where I'm heading, Roberta. My idea is to broaden our base and our buying power with a second shop, then, in a small way, to begin to develop a mail-order business. That's a whole different technique. Buying the right mailing lists is crucial, for example. So is shipping – wrapping and packaging and mail rates. So you start small. Just one little catalogue with what you hope are sure-fire items. Then two a year. Then four a year. Then, leaping ahead to a glorious future, I see you and me flipping a coin to see who gets to go on the next buying trip to Europe.

'In other words, I don't want to stand behind a counter all my life, do you? If I'm going to work as hard as I do, I might as well try for the gold ring – running a real business from executive offices and enjoying the profits thereof. People do it. Why shouldn't we?'

Roberta had been listening enthralled. Jane was so good at painting word pictures that Roberta had found every step entirely imaginable.

'Jane, if you weren't an enterprising retailer and a future mail-order queen, I swear you could make a name as a lady evangelist. You're *inspiring*.'

Jane laughed. 'It's easy when you're a true believer. Faith is everything. You have to dream something before you can do it, don't you agree? Anyway, now you know what my plot is. The first step is the place on Route 12. Let's go into the living room and be comfortable. I've got some rough figures to show you.'

It was dark when Jane shoved the papers back in the

folder. She had outlined every phase of the project: the probable cost of the building, cost of renovation, initial stock, and how long it would take to get to the break-even point.

'Remember, these are just guesstimates,' she said. 'Everything always costs more and takes longer than you think. Although I tried to make my calculations very conservative. Believe it or not, I'm cautious by nature.' She ran her hand across her eyes. 'God, I'm tired. How about a drink?'

Roberta jumped up. 'You're tired. Let me get it. Where?'

'Lower right-hand cupboard in the hall. Scotch for me, please.'

When Roberta came back with the highballs, Jane said, 'Well, Robbie, how does it grab you?'

Roberta stirred her drink, thinking. 'It grabs me a lot, Jane . . . and it scares me to death. In about equal parts.'

Jane nodded. 'Right. You'd be crazy if it didn't. It scares *me* – when I let it. At the same time, I'm convinced it's a sound proposition.'

'But I've got a funny feeling that this can't be meant for *me*, as if I'd gotten mail meant for somebody else. I can't imagine myself as a . . . well, an entrepreneur. I've always admired career women, but I've never considered *myself* the type. You can't imagine what a mental leap it took for me just to look for a beginner's job.'

'And little did you dream that a year later you'd be propositioned to buy a partnership and a building,' joked Jane. 'But seriously, Robbie, I know what you mean. I never thought beyond wife-and-mother either. When I finally faced the fact that my husband was an alcoholic, I *had* to go to work. It's funny, Robbie. You find more selves than you thought you had.'

'More selves. That's an interesting idea.'

'It's true. You sort of typecast yourself into an image, a kind of self-limiting image, and let it go at that until life forces you into another dimension. Or until you force yourself, because you're tired of your limits. Then you find you're also somebody else. But what am I doing philosophizing again?'

'Opening new vistas.'

'Well, they're there – if they turn you on. Do they? Or are you pretty sure this is not for you?'

'Not at all sure, Jane. It's a great big question. I don't trust myself to answer until I've given it a lot of thought.'

'Absolutely. And don't, for God's sake, Roberta, commit yourself unless you're really sold. Also, don't take my word for anything. I'm prejudiced. Look, there are copies of my rough figures in that envelope. Take it with you, and don't make a move until you have everything checked by someone you trust. Of course, that includes our partnership agreement, if and when.'

Roberta picked up the envelope and rose to go.

'And remember this, Roberta . . .'

'Yes?'

'You could lose your shirt.' Seeing Roberta's expression, Jane laughed. 'You *could*. I could. But I'm prepared to risk my last cent. That's how much *I* believe.'

'Me, too, Jane,' Roberta said. '*Believe*, I mean. I *think*,' she added.

'Now you've got it! Who wants an impulsive partner? Feel your way, kid. See you tomorrow.'

When Roberta got home she did not notice that the house was empty and silent. Her mind was on a new kind of future.

The question had two parts. One, did she want to commit herself to years of hard work? Two, did she have what it takes? *Was* she the type?

In the days that followed her discussion with Jane, Roberta thought of almost nothing else. The prospect of buying into a business was a total switch from her lifelong perception of herself. As she had frankly told Jane, it almost seemed like a case of mistaken identity; it couldn't be meant for her, Roberta Marston. Or could it? Jane said you find more selves than you thought you had. That phrase kept coming back to Roberta.

Well, what kind of 'self' did it take? Probably, she decided, a totally different mind-set. A drive toward independence, and the drive not just to make money but as much money as possible. Even if you didn't particularly need it – just to prove you could. You had to get a kick out of competition, for its *own* sake. Better mousetrap.

She thought of Mingo and Carole, two dedicated career women if ever there were such. Mingo, she knew, 'got her jollies' out of spotting the coming designer or artist or model before her arch rival, the editor of the other leading fashion magazine, did. Carole had said that in the world of TV commercials, it wasn't only the work, it was the predators. Even gentle Mary Blair had a gleam in her eye recently when she'd told Roberta that Richard West & Associates had just snatched a new account from the jaws of another ad agency.

What you need, Roberta thought, is the same motivation that drive men up the corporate ladder or into entrepreneurial gambles: the challenge, the kick from achievement, the desire for material rewards.

One thing she was sure of: committed working women worked like dogs. You ate it, slept it, dreamed it. 'Nobody here works overtime but the boss.' Nine-to-five was for clock-watchers.

On the other hand, wasn't challenging hard work supposed to be one of life's joys? Wasn't it, in fact, supposed to be the panacea for life's blows: loss, grief, frustration, or just plain loneliness?

She had already reached the point, due to her brief experience at the shop, where she couldn't imagine life without *some* work. What on earth would you do with twenty-four hours if you didn't have a structured work-day? Still, it was a dizzying leap from employee to co-owner.

Thus Roberta circled around the question, trying to find the angle of vision most true to her own inclination.

Suppose, she let herself fantasize, Whitford & Marston really did launch a mail-order business. Suppose, eventually, they really did run it from executive offices. Suppose she, Roberta, really did get to – oh, say *China* – to ferret out wonderful new items to sell? Well, as Jane said, you *did* have to dream it first.

She felt a little spark of excitement ignite within her. That would be Phase II of her life. Phase I – wife and mother. Then, a short interval between the acts, while she switched locales, realized her children were going to lead their own lives, had an affair, got romance out of her system. Almost out of her system. Next, Phase II – Roberta Marston, partner in a growing business, testing her skills and talents in the marketplace.

I'm forty-eight. I'd have twenty years to put into it. In that amount of time maybe Jane and I could make a dent. Then, Roberta smiled to herself, we could look forward to a triumphant retirement.

We could also flop and lose our investment. Do I really want to take that risk? I could let Paul Reston put my cash into something that would yield an income, without my lifting a finger. But then what would I actually *do* – just mark time?

At the end of two weeks of soul-searching, Roberta found that her spark of interest in 'Whitford & Marston' had produced a considerable glow. When she put down a magazine called *Successful Women* and realized that she'd been imagining photos of herself and Jane on its pages, she knew she had a streak of competitiveness and ambition, after all.

The next morning she told Jane she was seriously interested.

'Oh *good*! Terrific! Listen, we're a long way from a deal, of course, but I couldn't be more happy.'

'Well, you're a confidence-inspiring lady, Jane.'

'You too, Robbie.'

'So what's the next step?'

'The next step is to call in some contractors for estimates on the renovation of the new place, so we'll know what it will *really* cost.'

'Right.'

When Paul Reston's secretary said, 'Mrs Marston on five,' he felt the quick rush her name had always evoked. There was nothing he could do about *that* – it was pure reflex. But he was sticking to his decision to end his no-win situation with Roberta. He had visualized one further meeting with her, concerning her investments. And that would be . . . that. He waited a moment to remind himself of this before he lifted the receiver.

'Paul?'

'Roberta, how are you?'

'Fine. Marvelous in fact.' She did sound elated. Bubbly. Fear gripped him. Was she calling to tell him she was going to marry some undeserving bastard who was free? As he, Paul, hellishly was not? Paul clenched the receiver. Steady. Listen to what she's saying, for Christ's sake.

'. . . are you, Paul?'

'Fine, thanks, Roberta.'

'And Alicia?'

381

'Alicia's well.' The words stuck in his throat.

'You sound busy, Paul. I'll get to the point. I'm calling about the money from the sale of the apartment.'

'Yes, we're planning a portfolio for you.'

'Paul, I'm considering investing it in a business.'

'You what? Roberta I couldn't have heard you correctly.'

Roberta laughed. 'You sound as appalled as if I'd said I wanted to invest in a cocaine ring. Paul, the woman I work for has offered me a partnership. We want to start a second shop – we've already found a building.'

'Roberta, do you know how risky that is? Do you know the mortality rate of new businesses?'

'Yes. High, But, Paul, it's not a new business – it's an expansion of an established business.'

'Roberta, promise me you'll do nothing – above all, sign nothing – until I can look into this?'

'Of course, Paul, I wouldn't *dream* of it,' she said, to calm him down. 'In fact, that's why I'm calling you. To *consult* you. Could you possibly meet with me and my partner – my proposed partner, I mean – to go over the preliminary figures?'

'Of course, Roberta. When?'

'Would Sunday be possible? If Alicia wouldn't be too bored while we talk business, I'd love to have you two to dinner . . .'

'Alicia will be out of town next weekend.' Actually he didn't know where the hell Alicia would be, and didn't care. 'I'll come, and I'll take you to dinner . . .'

After he hung up Paul stared unseeingly at the phone. So much for his resolve to put Roberta out of his life. But he had no choice, he rationalized. It was his duty, his responsibility, to prevent her from going into this thing. It was absurd, a woman like that slaving at some shaky little venture. If there really *is* a venture, he thought darkly. It was possible that Roberta had told this 'partner' that she had sold her co-op so the partner was about to relieve her of her assets.

He had no choice but to see her, for *her* sake. Face it, he told himself, for your sake too, old boy. Admit it. Maybe, after all, you'd rather stay on the fringes of Roberta's life than not see her at all.

An image of Alicia, beautiful and mocking, rose before him. He shut his eyes, imagining his hands closing around her creamy throat. He opened his eyes, appalled.

34

Jane Whitford's first reaction to Paul Reston was: My
God, what a glorious man. Why didn't she tell me?
Her second reaction was: He's dead set against this
partnership.

She also sensed why. He's mad for Roberta, she
realized, dismayed. There goes the ballgame! But as the
meeting went on, she began to have doubts. There was
nothing in Roberta's manner to suggest the slightest
awareness of his interest in her. She treated Paul Reston
with the easy affection of long acquaintance . . . but
nothing more. Doesn't she *see*? thought Jane incredulously. Is she deaf, dumb and blind? Undoubtedly, he's
married. Still . . .

But Jane had to admit that, whatever this man's motive
for not wanting Roberta to tie herself up in a business, he
was being objective about the issues at hand.

'Yes, Mrs Whitford,' he was saying, 'I can't see any
obvious weaknesses in the figures as you've projected
them. Beyond, of course,' – what a smile, thought Jane –
'the speculative nature of *any* new venture.'

'But don't you agree, Mr Reston, it's not nearly so
speculative as starting my first shop? That was really
bootstrap. And we made it.'

'Quite an achievement, I agree. But this time you're
buying property. I'm uneasy about that. And beyond the
property itself, there's also the area to consider. The
potential for future development, zoning changes, taxes.
I'd strongly advise my client, Mrs Marston, against this
venture unless I were satisfied on *all* those scores.'

Jane looked stubborn. 'Mr Reston, I'm convinced Route 12 will develop westward, in our direction.'

'You may be right, Mrs Whitford, but I think you need more solid evidence. May I suggest this: My firm has contacts in New Jersey so I can get a confidential report on the property and projections for the future of the area. Would you care to have me do that?' he added, turning to Roberta.

'Oh, Paul, would you?'

'Of course.' He felt like a traitor. He hoped the report would say: Don't touch it with a ten-foot pole.

When they finished their discussion, Jane and Paul said polite goodbyes in front of the shop. Jane left still thinking: He's going to try to talk her out of it.

'Paul,' Roberta said, 'I'd love to show you the new place – the *prospective* new place, I mean. It's not far . . . have you time?'

'All the time in the world, Roberta. I'm taking you to dinner, remember?'

She'd forgotten he'd mentioned dinner; she'd been so totally intent on 'Whitford & Marston.'

When they pulled up to the Route 12 place, she said, 'There! What do you think?'

Paul saw an out-of-date building in the middle of nowhere. He searched for the right word. 'Nostalgic,' he said.

'*Isn't* it! We plan to play up those windows for all they're worth, of course, and – '

'But, Roberta, it's so isolated. There's almost no traffic.'

'Oh, I know. Believe me, Jane and I gave that a lot of thought. It does look like a back road. but you see, in three minutes you're in Flemington, and Flemington is *teeming* with people. Shoppers. That's what we're banking

385

on, luring people from there; it's so close. And we're going to run lots of little ads . . .'

She looked so eager one part of him wanted to wrap the place up in ribbons and hand it to her as a love gift. But the prospect of a woman like Roberta breaking her back at *shopkeeping* was hard to take. Still, what right had he to discourage her?

At dinner in the restaurant Roberta had chosen, Paul said, 'But Roberta, it's difficult to imagine you as a . . . as a . . .' He didn't want to say *shopkeeper*.

Roberta said it for him. 'Shopkeeper?' She laughed. 'But I'm a shop employee now. I hope to be a shop owner, isn't that a step up? But I haven't even mentioned what our real aims are, Paul, because I knew you would think it was . . . well, pie in the sky. But you see, our goal is really a mail-order business.'

She told him about the mail-order trade papers she and Jane had been studying, the variety of products sold through catalogues, the ever-increasing interest in serious cooking, and in professional cookware, and . . .

She broke off abruptly. 'Paul, I'm embarrassed. I've been gabbling on nonstop – talking your ear off, probably boring you to death.'

'I'm very interested.'

'And I'm an egomaniac. No, not another word about me. I'm sorry, Paul, I haven't even asked about what's happening with you . . . and Alicia. Funny, just the other day I was thinking about that week Brad and I and you two spent in Bermuda. Remember? And it rained the whole time?'

'I remember.'

'How is Alicia?'

Paul twirled the stem of his glass. Then, coming to a decision, he looked Roberta in the eye. 'Alicia and I are

386

living apart in everything but name, Roberta. We have been . . . for years.'

'Paul! Oh, Paul, I'm so *sorry*.'

'Alicia is involved . . . elsewhere.'

Roberta felt a quick stab of pity. 'Another man? Oh, Paul . . .'

'Another woman.'

She could not have heard him. He saw the look on her face.

'Another woman,' he repeated.

For a moment she was speechless. *Alicia*? That fragile, exquisite creature? Feminity incarnate? No. She rejected it. It couldn't *be*.

'I know what you're thinking, Roberta. You don't believe it. Some things *are* impossible to believe. That's how I felt when I found out Brad . . .'

He realized the slip he had made. He paled.

'What did you say?'

He made a valiant effort to undo it. 'A slip of the tongue. You just mentioned Brad . . . his name was in my head . . .'

There was a silence.

'So you knew about Brad's affair,' Roberta said quietly.

Paul looked at her. He saw there was no use dissembling.

'Roberta, I'd give my right arm to unsay what I never meant you to hear.' Roberta was staring at her demitasse. Paul was staring at Roberta. The successive shocks of the past few moments had numbed them both. Then the implications, for Paul, sank in.

'Then . . . then *you* knew,' he said.

'Yes, I knew. Brad told me.'

'Told you . . .' Now he was incredulous.

'Yes. The day before he died.'

387

'My God,' Paul Reston whispered. 'And you went all through that, knowing.' The courage. The dignity. If it was possible for Paul Reston to fall more in love, he did so now.

'You see, Paul, you mustn't feel you have betrayed anything, because you haven't.'

Because there is nothing *to* betray, he thought. Nothing for *Alicia* to betray. Nothing she can tell Roberta which Roberta does not already know. *Nothing to keep him tied to Alicia.* He was free.

Paul Reston could not remember how he signed the check, drove Roberta to her door, refused her invitation to come in, promised to send her the appraisal report.

But when he got to a remote spot on Route 78, he pulled over, put his head on the steering wheel, and cried as only a strong man can. He felt release from the years of pent-up frustration. The shock of having the shackles drop off so abruptly shook him, but the stormy reaction was brief, followed by a soaring high.

He mopped his face, pulled onto the highway, and pressed the accelerator to the floor. He had wanted to say to Roberta, right there in the restaurant, 'Then I can tell you I love you.'

But a deep-rooted sense of honor demanded that he be quit of Alicia first. He had to get to the city, confront Alicia, leave her, file for divorce.

He got a speeding ticket. 'Where's the fire?'

'In my heart.'

The cop peered at him more closely. He didn't look drunk.

'Let's see your license and registration.'

Paul handed them over. 'Sorry, officer. I *was* speeding. You see, I just had some good news – *tremendous* news . . .'

The cop laboriously wrote out the ticket, taking his time. Being human, he'd give a lot to know what news was great enough to give this guy such a high. He looked like Somebody too. And so did his Mercedes.

Roberta went to bed, still stunned by the revelations at dinner. The fact that Paul had known of Brad's affair had had less impact than the news about Alicia. It was natural, she supposed, for a man's best friend to know about an affair – a temporary affair, as she had now come to consider it.

But Alicia! Was nothing what it seemed? Did everyone lead some secret life behind the façade presented to the world? She thought again of Carole Harcourt's revelations about Greg, Mary's outpouring about Dr Blair.

But why does Paul put up with such a situation? He deserves far better, she thought indignantly. Paul Reston can attract a number of women, women who would give him the devotion he deserves. Why doesn't he simply leave Alicia? How strange . . .

What can I do to show my support and sympathy? He's certainly knocked himself out for me. Well, I'll try to express it, at least, when he calls about the report on the property.

The property. That sent Paul out of her mind. She fell asleep thinking only of the subject which now absorbed her – Whitford & Marston.

'Miss Clark, will you try to reach Mrs Reston, please?'

'Certainly, Mr Reston.'

Dorothy Clark knew what that meant. She hadn't been Paul Reston's secretary for twenty years for nothing. First try the apartment, then the gallery in SoHo, then the place in Connecticut. Mr Reston rarely knew where that bitch of a wife was. Why did bitches always wind up with the best men? Mrs Reston and her artist pals! No better than they should be, any of them. If anybody wanted to know Dorothy Clark's opinion – no, not opinion, she was *convinced* of it – Alicia Reston was having an affair with some so-called painter. Probably supporting him in a loft somewhere.

She pushed the button on the intercom. 'Mrs Reston on three, Mr Reston. From Connecticut.'

'Alicia, meet me at the apartment at six this evening.'

'Impossible.' Alicia's voice was irritated. 'I'm extremely busy.'

'It's important, Alicia. *Be* there.' He hung up.

She came in promptly at six, a blond angel, her face framed in delicate fur.

Paul rose as she entered the vast, stark living room.

'Good evening.'

'I hope this really *is* important, Paul.' She glanced at her watch. 'I have exactly a half-hour.'

'It won't take that long. Sit down, Alicia.'

She sank indolently into a chair.

'Well?'

'I'm leaving you, Alicia. Tonight.'

She looked merely annoyed. 'Really, Paul, how tiresome of you. Did you call me back from Connecticut for this? You surprise me. We settled this some time ago. You *can't* have forgotten.'

'I have not forgotten, Alicia. It would not be easy to forget viciousness like yours. But you can no longer threaten me. And you can't hurt the woman I love. You're powerless to do so. Roberta already knows about Brad's affair.'

Alicia had not moved a muscle, but her angelic look had disappeared. What Paul saw was a cat, eyes narrowed and feral, every nerve wary and alert.

'You've been declawed, Alicia.'

390

Slowly, insolently, she turned away, picked up a cigarette, lit it. Only when she had taken a deep drag and lazily expelled the smoke, did she meet his gaze.

'I don't believe you.'

'It's easy enough to test.'

She looked at him, measuring, estimating.

'Very well. I shall.' She opened a drawer, took out an address book, flipped through. 'Marston. Greenwillow, New Jersey. Two . . .'

She picked up the receiver, hesitated. 'You're bluffing.'

'Try me.'

She dialed, her eyes never wavering from his. Paul could hear the ringing sound, could picture the hall in Roberta's house. He heard Roberta's 'Hello?'

Alicia did not speak, but her eyes dared Paul, expecting him to wrench the phone from her.

He sat motionless. Seconds passed. He could hear Roberta say 'Hello' again. Alicia opened her mouth, closed it. Then she slowly put down the receiver.

'So you've won.'

'Yes. My freedom.'

She was across the room in a flash, raking his face with her exquisite shell-pink nails. 'You don't think I *ever* loved you, do you? I used you . . . for my own purposes.'

He gripped her wrists, forced her into a chair.

'Either I file for divorce or you do. Which?'

Even in moments of high emotion, Alicia Reston was capable of considering her own best interests. Her instincts now told her to sue Paul for all he was worth, and name Roberta Marston as corespondent. But that would cut her off from her inheritance from her Catholic grandmother. If Paul sued her, he probably wouldn't reveal the facts. She knew him – he wouldn't stoop to that. In that case, her grandmother probably would consider her blameless. Of course, she would still be married in the eyes of the church.

'You file,' she said.

'Sam Strauss will represent me. Have your lawyer get in touch with him.'

Paul went to his own quarters, dabbed the blood from his face and packed a bag. Twenty minutes later he checked into a hotel.

35

'Don't buy that shop. Roberta. Marry me instead.'

Was she dreaming? Paul Reston had just finished telling her that the report on the property was favorable when he'd suddenly flung the papers onto her coffee table and said . . . *Had* he said it?

'Marry me, Roberta.' He took her in his arms and kissed her. It was a long ardent kiss, a hungry kiss, a kiss that had waited too long to happen. Roberta stiffened – he wasn't Zack! Then, as the kiss went on she felt herself responding.

At last he let her go. 'I love you, you see, Roberta. I've loved you for years. And I won't apologize for kissing you. It was a force of nature – I've dreamed of it so long.'

'Paul . . .' Her knees were shaky. She sat down.

'Roberta, I've shocked you. I know damned well you've never thought of me in that way . . . but, Roberta, I fell in love with you years ago. It was impossible. It was hell. My best friend's wife. I had to live with it – hide it – and I did. Then when Brad died and you were free, Roberta – I had asked Alicia for a divorce even before Brad died – I asked her again, on any terms. But . . .' He felt it would be repugnant, even now, to tell Roberta of Alicia's blackmail. He felt it would somehow sully Roberta; he still wanted to protect her from it.

'. . . but Alicia put an obstacle in my way, an obstacle that could have hurt innocent people. That obstacle's gone now. I have filed for divorce. I'm free to offer my love – and my life.'

'Paul, dear friend . . .'

'Roberta, I could use a drink.'

'Of course.' Roberta got up a little unsteadily, glad of a respite from the intensity of the last few minutes. She still half felt she was dreaming.

Paul paced the living room. He wanted to say bluntly: Look, Roberta, I know you don't love me. But could knowing I love you make a difference to you, to your plans for the future? This shop you're becoming involved in?

No, he decided. Too demanding, too possessive. To a woman like Roberta, always protected but now developing independence, it might even seem chauvinistic. Don't bother your little head, I'll take care of you. Careful, Reston, he told himself. Don't begin by undermining what is so obviously important to her. Paul Reston was strong enough to love a woman who was becoming strong in her own right.

When Roberta came back with the drinks, he took the tray from her, handed her a glass, and sat down opposite her.

'Roberta,' he said gently, 'I know you're wondering how to tell me I'm an old friend, period – that you've never thought of me in any other way.'

'That's true, Paul. You *are* a cherished friend. But . . .'

'But. But it's a long leap from old friend . . . to lover. I understand, Roberta. Darling, I know I took you by surprise, caught you off guard. Trust me, Roberta. I don't intend to rush you off your feet. But it's only fair to tell you I hope to make you love me. Will you let me see you? As a free man?'

She looked at him. How could she say no to a man who had done so much for her?

'Paul, of course. I like being with you. But . . .'

394

He had to ask. 'Is there someone else?'

She hesitated. 'No. There was.'

She saw him wince.

'That was inevitable, I suppose. I can't imagine a man meeting you without wanting you.'

'Paul, that's ridiculous.'

'Not to a man as deeply in love as I am.'

He stood up. 'Roberta, I'm going to leave now. I have told you what I wanted you to know. I love you – just that. And I'm going to give you plenty of time to get used to the idea. No importuning, I promise.'

At the door he looked at her, his heart in his eyes, but he did not kiss her, not even on the brow. Then he seemed to turn into a different man. Suddenly he looked confident, mischievous. There was a laughing challenge in his smile, and he said something totally uncharacteristic. 'Have you heard old friends make the best lovers, Roberta? *You'll* see.' And he was gone.

The split-second glimpse of a stranger was almost as unsettling as the rest of the evening. Roberta went back into the living room feeling distinctly weak-kneed. She sat down, thinking ten thoughts at once. Uppermost was 'My God, what *next*?' Was there no end to life's abrupt reversals and turnabouts?'

Had that conversation really just taken place in this room? It was impossible to think of Paul Reston as a man – a potential suitor, lover, husband. Next to impossible. He was too deeply etched in her mind as a platonic male acquaintance. He had a fixed role: Brad's roommate, Brad's best man, Brad's best friend, protector of Brad's widow's best interests. And, of course, Alicia's husband.

She had never thought of him, for a minute, as a *male*. He didn't . . . turn her on, although she knew he was very attractive to women. She remembered a woman who had made a fool of herself over Paul on a cruise ship. But to Roberta . . . No, wait a minute. That kiss. At first she'd been too stunned to feel a thing, but then . . . Involuntarily she closed her eyes, remembering. Yes, she had responded to that kiss. But that was probably just sexual. Maybe she could respond to more men than she knew? How funny! As for falling in love with Paul, you couldn't fall in love on request – even if you wanted to.

And she didn't want to. She'd had love. Now she was turning her life in a new direction. She wanted to test her powers, learn the limits of her capabilities. *That* was what turned her on nowadays.

Unreasonably, she found herself getting a bit angry with Paul. Damn it, Paul, why do you have to spoil everything! Just when I'm starting something I'm very serious about, you *complicate* things. Why couldn't you stay as you were, my good friend I can call on!

She realized, with shame, how irrational that was. My God, Roberta, how selfish can you be? And how *callous*? Here is this man – quite a man, really, if you weren't so close you couldn't see him – offering you his love, and you're *irritated* – because you have other plans. And because you've relied on him, without even recognizing it, to *be* there if you have problems. Think about what it's like for *him*.

She went up to bed, but couldn't sleep. He'd said he had loved her for years. That must have been awful for him. And that situation with Alicia – pure hell. Apparently Paul had endured a lot of pain heroically. She wished she had shown him more warmth, told him she was honored, *appreciated* him more.

But if she did see him, as he'd proposed – had dinner with him, spent time with him – how would that be for *him*? With one loving, and one not. That couldn't work, could it? Yet not seeing him was unthinkable. She *was* fond of him.

What a tangle. Well, see what tomorrow brings, as my favorite grandmother used to say, she thought. Which reminded her that tomorrow she would show Paul's report on the property to Jane. They had agreed that if the report was favorable – and it was – they would make an offer on the building.

She fell asleep with that thought in her mind.

On a gray day in November Roberta Marston and Jane Whitford became co-owners of a building and ten acres on Route 12, and full partners in Whitford & Marston, Inc.

Paul Reston was not present at the closing, but he had chosen the lawyer who represented Roberta and had guided the transaction behind the scenes. He sent flowers to the new firm. On the card that accompanied them was written: 'Success as you've dreamed it.'

Both women had handed over checks for what suddenly seemed frightening amounts, and both had signed the mortgage documents, committing themselves to long-term debt.

Afterward, with the keys and the deed to the new property in their possession, they celebrated at lunch. At the hotel in Frenchtown they toasted each other with champagne and did a lot of giggling, a reaction to the serious step they had just taken. As Jane had said, they *could* lose their shirts – but they didn't intend to.

'Here's to you, partner.'

'And to you, Ms Whitford.'

'Now all we have to do is . . . *do* it.'

'What's to stop us? But this is probably the last lunch we'll have time for until who knows when, so let's order wild.'

They were aiming for a Memorial Day opening.

The next day Roberta called Paul to thank him for the flowers.

'They are beautiful, Paul. It was sweet of you. Jane was thrilled too. I'm sure she's writing you a thank-you.'

'Hang Jane. I'm pulling for *you*, Roberta. So much so that I'm going to make myself scarce for a while. I know you're going to be working very hard – and I promised not to importune, remember? And I'm going to be quite busy these next few weeks myself.' The settlement with Alicia would be sticky and time-consuming. Besides, instinct told him to give Roberta time and space. 'I'll call . . . say in a month or so.'

'Fine, Paul.' She was relieved. 'We do rather expect to be up to our necks.'

'Of course you do. And Roberta . . .'

'Yes?'

'You've come a long way, baby.'

Roberta hung up laughing. Coming from Paul, that remark struck her as hilarious. Such slangy language, for *him*. Yet it's meaning was exactly what she wanted to hear. She *had* come a long way, considering. It was nice to have someone recognize it.

From then on, the official shop hours were meaningless. Jane and Roberta simply worked until they dropped. The Christmas rush would start the day after Thanksgiving. They were frantically busy receiving shipments, stocking the shelves, decorating the shop. 'Pray that we beat last year's figures!' said Jane. 'Oh, I am, I am.' Roberta had already learned the difference between ringing up a sale in a shop where she worked and ringing one up in a shop she co-*owned*. 'You know,' she laughed to Jane, 'I think I'm developing a *lust* for money. I'm getting such a kick out of the sound of the cash register.'

'Makes the blood race, doesn't it, partner?'

They agreed they had to have more help than last Christmas. 'And not just part-time kid help,' said Jane. 'With either one of us having to run out on SS business' – SS was a term they'd coined for Second Shop – 'don't you think we ought to have someone halfway adult, preferably with common sense? Do you know anyone who fits that description?'

'Not off the top of my head . . . no, wait a minute. I *do* know someone who might work out. She's seventy, Jane, but able-bodied and smart. I've always liked her. She's feisty and quick-witted, worked in the city for years. I have a hunch she's hard up and wouldn't mind earning some money. She's quite dignified-looking too. Shall I try her?'

'Grab her, if she'll come.'

Sarah Smith was delighted. 'Oh, Roberta,' she said, 'this obligatory retirement is boring me to death. Let me at it – whatever it is.'

After hours, Roberta broke Sarah in, just as Jane had broken her in fourteen months ago. Within a week, both Jane and Roberta felt they were in luck. Sarah Smith was a godsend, and obviously the full-time employee they would need when they expanded.

Jim came home for Thanksgiving, and he and Roberta drove to the elder Marstons for Thanksgiving dinner. Susan had begged off, apologetically explaining that she was going to spend the day with Bob Giordano's family in Brooklyn.

'Your grandparents will be very disappointed, Susan, and so am I.'

'I know, Mother. I feel rather lousy about that myself. But that's the way it is when you're involved in two families, isn't it? You have to sort of divide yourself up.'

Involved with two families? Then Susan *was* serious about this still-unknown Bob Giordano.

'Anyway, Mother,' Susan went on, 'of course we'll be with *you* on Christmas.'

In a way, it was pleasant to have her son to herself. Jim seemed to have become quieter and more thoughtful in the eight weeks since he'd been gone. When she told him about her project with Jane Whitford, he asked all the right questions, cheered her on, and wisecracked, 'My mother, the entrepreneur.' But she had a distinct impression that Jim had something on his mind.

On the way back, she found out what it was. They had been riding in silence for twenty minutes or so, momentarily talked out. Roberta was drowsily thinking of things she had to be thankful for. One of them was returning to an orderly house, and not having to face postholiday chaos in the kitchen. She was already worrying about how she would manage Christmas, with the long hours she and Jane were facing.

'Mother.' Jim broke the silence. 'Mother, I have something to tell you. For the last twenty miles I've been trying to decide whether this is the time, and I think it is.'

Roberta turned toward him in alarm. 'Trouble of some sort, Jim?'

'No, no, not trouble. But something I'm afraid will distress you. Mother, I think I may want to drop out of law school.'

'*Jim!*' She could not have been more unprepared. If there was one thing she had considered settled in an unsettling world, it was that Jim would practice law, like both his grandfathers. As far as she knew, Jim had always *wanted* to be a lawyer. 'But why, Jim?'

'It isn't so much that I'm not interested in law, I am. It's just that something else interests me much more – a kind of life I'd rather lead.'

'And that is?'

'Mother, I'd like to make something of the farm.'

'Be a *farmer*?'

'A nurseryman. Establish a tree and shrub nursery. A special one with fine quality specimens. With Midge, of course.'

Roberta was silent. He had fallen hard for Midge Blair, and because Midge was so consumed with her own career dream of landscaping, her son was ready to throw up the career he'd planned for years.

As Jim so often did, he seemed to read his mother's mind. 'I know what you're thinking, Mother. I'm about to go off half-cocked because of my girl. What else could you think?' He reached over and patted her hand. 'But it isn't that way, Mother. Midge *is* the girl for me. I'm sure of that . . . and so is she. But neither one of us is going to do anything rash. Anyway, I haven't quite made up my mind yet, about dropping law, I mean. But I can feel myself going in that direction. I felt I owed it to you to let you know in advance.'

'Jim, it's such a serious decision. Something you decide now, under the influence of strong emotions, could change the course of your life. You might make a mistake you'd regret forever after.' Like my almost marrying Zack, she thought. And I wanted to, so much.

'I know.'

'Promise me one thing?'

'Which is?'

'Promise me you'll finish this year of law school.'

Now it was his turn to be shocked. 'Mother, of *course*. Did you think I was going to kick school this minute? I not only intend to finish this year, but to give it my all . . . and to keep an open mind. Maybe I'll find out it's for me, after all.'

'Oh, Jim, I think that's so wise.'

401

Then he spoiled it. 'But if it's *not* for me, I don't suppose having a year of law under your belt *hurts* any if you're a nurseryman.'

'I suppose not,' she said faintly. It seemed all too clear that this vision of living off the land had a powerful grip on him. 'But can you make a living with a nursery? A decent one?'

'More than decent if you do it right. Listen, Mother, let me tell you about nurseries.'

They were pulling into the driveway at the farm. Jim picked up the hamper of holiday leftovers the elder Mrs Marston had packed for them.

'Can you believe I'm hungry again? Come on, Mom, let's have a turkey sandwich and a glass of milk.'

When they were seated in the kitchen, Jim went back to their discussion. 'In answer to your questions about nurseries making money, Mom, one of the reasons I brought this up tonight was listening to you talk about *your* new business. How carefully you and Mrs Whitford are casing the possibilities. Nurseries are the same. There's a lot to learn and you can make a lot of mistakes, but if you're scientific about it – if you do your homework – there's real potential.'

'I'm sure there is, Jim. But doesn't it take forever for the stuff to get big enough to sell?'

'Not forever. About six years. And Midge and I have a special angle, You see, landscape architects buy nursery stock from growers. We want to do both, landscaping *and* growing our own stock. A sort of double whammy, Mom. We've got it all planned. As soon as she graduates, Midge will sign on as a beginner with a landscaping firm, and I'll offer my brain and brawn as a lowly nursery hand – to learn the business from the ground up.'

'Pun intended?'

'Pun definitely intended.' He grinned affectionately and

patted her hand. 'Meantime, during spring vacation, we'll plant ten thousand Christmas trees, for a faster cash crop. Then the next year, we plant *another* ten thousand, and so on. That guarantees us some future income later for equipment and stock. And another thing, it puts this wonderful land to use instead of wasting it. What do you think, Mom?'

'I think you could sell snowballs to Eskimos.' She smiled at this eager young man she loved so much. 'Of course, Jim, you must make your own choices. Please just be sure you're sure.'

'Haven't I already promised?'

'Yes, you have. And I have confidence in your good sense. But now my good sense tells me to get some sleep. Our holiday rush begins tomorrow.'

'I hope you sell up a storm, Mom.'

Undressing, Roberta thought that Jim's enthusiasm was as infectious as Jane Whitford's. The same sense of vision, coupled with the same pragmatism. Still, she could not undo in hours years of expectation that her son would make law his profession. Nonetheless *one* aspect of his plan appealed to her: having him on the farm. Visualizing her own future as she now saw it, that of a single working woman, it would be wonderful to have her son living at home.

But that shouldn't influence a decision as important as his future, she reminded herself. Maybe Paul Reston could talk to him, perhaps give him another perspective on the rewards of law?

Paul. There she was again, relying on Paul in time of need. It was a disturbing thought. Paul had permanently altered the nature of their relationship. It was not right to continually ask for his help, considering his feelings for her.

The truth was that in her absorption in her new enterprise she'd actually forgotten Paul's declaration of love for days at a time. And when she remembered it, it was with a sense of surprise rather than a thrill. She was flattered, naturally – any woman would be – but she had so many other things to think about. Looking forward to seeing Susan, meeting Bob Giordano, and, as of today, Jim's change of direction. Always, of course, her time and thoughts were occupied with having the new shop ready by the target date.

What was she going to do about Paul? Put the question on Hold, at least for now.

Eventually, though, she'd have to decide whether it was possible to go on being friends with a man who wanted to be a lover.

36

'There's *supposed* to be a month between Thanksgiving and Christmas,' said Jane Whitford, 'but I could swear it's just a speeded-up week.'

Roberta agreed. It did not seem possible that today was December twenty-first, or that Jim, who had seemingly just left, would be back in two days and that Susan and Bob Giordano would be waiting for her at home tonight.

'Not to *knock* it,' Jane added. 'We've been doing great, pardner.'

They had. Business had been brisk and continuous at the Smith's Mill shop. At peak hours they'd had the pleasure of being jammed, with a line of customers at the cash register.

'And just think,' said Sarah Smith, 'next year at this time you'll have *two* of these circuses going.'

'With your help, Sarah, I hope,' said Roberta. 'I don't know how we would have survived without you.'

The shop was open from nine until nine. The three women took turns leaving at six, so each got every third night off. But tonight Jane bore down on Roberta at five, carrying her coat. 'Beat it while the going's good,' she said. 'Your daughter's waiting for you, isn't she? First things first.'

Roberta gratefully accepted. Susan had called the shop in the early afternoon, to say that she and Bob had arrived.

Roberta had been in a fever ever since. She had not seen her daughter since last July. Was she really as changed as she seemed to be over the phone? Roberta couldn't wait to find out.

The door of the house flew open as Roberta came up the steps, and Susan was smothering her in a hug. 'Oh, *Mummy*! I'm so glad to see you! Let me look at you. You look terrific – being a career lady agrees with you.'

'Susan, darling . . .' Roberta kissed her daughter, again the exuberant, lovable girl she had been. 'It's so good to have you home . . .' Her eyes filled.

'You're not crying, Mom, are you?'

'Just so happy,' Roberta said, mopping her eyes.

'Me, too.' There were tears in Susan's eyes too. 'Oh, Mother, I know I was impossible – forgive me. But why are we standing here? I can't wait for you to meet Bob.'

Roberta's first impression of the young man who rose when they entered the living room was . . . unsuitable. He looked nothing like the boys Susan had known in New York, nothing like Jim's friends. He was a totally different type from any young man she had visualized for Susan. Not that there was anything wrong with his looks – he was darkly good-looking, in a Latin kind of way – but he was different. She realized what the difference was: He was not a WASP. But was that important?

'Mother, this is Bob,' Just 'Bob.' Susan said it proudly, as though that were enough. As though Bob were *sui generis*, his desirability self-evident.

The young man shook Roberta's proffered hand firmly, and said, 'Mrs Marston, I am happy to meet Susan's mother.' Manly enough. Direct, thought Roberta.

They made the kind of small talk people do when they are strangers. 'What a terrific house, Mrs Marston.' 'How was your trip down?' 'We just beat the traffic.'

He was more articulate than many young people, Roberta thought, but she noticed the trace of Brooklyn accent.

Then Bob said, 'Mrs Marston, Susan thought you might like a fire. May I bring in some logs?'

After Roberta directed him to the shed, Susan said, 'See how tactful he is? He wanted to give us a chance to talk alone together.'

'Well, that is rather sensitive.'

'You bet. And he has great respect for *mothers*. You ought to hear him talk about *his* mother.'

'That's rather nice too.'

'Yes, it is.' Susan was silent a moment. Then she said abruptly, 'Mother, I'm crazy about him.'

'Are you, Susan?'

'Yes. Know why? He brings out the best in *me*. It's crazy, but he makes be feel protected. Yet at the same time I have to meet some sort of standard. I have to be *responsible*. Grown-up, I suppose you'd call it. Not a big brat, the way I was when I met him. Oh, wasn't I awful!' She shuddered.

'You went through a . . .phase.'

'You shouldn't have put up with it. You were too permisive. You should have thrown me out of the house. Bob's mother wouldn't put up with that sort of behavior for a *minute*.'

Roberta felt a surge of indignation. Then the humor of the situation hit her: the young, making every possible demand on their elders, then bawling them out for being permissive.

'And listen, Mother, all right with you if I put Bob in my room. With me?'

A moment ago Roberta would have said yes. To do otherwise would have been silly, since it was now obvious that Susan and Bob were indeed living together.

But what she said was: 'No. Not in my house.'

Susan stared at her, floored for the moment.

'Besides, what would Bob's *mother* say?'

Susan burst out laughing. 'Touché, Mom!' She looked at her mother with admiration. 'That's what I get for setting you straight on parents and kids, right? Oh, Mother, you're something!'

Bob came back with the logs.

'Mother, would you like me to make you a drink?'

'That would be nice.'

'Just sit right where you are. Bob will make the fire, I'll make the drinks, and then I'll get going with dinner. You're not to lift a finger. And we're going to do all the Christmas chores too, from stuffing the turkey to hanging the garlands. You're the working lady, and you're to take it easy at home.'

'I've never had it so good.' Roberta smiled.

Roberta went to bed in a glow of happiness. Tomorrow her father would arrive – on the following day Jim and Mingo. She had arranged to take all next week off, to bask in the warmth of her nearest and dearest.

Roberta was glad that Paul Reston had turned down her invitation to Christmas dinner. She had thought it over and had decided it was obligatory to ask him. Considering that he was now newly 'alone' and remembering all he had done for her, it would be a sin of omission not to make the gesture.

But to her surprise and relief, he'd declined. He was going to Switzerland with friends to ski. He didn't say so, but Roberta had the impression that Paul's idea of seeing Roberta did not include a lot of other people. For her part, Paul's presence would have been an unsettling distraction – how could it not be? So she was grateful there would be just family and Mingo.

On the afternoon of the twenty-fourth, Jane, Roberta, and Sarah Smith had a quick Christmas drink in the back room while they left the shop in the hands of two part-timers. This time, it was Sarah who was surprised by a Christmas bonus check. There was a sprig of holly pinned to her cardigan and a twinkle in her eye as she opened the envelope. 'Oh!' she said. 'I'm going to frame it!'

Sarah had offered to keep the shop open until nine. 'What, you want to close early and lose all that last-minute business? Foolish! Let me stay.'

'But what about your own Christmas, Sarah?' Roberta protested. ''Don't worry about me,' Sarah replied staunchily. 'Tonight Terry Fenton and her kids are picking me up to go to midnight services. Tim still can't get around very well, but he's coming along. Tomorrow I'm going to my sister's, so I'm all set. I can keep the shop open while the last customer wants to spend a dime . . . if you like, that is.'

'You bet we like,' said Jane. 'Come on, Roberta, let's make our escape before this generous woman changes her mind.'

When Roberta reached home, the wreath was on the door, candles glowed in the windows, and inside Christmas had taken possession of the house. She found Jim and Bob Giordano putting up the tree, her father unwrapping ornaments, and Mingo and Susan busily chopping and peeling in the kitchen.

'Mother, the most enormous package just arrived,' Susan greeted her. 'Christmas goodies, from the look of it. Let's open it!'

The handsome basket, a gift in itself, contained Belgian chocolates, glacéed fruit, marzipan, a crock of pâté, a jar of caviar, and, cradled in wicker, six bottles of Mumm's.

'My word,' murmured Mingo, eying the caviar, *quel luxe*!'

'But who's it from?'

Roberta opened the little envelope and drew out the card.

'Paul Reston. "Holiday cheer to all the Marstons,"'

'What a spread,' said Jim. 'But then I always thought Uncle Paul was a generous guy.'

'Me, too,' sad Susan. 'Remember how he used to buy out F.A.O. Schwarz when we were kids?'

Privately Roberta thought the gift too extravagant, much too expensive. But then, Paul had always sent the Marstons holiday gifts, in his and Alicia's name. This time there was only his name. Well, she hoped he was enjoying himself in Switzerland. If anyone deserved it, he did. Then she forgot him and she joined the others for the tree trimming.

When the tree was glowing and perfect, they sat around the fire with eggnog and fruitcake. It was the traditional Christmas Eve Roberta had hoped for.

Around eleven someone said, 'Look, it's snowing!'

'Oh, let's go out for a few minutes,' said Susan. 'Come on, it's so beautiful.'

They bundled up and walked through the whirling flakes down to the edge of the creek. The quietness of the earth, the rushing water, the snow already clinging to the evergreens moved them all to awed silence. Then Jim began to sing, softly, 'Silent Night.' They all joined in. Roberta had to fight back tears. Susan, noticing, gripped her mother's hand, misty-eyed too. When they walked back to the house, the ground was covered, and they left footprints.

Christmas Day was better than merry, Roberta thought. There was a lot of laughter and gaiety, but what made it heartwarming was the sense of family unity. Everyone tried to make everyone else happy.

Jim and Bob Giordano seemed to hit it off, she noted. When she and Jim had a moment alone, he said, 'A straight arrow, Mother. Not what you expected, maybe, but a good guy. Bright too.'

'Is he?' Roberta realized she was surprised.

'*I* think so. But even if he weren't, Mom, have you ever seen Susan so *shining*. Isn't that worth the price of admission?'

On Christmas night Roberta went to bed feeling that the holiday had been a total success, not flawed in any way. Sometime during the coming week she would spend some private moments with her daughter, to learn more about her plans with Bob Giordano. And she would also talk with Jim about his future; she was still concerned about him. But at the moment she was inclined to put her faith in her son's and daughter's judgment.

Roberta was surprised to find it was eleven o'clock when she awakened the next morning. Downstairs she found that Jim had picked up Midge Blair, and the four young people were sitting around the kitchen as though they'd known each other forever.

'Mother, Midge is going to go and visit Grandma and Grandpa Marston with us. Isn't that super?'

'Super indeed,' Roberta smiled. 'And where's your other grandfather? And Aunt Mingo? Still sleeping?'

'Not on your life,' Jim said. 'They're out walking, can you imagine? Grandfather said he wanted to take his constitutional. Mingo said it was years since she had seen unsullied snow.'

'More energy than *I* have this morning,' Roberta said, accepting the cup of coffee Susan had jumped up to pour for her. 'It's a lovely day to laze and eat leftovers.'

The call came just after Mingo and Roberta's father returned, stamping snow from their boots.

Jim answered the phone. 'For you, Aunt Mingo. Your housekeeper.'

Mingo looked puzzled as she picked up the phone.

'Mrs. MacCochrane?' She listened. Roberta saw her face turn pale. 'Yes. Immediately. Call them back and tell them, please. About two and a half hours.'

She hung up. 'My father. They've sent for me. I must go.' She rushed from the room and up the stairs.

Jim rose at once. 'Mother, I'll drive her. Where it he?'

'Connecticut.' Roberta thought quickly. It would be a help to have Jim drive, and Roberta would of course go too, but she sensed that it would be easier for Mingo to be alone with her best friend. 'Thank you, Jim, but it will be better if only I go. You stay here and hold the fort. Go on with your plans.'

'Take good care of your grandfather,' she whispered to Jim in the hall. 'I'll call you from Connecticut as soon as I know how things stand.'

She flew upstairs, where Mingo was throwing things in a bag. 'Mingo, I'm going with you.'

Mingo was weeping. 'Oh, Roberta, *would* you? But it's your week off, and your kids are home.'

'Nonsense. I'll be ready in ten minutes.'

37

On the way, Mingo said only: 'They said Father was asking for me. In all the years I've been going to see him, he has never said a single word.'

They drove through the gates into the impressive grounds of The Pines. It was a place which suggested peace and beauty. A place where the severely disturbed or the hopelessly deranged could be kept safe from the eyes of the public. A place where people could live in protected private hells, all signs of their inner chaos discreetly concealed from the world. Inside the large entrance hall, very like that of a privileged private home, stood a Christmas tree.

The director was waiting for them. White-haired, dignified, concerned-looking. 'Miss Darcy, your father is waiting for you. It will mean much to him that you are here.'

Mingo had difficulty in speaking. 'But, Dr James, you know he has never recognized me . . . since he has been here.'

'He is lucid right now. It sometimes happens. Come, Miss Darcy. Let me take you to him.' Holding Mingo's arm, he escorted her up the wide curving stairway.

Instantly an attractive young aide appeared at Roberta's side. 'May I offer you some luncheon? The dining room is in the East Wing? Or perhaps you'd prefer the sun porch? It's such a lovely day.'

Sitting among the green plants of the glassed-in porch, Roberta watched groups of people move around the snowy grounds outside. They were of varying ages, and they were wearing the latest in winter sports clothes. It could have been a resort.

One face looked familiar. Suddenly she realized why. It must be the son of that world-famous comedian. He looked exactly like his father. She had heard he was here. She noticed a young boy, not more than sixteen, who reminded her of Jim. He was making snowballs, raising his arm to throw them, then carefully placing them on the ground instead. The young woman accompanying him made and threw her own snowballs, encouraging him to do the same. Always in such places, the staff and patients looked very much alike.

Roberta thought of her son and daughter. Both Jim and Susan were choosing paths other than the ones she had always assumed they would pursue, but compared to the tragedy of these lost minds, her children seemed models of health and normality. How do families bear it? she wondered.

Dr James opened the door of Mr Darcy's room for Mingo, nodded reassuringly, and left. Her father lay on his back, his hawky profile clear against the light, his slender height apparent even under the covers.

'Mignonne?' he said.

Mignonne! It was her real name. No one had called her that since childhood. Fighting back tears, Mingo said, 'Yes, Father?'

She moved toward the bed. She took his hand. He turned toward her, his eyes reflecting the clear intelligence she had been so in awe of as a child. 'My daddy is the smartest man in the world,' she had thought proudly. 'A physicist. Why, even the President of the United States has asked my father for his opinion.'

But now there was an urgent pleading behind that intelligence. 'Mignonne,' said her father, his frail hand gripping hers. 'Daughter, can you forgive me? Tell me you forgive me.'

Mingo was too overcome to speak.

Mr Darcy closed his eyes.

'No, of course you don't.' He turned his head away.

Mingo wanted to cry out: 'Daddy, do you forgive *me*?' She had always felt responsible for her parents' unhappy marriage. She had thought that her beautiful mother's bitter disappointment in her homely daughter had caused the rift. She'd wanted her father to give *her* solace, to tell her that was not true. How could she 'forgive' her unhappy, suffering father? There was nothing to forgive him for. That long-ago terrible incident had not been his 'fault'; it had been the blind act of a man seeking human closeness. But she realized her father had to hear her absolve him.

Forcing out the painful words, she said, 'Father, of course I forgive you.'

The pleading eyes searched hers. 'Totally? Without reservation?'

'Totally. Without reservation.'

He sighed. 'You have lifted a weight – a stone – from my heart, Daughter.'

He was silent. Then he said, 'You know, Mignonne, don't you, that I never meant . . . that I can't account for . . .' He couldn't go on. He tried again. 'You were the most precious thing in my life, Daughter. Your mother, you see . . .' He trailed off.

'I know. Father. I know you loved me.'

He tried to raise his head and failed. He was whispering now, visibly weaker. 'Daughter, please . . . for my sake . . . don't let my . . . sin' – the word was barely audible – 'don't let that . . . that incident . . . keep you from loving. Don't be afraid of love, Mignonne. It's worth the risk.'

'Yes, Father.'

'You promise?'

'I promise.'

He closed his eyes peacefully. She held his hand. He spoke no more.

She sat until Dr James came and led her away.

The next day Philip Darcy was cremated. Mingo said only that she was certain it would have been her father's preference. With Dr James's help, the simple ceremony was smoothly and quickly arranged. Mingo held tightly to Roberta's hand as the coffin slid from sight and the curtains closed. Later, she would arrange a Memorial Service so that those of the academic and scientific community who had honored Philip Darcy for his distinguished career could pay their respects.

Over Mingo's protests, Roberta drove her back to Greenwillow. 'I couldn't have gone through it without you, Roberta. But you've already sacrificed too much of your week off. Your kids are waiting, and your father. I'm spoiling your holidays.'

'Hush, Mingo,' said Roberta firmly. 'Of *course* I wouldn't let you be alone. Anyway, the kids will be gone for a couple of days, visiting their grandparents. It will just be you and I and Father. We'll have the quiet you need.'

'Oh, Roberta,' Mingo's voice broke. 'I thank God – you can't know how grateful I am – that Daddy spoke to me before he . . . left. I couldn't have *borne* it if he'd died without our making contact. Even though he's gone, I feel as though I have my father back again.'

She wept quietly all the way back to the farm.

By the time Susan and Jim and Bob returned from visiting the elder Marstons, Mingo had recovered. She was quiet and subdued, but composed and smiling. She disappeared for long walks, in order to give Roberta private time with Jim and Susan.

'And please don't change any of your plans because of me, Roberta,' she begged. 'I'm sure you were going to ask some of your local friends in this week. Don't cancel anything for my sake. Robbie – I'm fine, really.'

Roberta used her own judgment about that. She had planned to ask people in for an informal holiday evening. But she decided that expecting Mingo to socialize with strangers would hardly be kind.

Nevertheless, when Luther Hodges dropped in unexpectedly and sat talking with Mr Barclay while the women made tea, Roberta whispered to Mingo, 'Are you up to having a guest for dinner?'

'You mean that interesting-looking gent who just arrived? Of course, Robbie.'

'Sure?'

'Absolutely. Nice idea.'

After dinner, Mr Barclay said, 'Since we have a foursome, could I interest anyone in a game of bridge?'

Mingo and Luther, it turned out, made a lethal team. 'Well *done*, partner,' said Luther admiringly when Mingo executed a double finesse for a tricky little slam. And he's not just admiring her bridge, thought Roberta. Tonight Mingo was wearing a dress so simple it was a work of art, wearing it as only Mingo could, with her superb carriage and classic chignon. Not every man appreciates Mingo's elegance, Roberta thought, but apparently Luther has a discerning eye.

'Now, that's what I call bridge,' said Mr Barclay, as he added up the score. 'Even if they did put us to shame, Roberta.'

'And I don't know when I've enjoyed an evening more,' said Luther. 'Would you give me the pleasure of repeating it at my house on Friday?' He turned to Roberta. 'That's New Year's Eve, of course. But I thought if you *were* planning a quiet evening at home . . .' He was delicately referring to Mingo's loss of her father, of which Roberta had told him.

'Luther, how kind of you . . .' Roberta looked inquiringly at her father and Mingo.

'I'd be delighted,' said Mr Barclay, 'but of course Mingo is our concern, Mingo, my dear?'

'Thank you, I'd like to come very much.'

'Good!' Luther looked very pleased. 'The fact is, I've made it a practice to stay home on New Year's Eve these last few years. I look forward to seeing you. Seven-thirty?'

On Friday, Luther Hodges provided them with a memorable dinner, beautifully served in his paneled dining room. 'But Luther, this could be just off Fifth Avenue,' exclaimed Mingo. 'A New York townhouse in the *country*?'

'My great-grandmother was a New Yorker,' explained Luther. 'The legend is that she refused to marry my great-grandfather because she couldn't bear to leave the family house. So he built this one for her, by way of persuasion . . . to the amusement of the local farmers.'

It was an extremely pleasant dinner. They talked architecture, books, and theater. Luther asked pertinent questions about the magazine world, and Mingo responded with amusing anecdotes. Luther looked enthralled.

'And yet you know,' Mingo said, 'I find this *much* more appealing than the gilt-chair circuit where I usually find myself during the holidays.' Luther looked gratified.

After dinner they played bridge in Luther's second-floor back library. At eleven-thirty his houseman brought in champagne and a refreshment tray. At midnight they toasted the new year, and everyone kissed everyone else on the cheek.

Shortly afterward, Roberta noticed that her father, who had been enjoying himself hugely, had begun to look tired. 'Luther,' she said, 'I hate to break this up – it's been such fun – but Father will be leaving day after tomorrow, and . . .'

'Of course, Roberta, I understand. But won't you and Mingo stay a little longer? Henry can drive your father home . . . if that's all right with you, sir? I'm being selfish, I know, but this is the nicest New Year's Eve I've had in years – I hate to end it.'

'Luther, I'd love to stay. But you see the kids are at a party, and Id like to be there when they get home. Jim's leaving tomorrow, rather early.'

Luther turned to Mingo. 'Mingo, keep me company? I couldn't sleep if I tried.'

Mingo smiled. 'You know, I don't think I could, either. I'd love to stay, Luther.'

Roberta was awakened by a whispered 'Robbie!' She groped for the light. It was Mingo, looking star-struck as a sixteen-year-old.

'Forgive me for waking you – it's five-thirty in the morning – but I *have* to tell you . . .'

Mingo plopped down in the boudoir chair and looked at Roberta wordlessly, as though she didn't know where to begin. Why, she's *beautiful*, Roberta thought groggily, not homely at all. She's radiant . . .

'Oh, Roberta, the iceman *wenteth*.'

'What?'

'I'm not frozen anymore. Not frigid . . . not at *all* frigid. Luther – oh, my God, Robbie – I never knew, I never felt like a woman. But now . . . Luther . . .'

She burst into tears, half laughing, half crying, a little hysterical.

So Mingo and Luther had gone to bed . . . obviously with a transcendent effect for Mingo. Roberta was so moved by what was clearly a vital turning point for Mingo that she hardly felt surprise at the event itself.

'Mingo dear . . .'

Mingo dried her eyes and smiled. 'I'm in love, Robbie. Did you ever believe it could happen like that, like a bolt of lightning?'

'I believe it *now*.' Roberta jumped out of bed and hugged her friend. 'Mingo, dear, I've never seen you look so happy.'

'I feel as though I've been born again. No, not again. For the first time. Imagine, at my advanced age!' She laughed. 'But, Roberta, you must be dead for sleep. Look, I'll leave you in peace and tell you the rest tomorrow.'

'Not on your life. Do you think I could sleep now?' Roberta propped herself against the pillow. 'Go *on*.'

'You'll never believe what brought us together.'

'Mutual attraction, of course.'

'His wife . . . and my father.'

His *wife* and ?. . .'

'After you and your father left, we played that question-and-answer game people play when they don't know each other. *You* know, "Have you always lived in Manhattan?" and "Do you have grown children?" He told me about his wife. Do you know she has Alzheimer's?'

'Yes. I've heard.'

'She's beautiful, Robbie. He showed me a photo. She's been in an institution for ten years. He goes to see her every week, and she doesn't *know* him. Well, I know all about that, of course. Institutions . . . and not being recognized. Father used to look at me with the most terrible blankness . . .'

Mingo lapsed off, remembering.

'And, Mingo?'

'And then I told him about Father. How could I resist? Only someone who has been through it understands someone else who has been through it.'

'Yes, I see that. It's a bond.'

'Then – I don't know what made me to it, Robbie, I've never told a soul except you – I told him everything. *Why* Father was at The Pines – the whole enchilada.'

When Mingo was most serious, she was most flippant, Roberta realized. How painful that must have been for her, and how brave of her to do it.

'And then Luther' – she said *Luther* as one would say *the Sun, the Moon, and the Stars* – 'Luther took me in his arms and said "You poor little thing" Poor . . . little . . . thing. Me! Oh, Robbie no one has ever called me a poor little thing – even though I *was*. Under my glacéed exterior. That did it. I put my head on his shoulder and then' – she paused, remembering – 'and then we . . . found each other.'

'Mingo, it's wonderful to see you so – '

'Robbie, you know I've had my flings. But they were *flingless* flings. Nothing. Like Novocaine. You don't feel a thing, and then some. But with *Luther* . . .'

Roberta nodded, thinking, for a fleeting moment, of Zack.

'Do you know that old joke about Queen Victoria?'

'Which one?'

'The one about her wedding night with Albert. Afterward, she asked him "Do the *common* people do this?" And when he said yes, she said, "Well, it's much too *good* for them."'

Roberta laughed. Mingo was wearing her familiar wickedly sardonic look, but she became serious again.

'Are you shocked, Roberta?'

'Of course not.'

'You're not? Most people would be. Daddy has been dead less than a week.'

'Life offered you something and you accepted.'

'Bless you, Robbie, you *do* understand. In a way, I did it *for* Daddy. No, that's crazy. I did it for me. But it was almost like a tribute to Daddy. His last words to me were not to be afraid of love. He made me promise. He said it was worth the risk. I think if Daddy could know . . . he'd be glad.'

'I think so too, Mingo dear.'

'And Robbie, of course I'm not just talking about – well, I can't top Hemingway – the earth moving. I'm talking about love. I know I love Luther Hodges – irrevocably, permanently, forever. And he loves me. I *know* it. Don't ask me to explain it. We just met; it makes no sense. But it's true. We *recognized* each other. And I'm so *happy*.'

'I've always wished it for you, Mingo.'

'I know you have, Robbie.' Mingo got up. 'My word, it's getting light. I hope you can still get a little sleep. Happy New Year, Robbie, I'm off.' She left and then popped her head back in again.

'And, Robbie, forgive me if I leave earlier than planned? Luther's coming to town with me.'

Roberta threw the pillow at her.

It was an auspicious beginning for the new year.

38

In January, Roberta was surprised to find that she was glad to be alone. This time, the transition from a house filled with voices to a silent house was actually welcome. It had been wonderful to have the family at home, but she'd realized, even at the height of the holidays, that part of her mind had been on Whitford & Marston. As for her son and daughter, she had managed private talks with each of them. They were affectionate talks, but they left her recognizing, and accepting, that Susan and Jim were going to go their own ways – quite independent of her, which left her independent of them.

Now her energies were focused on a single goal: the opening of the new shop in May.

She got to work at seven forty-five on January second, beating Jane by five minutes. 'Well, partner, thank God that's over, right?' Jane greeted her.

'Right! There's something to be said for a nice plain weekday *workday* after all, isn't there?'

'You said it, Robbie. Let's go. I don't suppose you had a minute to think about the contractors? Whether we should go with Chet Slade or Boynton Brothers?'

'Yes, I did, Jane. Slade's estimate is lower, but I think Boynton is a better bet because . . .'

They plunged into the complex job of renovating and planning the new shop, while simultaneously running the original one. Life became a round of work and sleep. Roberta loved it. As Jane had said, she was experiencing a self she'd never known she had. The kick lay in making decisions and daring to believe they were right, and in coping with the delays, frustrations, and setbacks typical of any new business. The display-case supplier had sworn that he would make his delivery date, now he said he'd need another six weeks. The electrical contractor tried to substitute a track-lighting design different from the one specified. There were problems with the man paving the parking space.

As the work got under way, either Roberta or Jane shuttled back and forth to the new shop, to ride herd on the workmen. You had to *be* there, to make sure that the shelving was not one inch higher, lower, or deeper than you wanted, that the stamped tin ceiling was left untouched. Roberta arrived one day just in time to prevent the old oak display case from being carted away.

'Can you believe that?' she later asked Jane indignantly. 'Our prize piece!'

'Eternal vigilance is the price of renovation. To say nothing of cash, and lots of it,' Jane responded.

One Monday when the shop was closed, they went to New York to cover the cookware market. Visiting the wholesale showrooms on lower Fifth Avenue, dashing down to the Bowery where the restaurant supply houses were, being introduced as 'my partner, Roberta Marston' – all these added up to a new kind of thrill for Roberta. Was she actually a wholesale customer 'in the trade'? Was she really investing her own money in stainless slotted spoons by the *gross*? Betting they'd sell and pay off? She was.

Roberta found herself going to bed with an armful of price lists and a yellow legal pad.

Mingo called frequently, still on cloud nine, to report on her romance with Luther Hodges. 'We just had the most divine weekend. It's real, Roberta. I knew it was. But I bet you had your doubts, didn't you?'

'Yes and no. I trust your instincts, Ming, but – '

'But we had just met, and I could be having midlife craziness.'

'No, really . . .'

'Plus he's married. Well, you can't have everything, Robbie dear.' Roberta could almost see Mingo shrug her elegant shoulders. 'We've come to terms with that. Roberta, Luther's wife is . . . *gone*, poor soul, in everything but fact. Luther is really a widower, except technically. He'll always be devoted to her well-being, that goes without saying, but we see no reason to pass up happiness for a silly legality. Anyway, Robbie, You know I don't give a damn about convention. Neither does Luther. When he isn't here on weekends, I'll be at his house. Just think, Robbie, I'll be your country *neighbor* – can you top *that*?'

'Not possibly.'

'Oh, and while we're in the moonlight-and-roses department, did you know the Paul Restons are divorcing?'

'Yes, I sort of gathered. But why moonlight-and-roses?'

'Because I always thought Paul had a thing for you, Robbie. You know my antennae – I pick things out of the air. It amazes me that *you* didn't pick up on it. But of course you were always blind to everything but Brad. Anyway, there's another beautiful man up for grabs – next to my Luther, I mean. Could you be interested, Robbie?'

'Oh, I don't know, Mingo. I think maybe you and I are going in opposite directions at the moment. You're discovering romance, and I'm discovering work. I'm pretty much committed to being a late-blooming single career lady.'

'Hmm. Well, it's true, hard work provides its own highs – oh, there's my other phone.'

Roberta laughed. 'I know, it's Luther, right? I can take a hint, Mingo dear. Good night.'

She hung up and thought about Paul Reston. Paul had called early in January, within minutes of his return from Switzerland, apparently. He'd asked if she were free for dinner the following Saturday. She'd replied truthfully, that she and Jane were going to be tied up with paperwork that weekend.

'And the following Saturday?'

'Paul, you won't believe this . . . but ditto. We'll be making out our final orders for stocking the new shop. You see, Paul, there's so much involved in the new place that we . . .' She realized she was rattling on, sounding apologetic, overexplaining. 'It would be lovely to see you, Paul. I want to hear all about your ski trip' – that was ridiculous! – 'but right now – '

Paul's voice cut through hers.

'Roberta. I understand. You're very busy.'

'Yes, you can't imagine.'

'And enjoying it?'

'It's exciting.'

'Good. I'm very glad, and I won't keep you. Until we meet, then, Roberta . . .'

That conversation had been a little disturbing. She felt vaguely guilty. Was she treating Paul cavalierly? But she and Jane *were* up to their necks. Still, Paul had always made time for *her*.

Now, having just heard Mingo mention Paul's divorce, Roberta found herself wondering about him. It was two months since he'd called. She hadn't heard from him again. Wasn't that a little odd . . . under the circumstances?'

But look how inconsistent I am, she thought. This is the kind of inconsistency men *accuse* women of. He asked me to marry him, and I told him he was my dear friend.

426

He asked me out, and I said I was too busy. Talk about being illogical! What in the world do I expect? And why am I going on about this?

Well, I *have* known him forever, and I'm naturally . . . just curious. How is he doing, and what is he doing? Maybe he's found someone more responsive? That's certainly possible.

She finished getting ready for bed, thinking, rather regretfully, of what a gap there would be if Paul Reston disappeared from her life altogether.

Mary Blair walked around her new house and counted the closets again. If you counted the triple in the master bedroom as three, and the doubles in the other three bedrooms as six, and the huge coat closet in the foyer, and the storage closet in the utility room, and the linen closet and . . . fourteen! Was it possible! Her old house had three.

It was a year-old contemporary split level. The unfortunate first owners had been transferred, Mary was renting it furnished, with an option to buy. Which she intended to do as soon as her divorce was final and she received her equitable distribution of John's assets. No, her and John's *joint* assets. That's the way her lawyer said the law regarded it.

She was paying for the house out of a temporary agreement. She was surprised at how readily John had accepted the terms. It was though proud, aloof Dr John Blair, always above material benefits, was also above quibbling over them. He'd had to sell a piece of land to come up with the funds. 'That's the way it's done,' Mary's lawyer had told her. If all a man's assets were tied up in property, he had to liquidate some to meet his obligations.

But last night Mary had awakened from a sound sleep in a fit of cold fear. What was she doing in this strange house? In this strange situation? All the old inadequacies swept over her. She was Mary, a docile, dependent wife, scared of her own shadow – how did she get here? She switched on the light, shivering, and looked at the unfamiliar walls. What made her think *she* could face life on her own? And how could she handle Billy, who was acting up because he was disturbed by the separation? Where had she gotten the idea she could become self-supporting? She had a beginner's job, she was forty-two, she had started too late, she'd never make it – she was scared to death.

Then her fear turned to sadness. She wept for the lost years, the years which would be wiped out when she faced John in a divorce court. What a horrible, cold, *final* word . . . *divorce*. What hurt the most was the death of love. She had loved John so unreservedly, so long. But she loved him no more. That was the real pain, that love could end. And she felt sad for John too, lost in his tunnel-vision absorption in work, missing so much. She fell asleep on a tear-soaked pillow.

In the morning, however, with the sun pouring through the windows of her streamlined house, her fears were gone. In Midge's room she looked at the full-page photograph of herself which had appeared in *Home Woman*. Midge had proudly framed it. Mary looked at the piquant face with the tip-tilted green eyes. 'Is that me?' she said aloud. The same image looked back at her from Midge's mirror. Of course it's me. Always has been, I just didn't know it. But now I do. And last night was just . . . heebie-jeebies. To be expected.

She went to the kitchen to make lunch for Roberta. She couldn't wait to show Roberta the house.

As Roberta drove to Mary's she realized that this would be the first socializing she'd done in weeks. She could *use* some relaxation, and she was eager to see Mary's new home. What a major switch for Mary.

Mary greeted her at the door in snappy pants and top, and earrings to match her eyes. 'Mary! You look like a page from a magazine!'

Mary laughed. 'Always the ego booster! Roberta, am I glad to see you. *You* look marvelous. But then, you always *do*. Come on, I can't wait to *show* you . . .'

Mary showed Roberta every inch of the house, including the laundry room. 'And everything *works*,' she said. 'The washer, the dryer, the garbage compactor, the icemaker, the smoke alarm, the doorbell. Oh I know I sound like a lunatic, but *nothing* worked in the old house. And you should have seen the bathroom. Prehistoric. Look, Roberta. Besides the two and a half bathrooms upstairs, there's even this little john next to the utility room.'

'Convenient. It's marvelously well-planned, Mary, and easy to take care of, isn't it?'

'Very. But you know what really sold me on it?'

'The microwave oven?'

'The driveway. Look out the window – see? Flat as a pancake. You remember our lane? The potholes?'

'Indeed I do.' How could she forgot the crazy-angled car, with Mary sobbing within it?

'Well, those potholes were my symbol of everything that was wrong with my life. That's why this place is such heaven for me.'

At lunch Roberta asked, 'And how are you doing, Mary? Inside – where it counts?'

'Inside, where it counts.' Mary looked thoughtful. 'Mixed, Roberta. I feel I've done the right thing, but every once in a while I have strong doubts. Last night I woke up with the most awful case of night terrors. I wondered how I can face life alone. I felt as though I were in a paper boat on a stormy sea – with no oars.'

Roberta smiled at the image. Total terror, right? I know the feeling. I used to feel I was in outer space – with nothing to cling to.'

'You felt that way?'

'Of course. I think everyone does, sometimes. When you realize there's nobody in charge of your life . . . but *you*.'

'Exactly. But then, it's funny . . . The very thing that scares you suddenly reverses and bucks you *up*, because, in a way, if you're in charge of your life . . . then there's nothing to *stop* you.'

'That's the way it works, isn't it? I'm certain it's going to work for you, Mary. You're going to be *fine*.'

'You know, Roberta, I think so, too. Most of the time.'

'Most of the time is *enough*.'

They laughed, pleased at their mutual confidence.

'And how are the kids adjusting, Mary?'

'The twins are taking it in stride, but I'm having trouble with Bill. He's at that terrible, vulnerable age, thirteen – you know, puberty – and he's blaming the whole thing on me. I'm the one who left, you see. Roberta, he acts as though he hates me, and he's furious because I go to work.'

'Oh, Mary, I know what you're going through. I went through a miserable period with my daughter after my husband died. She bristled with hostility – and she was a lot older than Billy.'

'It's so hard to know how to handle, and – *mercy*!' The front door had been slammed violently. Both women had jumped. 'That's Billy.'

A moment later, the boy appeared, scowling, in the doorway. Mary introduced him, and he responded with a

430

grudging, barely audible 'Hi.' Abruptly, he left the room. Seconds later, a stereo blared.

'Excuse me,' said Mary. When she came back, the volume was down. 'You see?'

'He's a furious young man, all right.'

'But what do you do?'

'All you can do is show him your own strength. He's suffering, of course. He feels his world has fallen apart. Your standing firm will reassure him, even though he won't admit it. The trick is to let him know you love him – without letting him get away with anything. Not easy, I admit. And, of course, it takes a lot out of you. But it can be done.'

'You think so?'

'I do. Don't worry, Mary, he'll live through it . . . if *you* will.'

'I hope so. Anyway, I shouldn't complain. Midge gives me lots of moral support. She loves her father, but she's a sensitive girl. She's always understood that John's whole life is medicine, that he had nothing left over for me. She understands that I had to leave, to survive. I'm grateful for that.'

'She's a wonderful girl, Mary.'

'Your Jim's pretty impressive, too.'

They laughed. 'Well, that's certainly the way they seem to feel about each *other*.'

'Looks serious, don't you think?'

'I have that impression.'

'Me too. But who knows, with the young? We may, or may not, wind up being opposite number mothers-in-law!'

'My word, are we ready for *that*?' It struck them both as a funny idea – the mother-in-law role applied to *them*.

Then, for the rest of the afternoon, they forgot their

children and their marriages, and talked shop. They were two women new to the work world, and reveling in it.

Mary told Roberta that her agency had been stuck for a headline to fit a difficult layout, that she had dared to suggest one, and that the client had liked it. Roberta told Mary about the new shop, and the future plans for a mail-order business.

They were so absorbed in their discussion that Roberta wound up staying for supper and they talked on into the evening.

As she was saying goodbye on the doorstep, a thought struck Roberta. 'Mary, I just figured out why men aren't supposed to have as good friendships as women. It must be because men compete with each other while women *support* each other.'

'Thank heaven for *that*!'

39

Carole Harcourt, of course, was a different story. She called Roberta from the city and asked if Roberta could spend Saturday night with her.

'Roberta, I'm going to rent the Greenwillow house . . . as you suggested. Remember? I *do* need the money. I have a date with a real estate man on Sunday. And listen, don't think I don't know this sounds ridiculous, but I can't face being there alone. Could you possibly sleep at my place and stick around Sunday, if it's not too much to ask?'

'Carole, don't be silly, of *course*. It's time we caught up with each other, anyway. I'll come straight from the shop, about six-thirty. By the way, how are you getting here from the city?'

'Bus.' Carole forced a laugh. 'First time I've been on a bus since my steno days.'

Roberta hung up, marveling that a woman who had worked her way up from being a secretary to a powerful job could be so fearful of being alone. It was easier to understand Mary Blair's fears than Carole's. No two women could possibly be more different. Yet both women had reserves of courage, laced with strains of insecurity. Don't we all, thought Roberta.

Well, she was more than glad to lend Carole all the moral support she could. Certainly Carole's all-out friendliness had helped *her* in those early days when *she'd* needed a support system.

Over the weekend, Roberta saw Carole's volatile personality swing from high to low and back again. When she reported her progress in setting up her own production business, she sounded authoritative – tough, even. 'Listen, Roberta, in my field people do *anything* to get the business, and I'm ready to do just that. I've managed to land three accounts: two small ones – Mickey Mouse, really – and one medium-sized one. I undercut a guy I used to work with for that one, but that's the breaks.'

Her pugnacious look was so at odds with her petite figure that Roberta laughed. 'You're not red-haired for nothing, Carole.'

'Right. But my big deal, Roberta, what I *hope* will be my big deal' – she crossed her fingers – 'is the lead *you* got me. Lure, Inc. Thanks to the word you dropped to your friend Mingo Darcy and the word she dropped to Lure, I did get a foot in the door. I spoke to Milt Bergman himself, no less. Of course, he *had* to see me, as a courtesy to Miss Darcy. But he could have been polite for a half-hour, then brushed me off. That's the usual procedure. But he didn't. I think I got through to him. Anyway, I'm making a bid to his ad agency next week. Lure's bringing out a new line of eye makeup, and that's right up my alley. But pray for me.'

'Oh, I will. But, Carole, if you look half as sure of yourself as you do now, prayer's the last thing you'll need.'

Carole was all right when she was talking about her work, but as soon as she spoke of her personal life, the feistiness vanished. 'Oh, Roberta, I can't tell you how I hate that word *single*! To me, a single is a woman – at my age, anyway – not smart enough to hang onto her man. A loser. I'm a loser. I let another woman steal my man. That *bitch*! That' – she was fury incarnate – '*cunt*!'

She bit off the ugly word, like a woman biting off a thread.

'Sorry for the gutter language, Roberta. But in this

case it's *appropriate*. If I ever wanted to kill anyone, it's that – that – lady.'

'Get it out of your system. But, Carole, you know what?'

'What?'

'I'm no analyst, but maybe this anger you're feeling for this woman, whoever she is, is really anger at *yourself* . . . for putting up with Greg for so long?'

Carole looked at her, thinking it over. Then she said slowly, 'You know, maybe you're right. Hell, of course you're right. If I want to kill anybody, it should be Greg – for exploiting me. And if I want to kick anybody, it should be me – for letting him.'

'And another way to think of *her* is – Greg's next victim.'

'Right! Lucky her!' Carole smiled. It was easier for her competitive spirit to think of the other woman as *had* than as triumphant.

They were silent a few minutes, each thinking of men with women, women with men . . . the varieties of relationships.

Carole got up to bring more coffee. They were having Sunday breakfast. When she came back, she said, 'You really turned me around, Roberta. You're right. I haven't lost a thing. As I told you in the city, I *knew* Greg wasn't much of a man, more of a *prop* really. Like the props I use on the set. "This shot requires one easy chair, one lamp, one newspaper – and one man." But the dumb thing is . . . I feel lost *without* a prop, as if I've been cut off from a large hunk of my life.'

'What hunk, for heaven's sake?'

'The social part. I can't make myself go places and do things alone or with another woman – you know, screenings and openings and all that. I feel as though I'm wearing the Scarlet Letter – A for Alone. I even feel

435

funny going in and out of my building alone all the time. I imagine the elevator men saying "That's Mrs Harcourt. Her husband left her." You see, Greg and I used to have hordes of people around. Now, no Greg – no people.'

'Carole! I can't *believe* you! How can a dynamic woman like you have so little faith in yourself? Why do *you* care what the elevator men think! And why can't you entertain hordes of people on your own? I had the strong impression that all those people I met here were *your* friends, not Greg's.' Roberta remembered the drunken actress who'd muttered. 'Love her, loathe *him*' at the Labor Day party. 'Weren't they?'

'Come to think of it, yes. Practically all of them.'

'There you are.'

'Roberta, you must think I'm an idiot. The truth is, under my tough exterior, I'm a basket case . . . sometimes. But right now' – Carole's mercurial face changed again – 'right now I'm loaded for bear. Could you stand coming upstairs with me while I pack Greg's things? I *had* been dreading it . . . like shipping a body. But now I can't wait to get rid of them.'

Upstairs, Roberta helped as Carole quickly emptied the closet where Greg's country clothes still hung. 'See this?' Carole held up a safari jacket. 'I got it for him at Hunters' World. And this raincoat from Burberry. And those boots to cheer him up when *he* lost a job. I'm going to send the whole kit and caboodle to *her*, and I'm going to throw in my engraved stationery – the stuff that says Mrs Gregory Harcourt – with a note saying "He's all yours, and welcome."'

Roberta laughed. 'Carole, do you really think – '

'Oh, I know it's childish, Roberta. Not dignified. But I'm going to do it anyway. Just for the hell of it.' She slammed down the top of the carton, and kicked it into a corner. 'There! I feel better already!'

The real estate agent came at two o'clock. Roberta was struck by the speed and decisiveness with which Carole conducted her business with him. Within an hour he had looked over the property, they had agreed on the rent and the agent's fee and Carole had signed a contract and handed over a set of keys. No wonder she's good at her work, Roberta thought.

'I hate to give up this place, though,' Carole said, after the man had left.

'It's only for a year, Carole. A year goes fast when you're working hard. Anyway, anytime you want a weekend in the country, come and stay with me.'

'Could I?' Carole brightened. 'Oh, Roberta, that would make it so much easier. I'd hate to feel I was losing the country. And you . . . and the whole Greenwillow gang, for that matter.'

'Well, you're not. Next year you'll be back here in full swing, entertaining up a storm . . .'

'And buying party stuff at your wonderful new shop! Listen, how about a little socializing right now? Do you suppose we could round up some of the gang for drinks?'

'That would be fun.' Roberta could almost see Carole's need for nonstop company rising to the surface. She also sensed that, perhaps unconsciously, Carole was testing her power to attract people on her own.

'Let's!' Carole was already at the phone, flipping through her book. 'Hodges, Luther . . .'

'Oh, dear. I happen to know Luther's in the city . . . and Sarah's away too, come to think of it.'

'What about the Fentons?' asked Carole uncertainly.

'I haven't seen much of them. But I know Tim is walking again, with a cane.'

'I've always felt so guilty about that accident. If I hadn't given that wild party . . .'

'That's silly, Carole. It happened.'

437

'I'd *love* to see them, *if* they want to see me. Well, I'll call, anyway.'

Tim and Terry Fenton were peacefully reading the Sunday papers when the phone rang. Terry answered. The moment she heard 'Terry, this is Carole Harcourt . . .,' she experienced an instant replay of one of the most horrible moments of her life. She saw Greg Harcourt, handsome and indolent, in her doorway, she heard him say 'Tim's susceptibilities'; she felt his mouth on hers, his hands at her breast. She felt sick. '. . . could you and Tim possibly drop in? I'd love to see you – and Roberta's here, too,' Carole was saying.

Terry moistened her dry lips. 'Carole, thanks, but I don't think Tim is up to going out!'

'I'm renting my place in Greenwillow, you see . . . so this will be my last chance to see you for quite a while. Oh, and I'm out of a job and out of a husband' – Carole's voice came clearly over the phone – 'and I want you to be among the first to know, I'm divorcing Greg, that total S.O.B. . . .'

That total S.O.B. Exactly what Terry considered him. And apparently Carole did too, only more so – and with more reason.

Coming out of the blue like that, it was too much for Terry to handle. 'Carole, could I call you back? Tim's in the shower,' she fibbed. 'I'll have to see how he's feeling.'

She went back into the living room.

'Who was it, Terry?'

'Carole Harcourt.' Terry saw Tim tense just as she had done. 'But everything's changed. She's getting a divorce, she's out of a job, and she's renting their house.'

'And I thought people like that *never* had trouble.'

Terry knew what he meant. With their limited experience and their open, trusting natures, the Fentons had

438

glamorized the Harcourts beyond all reality. But now, in their attempt to readjust their lives, glamour was the least of their concerns.

In the six months since Tim's accident, both Terry and Tim had struggled toward new insights. Terry had finally admitted to herself that she had always known Tim could be latently homosexual. Indeed, she had loved him precisely because he was *not* like her macho father, because he was gentle, sensitive, responsible, and devoted. And *good*.

Tim was slowly losing his burden of crushing guilt. At Terry's urging, Tim had had several sessions with a psychiatrist while he was in the hospital. 'It is *not* a disease, Tim – not wrong. It's a fact of your being, like the color of your eyes. There are thousands of men with the same psychosexual characteristics. Some of them very distinguished, by the way.'

The doctor did tell Tim, however, that inconceivable as it might seem, he could easily experience another homosexual encounter, given the right circumstances. But that it need not necessarily ruin his marriage.

He told Terry the same thing, with Tim's permission, when the Fentons had a joint session. 'As long as you have common bonds – your children, your home, your values – you can have a good relationship. It's hostility that destroys marriages. Between you two, I see very little. You're on the same side, and you need each other.'

Carole's call had evoked the same thoughts in both Fentons. Terry came back to the present. 'Tim, I promised to call Carole back. Shall I just say you're still staying off your feet as much as possible?'

Tim thought of the Harcourt's house, which he and Terry had admired so extravagantly. He thought of the piano on which he had played Cole Porter. He thought of the blond stranger, David . . . 'You ought to be in the city.' The Harcourts' house was where the nightmare had started. He couldn't face it . . . yes, he could.

'I think we should go, Terry.'

'You do?' Terry was surprised.

'Yes, It's only a *place*. It didn't cause our . . . problems.'

He didn't have to explain. The Fentons often used verbal shorthand; their reactions were so identical.

'Of course, Carole didn't cause our problems either,' Tim added.

And she's certainly not responsible for Greg's behavior, Terry thought.

'Carole did sound awfully eager, almost as if she *needed* us.'

'Then we *should* go.' Tim took the Golden Rule seriously. He rose from his chair, holding onto the arm and reaching for his cane.

Carole was overjoyed to see them. She had tears in her eyes when she saw Tim's cane. 'Oh, Tim! How *good* of you to come!'

Both Roberta and Carole thought the Fentons looked as though they'd been through a wringer, but had survived. And they seemed more quietly confident than before.

Both showed concern, sympathy, and supportiveness for Carole's new situation when she candidly described it. Tim said he'd bet that when Carole got her new venture going she'd think the divorce was the best thing that had ever happened. Terry said that when Carole wanted a country weekend, the Fentons would love to have her visit.

'See?' said Roberta. 'That's *two* standing invitations, Carole.'

Carole looked at them. 'My God, people . . . I feel as

440

though I have a *family*. I never had one, you know. I was
an orphan.'

'Well, you have one now,' said Terry.

At ten o'clock the Fentons drove Carole to the New
York bus. Roberta went with them. As the bus pulled
out, Carole blew kisses and mouthed '*Love* you.'

40

Jim came home for spring vacation, preceded, the day before, by the delivery of a huge crate addressed to him.

'What in the world's in that box?' Roberta asked after she had welcomed him.

'Thirty-five hundred Christmas trees. And that's just for starters.'

Roberta had forgotten about Jim's plan to plant Christmas trees. 'Thirty five hundred? In that one box?'

'Sure. Look, I'll show you.' He pried open the crate and took out what appeared to be a small bunch of tiny branches with dangling roots. 'This is twenty-five Norway Spruce. In six years they'll be twenty-five beautiful trees. Isn't that kind of a miracle?'

'Yes, it is, Jim.' Jim looked almost reverent as he placed the seedlings back in the crate. It was clear that his heart really lay in the land. He had kept his promise about law school, and his grades had been good. But Roberta sensed that when the school year was over he would tell her he would not be going back.

'But Jim, how can you possibly plant thirty-five hundred trees in one week?'

'Easy. You work 'til you drop. I jam a wedge-shaped hole in the ground; then Midge drops in a seedling, kicks the dirt in the hole, and stamps it down. Thirty-five hundred times!'

'Good Lord. That *is* backbreaking.'

'Labor of love. But Mom, I'm afraid you won't see much of me, because we'll be at it pretty much nonstop.'

442

Roberta jokingly reached up and patted his head. 'That's okay, son. I'm pretty busy myself.'

Jim hugged her. 'Sure you are. Mother, the entrepreneur. Mom, did I ever tell you you're terrific?'

'Tell me now.'

'You're terrific.'

'So are you, Jim.'

For the rest of the week she did, indeed, see little of Jim. Midge arrived every morning at six, and the two young people worked until dark. However, Roberta and Mary Blair managed two family dinners. Mary and her children came to the Marstons one evening, and Jim and Roberta went to the Blairs in return. Both mothers came to the conclusion that Jim and Midge would certainly marry. But both mothers hoped they would wait, be absolutely sure, not do anything impulsive. Both mothers realized they would do exactly as they chose.

On the morning of the Sunday when Jim had to return to school, he asked Roberta to come and see the tree plantation. As they rounded the curve past the carriage house, Roberta realized she had not walked that path for a long time . . . and she realized why. Too many memories of Zack. Ah, Zack. A very special, very sweet romance. And one that had occurred at exactly the right moment, for both of them. But, thank God, she had been wise enough – and strong enough – to recognize it as what it was, a lovely interval.

The carriage house reminded Jim of Zack too. He snapped his fingers. 'I knew there was something I wanted to tell you. Guess who's getting married?'

'Haven't a clue.'

'Our former tenant. Zack Owen.'

In spite of what she had just been thinking, Roberta's heart skipped a beat. She felt the pang every woman feels on learning that a man who once loved her loves someone else.

'Did you . . . did you run into him?'

'No, I just happened to see it in the *Washington Post*. Her father's in the State Department. Beautiful girl, from the photo, anyway.'

Of course. Beautiful. And young. I hope she's good enough for him. I hope she makes him happy. She'd *better*. But I wish I hadn't left him thinking I really didn't love him, there in the airport. Because, at the time . . . I did.

They walked on, Roberta pensively thinking how often we hurt most the people we want to hurt least. But as they came to the high open fields, she felt a rush of euphoria. There, spread before them, lay spring. The land was hazed with tender green. On the hills opposite, the dogwood buds were swelling. The earth seemed full of promise. And so does life. She thought. I have my kids, my home, my work – and all this beauty. I'm blessed.

'There they are,' said Jim. He pointed to rich dark acres of newly turned earth planted in long straight rows of seedling trees. 'Aren't you impressed?'

'I *am*, Jim. It looks so professional. And the rows go on forever. How'd you keep them so straight, on a slope?'

'Stakes and measures. They're six feet apart, in both directions. Come on, let's walk down this row and I'll show you . . .'

Roberta interrupted him. 'Why, look, Jim. Somebody's coming.'

'Somebody's coming? Where?'

'Way over there – at the far end. Where our line joins the Harcourts' line.'

Jim looked. 'So there is. And he seems to be coming in

our direction. That's strange. Well, let's meet him half-way, whoever he is.'

The tall figure in the distance was covering the ground at a fast, purposeful clip. In a moment Jim said, 'Mother, I could swear that's Uncle Paul. That looks exactly like Paul Reston.'

'Paul *Reston*? In the middle of our field? It couldn't be.'

It was Paul Reston. When he was within hailing distance he waved and called 'Hello!' and minutes later he was at their side.

All three talked at once.

Jim said, 'Uncle Paul, where'd you park your helicopter? Did you drop from the sky?'

Roberta said, 'Paul, what in the world? . . .'

Paul said, 'I wanted to surprise you. I see I did.' He stood smiling at them, a well-knit man in jeans, jacket slung over a shoulder, hair roughened by the breeze.

'Yes, you did,' said Roberta. 'Paul, I'm so glad to see you.' It was true. It took a minute to realize how very true it was. But the sight of this good friend, whom she'd known so long, *was* a pleasure. Maybe even a reassurance . . .

. . . because, as she'd admitted to herself earlier, she would hate to have Paul out of her life entirely.

'But no kidding, Uncle Paul, how *did* you get here?'

'I'm your new neighbor.'

'Neighbor!' Roberta and Jim stopped dead in their tracks.

'I've just rented a house on the next road, owned by a Mrs Harcourt. For weekends, and so forth.'

'But how *come*?' Jim asked the question with the bluntness of the young.

'Well, you see,' Paul said blandly, addressing himself to Jim and not looking at Roberta, 'I've turned the Greenwich place over to Alicia. By the way, Jim, did you

445

know we're being divorced?' Jim nodded. 'You know the city in summer,' Paul went on matter-of-factly. 'You have to get away, so I asked my secretary to keep an eye out for possible rentals in the *Times*. And she turned up this place.'

'Wow.'

'Of course,' Paul said, turning innocently to Roberta, 'I knew it was in your *area*, but isn't it an amazing coincidence that it actually adjoins your property?'

'Amazing,' said Roberta faintly.

'Not only amazing, it's *great*!' said Jim. 'I can see more of you, Uncle Paul. You can even watch my trees grow!'

'Yes, what *is* all this?' Paul eyed the rows of seedlings. 'Are you trying to corner the evergreen market?'

While Jim told Paul Reston about his project, Roberta tried to sort out her emotions. The last time she had seen Paul he had asked her to marry him. Then she had not heard from him for weeks. Now he had made an overt move, both figuratively and literally, to be near her. That was inescapable. It *was* a coincidence that Carole's house happened to be available, but it was uncharacteristic of a man like Paul Reston to choose a place like Greenwillow. Unless he had a motive.

Apparently his declaration of love and his stated intentions had remained unchanged. He was going to . . . *pursue* her. Court her? Woo her? And how did she feel about it?

In her surprise at having him drop from the sky, she didn't know. It was so hard to think of Paul as *unattached*. Now looking at the attractive man talking to her son, she wondered about him. She had always thought of him as conservative, successful, and, of course, chivalrous. But that little act he'd just put on, explaining how he'd just happened to land on Rimble's Lane, and that glint of challenge as he'd finally met her eye, as if he was daring her to doubt it. *That* had not been conservative.

Roberta realized that she was *curious* about Paul. And that, obviously, she would have to invite him for lunch.

Immediately after the meal, Jim left for Georgetown. Roberta and Paul saw him off, together. As soon as Jim's car had disappeared from view, Paul took the direct approach.

'Roberta, of course you know why I'm here. I've already told you I love you, and that I hope you'll be my wife. I'm repeating that now, darling. I love you. But, Roberta, I do not intend to pressure you or get in your way . . .'

'Paul – '

'Listen, Roberta. It's important that I make you understand. I regret blurting out my love when I did. It was stupid of me, clumsy. Of course I shocked you. My only excuse is that *I*, too, was shocked then I found out, almost by chance, that I could finally free myself of a sham marriage. The sense of release was so sudden that I lost my head. Because I had loved you secretly for *years*. You must have thought me mad, Roberta.'

'No, Paul, of course not, but . . .'

'And there was another thing. I had this wild idea I had to stop you from buying that shop. That a woman like you should not be tackling such hard work, that you should be protected. I wanted to be your protector, to take care of you, to make life perfect for you. How's that for egotism?'

Paul laughed, then surprised Roberta by changing pace. 'And how's the new shop coming along?'

'Fine. It's taking shape. We expect to open at the end of May.'

'So soon? That's marvelous. I'm glad.' He looked as

though he really was glad. 'I know you'll make a success of it.'

This was certainly a Paul she had never seen before.

'Do you really mean that, Paul?'

'I do, yes. You know, Roberta,' he said reflectively, 'I've made a three-hundred-and-sixty-degree turn since I've left Alicia. Not only do I feel free, I see life as free . . . and full of choices. Your shop, for example. Why did it take me so long to grasp that this is a challenge you *want* – a choice – not something you have to be rescued from?'

'Well, it took me a long time, too, Paul. I never thought that sort of choice was open to me either, until I got a new slant.'

'It does take time, doesn't it? And so does love, Roberta. Darling, hear me. I'm so happy to be near you, I can afford to wait. I haven't called because the telephone seemed the wrong way to communicate with you. Besides, I wanted to get the divorce under way. It will be final in a few months, and now that I'm here, I want to share as much of your life as you'll allow. I think you know I won't intrude, and I promise not to make passes at you. For the moment, anyway. But I'm going to be practically next door. So as a new neighbor and old friend' – he put a slight ironic stress on *old friend* – 'I'll rely on you to show me around. After all, I don't know a soul in Greenwillow. Will you?'

Put that way, there was only one possible answer. 'Of course.'

'And there's one thing I'd like to do right now.'

She couldn't guess. He had just said he wouldn't make passes, but there was a look in his eye . . .

'What, Paul?'

'Take a look at your new shop, before I head back to the city.'

On the way to the shop, she reflected that Paul Reston certainly knew how to reach a woman where she lived. It was rather exciting, seeing an unexpected side of a man she thought she knew well. Almost like meeting a new man.

A month later Roberta found herself wondering how Paul had managed to weave himself into her life so quickly. Because he certainly had. Tonight was Saturday, and he was taking her to dinner. Last Saturday, she and Paul had spent the evening with Mingo and Luther Hodges, at Luther's house. *That* couple now spent every weekend together. Roberta suddenly realized it was almost understood that she would see Paul every Saturday evening and most of Sunday. So much so that tonight, as she'd stroked mascara onto her lashes, she knew she would feel a little lost if she were not dressing to go out.

But how had it happened so fast? Well, she thought with amusement, it must be that Paul is what the kids call an 'operator,' and a very subtle one at that. A week after his surprise appearance, he'd called to ask if she could possibly find a housekeeper for him, a local woman to take care of the Harcourt house from Thursday through Monday. With Terry Fenton's help, she had. Then he'd called to say he would be entertaining clients for lunch on Sunday. Would she bail him out of a lopsided situation and act as hostess? He said he hadn't quite got the hang of bachelor entertaining. Paul was making demands on her, in the name of friendship, in ways she couldn't refuse.

And why would she want to? He was turning out to be an amusing companion. At Luther's, he had displayed flashes of dry wit which kept the others laughing and sparked Mingo's most wicked ripostes. It had been the kind of successful evening that had prompted everyone to say 'We must do this again soon' and *mean* it.

And he seems so . . . so ready for anything, Roberta thought, eyeing herself in the pier glass, happy with her new dress. If I had to pick one word to describe Paul right now, I'd choose *vital*.'

So why am I feeling so *funny* about going out with an attractive, witty, vital man? Because it's so different from what I'd envisioned. I was going to pour my heart and soul into work, enjoy my kids when I saw them, be grateful for my friends. Period. Yet her I am with a sort of steady date. A man I've known for years . . . and don't know at all. *That's* why I feel funny.

Not that Whitford & Marston isn't still my first priority, she hastily added to herself.

41

A week before the opening of the new shop, Roberta and Jane sat parked across from it, looking at it critically.

Painted a warm yellow with shutters of soft sage green, it stood alone, surrounded by fields. Jane and Roberta had spent one Monday on their hands and knees, planting a low yew hedge along the path to the entrance. The landscaping firm they'd called had wanted an arm and a leg. 'No wonder Midge Blair says landscaping is profitable,' said Roberta, shocked.

'We'll do it ourselves,' said Jane.

They also planted annuals along the foundation. Marigolds, zinnias, snapdragons, and primroses now in early bloom, a blaze of color.

Inside, the atmosphere was that of a large country kitchen. The wall displays were designed to suggest Welsh cupboards. An old Hoosier cabinet offered mixing bowls, and its open doors held racks of kitchen utensils. Chintz-covered chairs invited shoppers to sit and rest, each strategically placed to draw the eye to a special group of wares.

'Well, it's got eye appeal,' said Jane. 'Now let's see if it has buy appeal. We *hope*.'

Both women were keeping an anxious watch out the front windows. There wasn't much traffic and they were both suffering from cold feet. Suppose, on this quiet road, nobody knew they were there? Suppose they flopped?'

'Worried, partner?' asked Jane.

'A little. There's nothing moving on the road.'

'I know. It scares me, too. Listen, it's classic. Opening-night jitters. But, Roberta, we knew up-front about this road. Remember, if we were on a major highway, we'd be surrounded by gas stations and tractor dealers. Anyway, we're not a drive-in, impulse operation . . . like a fast food chain. We're a quality operation. We have to rely on word of mouth from our *discriminating* clientele. When people really want good stuff, they'll go out of their way to get it. Won't they?'

Suddenly Jane looked so uncertain it was Roberta's turn to back *her* up. 'Absolutely. You already proved that with the Smith's Mill shop. And let's not forget the ads we've been running in the *Democrat*.'

'Right! And the publicity story they're giving us.'

The newspaper had sent a young girl reporter and photographer to cover the shop opening. The angle, said the reporter, would be 'Ex-Manhattanites Bring City Sophistication to Countryside.'

'Please put in "Five minutes from Flemington," will you?' Jane had begged.

'Oh, I will, Mrs Whitford, of course,' the young woman promised.

She had been visibly impressed by the shop, and somewhat in awe of its owners. 'I'm sort of a beginner,' she had confessed to Jane and Roberta, 'but women like you are so *inspiring*. You make me feel women can do *anything*.'

The photographer had taken exterior and interior shots, including one of Roberta and Jane next to the Hoosier cabinet. The paper would come out the Thursday before the Saturday opening.

'That plug should bring in at least a few of the simply curious,' Jane now said to Roberta.

'And maybe a few of our loyal customers from the Smith's Mill shop, especially with that little teaser Sarah dreamed up. "Bowls from Brazil. See them at our new branch.'"

The partners grinned at each other, Jane knee-deep in excelsior from a last-minute shipment of espresso pots, Roberta putting the finishing touches to their bakeware display.

On opening day, both women arrived at eight o'clock. By eleven they were still looking nervously at each other. At eleven-thirty a young couple in T-shirts entered the shop.

'Are you open?'

'Indeed we are.'

'May we look around?'

'Please do.'

'Wow,' said the girl. 'Look at these blue pots, Andy. I never saw blue ones. And look at this round thing – same stuff as a flowerpot.' They made their way around the shop, looking at everything, and audibly commenting. At the end of a half-hour, they edged toward the door.

'Just a moment!' said Roberta. She seized a little white coeur à la crème mold, hastily wrapped it, and handed it to the girl. 'Compliments of the house.'

'Bread upon the waters,' Roberta explained to Jane, after they left. 'For good luck.'

'And here comes a live one,' said Jane. 'See, it's working already.' A car was pulling into the parking area. Within moments a well-dressed older couple entered the shop.

'Why, what a charming place,' said the woman, running a knowing eye around the shop.

'Isn't it,' agreed the man. 'Elizabeth, you're in luck.'

'I don't suppose you have a twenty-quart stockpot, do you?' the woman asked Roberta. 'I know that's awfully large . . . and most places don't carry them . . .'

'Yes, we do have one,' said Roberta.

'Copper?'

'Copper. Made in France. *And* tin lined.'

Jane was already lifting the pot from the top shelf.

The customer was delighted. 'I can't tell you how pleased I am to find this – and here in the country, of all places. My husband and I have just bought a country place, and I'm stocking the kitchen from scratch. A whole new *batterie de cuisine*, you know. But this weekend hordes of people have threatened to drop in, so I thought a bouillabaisse . . . Of course. I need something huge, My dear, this is exactly what I wanted.'

She promised to come back later for some *serious* shopping. But as she chatted, she swiftly picked out other things, like a woman plucking items from a supermarket shelf: salad spinner, pepper mill, cutting board, dish towels. She handed her selection to her husband as she chose them commenting meanwhile.

'Look, Wilton, the nice linen kind with "glass towel" woven into them – a dozen, I think.'

When Roberta made up the bill, it came to $384.12.

'Three eight-four twelve, Wilton,' said the woman.

The man asked if they accepted credit cards. 'We're not set up for them yet,' said Roberta. 'but we'd be happy to take your check.'

'Right,' said the husband. He pulled out his checkbook.

After the couple had left, Jane and Roberta burst into shaky laughter.

'Oh, Jane,' gasped Roberta. 'Can you believe it? Jackpot, with our first paying customer!'

Jane was waving the check around. 'Mr Wilmot Williams, the Third – I love you!' She kissed the check. 'And you too, Chase Manhattan Bank!'

'I don't suppose that could happen again, not in a month of Sundays!'

'Not a chance. But it doesn't hurt for a little luck to splash on us going in, does it?'

'Proves luck *exists*, anyway. Oh, here comes another one. A *normal* one – a pound of cheese, maybe.'

The second customer wanted a plastic container for picnic food. They didn't carry that sort of thing.

In the early afternoon, the Fentons loyally turned up, and later Mary Blair came in and still later Luther Hodges and Mingo. All made purchases, and that bothered Roberta. It was sweet of them, of course, but it in no way represented genuine business. Jane confirmed that feeling. 'When we add up the day's take, we'll have to subtract the sales to our friends,' she whispered. 'Those are just opening-day handouts. But I must say their cars in the parking lot make the place look busy.'

Roberta nodded. She was amazed at the intensity of her commitment to the business. Even though she and Jane had been working toward this for months, today, when it was actually happening, she found she was involved heart and soul. She desperately wanted the place to succeed, and she was fiercely determined it would. Even as she smilingly accepted compliments on the shop, she had fantasies of the nation-wide – we ship anywhere – mail-order business she and Jane were aiming for.

So when Paul Reston showed up and began to select a suspicious number of things, Roberta got mad. Paul had already sent an opening-day gift: two miniature trees in terra rosa pots, to flank the front door. Now, here he was, pretending to need a set of saucepans, a salad bowl, butter pats, oil-and-vinegar cruets, and God knows what else. Did the man think Whitford & Marston were the 100 Neediest Cases?'

Jane was busy with a *legitimate* customer. Roberta cornered Paul in the back of the shop, where he was lifting a copper fish pan from the shelf.

'Paul, please don't.'

'Don't? Isn't this for sale?'

'Paul, you know very well what I mean. You have absolutely no use for all this stuff.'

'But, Roberta, I need a housewarming gift for a niece. And a wedding gift for one of our junior attorneys.'

'I don't believe you! Anyway, Tiffany would be more suitable, or Cartier!'

It was clear that she was really angry. Paul looked startled, then he smiled down at her.

'And don't say it!'

'Say what?'

'You're beautiful when you're mad.'

From the look on his face, she knew he had been going to say just that, and having expressed her anger, she took pity on him.

'Sorry, Paul, how ungracious can I be? You're being generous, as usual. But don't you see that your *gratuitously* buying things you don't want or need is exactly like giving us a tip? To encourage us in our little enterprise?'

Paul wasn't smiling now. He looked dead serious. 'You're right. It's like being offered trumped-up cases when you hang out your law shingle, when what you want is the real thing.'

'Exactly.'

'Forgive me, Roberta. It was an old reflex at work – sometimes they're hard to get rid of. But at least allow me to buy something as a souvenir of this red-letter day in your life?'

'Better than that, Paul.' She led him to the front of the shop, where she wrapped and handed him one of the *coeurs á la créme*.

'Compliments of the house, Paul.'

'Thank you.' He wanted to ask if there was any significance to the heart shape, but he didn't. Instead he allowed himself to think that when a woman was really angry at you, it had to be because she was emotionally involved with you. At least a little.

'Roberta, your shop is very impressive. I think you may find you have a hit on your hands, in a year or two. We'll drink to that tonight. I'll pick you and Mrs Whitford up at eight.'

He was taking *both* Whitford and Marston to dinner. He thought that after the rigors of opening day they would deserve some pampering, and he wanted to be the one to provide it.

The new shop got off to a slow, sporadic start. Some weekdays there were no more than three customers, and on one terrible day there were none. 'I told you,' Jane said, 'In the first shop, we waited a full week before *anyone* showed up.' Then, inexplicably, occasionally there would be a modest rush.

'The people who travel this road regularly are beginning to catch on to our Imported Cheeses sign,' Roberta reported over the phone to Jane at the Smith's Mill shop. 'I had three stopper-inners today, plus one word-of-mouth who said her neighbor had served our cheese. And a young couple came in clutching our ad. How are things at your end?'

'Brisk. I sold two Robot-Coupes this week – that's a record except at Christmas.'

'Terrific. Listen, Jane, the five-minutes-from-Fleming-ton idea is working. Here come five women with Flemington shopping bags.' Roberta went to greet the customers, thinking what a high it was to cast your bait and feel a tug at the line.

Roberta and Jane had agreed that Roberta would eventually manage the new shop while Jane would stick with the original. In the meantime, they switched every week, so that the new shop could benefit from their combined ideas, observations, and hunches.

Roberta was happy with the arrangement. Already she was thinking of the new shop as her baby. She couldn't wait to open up in the morning, because there was absolutely no telling what the day would bring. And, as she'd told Jane, on slow days she could always bone up on the mass of material they had collected on the care and feeding of a mail-order business.

Jim had finished his year at Georgetown and was back at the farm. As she'd felt he would, he announced his intention of leaving school. At first, Roberta had a panicky reflex. She thought of making a last-ditch effort to get him to reconsider, but hearing the decisiveness in his voice, she relaxed. His mind was made up. So be it, and bless him.

'Here's the scenario, Mom. I'll work at Princeton Nurseries for about a year. I applied yesterday, and they *jumped* at me.' He grinned in mock boastfulness. 'Just dumb physical labor, mostly, but an inside view of a successful nursery. Midge will be assisting a top land-scaper near Bedminster. Then, next spring, we should be ready to get our own nursery started. Do a lot of planting, and get set up for eventual selling. I'll work on that while Midge keeps her job. And I'll do some part-time work to bring in some cash. Then, the following year . . .'

He and Midge had apparently done some thoughtful planning.

'So what do you think, Mom?'

'Son, if it will make you happy, it will make me happy.'

'Thanks, Mom.' He squeezed her hand. 'And there's something else. Midge and I . . . well, of course you know we're serious about each other.'

'Yes, I know.'

'We want to be married, Mom. We thought maybe October.'

It wasn't really news. She and Mary Blair had both sensed it, even assumed it. But actually hearing it was still a little jolt. And so *soon*!

'Jim, I like Midge immensely. When you do marry, I'll be proud to welcome her as your wife. But Jim, you're in your early twenties. Don't you need a little time – I guess the word now is *space* – to be just yourself? Before you commit to so much responsibility?'

Jim smiled. 'But don't you see, that's what Midge and I give each other – space. So naturally, we want to share the *same* space.'

She didn't quite follow this line of reasoning.

Jim leaned over and patted her hand reassuringly. 'Not to worry, Mother. Midge and I know exactly what we're doing.'

'I hope so, Jim.'

How did it happen, she thought, after he'd left, that children suddenly acted like parents? Patting their own mothers on the hand, to calm their mothers' childish fears? The deadsureness of the untried!

What she needed now was a seasoned *adult* to pour all this out to. She would discuss it with Paul, tomorrow night.

It was a crammed-to-overflowing busy summer. Weekends were abbreviated, extending only from Saturday night to an early-to-bed Sunday. There was hardly time to socialize with Mingo and Luther and her other friends and she scarcely saw Jim. They both left early and worked late.

But busyness is beautiful, Roberta thought, riding a wave of exhilaration. It makes time so *precious*. At a red light she checked her makeup in the car mirror, and had the funny feeling she was seeing a different woman reflected there. It was as though she had never seen herself before. She tried to put her finger on the change. I suppose I feel . . . what, exactly? She groped for the word. *Enough*. I feel enough . . . in myself. Enough to handle whatever has to be handled. My God, I've just come of age!

The shop was doing well. Over the July Fourth weekend, they beat their opening figures without the moral-support purchases of friends and without the splurge of their first big spender, Mrs Wilmot Williams, III. Mrs Williams had come back, though, as promised, and looked fair to become a steady customer. Occasionally she even dragged some of her city friends with her. 'My discovery, Madge,' Roberta heard her say to her companion, indicating the shop with a possessive wave of the hand, '*so* much nicer than the crowds at Bloomingdale's.' Roberta had the distinct impression that poor Madge bought what she bought because Mrs Williams said she'd be a fool not to.

But it made a nice figure on the sales slip. And customer-watching was better than a course in psychology. What tricky little by-plays and interplays. No wonder the days flew.

42

On a hot night in August, Roberta could not sleep.

She and Jane had worked until ten in the back room at the Smith's Mill shop. 'God Robbie,' Jane had said, rubbing her tired eyes, 'won't it be heaven when we can afford a bookkeeper?'

'Heaven,' Roberta had agreed, through a yawn.

She'd gotten into bed expecting to sink instantly into exhausted sleep; instead, she was tossing and turning.

Please, not insomnia, she thought. That's such hell . . . and I'm so tired. Restlessly, she threw off the sheet and turned onto her back. She was wearing a short silk nightie. The accidental brush of her own hand against her bare thigh burned her skin . . . and she knew why she couldn't sleep.

Of course, she thought, staring at the dark ceiling. I want a man. A man's arms. A man's mouth. A man's passion. No, my *own* passion. She felt her nipples harden. She had never felt sex hunger this way before. Not alone like this, uninvolved with a man.

She got up, threw on a robe, and went downstairs to prowl through the garden. But the seductive scent of nicotiana, the dew against her bare feet, and the insinuating murmur of the creek made the moment even more sensuous.

But why right now? she asked herself, as she crossed the lawn to the evergreen grove. She thought of Brad . . . and Zack. The only two men she had ever known. In both cases, long-term husband and short-term lover, her fervor had been kindled by *theirs*.

461

Yet here she was bursting into flame on her own. Could it be because she was now *acting* in life, instead of just reacting? Had her new sense of being her own woman freed her to make her own physical claims?

Maybe, she thought. The question is, what do I do about it? Because she already knew the answer. Paul. Of *course*, Paul. Just because he was there, like Mt Everest? No, because he was Paul.

Leaning against the trunk of a hemlock – tall and strong, like Paul – she closed her eyes and *saw* Paul. She saw his thick dark hair, now limned with silver. She saw his handsome teeth, his hands – disciplined, with spatulate fingers – and his ears! She'd always liked his ears, carved flat to the head, like sculpture. It was as though she had never really *looked* before.

Roberta went back to bed, carrying a sprig of nicotiana with her. Half-awake and half-asleep, she deliberately allowed herself to fantasize that she was in bed with Paul. At length she sighed, released, and fell asleep.

The next morning, she thought she had dreamed the whole thing, including the walk in the garden. But no, she knew she hadn't. There was the nicotiana on her pillow. Anyway, she realized that, awake or dreaming, the meaning was the same. She had recognized a need in herself, and her view of Paul had changed.

He was on her mind all day. What struck her most was how long she had clung to her original image of Paul as old friend, no more, long after reality had invalidated it. He was *not* just a friend; he was a man who desired her and wanted to marry her.

And he had said that he had loved her for years, even before Brad had died. She realized, with something like shame, that she had hardly acknowledged that confession.

She'd heard him, but the words had simply not sunk in. They sank in now.

Disturbed, she thought of last night. Last night I was overcome by longing. For closeness. For sex. My god, what must Paul's longing be like? I must be the world's most insensitive woman . . . and selfish. I've been taking and Paul has been giving. I've been quite willing to let Paul take me to dinner and listen to my shop talk and discuss my kids with me. What a rotten *deal*, from his point of view.

But of course, she realized, Paul can hardly be starved for sex, as such. That's inconceivable. Naturally he has a woman . . . or women.

She didn't much like that idea. She *hated* it.

Roberta was in the shop, preparing a bank deposit. Now, feeling shaky and confused, she put it aside. She was too agitated to concentrate. Paul – familiar Paul – suddenly presented her with an urgent question. And she didn't know the answer.

She was grateful that a customer came in just then. It forced her mind back to work.

That night she took a long walk along the creek, trying to clarify her feelings. One thing was certain: the situation with Paul could not go on indefinitely. He would hardly put up with it much longer. Another thing was certain: she didn't want to lose him. She had never wanted to lose him, as a friend. Now she didn't want to lose him – as a man.

What *are* the possibilities. Could we just be lovers? Would Paul accept that? The new Paul was so surprising, she couldn't guess. If so, exactly how would that come about, since she had set up taboos and he had honored them? Did you just sort of say you'd changed your mind – no more taboos?

But what's wrong with me? I'm thinking like a child.

Paul wants to *marry* me. He won't settle for half-measures. Do I think I can arrange his life to suit myself?

She turned back toward the house. The walk had not clarified a thing. She knew only that she felt a compelling need to see Paul Reston . . . and next Saturday night seemed far away. This was only Tuesday.

On Thursday, Paul's secretary called Roberta at the shop. 'Mrs Marston, Mr Reston had to leave unexpectedly for London. He particularly asked me to tell you he tried to reach you last night, to tell you personally how sorry he is to break your engagement for Saturday. He'll be back in the country on the eighteenth.'

Thud.

She stayed home Saturday night, trying to read a book. Every so often she visualized Paul in London, at the Connaught or Claridge's, dining in the company of a dazzling woman.

On Monday he called.

'Roberta?'

'Paul!' The joy in her voice was audible even to her.

There was a split-second hesitation across the Atlantic. She had never said his name that way before.

'How are you, Roberta?'

It wasn't much of a conversation, really. He asked about the shop, about Jim, about the farm. She asked if he was enjoying London. He asked her to dinner the following Saturday. But when they hung up, she sensed that something had changed.

When she greeted him on Saturday, she felt oddly self-conscious. She wondered if she looked nice. She wondered if he thought so.

'Roberta, what would you say to dinner in the city? Change of venue, for variety's sake? I've made a reservation for eight-thirty.'

She said that would be fun.

All the way into Manhattan and during the dinner Roberta could hardly touch, she felt the tension crackling between them. And she felt absolutely certain that she and Paul were going to go to bed together.

But when, as they left Lutèce, Paul looked at his watch and said, 'It's only a little after ten – come and see my new apartment,' Roberta panicked.

She knew it was irrational and absurd, but she couldn't help herself. At that moment a lifetime of conservative training rushed to the fore. She felt inhibited by the idea of going to his apartment. Especially when she had designs on him.

Paul saw her hesitation and exploded. 'For Christ's sake, Roberta, you'd think we were back in the days of "Come up and see my etchings"! I'm Paul remember? We've known each other for years!'

He was as mad at her as she had been at him when he'd made all those pretend purchases at her shop. And he had a right to be. She was being childish.

'I'm sorry, Paul. I'd love to see your new apartment.'

It was a duplex on East Fifty-seventh Street, with a terrace and a view. Roberta wandered around admiring it. Paul made espresso and served it with cognac.

'It's a wonderful apartment, Paul. There *is* something about this city, isn't there? Something you never get over.'

'Nor would you want to. But the country grows on you, too. I'm beginning to want them both.'

'Really, Paul? But you're such an urban man. I've never thought of you as a country type.'

'I am now, Roberta. I've learned it from you.'

They made desultory small talk, which was punctuated by silences.

'More coffee?'

'No more, thanks.'

'Then,' said Paul deliberately, his eyes holding hers, 'shall we go?'

She didn't have to be brave after all. The words came of themselves. 'Why don't we just stay here?'

And as he had promised, old friends do make the best lovers.

The next morning, leaning on an elbow and stroking her bare shoulder, making it a spot more erogenous than she would have thought possible, Paul said, 'Roberta, Roberta, you're just the way I've dreamed you . . . for years.'

She smiled. 'And you're just the way I dreamed you . . . ten days ago.'

'Really?' He was delighted.

'Yes. I couldn't sleep, and I thought of you, and – '

His mouth stopped hers.

Later, he said, 'Roberta, I love you. I want to marry you. You already know that. What you *don't* know, yet, is that you love me, too.'

'Paul, I want you. I'm rather crazy about you, in *this* way . . . That's kind of obvious, isn't it? But . . .'

'I understand. We'll wait, Roberta. Until you're confident your project is under way, to your complete satisfaction. I calculate that will be . . . oh, next spring. By that time you'll realize that although work is one of life's great boons, God knows, it's not enough. Not enough for a woman like you. That's when I think you'll know we love each other, and we'll be married.'

He didn't say it dramatically, just as a statement of fact.

She mulled it over, trying to visualize it. Then she spoke aloud, in the middle of a thought. '. . . but you live in the city and I live in the country.'

'As though there aren't ways around that. I could be in the office four days a week, and in the country four nights a week. Hell, I could even commute. I understand there's a helicopter service from Allentown. Anyway, isn't that what working couples do, accommodate each other's schedules?'

Working couples. It seemed to reach the limits of incongruity that she, Roberta Marston, and he, Paul Reston, were discussing being a *working couple*. Yet it didn't seem . . . impossible. Especially with their mutual awareness of their warm bodies in a warm bed.

'Anyway, darling, as your business takes off, you'll certainly have to be in the city yourself for buying trips and trade shows, won't you? So we'll both need this place.'

He had it all planned.

They drove back to Greenwillow, holding hands, friends *and* lovers. They made love again, in one of Carole Harcourt's Victorian bedrooms, before Paul reluctantly returned to the city.

43

It was to be a double wedding. Jim Marston and Midge Blair would exchange their vows in a joint ceremony with Susan Marston and Bob Giordano.

When the kids announced their intentions, both mothers said the same thing. Wouldn't it be wiser to wait? If you really love each other, you'll still love each other a year from now . . .

Jim, of course, had prepared his mother in advance, and both Roberta and Mary had expected a wedding. Even so, Mary worried that her daughter was too young. 'Midge, you're the same age I was when I was married. Perhaps, if I'd been older and wiser . . .'

Midge tried to reassure her. 'I can understand your hesitation, Mother, after the way things turned out with you and Dad. But Mother, Dad is such an unusual man, kind of workaholic . . . I mean so dedicated . . .' She broke off, she was treading sensitive ground. 'I'm sorry you've been so unhappy, and I think it's wonderful you're building a new life. But it will be different for Jim and me. You see we'll be working *together*. How could anything go wrong with that?'

Mary, like Roberta, realized it was out of her hands.

When Susan broke *her* news to Roberta over the telephone, her voice was exultant. 'Mother . . . Mother, Bob and I are going to be married. And guess what! I'm pregnant!'

Roberta reached behind her for a chair.

'Mother? Are you there? Did you hear me? Isn't it wonderful?'

'Susan! Oh, Susan, are you sure?'

'Sure that I'm pregnant? Absolutely.'

'Sure this is right for you? You needn't be hasty, Susan. You need not rush into marriage, just because – '

'Mother, I'm so happy, I could squeak! I want a baby, terribly, and so does Bob. Mother, aren't you glad? You'll be a grandma! And, Mother, I want to be married at the farm – an outdoor wedding – okay with you?'

Only Bob's family, the Giordanos, in Brooklyn, offered no ifs ands or buts. They believed in young marriages, and when Bob told them about the pregnancy, of course, that clinched it. Privately, they shook their heads just a little, but then they reminded themselves that today things are different. Maybe even better. More natural.

It was Jim's idea that they have a double ceremony. If there were to be two weddings in the family, didn't it make sense to combine them? Besides, he liked Bob, and was happy for his sister's happiness. But first he naturally had to consult Midge. A girl's wedding day was the most significant day of her life. She was entitled to want it to be hers, and hers alone. Midge might understandably prefer to be married from her mother's house. For his own part, Jim would have settled for taking Midge as his lawful wedded wife barefoot, under a tree, at dawn.

Midge's response was spontaneous. 'What a great idea! Do *they* want to?'

'I don't know,' Jim told her. 'I wanted to ask *you* first.'

'Let's call them tonight and see what they say.'

An unusually clear-headed, direct girl, who knew exactly what her values were, Midge had no need at all for the queen-for-a-day role most girls covet. To Midge sharing her wedding day with the sister of her bridegroom seemed a nice, natural way to cement family ties.

Susan was by far the more romantic of the two girls. She *did* have stars-in-the-eyes visions of the moment she would exchange rings with Bob. She would *not* have wanted to share her wedding with another girl – *except* her brother Jim's girl. Susan adored Jim, and she felt this was a way of pleasing him and her mother.

Mary Blair had a conflict. On the one hand, she wanted to provide her own daughter's wedding, like any mother-of-the-bride. On the other hand, Roberta's lovely house and extensive grounds were more appropriate than her own place, pleased as she was to be living in it.

In the time she'd been working – a full year next week, was it possible? – Mary had begun to trust her own judgment. Having made the decision to end a bad marriage, she was now more decisive about other choices as they arose. Thinking about Midge's wedding, Mary weighed the pros and cons. One of the big pros was her warm friendship with Roberta. Another was that such an arrangement would halve the burden for her and for Roberta. But the biggest consideration of all was that Midge wanted it that way.

After Mary and Roberta spent an evening discussing it, they ended up in happy agreement.

'Mary, I think it will be lovely. We'll be co-hostesses.'

'I think it will too. But remember our deal, Roberta. I insist on our splitting expenses to the penny. I know John will insist on that too.'

'Agreed, Mary. Just think, we're going to be related by marriage.'

'As we suspected all along. But don't things happen fast? A year and a half ago we hardly knew each other. Roberta, I couldn't be happier it's my Midge and your Jim.'

'Me, too.' Roberta gave Mary a good-night hug.

'Mother, would it be too awful for you to have Daddy give me away?' Midge had been worried about that, and had been putting off the question. Still, it was

470

inconceivable to her that she should not walk down the aisle on her father's arm.

The flicker of distress on Mary's face vanished as fast as it had appeared. 'Of course not, Midge. Naturally your father will give you away. I've already spoken to him about it.'

'You have?' Midge's young face glowed with love for her mother. 'Mother, you're a fantastic woman, you know that?'

Susan had already decided to be given away by her maternal grandfather.

So the planning and list making and invitation mailing began. All agreed that it should be a simple wedding: one attendant for each of the principals, champagne and a light buffet at little tables on the lawn, dancing on the patio. Roberta and Mary worried about rain. The four young people blithely insisted it couldn't rain on *their* wedding. Even the *Farmers' Almanac* said so.

Mingo Darcy got into the act early. When Roberta told her about the plans on the phone, Mingo responded with characteristic enthusiasm. 'Jim and Susan *both* – in one fell swoop? What a thrill! Those kids! God, doesn't it make you feel old? Listen, Roberta, you've got to let me mastermind the girls' gowns. Look, some of the bridal houses are open on Saturday. If they're not, they'll open for me. Send the girls in, and I'll meet them on Seventh Avenue. Crazy to do anything else. I can get it for you wholesale. So that's settled.'

'Mingo! What a bossy woman you are.' Roberta had to laugh at Mingo's bing-bang approach.

'I know. Pushy. But after all, I've known them since they were tadpoles – and Jim *is* my godson. So you can't deprive me of the pleasure, can you?'

'Absolutely not, fairy godmother. And, of course, that will be an enormous help. Jane and I are up to our necks

471

with the two shops and Mary Blair is busy with her job, so it would be heaven to get the girls' dresses off our minds.'

'Listen, Roberta. A light buffet, you said? A *fête champêtre* in the garden? Look, I know just the man for you. "Mr Party" – a new young catering service. He does wonderful things. He'll make it as simple as you like – but superb. Shall I give him a ring?'

'Mingo, surely that would cost the earth. A Manhattan caterer, coming all the way out here?'

'Not if I arrange it. He's out of his mind with gratitude to *Cachet*. We gave him a nice plug when he started out – it helped him get off the ground – so I know I can get a price break for you. As for the distance, his vans go to Westchester and Fairfield County – they can certainly go to New Jersey. Just tell me how many guests and how much you want to spend, and he'll come up with some menus. Plus tables and chairs and a tent.'

'Mingo, that's too much to ask of you. You're doing all the work!'

'What is the point of having contacts, I ask you, if I can't use them for my best friend? Sure as hell, I'll never be able to arrange a wedding for *my* kids, so you must let me help with yours. Agreed?'

'Mingo, darling, you are the most generous of creatures. Of course, I'd love it. Mary and I were worried about finding a decent caterer locally. But I do have to consult Mary first. We're equal partners in this enterprise. I'm sure she'll be tickled pink – why wouldn't she be?'

'How *is* Mary?'

'Mingo, she's a changed woman. She looks terrific, she loves her job, her divorce is in the works, and she's making it on her own. I can't tell you how many times she mentions her gratitude to you. She says the magazine makeover you set up for her changed her life.'

'Amazing what a little uplift for the outer woman does for the inner woman. After all, that's the theme of my lifework.'

'And you know, I think there may even be a man in her life, or the hint of a man. She hasn't said anything, but there's something in her face when she mentions him – the art director at her agency.'

'Let's *hope* so!' said Mingo.

She hung up, and sat mulling over their conversation for a moment, in her starkly elegant contemporary office, a direct contrast to her becushioned townhouse.

Couples. Finding each other. Joining, making two lives into one. If any of her staff had seen her at that moment, they would have been surprised at Miss Darcy's expression. There was a look of wistfulness on that well-known sardonic face.

She'd found a man to love, who loved her. But she was denied a wedding of her own. Well, when could you have everything? She had Luther, and that was more than enough.

Between the shop and the wedding preparations, Roberta was endlessly busy. Yet she felt charged with energy, and zipped through her lists of 'things to do today' with ease and speed.

Was that due to the hours she spent with Paul? There wasn't much time for them to be together at the moment, but they managed to keep Saturday night sacred, dining out in the country, then going back to the Harcourt house, and falling into bed with a frank urgency that fulfilled them both.

There *was* something special about making love to a man you'd known well, as a friend, she thought. She liked him as much as she desired him. But did she *love* him? Strange how uncertain she was about that.

Mingo put it bluntly. 'Why didn't you tell me you're in love, Robbie?'

'What?' They had just had the wedding rehearsal.

'I told you I always thought Paul had a thing for you, from way back. Why didn't you tell me it's mutual, and then some?'

'Why do you say that?'

'Roberta, darling, you should see the way you look at him.'

Am I the last to know? Roberta wondered.

The young people's insistence that the first Sunday in October *had* to be beautiful turned out to be true. It was a lovely day, it's Indian summer warmth contrasting with the fall foliage. The sun shone on the fluttering canopy of the big yellow tent, the grass was still green, the creek glittered. The guests were assembled on the side lawn. Then Tim Fenton, thrilled with his assignment, struck up the wedding march from inside the house and the sound soared through the open windows.

Susan, on her grandfather's arm, and Midge, on Dr John Blair's arm, came through the side door and walked, in measured steps, to the rose arbor, where Jim and Bob Giordano awaited them.

The Unitarian minister was hardly older than they were. '. . . so long as you both shall live?' 'I do.'

Looking at the serious faces of her son and daughter, Roberta could not keep back the tears. Susan, who had gone through such a turbulent growing up, would be a mother herself next spring. And Jim, as yet untried, was taking on the responsibilities of a man. Roberta wept with love and pity for their vulnerability. They were so hopeful – and they had so much to learn.

Mary Blair silently prayed that her daughter's marriage would be happier than hers had been, and she felt a sad compassion for her ex-husband. This must be hard on John. He does love the children, in his way, she thought.

Rosalina Giordano cried unabashedly. Her son, her Bob, now belonged to another woman. A nice girl, though, from a nice family. But she hoped they would do it over again, with a Catholic priest.

Mingo clutched a lacy handkerchief in one hand, and gripped Luther's hand with the other. 'I'm always a *fool* at weddings,' she whispered.

Carole Harcourt tensed her determined little chin to keep from crying. I suppose it works for some people, she was thinking, innocent young people like these four. But if I married again, I'd pick another Greg, I know I would. That's what people do, repeat. Thanks, but no thanks.

Terry thought how beautifully her Tim had played the wedding march. Those cascades of triumphant sound. She remembered their own wedding, two people who didn't fit in, uniting against a critical world. And they had proved there was more than one kind of marriage – of triumphant marriage.

Sarah Smith didn't cry at all. She simply twinkled. 'Why, God bless them all,' she thought.

The young people danced on the lawn, first kicking off their shoes. The parents and their friends danced on the patio.

John Blair, dancing with his ex-wife, said, 'Could we try again, Mary?'

'It wouldn't work, John.'

'The hospital called me here a half-hour ago. I didn't go. I've learned, Mary.'

'John, I'm sorry. It's too late.'

'Is there someone else?'

'I think so.'

Roberta, dancing with Mr Giordano, felt Paul's eyes

on her from across the patio, where he was dancing with Mrs Giordano. She could read his message: *We'll* be doing this soon, you and I.

Would they?

For a few moments, Roberta forgot she was at her children's wedding, and was lost in searching her soul. *Do I love Paul?* Inside, she was still, waiting for the answer. *Yes*, answered her heart. *Then of course I want to be his wife. Yes. I do.*

But not yet . . . This was also her deepest self speaking, voicing her truest wish. *First I must meet the challenge I have set myself. But is that silly, quixotic, tilting at windmills? Is Whitford & Marston really that important, compared to the love of a man like Paul? But it isn't Whitford & Marston. It's me. It's a need in me to be my own woman, at last. A need I never filled, because I've always been protected. Besides, I'll have more to give Paul if I complete myself first. Then, I'll have everything.*

Everything. That's what young women demand today — love and marriage and motherhood and a career, all at once, right from the beginning. But I don't think you can have it that way, thought Roberta. *I think you have to suffer and learn and grow and ripen first. Then, if you've earned it, maybe you can have everything.* She felt a rush of exultation, then came back to the present.

The two couples left, in the traditional shower of rice. 'I love you, Mother, and thank you,' Susan whispered. 'Back in a week, Mom,' Jim said.

Jim and Midge were going to spend a week touring gardens, a busman's honeymoon. They would go to Longwood and Winterthur, ending up at Musser Forests, in Pennsylvania, to look at nursery stock for their spring planting. Then they would be back permanently to live in the carriage house. 'What luck your tenant is leaving,'

Jim had said. 'May we apply, Mom?' It would be good to have them so close.

Susan and Bob, more conventionally, were to spend a week on Grand Cayman. 'You see, with the baby coming, we don't know when we'll get another chance,' Susan had said. The baby. That will be the next milestone, Roberta thought. When she told Paul about it, he said, 'Step-grandfather. You know, that has a rather nice ring.'

After the guests had left and the caterers had packed up and departed, and the grandparents had gratefully turned in, Mingo, Luther, Roberta, and Paul relaxed in Roberta's living room. Paul opened a last bottle of champagne.

'It was a beautiful wedding,' he said, 'and they're beautiful kids. But I want to propose a toast: To us *grownups*.'

They all drank to that.

'Seriously,' Paul went on, 'and for adult ears only, isn't it wonderful to have life's slings and arrows *behind* you?'

'Is it ever!' said Mingo. 'You know you've weathered the worst.'

'Would anyone want to do it all over again?' Luther looked skeptical.

'Not if you could get from there to here *without* doing it all over again.'

'Ah, but isn't that the point?' asked Roberta. 'You can't get here without being there first. Here's to *here*.'

Her eyes met Paul's, and Paul's spoke back.

Mingo and Luther were sending their own messages.

Outstanding fiction in paperback from Grafton Books

Nicola Thorne

Yesterday's Promises	£3.50 ☐
A Woman Like Us	£1.25 ☐
The Perfect Wife and Mother	£1.50 ☐
The Daughters of the House	£2.50 ☐
Where the Rivers Meet	£2.50 ☐
Affairs of Love	£2.50 ☐
The Enchantress Saga	£3.95 ☐
Never Such Innocence	£2.95 ☐

Jacqueline Briskin

Paloverde	£3.50 ☐
Rich Friends	£2.95 ☐
Decade	£2.50 ☐
The Onyx	£3.50 ☐
Everything and More	£2.50 ☐

Barbara Taylor Bradford

A Woman of Substance	£3.95 ☐
Voice of the Heart	£3.95 ☐
Hold the Dream	£3.50 ☐

Alan Ebert and Janice Rotchstein

Traditions	£3.95 ☐
The Long Way Home	£2.95 ☐

Marcelle Bernstein

Sadie	£2.95 ☐

To order direct from the publisher just tick the titles you want
and fill in the order form.

All these books are available at your local bookshop or newsagent, or can be ordered direct from the publisher.

To order direct from the publishers just tick the titles you want and fill in the form below.

Name _____

Address _____

_____

Send to:
Grafton Cash Sales
PO Box 11, Falmouth, Cornwall TR10 9EN.

Please enclose remittance to the value of the cover price plus:

UK 60p for the first book, 25p for the second book plus 15p per copy for each additional book ordered to a maximum charge of £1.90.

BFPO 60p for the first book, 25p for the second book plus 15p per copy for the next 7 books, thereafter 9p per book.

Overseas including Eire £1.25 for the first book, 75p for second book and 28p for each additional book.

Grafton Books reserve the right to show new retail prices on covers, which may differ from those previously advertised in the text or elsewhere.